Her destiny was in the hands of a man who knew not love, but lust . . .

Alone and fed, Kate turned to the exciting prospect of a bath. She slipped out of her clothes, and with an eye to starting at the top and working down, she bent over the rim of the steaming barrel and dipped her head into the water. The biting heat felt wonderful. She took the bar of soap and began applying it.

It was not until she had rinsed her hair and was twisting the squeaky tresses into a knot that she sensed a visitor behind her. She turned and saw Jason Steele regarding her from the doorway. She voiced a squeal of indignation and virtually dove into the tub to hide her nakedness. She came up sputtering and lifted her head over the rim.

"What are you doing here?" she demanded.

Jason had not moved. He wore a thoughtful, half-quizzical look. "I happen to be captain of this ship."

"Does that give you the right to intrude on my privacy without knocking?"

"It gives me the right to do pretty much as I please."

"Well, get out or I'll scream!"

"That wouldn't do any good. Nobody would come."

"Then you're saying that I'm at your mercy!"

"I guess that's true. So you'd better pray that I'm merciful . . ."

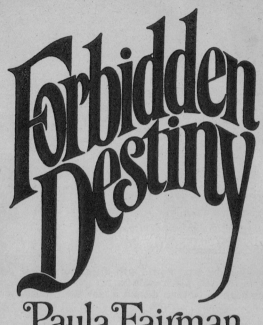

Forbidden Destiny

Paula Fairman

PINNACLE BOOKS   LOS ANGELES

FORBIDDEN DESTINY

Copyright © 1977 by Paul Fairman

Jay Garon-Brooke Associates
415 Central Park West, 17D
New York, N.Y. 10025

ISBN: 0-523-40-105-6

First printing, September 1977

Cover illustration by Stan Hunter

An original Pinnacle Books edition, published for the first time anywhere.

Printed in the United States of America

PINNACLE BOOKS, INC.
One Century Plaza
2029 Century Park East
Los Angeles, California 90067

To Jay Garon:
    dear friend—indispensable adviser

Dramatis Personae

Kate McCrae: Beautiful young orphan, who quickly learned to negotiate with her one marketable commodity—herself.

Jason Steele: Handsome, wild, irresistible, whose inborn pride nearly cost him what he wanted most in the world.

Peter Wells: A lamb in a world of lions, he loved not wisely but well.

Elizabeth Penn: It could have been written of her: whom the gods would destroy, they first make mad.

Chester Manson: Elizabeth's husband. An honest man who saw love and loyalty as one.

William Steele: Jason's grandfather. The complete gentleman, who quietly mourned the passing of an era.

Theresa Wells: Peter's sister. A rebel with a cause, she gathered strength from each defeat.

Bella Cantrell: A peacock with the voice of a nightingale and the instincts of a hawk.

Calvin Gentry: A roué, who learned that the glitter of wealth and position could turn to tinsel, without love.

John Saipan: Self-proclaimed servant of the Lord, his madness poured blood into the sea.

Lucas Peavy: He would perjure himself under oath for revenge and pride.

Contents

Part One:

THE WHALERS

Stonington, Connecticut, 1903

1.

Ever on her guard since Lucas Peavey had so blatantly made his intentions known, Kate McCrae waited to make sure the passageway to the tap room was clear before carrying in the cheese tray for the afternoon trade.

Had Lucas been able to trap her in that narrow confine she would have had to endure a hard pinching of her tender nipples and the pawing of his calloused hands as she sidled past him with flaming cheeks and murmured protests. But once in the tap room of the *Blue Mermaid* she would be safe—at least for the time being.

Peavey, a more complex man than one would have suspected from his simple background, was determined to have his way with the lovely waif he had taken in, but still he had acted with much restraint during the first three months; possibly even the anticipation of what he planned gave him pleasure. The delay could have been for another reason, of course; that of baiting his wife Clara, keeping her miserable while she waited for the infidelity that was sure to come. Jealousy and pain often flared out at Kate from Clara's cold blue eyes. But now, three months having dragged by, Lucas Peavey was growing impatient; and Clara was more desperate than ever in defense of her marital rights.

Her love for her brutish husband was far more a burden than a blessing, a trap wherein she distorted truth into falsehood as the only way open to her. He loves *me*, she would tell herself fiercely. It was not his fault that his virility attracted loose, predatory women. Obviously this lovely little eighteen-year-old snip of a girl was bent upon seducing her husband. And Lucas, while resisting to the best of his ability, could hold out behind the barricades of his moral strength just so long.

Clara had certainly been frank enough with Kate. "Child, you would be no match for him. Only a physically strong woman such as myself can weather him in bed. He would destroy you and then cast you aside out of contempt for your weakness."

Stunned by the accusation, Kate could only protest, "Mrs. Peavey, far from being attracted to your husband, I have tried to avoid him! He frightens me. Truly he does!"

"Naturally, my girl. Fear and fascination go together."

Perhaps Kate should have been more forceful. She could have explained that Lucas Peavey's gross, ugly bulk and his tobacco-stained mouth disgusted her; that his clumsy, lustful pawing made her skin crawl.

Such a frank confession might well have gotten her ordered from the tavern; and where in that frightening New England complex of shipbuilding and whaling could a friendless, penniless girl find shelter?

"No, Mrs. Peavey! No! Please do not think so badly of me. Please believe that I do not aspire to your husband's affections."

Clara sighed. This—this *actress!* Such a clever baggage with that look of innocence about her. Her natural loveliness gave her an insurmountable advantage over a woman worn by years of drudgery. But Clara would fight to keep her marital sheets free of greater stain than they already bore. There had to be a way to get rid of Kate McCrae. Child of misfortune though Kate was, Clara Peavey could not afford sympathy.

The sudden death of her father was the second great tragedy in Kate's life and the most shattering. The first, buried deep in her early childhood had become but an uneasy memory—the vague image of a mother who had not wanted her, who drank at times and screamed at her father for failing to live up to standards beyond his inclinations and abilities. The ill-mated marriage was brought to a shattering finish one terrible night as Kate cowered in her bed, listening to the screams from the room beyond. The next morning Jenny McCrae was gone. Clinton McCrae bundled up his four-year-old daughter, muttering, "Sweetheart, we're going to find a place where we can erase

5

our mistakes and start anew," and the pair left Richmond, Virginia forever. What those mistakes were other than the marriage itself, Kate never learned. Nor did they ever reach that place Clinton McCrae specified. McCrae, a wanderer by nature and an artist by talent, was no doubt sincere in his aspirations for a new home—a growing daughter needed a place to put down roots—but season followed season and the McCrae gypsy wagon crossed and recrossed New England and the Midwest, McCrae's brushes providing support. Many well-to-do farmers and merchants were happy to commission family portraits; landscapes and scenics done during off-times sold right from the wagon to art-hungry buyers in the hinterlands.

Impractical dreamer that he was—a weakness no doubt justifiably resented by his wife—Clinton should probably never have sired a child; he was ill-equipped for the responsibility. However, he did see that Kate received an education above average, and he was an able teacher. But beyond that there was only the love that overflowed and kept Kate bathed in its warmth and brightness. She adored her father and thus absorbed his joy of living. This characteristic, though laudable in itself, was unfortunate in the case of Clinton McCrae. Each of his days was so engrossing in itself that he never looked to the next; no thought of tomorrow ever disturbed his sleep. This was his great and sad disservice to the daughter he loved so dearly: Safe and secure in the aura of his immediate presence, Kate sensed no needs, present or future, beyond its scope.

At times during the early years, Kate asked about her mother. She was told very little, but not much was necessary. The lack of maternal instinct that had been displayed, tragic as it was, left Kate with no longings for the mother who had not wanted her, making her babyhood in Richmond a vague memory with her mother only a small part.

The last of the quicksilver years flowed past the red wheels of the gypsy wagon and the end to which Clinton had given no thought came in the town of Stonington, Connecticut in the spring of 1902. His death left Kate under the lustful eye of Lucas Peavey; where swiftly shaping events were to dance her about as if she were a puppet on destiny's strings.

What price survival?

2.

At that time, whaling was a romantic and dangerous adventure unlike the slaughterous enterprise it later became. Brave men went out to take the oil and the riches with harpoons as puny as hat pins when matched against the size of the behemoths they sought; where, in the main, they fought fairly, with the odds favoring the whales. Few of the ships ever returned from their two- to three-year voyages with full crews, whereupon New Bedford, Stonington, Mystic, and the rest of the whaling towns would console the new widows, throw blossoms on the waters, and the next ship would go off on schedule because reasonable success meant a living and great success could bring great wealth.

But more than courage was required. Enduring success went to those who were blessed with sharp business acumen and ruthless determination. Only men of that caliber formed the great whaling dynasties.

Two such Stonington families dominated the trade during those twilight years of the old order: the Steeles and the Penns. Their men went out in the wooden boats to take whale with simple weapons, the harpoon and the killing iron, and a stubbornness which could be traced to the two iron-willed patriarchs who ruled the two clans. This pair of ancients, William Steele and Jethro Penn, with their lives mostly gone, still found joy in the fierce hope that this ship or that would beat the other into port with sperm oil to the gunwales and proud victory flags flying.

The affairs of the two families were naturally grist for the rumor mill of Stonington, and in that spring of 1902 a situation existed that was calculated to keep the whispers flying.

The gossip concerned the flamboyant sea captain, Jason Steele, who was engaged to Elizabeth, the patrician daughter of the Penns. The betrothal had been effected prior to Jason Steele's present voyage and he was due to return shortly and claim his bride. It was not to be, however, for the drama was complete with a villain, one Chester Manson, the rejected rival for the golden Penn hand. Rejected, but not defeated: Manson, captain of the *Water Nymph*, a Penn whaling ship, had returned three months earlier and married Elizabeth, with Jason still at sea. And now the whole town awaited Jason's return.

It was natural during that era that whaling folk drew their heroes from the ranks of the mighty men who went to sea in wooden ships to find and kill the great ocean monsters, and young Jason Steele, handsome, dashing, excitingly erratic, stood high on the list.

A comparison between the two men was unfair, Jason's charisma carrying too much weight. While Chester Manson was as unspectacular as his name and had sent no unwed maidens into romantic fantasy, he was an industrious man and perhaps a better whaling captain than his rival of the flashing smile and impressive physique.

During their seagoing years, he had brought back more oil than Jason, but quietly, without the showmanship inherent in the latter's nature. Thus, lying to at the Stonington quay with twenty-two hundred barrels three months in advance of Jason could not have been merely accidental.

Manson was not a Penn; rather, he was the son of a sea captain who had served the Penns well and died on a voyage in their employ. Thus he started out in their affection but merited even more. He had gone before the mast and earned his way up by stolid and unspectacular hard work, while Jason Steele, in the direct line of the illustrious founder of the Steele whaling dynasty, conducted himself as a prince of the blood and had more than once tried the patience and love of his grandfather with his heroics.

Still, the old man's patience held. There was no meanness in Jason. He was warm and generous to a fault, though given to an explosive temper at times, and he cut a colorful figure. In William Steele's eyes Jason lacked only one attribute—maturity.

So it followed that the town's interest in Jason's arrival was high. How would their young Lochinvar of the seas react to finding that his lovely Elizabeth had gone back on her promise and leaped into another's man's bed?

The day had finally come. Word had it that

the *Gray Ghost* dotted the horizon and was approaching port with a fair wind. Jason would soon be at dockside and the townspeople gathered at the quay to wait. Jason himself could be distinguished, blue jacket with brass buttons shining as he brought his ship gently and skillfully to her mooring.

He lifted his hand to the onlookers and perhaps interpreted their unusual silence as a mark of respect. Their presence was no surprise because well-wishing crowds habitually met incoming whalers, but the traditional exuberance was certainly missing.

Jason turned the ship over to Guy Mapes, his first mate, and swung down effortlessly onto the dock where a surprise was indeed awaiting him: Only a single individual from the company was there to greet him; for generations, the head of the house of Steele had come down in person to grip the hand of a returning Steele captain.

He scowled at the man. "Where is my grandfather?" he demanded.

"He sends word that he wishes to see you immediately."

"And who are you?"

"I am Gerald Martin, sir. A clerk with the firm."

"A *clerk!*" It was not Jason's intention to insult the man. He was simply expressing consternation at this embarrassing change in protocol. "What has happened? Is my grandfather ill?"

"No, Captain. He is in good health. He is awaiting you in his private office. He specified he wishes to see you *immediately.*"

11

Obviously something was terribly wrong. The scowl on Jason's handsome face remained in place as he strode up the dock, pushing his way through the crowd which was not at all bashful in telling him what had happened.

3.

William Steele felt old. He sat behind his desk in his spacious oak-paneled office with his back to the window which framed a view of the *Gray Ghost* now fixed securely to her mooring posts. He felt his age, but not so much in the physical sense. For all its seventy-six years, his whipcord body had been "salted" and toughened in his seagoing days and he was pretty much free of the aches and pains usually brought on by aging.

It was more a weariness of the spirit, his somber mood brought on by his own entry, so to speak, into the new fishing world he regarded with sadness. It was an era of steel and steam and gunnery which had transformed whaling from what it had been into what he regarded as looting expeditions bent upon robbing the sea of its wealth with no thought of coming years; in a shorter time than men supposed, the whale in all its wonder and majesty would be gone. Perhaps his spiritual letdown was the preparation for his own departure along with the old order.

William Steele awaited his grandson but his thoughts, perhaps deliberately, were on the past; that bitter day when faithful Guy Mapes, first mate on the *Sea Flower*, brought the news of Gordon Steele's death into this very office:

The captain died valiant, sir. That sperm was fifty barrel if a pint and when it surfaced underneath, the boat went to splinters. The whale stayed about, sir, like it wanted the men down in the water and the captain manned a rescue boat himself. While they were pulling the men aboard, the sperm went for the boat with a belly full of hate and stove it in. The captain and three men took the deep six, sir, like I wrote in the log. . . .

The memory came back to William so clearly; the desolation he had suffered at the loss of his beloved son—and the rage. *The simple-minded fool, leaving his ship to rescue hands!*

Now his lament was somewhat different, for it was against the great waters themselves. The sea would not be cheated: It always demanded payment in kind; lives in return for the lives taken from its depths.

One blessed thing—Gordon had left a son, a bonny lad indeed, and now Jason was coming in off the sea to face disappointment. From William Steele's point of view, being bested in the marriage arena was petty, almost amusing, but he was sure his grandson would not find it so. And that, William felt, was forcing him to a decision.

The door opened then and Jason entered with the force of a sudden gust in a dead calm.

"Grandfather, what has been going on? What has happened? Are the rumors true?"

"Then you *have* heard."

The exchange might seem inadequate after

close to three years of separation but William understood. The young put less value on sentimental reunions and, as things stood, Jason could hardly be blamed for callousness.

Jason said, "They tell me Beth married Chester. That's too absurd to believe!"

"It is true, though, son. But first let me apologize for not meeting you. With that mob looking on I thought it best to suspend the old custom."

"Then they *are* married. I still don't believe it!"

"Sit down, Jason. Collect yourself. It is a shock, of course, but the world has not ended."

Jason obeyed. He sat ramrod straight on the edge of his chair. "Tell me what happened. What sort of devil's joke . . ."

William Steele lifted a restraining hand. "As I understand it—as Jethro Penn tells it—the thing began at sea. You did speak Chester Manson's *Water Nymph* off Valparaiso some months ago?"

Jason nodded. "We were happy to see someone from home. I had Chester and his first mate across for dinner."

"And there was a female aboard the *Gray Ghost?*"

"Quite true. A Jamaican girl, Marita. She helped in the galley and served the meals."

"That was it. Chester Manson saw her as quite something else by way of service. A woman for your personal use. He so informed Jethro. Jethro told Elizabeth."

"But to be rejected without a hearing—"

"There is something we must remember. Jethro Penn was never very enthusiastic about

15

joining the two families. I am sure he saw Elizabeth's insistence on marrying you as rebellion. He tried to discourage her even before the engagement was announced. The postponement until your return was his doing."

"But Manson—that blackguard—!"

"We cannot be sure that it is his fault. When Jethro relayed Manson's information to Elizabeth he could have made it sound far different than Manson intended."

Jason's hands had become fists. "That damnable swine!" he snarled.

William realized that his persuasions as to Jethro Penn's guilt had gone unheard. His outraged grandson saw Chester Manson as the guilty party, and Manson would pay—violently.

Which was precisely what William Steele was bent upon preventing. He saw no point in churning the already troubled waters into a bloody froth, and that would certainly be the case if Jason was allowed to proceed without restraint.

"Jason," he said, "I am not at all sure that what happened was not for the best."

"What do you mean? I don't understand."

"Perhaps Elizabeth was not the girl for you. At any rate, she is now beyond your reach and no action on your part will bring her back."

"It isn't a matter of getting her back! It is a matter of settling a score with a sneaking lickspittle who violated a code of honor decent men observe under all circumstances!"

There was also the matter of the authority that went with being the master of the house. "Jason, I think your wisest course is to go back to the sea immediately. What is the condition of the *Gray Ghost*'s hull?" William asked in a firm voice.

"It will do," Jason replied sullenly.

"You encountered no bad storms?"

"The weather favored us."

"Then I propose you make another run immediately. In forty-eight hours."

"It would not be possible to unload and then stock the ship in that length of time."

"On the contrary, it can be done. Guy Mapes is most efficient. He will handle everything while you remain with the family."

"The crew—"

"No problem. We treat our hands well. They are loyal." William leaned forward, now the sympathetic patriarch reassuring the troubled youth. "Jason, my boy, the sea is a wonderful place to regain one's bearings. She is our silent mother. Out there under the stars, she counsels and gives us her wisdom. You will profit in this time of your uncertainty and all things will again fall into the order of their correct importance."

It is true one turned to the sea to forget. But rather than a suggestion, the proposal was a command, where it did not occur to Jason to make counterargument.

"Dinner will be at eight, as usual," William continued. "And now you will want to pay your respects to your grandmother after these three long years."

This too was an order—and a dismissal. Jason withdrew.

17

4.

Kate McCrae had never set eyes on Jason Steele prior to the docking of the *Gray Ghost*. There in the tap room, she had of course heard about the impending drama, and when the place emptied she too went along to the quay, partly out of curiosity and partly in fear that Lucas Peavey would remain behind and use the occasion for further assault.

She had shown no great interest in the town's speculation on the coming humiliation of Jason Steele. The Penns and the Steeles and their commercial and social conflicts meant nothing to her. Kate's world of the moment was bounded by the four walls of the *Blue Mermaid*, escaping only in the memories of the past—the happier days with her father, growing up in the gypsy wagon. . . .

Had her descent into unhappiness come in gradual stages she would have been better able to handle it; she was not without strong character. As things were, she had plunged too suddenly into shock, confusion, and misery, and was thus vulnerable to any diversion from her bleak situation.

And so she got her first glimpse of Jason Steele.

Such a stirring figure as he quitted his ship and strode up the dock! A gray kerchief graced his throat. His fawn-tan trousers were caught at the insteps by stirrups that drew them skin-tight against his smoothly muscled legs. Aside from the blue jacket, his garb hardly seemed seagoing attire; more that of a shoreside dandy than a working ship's officer. But then Jason Steele was an exceptional seagoing man. Kate could only stare.

She left the quay ahead of the crowd, the memory of those tightly clad legs staying with her. So strongly masculine; so purposeful of stride; the broad chest, the erect head, the handsome, firm-chinned face.

Kate's sexual education had been nil, Clinton McCrae shirking that responsibility to his daughter. She remained a virgin, the sexual act a thing of doubt and fear better avoided than sought after. But approaching puberty had brought confusion wherein she needed a sympathetic ear and an experienced advisor. As such a person was lacking, all her thinking relative to men and sex remained unvoiced. Only once in her life had she appeared naked before a man, this when her father used her as a model. Kate had felt only pride that her father saw her as being worthy of his brushes.

Thus a war ensued between the purity of her maidenhood and the first stirrings of puberty. Believing that an inability to control erotic impulses was a moral weakness, Kate's unguided approach to womanhood was in essence a battle.

But there were times when her body won out. On these occasions she had then observed

19

with perplexity the banner of puberty manifest itself upon her body—first a soft shadow, then to thicken and coarsen into a black triangular badge which would have been worn proudly by some who were more skimpily endowed in that respect. Kate's reaction was fear. In her untutored young mind was the thought that it would continue to grow, that the hirsute decoration might eventually reach her knees; she wondered if grown women trimmed it in the secrecy of their toilettes. She instinctively kept her hands away from that region except when bathing, that being the only justification for touching it.

But a completely unguarded moment came during her fifteenth year: a dream just as dawn was touching the tops of the trees in which the gypsy wagon was partially hidden. The man in her dream was nameless, vague almost to the point of formlessness, but the impatient demands of her body fashioned him into the only male she really knew—her father. He was there in the ephemeral substance of her sleeping reverie. Hands touched her breasts—the nipples rose in response. They caressed her flat young belly and there was an outward movement of her thighs. Then came a most intimate handling of her private parts and the potential for orgasm latent in her being burst forth like a colored fountain. Her moans of delight were real, not a dreaming silence, as an ecstacy past all imagining flooded every fiber of her body.

Sharp wakefulness followed quickly, and to her utter shame, Kate found her legs splayed wide apart and drawn upward. Even her toes were curled, while both her hands were deep in the resulting cleft of soft flesh. With the delight having faded, there was some pain and Kate, in horror, saw traces of blood upon her fingers.

Panic gripped her. Her father slept just beyond the curtain which served as the forward wall of her makeshift bedroom. Had he heard her moans? She arose and peeked out. His bed was empty, but it had obviously been slept in. Had Clinton McCrae left the wagon after hearing his daughter enjoy her first orgasm? Kate peered out and found the surrounding area deserted. She went swiftly about the business of washing and composing herself before he returned. Later that day, when her father went off to paint, she scrubbed the blood-stained sheet in a nearby creek and hung it in the sun to dry.

It was beside the creek, from another itinerant woman doing her laundry, that Kate learned that she had begun to menstruate. . . .

But if Clinton McCrae witnessed Kate's self-introduction to sex, he gave no sign, and her ignorance in that area remained to plague her and confuse her later years.

There were other occasions when her body went ahead without her, so to speak, but its victories over her willpower were rare. She strove to take firm control of her strong sexual nature; she would not allow it to dominate her. She resolutely drove erotic thoughts from her mind. Decent girls did not think of such things. Fear of male attentions helped in this respect. Sex meant male participation; men sought only their own pleasures, or so Kate had come to believe, and nothing had happened since her arrival at the *Blue Mermaid* to change her mind.

But her first sight of Jason Steele was something else. Prior to that moment she had had to struggle with only the erotic stuff of dreams, and now the mere sight of this man had produced a reaction almost as tangible as if he had thrust his hand under her petticoats. This young god just off the sea had the power to make her knees tremble without his even knowing of her existence!

No thought of love entered her mind. Kate knew it was merely another trick of her body, and she fought to regain command. But even as she pushed through the crowd and rushed away, the sensations in her groin were overwhelming. Good God! Was she so weak that a man she had never before seen could ravish her from a distance? She would not allow it!

If she could not control her erotic impulses any better than it now appeared, it was a dangerous state of affairs indeed. . . .

5.

"Love as you young fools see it," said Rebecca Steele, "is illusion. Its thrust is not in the bedroom, as you suppose, but in the nursery and beyond; not into a lover's body but into a mother's heart. Only there does true love lie and it can be a special kind of agony. To love a child is to fear for it with no surcease; to suffer always in one's soul the perils it must experience on this dangerous earth. The ecstacy of the bedroom is deceitful nature's trick, nothing more."

Even in her late seventies, Rebecca still showed bright flashes of what she had been: earthy, physically attractive, lusty in spirit. Her back was ramrod straight and her head was held high as she sat in her morning room with her grandson just home from the sea. Her eyes were still as bright as a pair of jewels, aglitter in the wrinkled ruin of her face. All in all she was a queenly figure.

Jason Steele, while he honored his grandfather, was in awe of Grandma Becky. Now he sat listening to her philosophy on life and love. He had respectfully suspended preoccupation with his own problems to follow whatever lead she took in their conversation.

"Then you are saying, Grandma, that you never loved Grandfather Steele?"

"Fortunately we were well attracted to each other. Nothing can be more punishing than a family-arranged marriage with no spark of passion between the young victims. I wanted William and he fairly ached for me. That made our marriage quite interesting for some time. After the children came our marriage took its natural course. Habit, social position, pride held it firmly together and of course an affection remained, but my love was where it belonged—with my children. When your father died at sea, much of me died also. I suffered the agonies that love in its true sense demands. While William went on and on about bravery, character, and the nobility of dying well, I saved my sanity by loving you. You were the anchor that held my ship steady until time dulled the pain."

Jason was somewhat taken aback. Grandma Becky had never before opened her heart to him in this manner. For some reason this occasion had been taken as a time to sum up.

"Long before that, when your grandfather was at sea and began having mistresses, I wasn't much bothered. It touched my pride, I suppose, but only lightly."

Rebecca Steele paused to smile. "Your grandfather did have fire in those early days." She laughed softly. "The captain of a New Bedford whaler—I no longer remember his name—stole one of William's favorite mistresses in Havana. William bided his time, then met the man in a San Francisco saloon and beat him bloody. After that I often wondered. . . ."

She trailed off, into the past, until Jason asked, "Wondered what, Grandma?"

"How I would have felt if he had been fighting for me instead of some strumpet. Would I have been proud? Of course, William never had reason to fight over me." Her still lovely eyes twinkled now. "No reason at all. If there were times of infidelity on my part, he never heard of them."

A silence fell between them, broken by a soft sigh from Grandma Becky. "And now William is packing you off to sea in a mighty hurry. I suppose it is best. Nothing is ever really won by violence."

"Grandma, I have a feeling you do not agree with Grandfather ordering me to sail immediately."

She shrugged. "He is probably right. Age brings wisdom, or so they say. It has been said that the spirit must grow weary before it becomes truly wise."

"Who said that?"

"I don't recall. I no doubt read it somewhere. But now you must run along so that I may have my afternoon nap. I shall see you at dinner?"

"Of course."

When Jason bent down to kiss her cheek, she took his hand in both of hers and lifted her eyes to his face. "I wish we could have been closer while you were growing up, Jason. I should have asserted myself but your mother was a possessive baggage who brooked no interference in her child-rearing. But you needed more than she could give. You needed a confidant—someone you could talk to."

"That would have been wonderful."

She patted his hand. "But you were brave. You seldom cried."

"I think that was because of you. I didn't want you to think I was a sissy."

Her grandson left the room with a wave of his hand. After he was gone, Rebecca sat gazing out the window. Her vision was still quite good and the busy harbor below was not blurred in her sight. Nor was much of the past blurred in her memory.

She wondered briefly if William had ever actually fought over a mistress—if the story she had made up for Jason could be true. Possibly, but probably not. There were too many available women in the ports of the world to make a struggle to keep one worthwhile. Imagine ordering Jason to back away without knowing or caring what such a retreat would do to the boy's spirit! The wisdom of age, she thought, often went wide of the mark. . . .

She lay back and closed her eyes. She appeared to doze, then her lips moved and she whispered:

"Jonathon—my darling . . ."

But who Jonathon was and what he had meant to her was a secret she would soon take to her grave.

6.

After he was dismissed, Jason strode purposefully to the closest tavern, retired to a rear
booth, and ordered rum.

For a time he allowed his mind to roam generally over his grandmother's revelations.

So ingrained was the respect he had for his
grandfather it took a little time and several
mugs of hot rum, before he found himself able
to move mentally in the direction Grandma
Becky had pointed him. Gradually, resentment
and indignation surfaced.

The pious old hypocrite! Sitting there calmly
ordering him to beat a disgraceful retreat when
he himself had once exacted vengeance from a
man who had merely stolen his mistress! A
man of his own blood demanding that he sneak
off like a coward, leaving a despicable rival to
laugh at his sheepish ways.

Even as Jason drank and fretted, fretted and
drank, there was one surprising truth he completely ignored: After the initial shock, the loss
of Elizabeth Penn as a wife did not greatly
bother him. It was the manner of the loss that
demanded an accounting. God, how Manson
must be laughing at his humiliation!

After another flagon of hot Jamaica rum

Jason motioned a tavern hanger-on to his side. "You will deliver a message for me. . . ."

In no time, the news was all over town. *Jason Steele just called Chester Manson out!*

A fight between the two lordly clans of the town! How glorious! Not a mother's son in Stonington proposed to miss it. A revival of the drama which previously appeared to have petered out into nothing was welcome indeed.

Word of this latest development came quickly to the *Blue Mermaid* but Kate McCrae evidenced no interest. Her present troubles were enough to keep her occupied. Lucas Peavey had been drinking for most of the afternoon.

A steady, slow intake of straight rum was a rarity in his routine; he usually did not drink in his own tavern. Nor was he inclined to sit alone at a remote table and not join in the rough and bawdy conversations. That in itself was enough to make Kate nervous, but there was more: All during that time, his eyes never left her, the lustful brooding expression on his ugly face never changing. Kate could only wonder in helpless dismay.

As the day wore on and there were no new developments, she began telling herself that she had jumped to conclusions. Her employer was simply in a foul mood and she was making too much of it.

After all, the *Blue Mermaid* was a tavern, not a convent. True, she *had* suffered attentions while serving there as a bar maid that would have been insulting in most other establishments. But men came to the *Blue Mer-*

maid to relax, to chat and laugh and forget their troubles. In that vein a bar maid, especially a pretty one, had to expect a bit of ribaldry. Her nether cheeks had been pinched more than once, but it was a cheerful gesture rather than one with true lustful intent—more complimentary than otherwise.

No doubt there was the yearning of lonely men in the eyes which peered into the cleft of her bodice, but other men would have come quickly to her defense had anyone presumed too much.

For those reasons she could give the clientele the benefit of her doubts, and in desperation she tried to give Lucas Peavey that same benefit.

After all, his pinches had been no more punishing than the others she had received. And perhaps the pawings and maulings in secluded passageways were more mischievous than otherwise. There had been kindness and compassion certainly in his offer of sanctuary when she had not known which way to turn:

You just move right in, lass, and don't you worry about a thing....

That well-remembered welcome must merit her gratitude, she told herself, not her suspicions.

She must not be guilty of judging Lucas Peavey too hastily.

7.

The fight that was to become legendary in local chronicles took place that night behind one of the Penn warehouses under a bright moon.

Upon receiving Jason's challenge, Chester Manson sent back word that he would accommodate his former rival at such time and in such place. The acceptance was delivered by a close-mouthed messenger so that only a scant dozen spectators were present at the event. Thus, accounts of the battle expanded with each telling. Still, it was savage enough for the most bloodthirsty.

Chester Manson was already there when Jason arrived. Jason was alone, no friends or seconds accompanying him. When he reeled slightly, Manson scowled and said, "I refuse to fight with a drunken man."

"You'll fight me, you scaly blackguard!" Jason roared back. "The rum I've had will even us up but I'll still beat your lying tongue back into your throat, you low, sneaking, cowardly swine!"

Manson's reply was mild under the circumstances. "Jason, I fear you are overwrought. Perhaps we should talk—"

Jason's right fist slammed the first blow into Manson's face.

Manson backed away and spat a tooth to the ground. His eyes narrowed to slits. "You fool!" he muttered, his reputation for coolness notwithstanding. He moved forward.

The fight was a match of speed versus more slow-moving endurance: Jason's slim, whipcord build against Manson's solid physique. Obviously Jason would need quick reflexes; he was giving away at least forty pounds and it was a question of whether too much rum had clouded his mind.

This did not seem the case. Although he allowed Manson to move in and drive a fist at his jaw, a blow which might have ended the fight but did not, he was able to throw two light lefts and then veer away, leaving a jagged, bloody slash from his signet ring along Manson's cheek.

Manson staggered past, turned, and now Jason, made overconfident by his success, waited too long. Manson threw a ponderous right fist and Jason ducked the blow only partially. The fist, a sea-hardened bludgeon, slammed high against his temple and sent him reeling, dropping him to one knee.

The difference in their attitudes became apparent now. Manson took no pleasure in the fight; he experienced no elation from landing a successful blow. The battle was a job forced upon him, no more.

Jason exhaled a curse as he stumbled to his feet. Regaining his balance, he drove forward with amazing quickness for having been so recently stunned and broke Manson's nose with a vicious right-hand jab.

Manson snorted in pain and back-pedaled as he tried to clear his nostrils with a bull-like shaking of his head. His right eye was almost closed from a previous blow and Jason saw his opportunity: If he could seal it completely and wreak similar havoc upon the other one, he would assure himself of victory.

He stepped in with his target in mind, but in his zeal he became careless and Manson braced himself and buried a fist deep into Jason's belly. Jason sensed his spine bending as a squall of pain burst from his lips together with whatever air remained in his lungs. He doubled over as he fought sickness and nausea.

Manson could have taken better advantage of Jason's condition if he had not been preoccupied with his nose. It was now useless for breathing and blood from smashed cartilege was filling his mouth. He spewed out a red sheen and moved forward, more from instinct than intent, and was towering over Jason before the latter was able to straighten up. But this opportunity too was lost as Manson threw an aimless punch which did little damage. Jason rolled aside and Manson peered down through one eye trying to locate him.

The spectators cheered. This was turning out to be one hell of a fight!

Anger now took hold of Manson. In a desperate effort to end the fight, he rammed a bent knee in the direction of Jason's head, the latter still not back on his feet. Jason avoided the thrust and Manson's knee smashed into the brick wall of the warehouse, Manson gasping at the pain that shot up his thigh.

Still fighting nausea, Jason came finally to his feet. He staggered a few steps along the brick wall, then turned to see Manson limping stubbornly in his direction, grimacing with every step. There was something admirable in his determination, his leg barely supporting him and blood spewing from his mouth at every breath.

Weariness was now reflected in both adversaries. There were no more mindless rushes brought on by pure rage; they squared off after the fashion of professional boxers and for a time they unwittingly observed the Marquis of Queensbury rules. This was to Jason's advantage; he aimed quick thrusts against Manson's ponderous attempts at a single finishing blow, beating a veritable tattoo on Manson's bloodied face. Then one of Manson's haymakers connected.

Jason had no recollection of going down but once on the ground he regained consciousness in time to see Manson limping toward him.

One of the spectators cried, "My God! He's going to stomp him!"

Indeed that seemed the intent. His weight and strength driven into Jason's prone body could bring serious damage.

Manson's injured knee saved Jason. As he sought to end the fight then and there, his leg gave way. He teetered, lost his balance, and while he tried to regain it, the heel of one boot ripped across Jason's face, opening his cheek.

The fresh pain stirred Jason into clearer consciousness. With a strangled snarl, he came half-erect and seized Manson's unsteady legs, bringing him down. In moments, he was astride his foe, hammering bloodied fists into his face.

It was the lack of resistance on Manson's part that brought back a touch of sanity, and unpredictably it turned out to be Jason who ended the battle. Sobbing out his final frustration, he arose and staggered off into the night.

The watchers stood for a time, awed by what they had seen. Then some of them moved forward to give Manson aid. The latter was slow to react. When consciousness seeped back, he struggled to his knees and brushed them away.

"Keep word of this to yourself," he ordered before he too staggered away.

But of course they would not.

8.

That same night, Kate McCrae learned that giving Lucas Peavey the benefit of the doubt was dangerous.

After the tavern emptied she had gone to her room and prepared for bed. Suddenly the door opened and there stood Peavey, casting a monstrous shadow on the wall behind him. Kate stood frozen.

"All right, lass," he growled. "Let's have done with this maidenly nonsense. It's high time you paid for your board and keep."

"But I do," Kate quavered. "I work very hard all day long. . . ."

He didn't bother to reply. Taking a long pull from the bottle of rum he was carrying, he advanced upon her, forcing her back, trapping her in the narrow space between the bed and the wall. She could see the red veins in his eyes by the light from the bedside lamp. With his jet-black beard and open red mouth, he could have been the devil's agent come for her soul.

But it was her body he wanted. Kate tried to turn her face from the fetid boozey breath but he gripped her chin and forced her lips to his as he pressed her against the wall. His tongue probed in an effort to push between her clenched teeth to the inner surface of her mouth where her own tongue was curled back as far as it would go.

Just when she thought she could stand it no longer, Peavey took a backward step. He seized the neckline of Kate's night dress and jerked downward. She staggered, gasping, and found herself naked to his gaze.

The bottle of liquor fell unheeded to the floor as Peavey stared spellbound at Kate's lush body.

Her skin was not the milky whiteness so prized by fashionable women. Instead she was golden, flawless from head to toe. Peavey's gaze traveled slowly down her torso to rest on the jet-black triangle. For long moments they stood suspended in a kind of frozen tableau.

"Please," Kate whispered. "Please—"

"Easy, pet, easy . . ." Suddenly he grasped Kate's protruding nipples between his fingers. Her quick scream of pain was choked off. "Yell like that again and I'll pop your titties like grapes. You wouldn't like that, would you?"

Kate's face remained rigid, her mouth strained but no sound coming forth.

Peavey grinned. "You don't think your innocent ways fooled me, did you?"

"I—I don't know what you mean," she gasped.

"Oh, yes you do, you little tart. Don't tell me you ain't never been pleasured by a man. I'll wager there was plenty of times before you came here."

"No! Never! I've never been with a man in my life!"

He laughed as he teased her now-hardened

nipples with rolling movements. The automatic reaction to his attentions was not lost on him.

"I'll wager different. But if that's true, then I bet you do it to yourself," he taunted.

An old memory flashed into Kate's mind: those first moments of ecstacy her burgeoning body had demanded. It was as though this evil man had discovered her secret; Peavey's knowing leer stripped her more naked than even the baring of her body; for it laid open to him the tender recesses of her mind. She lowered her eyes and a blush came unbidden.

Peavey realized that he had struck home. He laughed, spewing out his nauseating breath. "I thought so. All you young wenches have your private ways. Maybe you ought to show me how you do it."

"Mr. Peavey! Please! You're hurting me. I've done you no harm. I've worked hard. I've tried to please you—"

"And now you can please me a lot more. Undress me," he ordered.

"What?"

"I said undress me!" Again that fascinating black triangle proved a magnet for his lustful gaze. "Unbutton my shirt, then my trousers. If you were never with a man it's time you saw the genuine article," he bragged.

The conceit of his statement was lost on Kate. There was only the fear of what was surely to come.

Releasing her nipples, he forced her to her knees and pressed her head toward his body in silent suggestion. Kate resisted the pressure as she fumbled with his buttons. Then, along with the fear, anger stirred within her. Why did her first time have to be *this* way, with this horrible man? Why couldn't it have been Jason Steele standing before her, gently embracing her?

She was looking up at a chestful of thick, black hair above a paunch still partly covered by trousers.

"Now caress me."

The term seemed out of place in the situation, grotesque in relation to that repulsive body above her. But Peavey's fingers twisted in her hair and Kate lifted her arms to his chest. She found his nipples and touched them tentatively, hating him with all her might.

"Now the trousers, lass," he urged. "Unbutton them, and drop them to the floor."

"No—please—I—"

"Do as I say."

One thought gave Kate dubious comfort: At least he was not pawing *her* body now. She unbuttoned his trouser front. They fell away easily and with his shirt open, he was to all intents and purposes as naked as she.

Kate forced herself to caress the paunch now presented to her, in the vain hope that would satisfy him. "Lower down," he growled. "You know what I want."

Indeed she did. In an effort to lessen her sense of revulsion so that she could perform the task, she sought to turn her mind away to the world of fantasy not made disappointing by the intrusion of flesh's reality. Destiny was cruel in substituting what stood before her for the slim, male youthfulness of which she had dreamed. And Jason Steele's magnetic image surfaced once again. Why had this humiliating initiation been decreed in place of the tender, exciting exploration which should be every virgin maiden's introduction to a lover?

In sullen obedience, she allowed her hands to slip lower on Peavey's body.

She encountered a great, hairy softness, a flaccid male extension nestled in its lair; limp, supine, entirely indifferent. Peavey spread his feet apart to form a wider V.

Immediately his manhood, a lank, harmless snake, fell its length with its head pointed dejectedly toward the floor.

This sorry demonstration further allayed Kate's fears. Her sudden contempt was instinctive. Sensing that there was no immediate danger, Kate curiously, lowered her questing hands toward the great, soft sac from which Peavey's unloaded weapon was suspended. She found what seemed like two round eggs in a bag. Guessing that this was the area of greatest male vulnerability, Kate felt an urge to squeeze, to hold the two globes hostage in exchange for the ransom of this monster's retreat from her room. The thought was clear but the courage was lacking.

"Well, get on with it," Peavey snapped.

"Get—get on with what—sir?"

"Don't be stupid! You know what to do!"

"I'm sorry—I—I do not."

Snorting in disbelief, Peavey seized both her hands and sought to educate them. He cupped her right hand and curled the fingers around his hanging member. He pressed her other thumb and forefinger so that they gripped the soft head and drew it taut. Then he grasped her right wrist and moved her hand up and down.

The results were nil.

"Damn!" Peavey cursed. The realization that his drinking had rendered him impotent sent him into a fierce rage.

Kate was filled with terror as his rage exploded into anger directed at her. Muttering "Bitch" over and over, Peavey threw her across the bed. He grasped her ankles, pushing her legs up until the pain made her cry out. Then he mounted her, her face buried in the thick hair of his chest as he thrust his hips again and again against her helpless body.

But the frantic pounding was fruitless. Ironically, Kate felt laughter bubbling up in her taut throat. Born out of her fear, she had a sudden hysterical vision of the tap room and the howls of laughter that would have prevailed had the rum-and-ale trade been privileged to watch Peavey's sad performance.

With Kate close to smothering under the weight of him, Peavey suddenly came up on his knees, maneuvering her roughly, and Kate again found herself a helpless prisoner beneath him. But her face was no longer buried in his chest. Although still upon her back, her head was now between Peavey's widely spread knees, the ineffectual tool with which he had endeavored to skewer her dangling harmlessly from above.

When Kate felt the wet, slobbery mouth pressed between her legs she hardly knew what to make of it. Had there been pain it would not have been so confusing. But there was none; what she felt was an undefinable, rising excitement, and, though she tried to deny it, a pleasure new to her experience.

Gritting her teeth she cried out in the silence of her mind: *I am not enjoying it! He is a monster! I could not enjoy what he is doing to me!*

But her body was hungry, and fires so long held in check flared unbidden. Waves of savage sweetness engulfed her.

Heaven forgive me, I want it! I want it!

Even as she begged forgiveness her hands moved of their own to Peavey's head to push his face deeper—deeper.

"Oh yes—yes—yes!" she cried.

When it was over, Peavey unstraddled her in silence. He seized his garments, hauling them on as he rushed from her room.

Kate lay still, her rebellious body in weary repose, her mind not yet ready to consider what had occurred.

Finally she rose and went to her pitcher and bowl, where she tried to wash away the feel of the vile mouth that had yet so pleased her disobedient body. Would Lucas Peavey be satisfied with what he had taken from her? Perhaps the next time he would not be filled with alcohol, and that harmless, dangling appendage would turn into an unyielding rod. . . .

A knock at her door came to spare Kate the rest of that terrible image. When she opened it Clara Peavey stood there with a lamp in her hand.

Oh God! Clara knew!

But there was no accusation. Obviously distraught, Clara said only, "Come, Kate, I need help. You must follow me at once."

Clara turned, her light not penetrating to Kate's bed, where the disarray of the bedclothes attested to the previous goings-on.

Thankful for the comparative darkness, Kate slipped into her robe, wrapped it tight around her, and tied the sash. Then she followed Clara out of the room and into the narrow second-floor hallway.

At the foot of the sharply angled stairwell to the third floor, Clara stopped. "The water on the kitchen stove must still be quite warm. Go down and bring a pail up here to the attic room. Also an armful of bar towels. Be quick about it!"

Kate could only wonder at the urgency in Clara's voice while hurrying to obey her orders. What had happened? When she arrived, heavily laden, at the upper floor, however, she almost dropped the bucket she was lugging.

A man lay on the bed in the attic room. He was naked save for a sheet thrown over his middle. He appeared to have been in some terrible accident. His face was so bruised that portions of it looked like raw meat. His left side was covered with huge, purple swellings. There was a long gash along his outer left thigh that looked as if it had been inflicted with a dull, jagged blade. And the man was smiling!

Kate had come to a stunned halt, staring at this bloody midnight apparition. Clara's harsh voice brought her to her senses.

"Well, don't just stand there—bring me the water and towels!"

The man had a soft, drawling voice. "Easy, pet. The girl is understandably surprised by my appearance."

"That's no excuse," Clara replied tartly. Then to Kate, "He isn't going to die, if that is what you're afraid of. He is too stubborn a

42

specimen for that. He is just a mess and no more. You are to clean him up, and try to make him look at least partly human again."

"Yes, ma'am," Kate replied out of habit, but she wondered why this gruesome task had been allotted to her.

She found out quickly enough when Clara addressed the fallen warrior. "I must go now. I've tarried much too long. Lucas is bound to awaken and come seeking me."

Not surprisingly Kate took comfort from Clara's words. She obviously knew nothing of her husband's actions. Clara's accusations, on top of the attack itself, would have been too much for Kate to bear.

She warily approached the bed.

9.

"Great God in heaven, what happened to you?"

Clara Peavey had been quite taken aback to find Jason Steele at the rear door of the *Blue Mermaid* after his fight with Chester Manson.

"A little argument with a friend," Jason replied, a ghoulish grin revealing bloody teeth.

It was logical for Jason to come to Clara Peavey in the manner of a hurt child seeking help. Their close, highly private friendship had begun years before when Jason, fleeing a boyhood mischief which would have earned him a tanning, ran into the tavern for some long-forgotten reason—and found sympathy. Clara, childless and lonely, was happy with the boy's continued visits, pleased to comfort him during juvenile disappointments and give him the kind of counsel he could obtain only from an adult friend. After that first time, he always came in the back way. It was not seemly for a child to enter the tap room. Perhaps it had remained that way through habit, for even as a man, when Jason brought his "Aunt" Clara gifts from afar after each voyage, he entered through the living quarters.

Clara's role was not all praise and ego-tend-

44

ing. She could be sharp, even acid in her criticisms when Jason's transgressions warranted.

"Jason, you young fool! What insanity have you been up to?"

He leaned wearily against the door jamb. "If you keep me standing out here I won't tell you a blessed thing."

"Come with me. We'll go up to the attic. It's best Lucas doesn't know."

"Lucas!" Jason snorted.

Clara ignored that. "Can you get up the stairs without help?"

"What do you think I am, a cripple?"

"For the life of me I don't know what you are. You look as though you've been put through a meat grinder."

"He tried to kill me," Jason said with remarkable cheerfulness. "It was a glorious set-to. They'll be talking about it for years."

"You fought with Chester Manson!" It was an accusation.

"You must've known. Word of the fuss had to reach the tap room."

"I heard but I thought it was just talk. Over that Penn girl? Insanity! Did you think you could change things by brawling in the street?"

"It wasn't that—it wasn't losing her. . . ."

They had reached the attic and Jason sank down on the bed.

"Rest here," said Clara, "while I get salves and bandages. By rights we should call a doctor."

"I want no sawbones, nor any salve. I need a good jolt of rum and a breather. Bring me a bottle."

"Stubborn—stubborn." Clara shook her head

all the way to the bar. She returned with the rum Jason had demanded. He swallowed down a goodly amount, then turned on Clara.

"What are you staring at. Have you never seen bumps and bruises on a man before?"

"Bumps and bruises indeed! I've been waiting for the rum to leak out through the holes in you."

"I'll be right as rain in a little while."

"At least let me stop the blood oozing from your cheek."

Clara formed a makeshift bandage from a kerchief. "The fight was not about Chester Manson taking Elizabeth Penn from you?"

"Only after a fashion."

"That wants explaining."

"It is a simple case of a blackguard coming into his own."

"How so?"

"It goes back some four months to when we spoke the *Water Nymph* off Valparaiso. Manson was on his way home and as a friendly gesture, I invited him and his first mate to dine with me on the *Gray Ghost* that evening. I knew full well he would come only to crow over his lucky cargo of sperm and beating me back to port, but I didn't mind that, and it was a pleasant evening. I did not know then what I'd done—to wit, entertain a sneaking bilge rat at my table."

"What did Chester Manson do to deserve such contempt?"

"He'd hardly dropped anchor here in Stonington when he rushed to Jethro Penn with a tale that I had taken on a Jamaican lass. I should have known what was in his mind when his pig eyes were glued to her during dinner. She went back and forth to the galley and his scheming gaze never left her."

"And he told Jethro Penn that you had the girl aboard for your own purposes."

"Exactly. Word traveled from Jethro to my grandfather and my wedding was not only called off but Jethro was only too happy to push Elizabeth into Chester's arms."

"Are you sure that is how it was?"

"Of course. Jethro only agreed to the marriage of our two names because there was nothing he could do to prevent it: Elizabeth and I had made up our minds. He never really wanted it."

"I see. And Elizabeth listened to Chester Manson's lies—"

"Lies?"

"He was telling the truth?"

"Certainly. Chester is no liar. But what has that to do with it?"

"But if what he said was true—you were keeping a whore on your ship—"

"No man of decency would stoop so low as to tell that to his fiancée."

"Is it the custom of whaling captains to carry loose women on their voyages?"

"The captain of any vessel is its absolute master."

It was Clara Peavey's opinion that the answer to the question Jason had evaded was negative. She had never heard of mistresses or concubines being taken along on those perilous runs after the great whales. What happened in port was another matter. However, all men were deceitful; they were all animals where women were concerned. Heaven only knew what actually went on aboard those vessels.

Clara was not really concerned about Jason's morals. His story interested her only insofar as it inspired the germ of a plan. Perhaps Jason's ideas on the rights of sea captains could be put to good use solving her own troubles.

"I don't like that word you used," he was saying now. "Marita was not a harlot. She was a sweet little thing and I treated her with respect and when I put her off I saw to it she was well provided. The girl was definitely not a whore."

The semantics did not interest Clara. With all her tempting ways, she knew that Kate was not a whore either, but certainly women who exchanged their virtue for anything but holy wedlock were of a different cut and merited the contempt of decent people. Therefore the plan . . .

"I must not tarry here," Clara said. "Lucas will miss me. I will send our girl up to tend you—our bar maid. You will find her efficient, I am sure . . ."

Thus was Kate about to care for Jason Steele, and even in his condition, Jason was not too far gone to appreciate her charms. The bulky robe concealed her figure effectively but there was shining black hair flowing down her back, and lovely features of an innocent cast.

There was also the timid uncertainty of her approach, which Jason found rather pleasant. "Don't be afraid, lass. I am quite harmless."

"You have been terribly injured."

"Not as badly as it appears. If you could

48

wash the abrasions and perhaps affix a bandage
or two . . ."

"I'll do my best, sir."

Using a bar towel, Kate went about a nurse's
duty, gently bathing Jason's wounds while he
lay watching her.

"You were not in the tavern when I was last
here."

"No, sir. I came only a few months ago, after
my father died."

"I'm sorry."

"Thank you."

There was silence while Kate ministered to
Jason's battered face. Though she was as gentle
as possible, there was a certain unprofessional
clumsiness and Jason did his best not to grimace at the pain.

Quite soon, there was a diversion which
helped greatly. As Kate became totally preoccupied in her work, she did not note that the
sash of her robe had loosened. Jason had only
to angle his eyes and behold two firm young
breasts with bold, dark nipples of surprising
maturity. When Kate bent to inspect the great
swollen bruise on Jason's side, the robe fell
slightly more open and the rays of the bedside
lamp displayed her smooth young body to her
knees. The sight of the flawless skin with its
slightly dusky quality, the light transforming
the black triangle to a surface of silver threads,
caused Jason to react sharply under the sheet
thrown carelessly across his middle.

Kate caught the direction of Jason's gaze,
straightened up and bound the sash securely. A
blush came to her smooth cheeks. Jason closed
his eyes and for reasons beyond him, actually

felt shame. He had always been most overt in the presence of females of lower station in the past, his tendency in that direction often having brought him trouble.

Trouble. His present trouble. The *Gray Ghost* would ride out upon whatever tide William Steele decreed. Jason did not doubt that. Of course his grandfather's decision had been made prior to his calling Chester Manson out, but nothing really had been changed by that action. The sea would probably be the best place for a time—at least in case Jethro Penn resorted to legal action. Unlikely, though. Chester Manson had stooped low but he would not go whining to the authorities.

Not one to worry too greatly under any circumstances, Jason really had but one regret: He should not have soaked himself in rum; it was that gesture of self-pity which had reduced him to this sorry state.

And so Jason reached for the flagon and had another drink. Thus preoccupied he was paying no attention to Kate as she tended his discolored side. Had this not been the case, he might have been amused at her reaction and the interest she was trying to hide.

This interest centered upon the manifestation of Jason's manhood brought on by his inspection of her lush charms. She glanced up to see his eyes still closed. A lowering of the sheet's upper edge a scant inch and the organ would be revealed. Curiosity and excitement merged as she placed a bandage over the bruise she had cleansed and anointed with salve. She felt none of the revulsion she had known at the onset of Lucas Peavey's attack; only the remnants of a natural reluctance to completely disrobe a total stranger—even such a one whose body excited her so much. With a groan, Jason suddenly turned upon his stomach, wincing at the discomfort.

"I'm going to nap for a while, lass. Thank you for your kindness."

Kate reached for a folded blanket but before she could spread it over him, Jason said, "The sheet will be enough."

Good heavens, she thought. Had he known what was in her mind?

She hurried from the room.

10.

Midmorning of the following day, Clara found an opportunity to slip up to the attic without being seen. Jason was seated on the edge of the bed having just awakened from a long, sound sleep.

"Not bad," he announced. "Even the swelling has gone down."

"Your face still has that meat grinder look," Clara told him. "Are you hungry?"

"Ravenous."

"Good. Whether I feed you or not depends on you—I want a favor."

"Aunt Clara, you have only to ask. You know that."

Clara regarded him with affection. Even with his face chopped to ribbons he was still handsome, his exuberant love of life shining through.

"It's about that girl who ministered to you last night . . ."

"An attractive lass. Her presence must help the trade downstairs."

". . . I want you to take her away with you."

"Aunt Clara—"

"Why not? You are going to sea again. You've demonstrated that female company is quite welcome. And that little tart is a living beauty—no one can deny that."

Jason was not slow to understand the situation. "So that's it. She is too beautiful for your comfort, with Lucas no doubt stalking her like a shark after a dolphin."

"Jason! I ought to slap you! Lucas loves me. He does not chase women. I am quite enough woman to satisfy him. But all young and unattached females are predatory at heart. Lucas has resisted her advances so far. But he is still a man, and—"

"Of course. I understand. He has just so much resistance. She spells trouble for you."

Jason's understanding went beyond that. In his affection for Clara, he knew she believed what she had to about the lecherous brute she had been condemned by fate to love and need. Her false vision of the man and his nonexistent virtue was a necessary support to her pride.

"I'll do what I can, Aunt Clara—I certainly owe it to you. But I can't tie the girl in a bundle and haul her off. Shanghaiing females is out of my line."

"That will not be necessary. When will you be leaving here?"

"As soon as possible. Probably right after nightfall."

"There is already concern about what happened to you."

"They probably think I'm in my cabin on the *Gray Ghost*."

"You *are* going back to sea."

"Ha! My sainted grandfather is seeing to that. When I talked with him last, he gave me forty-eight hours."

53

"Can your ship be ready on such short notice?"

"With Guy Mapes handling the refitting, it can. If we are short of supplies we will take them on somewhere down the coast. Grandfather Steele wants me out of town. And probably more so than ever now."

"That will work out fine. You can drop the little hussy at whatever port you choose."

"Aunt Clara, you can't be that cruel! You can't expect me to put a penniless girl ashore on a strange dock—"

"Of course not. I expect you to give her money. Enough to salve your conscience before you cut her loose."

"You *are* a cruel woman. I wish very strongly to lessen my debt to you with a favor, but what you are asking me to do—"

"I know. It is against your principles to shanghai females no matter how much they deserve it but in this case it will not be necessary. I shall go down and order the young lady off the premises; I will give her until evening to get out bag and baggage. She is without friends or resources so she will have no place to go and will be very happy to accept your invitation."

"It *does* seem cruel—"

"Cruel? To be put ashore with the money you will give her? I'd say it was a *kindness*. That way she is not put out to wander off and survive as best she can."

Jason lifted his hand. "All right—all right. I'll do as you ask provided she comes with me of her own free will."

"That she'll do if she isn't seven kinds of a

fool. I shall go down now and tell her she must leave the tavern. Then I'll send her up with a tray for you. You do the rest."

Jason nodded in silence. At the door, Clara turned. "Please understand that whatever you do with her when you get her on your ship is a matter of no concern to me."

Jason laughed. "Aunt Clara, you are a hard woman. Now don't wait too long to send me something to eat or I'll be down there gnawing on your bar."

11.

Clara lost no time in seeking out Kate McCrae. When she descended to the tap room she found it empty save for a single townsman quietly sleeping off a night of overindulgence in a far corner.

She called Kate in from the kitchen and eyed her sternly. "My husband and I have come to a decision," she said. "We have been very kind to you but it cannot go on forever. You are to leave the *Blue Mermaid* immediately."

"Immediately? I—"

"Frankly, your overtures to my husband are wearying to us both."

"Overtures! But Mrs. Peavey, it has been quite the other—" Kate broke off. If she told Clara Peavey what had happened in her bedroom she would only be accused of lying. Desperately she went off on another tack. "I do my work well and the work is here to be done. Before I came there must have been far more than you could do yourself."

Clara saw no point in explaining that obtaining and disposing of bar maids was a game she and her husband had played for a long time; that she was quite willing to work all hours to protect him from the wiles of predatory temptresses. In turn, they had been on both sides of that fence. Lucas had found excuses to get rid of two unattractive, middle-aged females and had refused to hire a likely young man, while Clara had gotten rid of a busty young woman by finding a willing swain and arranging an elopement.

"Tonight," she ordered. "This very night. If you do not leave of your own accord, I shall solicit testimony from certain of our patrons concerning your lewd suggestions to them."

"Mrs. Peavey!" Kate gasped. "I have hardly spoken to any of the patrons except to ask for their preferences."

"Their preferences?"

It was no use; Kate realized that Clara Peavey had resolved to banish her and would use whatever lies and deceit were necessary.

"But I have no place to go!"

"There is always the street. Now I have a chore for you," Clara said sternly. "Our guest in the attic bedroom is ready for nourishment. You will take a tray up to him. Hot tea, toast, and a bowl of cornmeal mush. Get to it, girl, no dawdling...."

Fighting back her tears, Kate went into the kitchen and prepared the tray. She carried it to the attic and found Jason Steele regarding his battered face in the mirror.

"Mr. Steele," Kate admonished "I am sure you shouldn't yet be on your feet. You were badly mauled—"

"And I mauled right back with very good effect. I think Chester Manson will not be out of bed for some time."

"I have brought you something to eat."

57

Jason regarded her thoughtfully as she set the tray on a small table and pulled up a chair for him. "The bandage on your side—would you like it changed?"

"No, it's fine. In fact I am about to discard it."

"Do you think that's wise?"

"All my scratches were pretty superficial. I'm just a little stiff, that's all. A cup of tea would be just the thing."

Jason sat down while Kate poured the hot brew. As she did so, he recalled the loose robe of the previous night, the smooth young body under it. Kate was more demurely clad now in skirt and shirtwaist but the heady aura of her youth and beauty as she bent toward him were still much in evidence. Clara's idea was beginning to appeal to Jason very much.

She straightened and set the teapot down. "Is there anything else, Mr. Steele?"

"No, I think not. But why don't you sit a while and talk to me? I hate to drink my tea in solitude."

Taking the request as a directive, Kate sat down on the edge of the bed and smoothed her skirt over her knees. "What do you wish to talk about?"

"About you, my dear. To be perfectly frank, I cannot see you as a bar maid. You have much greater potential."

"As a matter of fact, sir, I have very little potential."

"Oh, I do not agree with you there. I see you as the sort of person who should not be trapped landside. Have you ever been to sea?"

"No, sir. Only on pleasure boats on the

James River as a very young child when I lived in Richmond. I can hardly remember it."

"Then sailing around the world would be a new experience for you, would it not?"

"Oh, certainly. I suppose you have been there many times—I mean, around the world."

"Often enough to be quite familiar with much of it. The world is full of exciting ports and places. It's a shame so many people stay landbound all their lives. They miss so much."

Jason poured himself another cup of tea, glanced at Kate's neat ankles, and tasted the cornmeal mush. Then he put down his spoon, the project at hand overshadowing his appetite.

"There is only one bad thing about being the captain of a whaling vessel—the loneliness. Months at sea with occasional stops at various ports could be quite pleasant with a female companion."

"I understand some captains take their wives with them."

"It does happen." Jason sipped at his tea. He was not getting the response he had hoped for, but perhaps he had expected too much. From Clara's description of this little package, she should have been showing some sign of coquettish interest at least. The direct approach, he decided: Get it over with.

"I am inviting you to go with me on my next voyage. We start immediately."

Kate was stunned. "Are you saying that you want me to go to sea with you—on your ship?"

"My dear, I could hardly put it any plainer."

"Are you asking me to marry you?"

It was Jason's turn to look stunned. "Oh, come now—"

The pressure inside Kate had been building. The violence inflicted by Lucas Peavey plus the abuse contributed by his wife had wound her into a tightly coiled spring. She had to snap sometime. She sprang to her feet.

"I won't allow you to insult me, no matter how important you are in this town! I am not a harlot waiting to run off with any man who asks me!" The tears came now, tears of anger and defiance rather than self-pity.

Jason's cup clattered back into its saucer. "But I thought—"

"I know what you thought. I guess Mrs. Peavey told you I'm a whore trying to seduce her husband. Well, it isn't true! I loathe the man, and he attacked me. I do intend to leave this awful place and I don't know where I will go or how I will fare but it will not be on your boat as your harlot!"

"Now, wait—I didn't mean—"

"I know very well what you meant. And what I'm telling you is that I will not be humiliated!"

And with that she stormed out.

Jason sat gaping at the door. What an outburst, and what a beautiful little figure she made, spouting her defiance like red steam coming from a South Seas volcano. Clara had lied about the girl, no doubt about that. She must have been the victim of Lucas Peavey's lust, from what she'd said. Jason poked at his mush and pondered the situation. He could only wonder how and why the girl had come there in the first place. What was her background? What was the depth and breadth of her misfortune?

Interesting questions indeed. However, they were unimportant in relation to his own problems. Suffice it to say that she was not a prospect for the role he'd had in mind for her—a pity, too; such a luscious little wench was bound to be led to grief, but some other man would escort her. He decided that Lucas Peavey would probably win. If Jason understood the man, and he thought he did, the tavernmaster's desire for the little beauty would transcend his respect for Clara's feelings, and with no place to go, the girl would stay where she was—and, in time, Lucas would break her spirit.

With that assessment, Jason dismissed the subject in favor of his own situation. All in all, he felt pretty good. The swelling in his side had gone down. It was still somewhat tender, but by favoring it he could get by. His face was still a caricature of his true one but he planned to stay out of sight anyhow so that made no difference.

He was surprised that Clara did not come to the attic again to get his report on Kate's reaction. He could only conclude that Lucas was watching her too closely.

When the day ended and it was quite dark, Jason slipped out the back door of the tavern and made his way to the dock where the *Gray Ghost* awaited. Soon he would again be at sea. He would attend to business and bring back many barrels, perhaps a record run. During the intervening years he was sure the town would forget. He was somewhat bemused at how little the loss of the fair Elizabeth had affected him.

It was the circumstances that had been important, and he had recouped his honor in that respect.

Jason shrugged. The affair was done with.

12.

Jason's guess as to why Clara Peavey did not visit the attic bedroom for the balance of that day had been entirely correct. She had learned over the years just how far she could control her husband, and as things had worked out she was on the brink. Under normal circumstances she managed him fairly well since he was not perceptive enough to realize he was being maneuvered. But his anger was something to be feared. Twice during their married years she had gone too far and had been badly beaten. Thus she had learned to be wary.

As things stood, Lucas Peavey's mood had been darkening throughout the day. He'd fallen silent, and he had not lifted a single flagon of ale, which in itself was ominous.

Clara wished that she had let him know of Jason's presence. Concealing it had been a spur-of-the-moment decision. Unaware that the true reason for Lucas' dark mood was his failure with Kate, she could only assume he suspected her of an intrigue behind his back. To reveal Jason's presence at this late date could bring her husband's wrath down upon her.

So Clara did not dare risk another visit to the attic as Lucas' baleful glare followed her about the tavern. Also, there was need of her presence in the tap room. Kate had not returned after delivering Jason's lunch.

Curiosity as to Kate's reaction to Jason's proposition got the best of Clara by late afternoon, and she made her way to Kate's bedroom. But Lucas' harsh voice intercepted her from below while she was mounting the stairs.

"Where are you going?"

"Kate must be dawdling in her room. She should be in the tap room helping me."

"Never mind about the girl. She's been working hard enough around here. She deserves a little time. Get out there with the patrons where you belong."

Lucas' glowering scowl remained on her as she slipped past him. He was doubly damned if he was going to let the troublesome old shrew interfere with his plans for the night. Let Kate remain in her room. That was just where he wanted her. . . .

After fleeing Jason and his "invitation" to sail with him on the *Gray Ghost*, Kate flung herself upon her bed and wept all the tears which had been clamoring for release. They provided comfort after a fashion, but Kate's spirit was drained rather than renewed—a bleak state of mind in which no single outrage or misfortune stood alone: Neither Lucas Peavey's attack nor its effect on her physically was prominent; Jason Steele's insulting offer still carried some sting but Kate's sharp indignation had faded. The only clear dread was that of making decisions that demanded to be made.

Time passed, darkness came, and the hope of any firm resolve by then dissipated.

When her door opened and Lucas Peavey entered her bedroom, all else faded from her mind.

Kate turned from her window to see a different man from the one who had come to her on the previous night. Lucas was stone cold sober, and the look in his eyes was one of grim determination rather than the eagerness of lust. For all appearances, he had come to correct the impression he had left her with previously, rather than to wrest pleasure from her body.

They were both silent. Lucas, clad in a robe, stood just inside the door. There was an air about him that implied he had thrown all caution to the winds and Kate sensed that screaming would do her no good, that Clara Peavey would only cower somewhere in the dark and wait.

Kate moved along the wall much as a trapped animal might, the unwilling prey of a hunter. Lucas regarded her with a cold smile.

"Easy, lass, easy," he murmured as he undid the sash of his robe and threw it open. He was naked beneath it.

Kate stared, shocked and terrified. Nor did she miss the pride and satisfaction in Lucas Peavey's face as he watched her reaction to his erectly poised weapon.

"Oh, please—" Kate barely whispered.

Lucas dropped his robe to the floor as he approached her. "It's time to settle up, lass. It won't be as bad as you're thinking. I'll make a woman of you once and for all and you may take that as gospel."

"Oh—no. No! Please . . ."

"Enough of this. Let's get to it."

He moved swiftly, pinning her to the wall beside the bed table. His naked bulk pressed against her and she felt the hard shaft against her belly.

Her arms flailed wildly about until Lucas caught her wrists and held her as easily as if she were a doll.

"No good to fight, lass. We're here to settle a difference, you and me."

With that he bent her arm behind her back and lifted her off the floor. He took a backward step, then with a quick, deft movement, he released her. Before she could react, he crouched low and caught the hem of her skirt, jerking it upward. He pulled it over her head and held it there, the material bunched in his fist. Kate's arms were trapped. She was helpless.

She heard his satisfied laugh. "This is a lazy man's way, lass, but it saves a lot of fight and gets the thing over with."

Kate was crying out, struggling frantically against the smothering trap. But Peavey held her there, still standing, and now with his free hand was stripping down the two petticoats which obstructed his sight of the loveliness he planned to violate. That left only pantalettes. These he hauled down with a new impatience, snatching them from the waist and leaving them bunched about her ankles as he threw her onto the bed. Kate felt the cool night air on her bare flesh. Immediately the weight of Peavey's naked body was on top of her, pushing her deep into the down mattress.

There was a growl and a curse as Lucas

strove to spread her legs against the constricting effect of the pantalettes at her ankles. His lust mounting, he tore them away and spread Kate's thighs with savage satisfaction.

There must have been pain but Kate hardly noticed it, nor was she clearly aware of Lucas' thrust into her body: "There—that makes you a woman, lass!" The need to draw breath blotted out all else. With Lucas totally preoccupied, Kate was in danger of smothering in her gown. Desperately she fought the thick material of skirt held fast over her head. Panic gave her the strength she needed to free one arm. Gulping a breath of air, Kate pawed about wildly. There were two objects on the bed table, a lamp, and a heavy brass candlestick, the taper half burned away. She gripped the candlestick at its top and swung it in an arc across the bed.

The thump of the base against Lucas' skull was the most satisfying sound Kate had ever heard. It was followed by another sound, a low moan, and the weight of the gross body under which she was pinned turned inert, as did the rigid rod which penetrated her.

After a few wary moments and gulps of life-giving air, Kate began wriggling and writhing out of her imprisonment. She twisted upward, heaving Lucas away to a point where she could come free. He lay unconscious. Kate wondered if he were dead as she saw that a section of his scalp was laid open and oozing blood. She did not investigate further. Sobbing, she straightened her skirt and ignoring her undergarments she fled from the room, down the back stairs, and into the street.

There she stopped to ease her tortured lungs. Returning steadiness brought a wave of dismay.

She had to return to the bedroom; there was something she had forgotten.

Although the idea frightened her, there was no doubt she would go back if the devil himself now waited for her there in the shadows. Still sobbing with fear and tension, Kate returned as she had come, her fright increasing at every squeak of the stairs. She peered into the bedroom. Lucas Peavey still lay where she had felled him and with a quick little whimper of gratitude, she tiptoed to the closet where she retrieved a rather bulky cylindrical object about three to four feet in length and tightly wrapped in cloth.

The rolled-up treasure consisted of two dozen canvases done by her father over the happy years they had been together. The canvases and some clothing were all she had brought with her when the Peaveys took her in. The wagon and horses had been sold to pay for her father's funeral. Except for a cloak, her father's paintings were all she took with her when she left the *Blue Mermaid* for the second and final time.

As she crossed the room Lucas Peavey groaned and stirred. Somewhat relieved that she had not murdered him, although she would not have regretted what she had been forced to do, she nonetheless hastened back into the night.

Alone and forlorn now, on dark Water Street, she stood and looked northward toward Lambert's Cove into which Captain Kidd had once sailed his infamous ship. But the historical background of Stonington was lost on her. What she saw in her mind was the cemetery off Robinson's pasture near the old Watch Hill dock where Clinton McCrae lay buried. She sighed deeply and turned away.

Across Water Street was Wanawaduck and to the west on Main Street the fine mansions of Stonington's wealthy townsmen. But none of them would provide sanctuary for her, she knew. Those people did not take in penniless bar maids on the run.

She walked south, the gas-lit street deserted save for less than friendly shadows. For all her sense of desolation there was a spark of pride glowing in her mind. She had stood up for her rights, fought back, ready to accept the consequences rather than submit slavishly to Lucas Peavey. And she wasn't beaten yet. An idea began formulating in her mind.

As she hurried along Water Street to disappear into the night, her sole possessions were the roll of canvases, the dress and cloak she wore, and the young body Lucas Peavey had violated.

And a stubborn, though tear-stained, courage.

13.

The *Gray Ghost* went out quietly on the early tide with Guy Mapes on the afterdeck and Jason Steele asleep in the master cabin. His side had swollen again and it was painful.

The *Gray Ghost* was a bark of 111 feet registered at 313 tons; a three-master with canvas typical to the whaler where endurance rather than speed was the prime requirement. Built in 1841, she was far from being an inexperienced ship, having weathered human and natural disaster from Arctic whaling grounds to sultry tropical waters in four oceans. Whales, reluctant to be hauled against her stays, had destroyed many a forecastle hand over the decades. Once she was even boarded by hostile natives off the Marquesas Islands, resulting in eighteen casualties before the decks were cleared, four of them hands who fought well.

Over the years, the *Ghost* had met every onslaught Neptune brought against her, though more than once she limped into port with masts down and pumps working. Now, on the brink of being exiled from the seas by the great floating factories built to turn whaling into a "rocking chair" business of scientific slaughter, she was as good a ship as when she had slipped her stays at Thomas Kane's boatyard in Stonington, an untested beauty.

This would be her last voyage and if ships have souls the *Gray Ghost* may have looked sadly upon Cannon Square, Stonington Point, and Noyes Rock as she was eased out toward the northwest trades.

Guy Mapes paid little attention to the landmarks. Frowning down from the afterdeck, his concern centered on the crew. The hands seemed happy enough. They were chanting a sea ditty as they heaved the anchor short:

Oh, Ranzo was no sailor,
He was a New York tailor . . .

The lilt was lighthearted but Mapes, troubled of mind, hardly listened.

Oh, Ranzo was no sailor,
But they shipped him 'board a whaler . . .

The trusted first mate had realized from the beginning that William Steele's bland confidence they could sign on good, loyal hands was overoptimistic. Men just back from three years on the sea were not inclined to enthusiastically turn about and go back again without a reasonable breather. There were wives and sweethearts to be considered; also, that prime enemy of ambition—money in the pocket. Whaling hands never worked for wages. Instead, they gambled along with the owners on the generosity of the sea. Their lay—or portion of the returns—was agreed to before sailing, its size dependent upon the importance of each man to the ship. A master could receive as much as a quarter of the profit, with forecastle hands dropping as low as a half of one percent. Disastrous voyages could net a hand as little as ten cents, although several hundred dollars was the usual share—not a great deal for years of work. The Steeles were eminently fair with their hands and never left them to starve ashore while waiting for a new berth.

> *Now Ranzo was no beauty,*
> *He would not do his duty . . .*

Thus the Steeles were able to maintain a sizable core of efficient seamen by virtue of good treatment, which was not necessarily the case throughout the industry. They were seldom forced to go to the crimps for manpower.

> *So they gave him lashes thirty,*
> *Because he was so dirty . . .*

On this occasion however, one of the agents had been contacted. Crimps functioned in every whaling port as labor agents and were always ready to furnish hands from the lists they maintained—men not always of the best caliber.

> *Now Ranzo is a sailor,*
> *The Captain 'board a whaler . . .*

This was what was bothering Mapes. He'd taken on five for the forecastle of whom he was uncertain, and one in particular. Of the remaining four, two—Louis Baptista, and Juan Castro—were Portuguese, a point much in their favor. Portugal had supplied the whaling trade with many of its sturdy sons, fine, efficient sailors who followed the ships wherever they went—high among the everyday heroes who took the perils of whaling as a matter of course.

The second pair, Antone Salas and Leon Ramos, were Jamaicans, totally unknown quantities.

He's known wherever them whalefish blow,
As the hardest bastard on the go....

There was another aspect to the situation. The *Gray Ghost* was going out with a short crew, only thirty-eight hands where the full contingent for the class of ship was closer to fifty; somewhat dangerous under rough conditions. With too few hands, however, there would be plenty of work and less time for the rot of discontent to set in.

But the signing on of the fifth man, John Saipan, was Mapes's main worry. Saipan was a "sea lawyer," the designation given to men with a cursory knowledge of maritime law and a penchant for causing trouble. It was not that Mapes, a fair man, wanted to abrogate any seaman's rights; it was just that there was no advantage in having a hand aboard who would deliberately foster discontent in the forecastle. In the case of John Saipan, there was more cause for concern. The man had sailed with Guy Mapes before, an unhappy circumstance, and there was something Mapes would have to face and settle in short order.

73

Mapes sighed and turned his gaze windward. He watched as the white flash on East Breakwater Point off Bartlett Reef faded and dropped below the horizon. His eyes were troubled even though his grizzled old face held its customary calm.

For better or worse, the *Gray Ghost* was on the high seas.

14.

Twenty-four hours out, moving south by southeast off the Grand Banks, the ship ran into a stillness most unusual for that time and place. The weather was unseasonably warm with the glass hanging low, short, sullen gusts bellying the sails only to fall away again into calm. Second Mate Peter Wells had the watch with Boatswain Cater MacRoy, a dour, weathered old Scot, at the wheel. MacRoy was muttering to himself, reliving his shrewish wife's reaction to his sudden turn back to sea:

" 'You are happy to go,' she says. 'You don't care a fig for me or the bairn,' she says. 'You come ashore and get me with child and then it's off again with a tip of your hat,' she says. 'This time you are turning your ugly face from us after one night's sleep.' "

There was truth in Hattie MacRoy's lament. Five times since he'd wed her, Cater had sailed off in Steele ships, each time to return and find a two- or three-year-old that he'd sired. He might have retired long since, but as he explained once to a shipmate:

"It's just that after a first night or two in bed with her, I can no longer stand the woman. The only time she's silent is when I'm on top of her.

75

Believe me, mate, she's got the capacity of a rabbit for duplicatin' her species. . . ."

Peter Wells smiled at the old Scot's grumblings. He was young for an officer's berth. A son of old-line wealth and a Harvard graduate, Peter rated favors through his father, a valued business associate of the Steeles. This was his second voyage, both under Jason Steele and the reliable Guy Mapes, and while any man at sea was required to take his chances along with the others, Peter had still not been allowed an oar in a whaleboat. His second-mate status was not out of line however. Peter was of good intellect, quick to learn, and not overbearing in authority. He had been given the duty of inscribing the log under Jason's—and at times Mapes's—dictation, because of his fine Spencerian hand, so the *Gray Ghost* log might well have been the most legible on the high seas; also the most literate and lyrical because Peter often transposed the dictation into rhetoric less harsh to his educated ear. All in all, Peter loved the sea and made an honest effort to pull his weight.

Now, under brooding, starless skies, he turned to the wheelman. "Mr. MacRoy, how long do you fancy this calm will last?"

"I don't know, sir," the Scot replied. "Heavy. Very heavy. Unnatural."

"Would you say it signals bad weather ahead?"

"Aye, it could."

At that moment, with atmospheric conditions exactly right, one of the rarest of ocean phenomena began manifesting itself on and about the ship. There was a sharp crackling as if of electricity. The last of a wind gust died against the sails and a thin green line leaped from a crossbeam of the foremast to the midmast. It hung there, quivering, like an illuminated bowline. A second, then a third eerie line was flung across and the iron topside, the cleats and rings and metal stays, took on an unearthly green glow.

It was as though some celestial magician was performing an Olympian illusion to confound the mere mortals. The phenomenon developed with awesome speed until the whole ship was enveloped in a tremulous green glow.

Peter Wells, watching from the afterdeck, was totally entranced. "Mother of God!" he breathed.

He knew what was happening, of course. The ship was being visited by St. Elmo's fire, a form of electronic manifestation which came about when atmospheric conditions were exactly right.

Hands were now appearing from the forecastle to view the awesome sight. They were silent as the green fire crackled and glowed about them. Several crossed themselves and there were those who muttered prayers; each man according to his nature.

Only Cater MacRoy remained exactly as he had been—unimpressed, hands on the wheel, his eye on the compass, holding the ship five points south by southeast. To the grumbling Scot, duty came before miracles.

The two new Portuguese dropped to their knees in prayer.

One of the hands broke the silence. "It's the death of us!"

"An evil sign, as God's my judge!"

A third disagreed. "Stow that bilge! It's a storm warning, nothing more and nothing less. We're in for some rough weather."

The timid were not convinced. "It will fry us all to death!"

"You're a shame of a sailor man, you are! You ought to be beached and forgot. Do you think it's going to burn you?"

Observing from the afterdeck, Peter Wells knew a touch of guilt. With First Mate Mapes and the Captain still below, it was his duty to go among the men and reassure them. But he observed the scornful one doing an excellent job without help.

Scowling disdainfully at those showing fear, he grasped a halyard tremulously aglow with green light and ran his hand slowly up its length. As he did so, the fire was erased leaving the metal clean where he had touched.

"There! Am I fried? Am I even burned?"

With intent to commend the man, Peter took a forward step. He had vaguely sensed a presence near him there by the rail; now he threw a glance rearward and froze. What he beheld was almost as startling as the stunning spectacle of St. Elmo's fire. A creature stood there, a human being, obviously, but bedraggled beyond description. A begrimed face below a tangle of hair in which mice could have nested, and a shapeless wrap of a garment completed the apparition.

"Good Lord," Peter gasped. "Who are you? Why, you're a—a female!"

The reply was tart, defiant. "Should I be ashamed of it?"

"Where on earth did you come from?"

"Down below, in the basement of this stinking tub. I couldn't stand it anymore."

"A stowaway?"

"I don't have a ticket, if that's what you mean."

Peter Wells continued to gape while the St. Elmo's fire began to fade, and up forward the self-appointed disciplinarian was ably completing his task. "You cowering pups! Stand up on your legs! There's nothing here to frighten you! What are you, sailors or tots out of a nursery? Get back to your posts!"

The hands turned to the companionway, with one exception. John Saipan moved into the larboard gangway where, out of sight of the others, he whispered harshly to God. "Oh, ye Lord of vengeance! I have beheld the sign Thou sendest me and I bow to Thy supreme will. I shall be the weapon. Thine own sword of flaming justice!" Tears rolled down his face. "Preserve me, oh Lord! Shield me from mine enemies that I may work Thy will."

Minutes later, when he joined his mates in the forecastle, he was again quite normal.

Meanwhile, Peter Wells was completely out of his depth. "A female stowaway," he said helplessly.

"*Must* you keep calling me that?" was the reply. "I have a name. I am Kate McCrae and I demand to be taken to the captain."

Wells attempted to collect himself. "Oh yes, the captain . . . well, I think perhaps Mr. Mapes."

79

"Well, for heaven's sake, take me to *somebody*."

Wells extended a hand, then withdrew it. "This way, Miss. Please follow me . . ."

15.

"You say you were invited aboard this ship?" Mapes asked.

"Yes," Kate replied defiantly.

"Who invited you?"

"Mr. Jason Steele."

"The captain? Then why did you slip aboard and hide out in the hold for all this time?"

Kate's defiance was a gesture of desperation. The pretense of bravery sprang from the fact that just about everything bad which could happen to her had already happened. Nothing was left that she could think of except, perhaps, being thrown overboard. After spending all those fearful hours behind a water keg down in the malodorous bilge-level of the *Gray Ghost*, being thrown into the clean ocean might be a blessing.

"I asked you—?"

"I know what you asked me and I refuse to answer. I refuse to stand here and be treated like—like a stowaway!"

"Madam, from my point of view that is exactly what you are. But I do not wish to be rude, so you may sit down."

"I don't want to sit down. I want to see the captain. I demand to be taken to Jason Steele."

"Not at the present time. Captain Steele is resting."

Guy Mapes' decision to handle the preliminaries of this affair by himself was based on precedent, a gentlemen's agreement between himself and old William Steele:

I know, Guy, that I lean hard against your loyalty by placing Jason on your back as a burden. But without you, without your good sense and solid experience to rely on, I fear that my grandson would eventually come to grief on the high seas.

I cannot entirely agree with you, sir. I grant that Jason is not cautious at all times, but a feel for the sea is in his blood.

A feel for the bottom of it, I sometimes suspect. Anyhow, I depend upon you to hold him in check at dangerous times, even from your place as second in command and knowing that if an issue is ever brought to judgment I might have to rule against you.

I understand, sir, and I'll do my best.

No one could ask for more, good friend....

Actually, Guy Mapes experienced no great difficulty functioning as Jason's guide and mentor. There was no meanness in the boy, nor was he a believer in strict discipline. He took advice easily and was content to leave the running of the ship, the mechanics of it, to his officers under Mapes' direction. Such was his attractive personality that he was not seen as remote or standoffish by the crew, so things had always gone well. Jason was called a generous captain by most hands.

As to finding this disheveled waif aboard, Guy Mapes was mainly intrigued by the details

of how the thing had come about. He was neither surprised nor skeptical that Jason had invited her—nor highly critical. A virile young
buck like Jason needed a woman upon whom to
release energies which might have otherwise
sent the ship into reckless actions.

He said, "Young lady, I think it would be wise
if you confided in me. I am not doubting your
word about being invited aboard, but certainly
not to hide in the bilge. That I do not understand."

"There was no place for me to go and I preferred any place on earth to where I was."

"But you said you were invited—"

"I rejected the invitation. I am no man's
plaything! Mr. Steele as much as called me a
harlot!"

Sensing a female outburst—women were
pretty much a mystery to the first mate—he
went on gently, "But you still want to be taken
to him?"

"I demand it!"

"It might be a good idea at that. If he saw
you now he wouldn't have much stomach for
you as a plaything, I'm pretty sure. You look
like a half-drowned rat." Mapes was inclined to
speak frankly.

"I can't help it," Kate replied in the same
defiant tone. "If you'd spent two days where I
did you'd hardly come out looking like a
lady."

"We are running with only two officers so we
have a vacant cabin aft. You might look to
your appearance before going to see the master."

Kate automatically ran her hands over her

filthy frock and gave silent agreement, where-upon Mapes called Peter Wells in from where he was waiting in the companionway. Facing Mapes but eyeing Kate, Wells saluted and said, "Yes, sir?"

"You will take this lass to the vacant cabin larboard and bring her a bathtub. Then to the galley and fetch some buckets of hot water."

"Yes, sir."

"That'll be all."

As the young officer stepped aside for the grubby little stowaway and followed her into the companionway, Mapes mentally commend-ed him. Respect for a female, regardless of her condition and social position, was the mark of a gentleman, he thought approvingly. He sighed. There was business to attend to. "Mr. Wells," he called out. "We have a fo'c'sle hand—John Saipan. Send him to me . . ."

Saipan entered a few minutes later and stood quietly awaiting Mapes' pleasure. The first mate regarded him thoughtfully, the silence stretching.

It was the change in the man that held Mapes. He clearly remembered another time, another ship, and the scornful rebel with whom he had dealt: the powerfully gaunt figure pos-turing defiance even at the whipping post.

That had been five years earlier. Still, the change in Saipan was arresting. He now had a flowing beard and long, silky hair to match. His manner as he stood there was passive, se-rene, so that it looked as though the erstwhile sea lawyer had mended his disruptive ways. Mapes could only wonder why he continued to distrust the man. Something, possibly the first mate's deep-seated instinct, was trying to get a warning through. Mapes pondered, taking his time. The red fire of scorn and protest—had it been extinguished, or transformed into a hidden, far more deadly blue flame?

Am I being unfair? Mapes asked himself. Then, "You no doubt remember me, Mr. Saipan."

"I remember you, sir."

"Aboard the *Martha Kane*. I had you flogged."

"I recall. And I forgive you."

"I did not call you in here to be forgiven. I'll be frank, Saipan. You would not be here if any other hand had been waiting on the dock."

"I am grateful for the berth."

"Don't thank me. Just do your duty. I'll be watching."

"Have no fear. Since we last met I have gone to the mountain and knelt before the Lord."

"Are you saying that you've found religion?"

"I have knelt before my God and received His blessing. I have been anointed into His holy army."

So the man had found religion. "Well, I can't quarrel with that. And I hope the Lord told you to step up smartly and heave with a willing hand."

Saipan nodded, then said, "I have a request, sir."

"Ask it."

"I ask to stay shipside and be spared the whaleboats."

"You've lost your taste for danger?"

"Far from it. But in obedience to the Lord, I cannot kill."

The man's request was a rare one but not unheard of. Mapes had known three such in his career, men with scruples against killing living things. But that had not stopped them from being willing and faithful hands aboard ship. "You were once a good man with the harpoon."

"Those days are gone. I dare not touch the irons."

"Very well. I'll respect your scruple. No man should be made to go against his conscience."

"I am grateful, sir."

"Is there anything else?"

"Nothing."

"Then back to your duties."

After Saipan left, Mapes sat staring at the space he had vacated. The first mate was far from satisfied with the interview, but was not sure why. Finding religion, even late in life, was not a mark against any man—so why the uneasy feeling? Why did an assurance of good conduct leave him more doubtful than if there had been open defiance? He could only watch and wait, alert to the unusual aspects of the voyage. First there was the order to return to sea on dangerously short notice, then a female stowaway and a becalmed sea at the very outset.

Those things, and St. Elmo's fire to top it off.

Guy Mapes was not a superstitious man but there was some comfort in the conflict of opinion concerning the green fire. Some said it was a good omen, and if so, there was that much less onus for the voyage to bear.

The grizzled old seaman rose from his chair and went to inform the captain there was a woman aboard the ship.

16.

Peter Wells stumbled over the sill as he preceded Kate into her cabin. He flushed, and glanced accusingly at the sill as though it had tripped him on purpose. "I'm afraid you will find this cabin a little cramped, Miss, but there is none any bigger except the captain's."

"It will be quite all right, thank you. I grew up in the back end of a wagon."

If Peter Wells thought that a curious statement he was too polite to react. But Kate did not really care. She was in the grip of an odd elation—half lightheaded from lack of food and half filled with a profound relief at coming through the crisis of discovery without being harshly treated.

Peter Wells's amazement had not yet abated. "Did you stay down in that hold all the time?"

"I was afraid to come out. I found water in the supply kegs, and I was cold most of the time, but—"

"You are a very brave girl." He looked vaguely distressed. "I'm afraid you've ruined your frock."

"After I've had my bath I'll try to wash it."

"I don't think Mr. Mapes would mind if I

looked in the slop chest and found you something."

"The *slop* chest?"

"It is really a supply bin where the hands can buy things against their lay—you know, soap, combs and brushes, extra clothing, things like that."

"I'd be grateful."

"What you'll want now is a tub and lots of hot water."

"And if I could, maybe something to eat. I'm ravenous."

"Oh, of course! How stupid of me. I'll bring you something the first thing."

Peter Wells backed out of the cabin, again stumbling over the high sill. He returned a few minutes later balancing a tray. Entering carefully this time, he said, "I brought you some biscuits. They're awfully hard, but you can soak them in this bowl of dog's body—"

Kate's stricken look made exclamation unnecessary. "It isn't what it sounds like," Peter explained hastily. "The cook takes pea soup and cracked-up biscuits and fat from the meat and some other things and makes them up all together. It's really quite good."

Kate looked skeptically at the greenish concoction in the bowl, then smiled bravely. "Well, I'm hungry enough to eat a horse, so I ought to be able to handle dog's body. Actually, it looks wonderful."

"I'm sure you'll enjoy it. I'll bring a bathtub for you now and then all the hot water you want."

Kate smiled her thanks. She waited to eat until the young officer left, not trusting herself to remain ladylike in her ravenous hunger. Alone, she literally plunged into the gooey dish. She found the dog's body delicious, but in her state that couldn't be considered true judgment. The biscuits were hard enough to endanger her teeth but soaked in the dog's body they became less like chunks of iron ore.

Soon there was a knock on the door and Peter Wells re-entered, lugging in a sizable barrel sliced off to two thirds of its height. The rough edges of the cut had been planed down, smoothed, and varnished, as was the interior of the crude utility.

"Take your time with your meal," Peter said. "It will take several trips to fill this tub even with two buckets at a time."

"Please do not overexert yourself," Kate said. "There is no great rush."

"I'll be right back."

Kate's appetite was now appeased to a point where she was eating with less gusto. Still, she emptied the bowl, not caring if anyone thought her an utter pig.

Five trips from the galley brought the water level to a foot from the top and on his last trip, Peter Wells came back with a slab of carelessly sliced brownish material he identified as soap.

"It is hardly what a lady would use," he said, "but it is all we have outside the captain's cabin and Mr. Mapes's."

"It will do fine," Kate assured him.

"And now I'll look into the slop chest and see what I can find for you."

He was off again in eager servitude, and Kate could only marvel. *The way I look, I certainly can't be in the least attractive to him, so he must be just a very nice young man.* Thus she reckoned without awareness of the glow of lovely young womanhood that would not have been obscured by a burlap blanket much less a frock, however filthy, which still bravely outlined her firm, young, upturned breasts and slim waist. Also, the rat's nest into which her hair had been transformed still had some faint shine to it, more than enough to stir the imagination of a loveless young man who had looked forward to months and even years of that same state.

He returned with several garments. They were clean, which was about all that could be said for them.

"There just isn't anything on board for a lady," Peter apologized. "I think this shirt and this jacket will come close to fitting you. And the trousers ... well, they're all of very rough material."

"I'll just have to make them do, won't I?"

"At least until your frock can be washed and dried. That shouldn't take very long. I'm sure the cook will let you dry it over the oven in the galley. Your frock and underthings."

Kate saw no point in confusing him with the fact that the only underthing beneath the frock was her own skin.

"Now, if there is anything else—?"

"Nothing, thank you. You've done too much already, Mr. Wells."

Peter's look said that he would be happy to stay around and do more. He gulped and said, "It's Peter, Miss. And that water is very hot." Then he left, lifting his feet absurdly high over the door sill in order not to stumble a third time.

Kate smiled warmly after him. His kindness had braced her spirits, which were skidding dangerously and liable to plummet into the depths at any moment.

Alone and satiated, she now turned to the exciting prospect of becoming human again. She slipped out of her filthy frock, the act bringing back thoughts of the underthings left at the *Blue Mermaid*. She shivered and deliberately turned her mind to the task at hand.

Her hair! Good Lord, it was a mess! With an eye to starting at the top and working down, she bent over the edge of the tub and dipped her head in the water. The heat biting into her scalp felt wonderful. She took the outlandish bar of soap and began applying it. There was some difficulty in getting it to lather but then the hot water took hold and Kate reveled in the white cloud of suds which resulted.

She scrubbed and rinsed, scrubbed and rinsed a second and a third time, completely preoccupied.

It was not until she straightened and was twisting her squeaky clean hair into a knot on her head that she sensed the visitor in the cabin. Bent over the tub, her back to the door, the splashing of water in her ears, she had not heard anyone enter.

Abruptly, she turned and saw Jason Steele regarding her from just inside the door. Kate drew in her breath, and with nothing close by to cover her nakedness, she jumped into the tub. The firm young derrière Jason had no doubt contemplated while Kate was bent over, disappeared along with the rest of her. Only her head showed above the water line.

"What are you *doing* here?" she demanded.

Jason had not moved. Nor had his expression much changed from a thoughtful, half-quizzical look. "I happen to be the captain of this ship."

"Does that give you the right to intrude on my privacy without knocking?"

"It gives me the right to do pretty much as I please."

"Well, *get out*! Get out or I'll—I'll scream!"

"That wouldn't do you any good. Nobody would come."

"Then you are saying that I am at your mercy?"

"I guess that's a good way of putting it. So you'd better pray that I'm merciful."

"What are you going to do?"

"I came to ask a few questions, if that's not too presumptuous."

Jason's attitude was in no way harsh. The bathtub episode appeared to have amused him.

"Exactly who are you, young lady?"

"You know who I am. We've met before."

"Correct—at the *Blue Mermaid*. Your name was Kate, I believe."

"It still is. Kate McCrae."

Jason came forward and seated himself on the edge of the bunk. This, what with the size of the cabin, put him in close proximity to Kate in her bathtub. She huddled down into the water, her arms wrapped around her breasts. From where he sat, Jason could see her face, now shiny clean, above the rim of the tub. She looked painfully young.

"Yes," Jason said, "I recall your name but that doesn't really tell me much."

"Couldn't we talk about it later?" Kate pleaded.

Ignoring that, Jason went on, "I recall a pretty enough little trollop I invited into my ship—one who got very indignant at the idea. Still—here she is."

"I can explain that."

"I would be most interested in hearing your explanation."

"I had no place else to go," she said simply.

"Why was it necessary for you to go anywhere? You had work at Lucas Peavey's tavern."

"His wife ordered me to leave. And—he attacked me again. I had to get out of there."

"You are saying that gentle, considerate old Lucas *attacked* you?"

"You are making fun of me!"

Jason gave the merest hint of a smile.

"Well, that old goat was not gentle and not considerate. Anyway, I hit him."

"No! What with?"

"A candlestick. It opened his scalp and I ran."

Jason's white teeth flashed in a real smile now. "You slugged the old reprobate? Marvelous!" He leaned back and laughed.

"I was afraid I'd killed him, but then he moved. I had to run away, though. I knew he'd call the constable. And I had no place to go."

"I understand that, but you didn't have to sneak onto the ship and suffer in the hold for two days. You'll recall that I extended an invitation to you."

"I do recall, but that was to be your mistress. Or rather less than that, I think—your whore. I refused you then and I refuse you now!"

In her defiance Kate forgot her situation and came up on her knees. She realized her position when Jason made no reply. He was staring hypnotically at two shiny young breasts with water falling in drops from their nipples.

She sank back into the tub even as she conceded that it did not really matter; Jason had already seen everything.

"Please! This water is getting cold. Won't you kindly leave or must I freeze to death?"

Jason came to his feet and moved toward the door. With his hand on the knob, he turned. "We'll talk later. But in the meantime, don't shout to the world that *I* came in here and raped you."

Again Kate almost came out of the tub. "Are you saying that you don't believe me about Lucas Peavey? That I *gave* myself to him willingly?"

"Let's say that I am withholding judgment for the time being."

With that, Jason left, Kate glaring after him, every nerve in her body aquiver with indignation. But what difference did it make *what* Jason Steele thought? She did not care one way or another about his opinion.

She stood up in the tub.

There was a single, sharp rap on the door and it opened. Kate turned in alarm to once more look upon Jason Steele's unsmiling face. She sank back into the water.

Jason said, "Mr. Wells evidently forgot you would want to dry yourself."

With that, he tossed a pair of bath towels into the cabin and promptly closed the door.

Kate leaped from the tub, seized a towel and began vigorously rubbing herself. The water, long since cold, and the chill of night had coated her with goose bumps. Soon her skin was aglow and she was warm. She held the towel up for inspection. It was white and fluffy and large enough to serve as a robe; a towel of luxurious quality with letters embroidered in purple along one edge. They read:

Jason and Elizabeth

Kate recognized the names. It was probable that Jason had purchased the towels on his last voyage and had them monogrammed in anticipation of his life with Elizabeth Penn as his wife. Throwing the towels almost contemptuously to a virtual stranger was no doubt a symbol of his bitterness. The poor man, Kate thought. Losing the bride of his heart must have been a terrible blow. It was the first time she had ever felt kindly toward him.

There was more to it, an irritation, vague but discernible. It concerned his having seen her naked, and his reaction—or lack of it. She did feel *some* shame, but more than that she was annoyed at his attitude. It had been one of amusement—as if a small child had tried to shield her body from the eyes of an understanding adult. In all honesty Kate had to admit she would not have resented a little of Lucas Peavey's lustful gaze in Jason Steele's eyes—enough to indicate that he was not totally impervious to her charms.

Not that Kate wanted his overt admiration. Oh no! Jason Steele meant nothing to her. For the time being, however, she was dependent on his good graces for her board and keep.

Dried, warmed, and comfortable now, she turned to the garments from the slop chest. They fit well, and that was all that could be said for them. However, Kate was in no position to complain. She dressed herself and then scrubbed at her dress in the bathtub.

She had just finished wringing it out when there was a tap on the door. This time the visitor waited to be admitted.

Kate was not disappointed when Peter Wells stepped into the cabin. She was not really aware of the picture she presented. She had braided and spiraled her hair, giving her a most mature crown. Below, the loose tunic effectively camouflaged her prominent breasts, turning her into a typical cabin boy. But the trousers terminated just above the knee revealing a pair of lissome legs which betrayed her sex most excitingly. All in all, Peter was enchanted. She was an adorable pixie, and certainly a lovely girl in strange clothing.

Peter Wells stared and gulped.

Kate laughed, earlier tensions vanishing.

"Good heavens, do I look that bad?"

"You look wonderful," he replied.

"I'm surprised that you found clothing so near my fit."

"They were for the cabin boy, I believe. But we do not have one on this voyage." He came forward. "If you will give me your frock I'll have it dried over the galley oven."

"Thank you. There *is* one more favor I'd like to ask."

"I'll be happy to do anything I can."

"I'd like you to run an errand for me, to the cellar at the back of the boat where I was hiding."

"The afterhold of the ship," Peter corrected.

"Yes. There are a lot of barrels down there."

"Water and ballast."

"I was hiding behind the barrels right at the back by the left wall."

"The larboard hull. I'll find it."

"All I brought on board was a rolled-up cylinder about three feet long, wrapped in heavy cloth. I treasure it and I would not want to lose it. Could you bring it to me?"

"I'd be glad to, Miss."

"My name is Kate. I've already called you Peter, so . . ."

"All right, Kate. I'll be right back."

"Then will you take me for a tour of the boat—I mean the ship?"

He hesitated in the doorway. Then he left, to return some minutes later with Kate's treasure. He examined it critically. "Lucky it didn't get into the bilge. Is what's inside perishable?"

"I'm afraid so. They're canvases my father painted. They are all I have to remember him by."

"Oh, your father was an artist?"

"A very good one."

"Paintings should have more protection. I think I can get the ship's carpenter to wrap waterproof oilskin around them."

"Peter, you're an absolute dear!" Kate stepped close to him, and laid her open palms

97

on his chest. She was enjoying the lighthearted flirtation. Peter reddened.

"I'd love to be shown around the ship."

"Maybe I'd better empty the bathtub first," Peter said. "You will want to get rid of it in this small cabin."

He seized a bucket, and began emptying the water out the porthole.

When the tub was almost empty, he rolled it out of the cabin.

"I'm ready to tour the ship," Kate said. "See? I'm learning to be a sailor. I said ship not boat. The boats are the little ones hanging on the ropes along the rail."

Peter nodded. "Miss—ah, Kate—I'm afraid I can't show you around."

"Of course. You have your duties and I've taken up too much of your time already."

"No, it's not that. It is Captain's orders. You are to stay in your cabin until further notice. You are not to go on deck." He paused. "I'm sorry."

Kate felt like a punctured balloon, the remembered fact that she was an unwanted stowaway rather than a welcome guest shattering her gay mood. Peter Wells's embarrassment at having to remind her was painful to him and Kate could only regret having taken too much for granted.

"Oh, of course. But thank you for being so sweet to me, Peter. I'm sure we shall see each other again."

"I'll be looking forward to it."

As he opened the door, Kate stopped him. "Peter, what do you think they will do with me?"

"I don't know, Kate."

"But you must have some idea."

"I think the captain will probably turn to port and put you ashore. Either that or wait 'til we put in for supplies."

"I see."

"I'm sorry. I truly am."

When Peter left, Kate tried to assess her situation in a calm manner. There seemed little doubt that she would be put ashore as soon as it could be managed; it was only a matter of where and when. She realized that once again she would be stranded in some strange place with neither friends nor prospects. Destiny had once again set her on a perilous course. . . .

17.

"You talked to the lass?" Guy Mapes asked.

Jason nodded pensively.

"Where do we turn in to put her ashore?"

"Nowhere," Jason said with sudden decision. "We're after a cargo. We aren't a packet running tarts up and down the coast."

Mapes was not surprised, although he felt that Jason was misjudging the girl. But this was not the time to plead her cause. Better to wait and see if basic Steele decency would prevail. Then, if Jason tried to seduce the lass—

"We could put her to work. We have no cabin boy and she seemed able-bodied enough. She could serve."

Jason grinned, then laughed outright. "Capital! They raised the roof at home when I merely had a female aboard as a guest. What will they say when they hear I've taken one on as a cabin boy?"

"She could be gone by the time we return— put ashore with wages to tide her over. But while aboard she should be restricted, not given the run of the ship. I'd say any place forward of the galley should be out of bounds—for her own safety.

"Will she do as she's told?"

"I'll see that she does," said Mapes.

"Peter Wells has been making her feel at home, I'll wager."

"He saw to her needs. He's a decent chap."

"Did I say he wasn't?" Jason frowned, closing the subject. "What have you to report concerning the crew?"

"Short. Mostly old hands. I signed on five new ones."

"Satisfactory?"

"I hope so. Two Portuguese and two Jamaicans."

"You said five."

"We drew a prize with the fifth. John Saipan."

"Not that goddamn sea lawyer!"

"I had to take him in place of even worse. We're still short as it is. I had a talk with him—warned him that any trouble it's a rope's end or irons."

"He must've snarled at that."

"No, he didn't. He said he too wanted no trouble and seemed sincere about it."

Jason was eyeing his first mate closely. "That didn't satisfy you?"

"I'm not sure. As I said, he *seemed* sincere."

"But he worries you. All right, see that he's watched closely. Any hint of underhanded antics and into irons he goes."

"I don't think that will be a problem. Saipan has never been underhanded. He has always brought his trouble out in the open."

"So much the better."

"How are you feeling, Jason? Does your side still pain you?"

"I'm as good as new. All I ask now is to lay

101

to on a pod of sperm right off—before I die of boredom."

"Amen!"

Guy Mapes left to go about his duties. Jason Steele's dark mood did not worry him. The boy was merely sulking, a logical state of mind given the treatment he'd received ashore. Soon he would come out of it and revert to his customary, unpredictable self. As a matter of fact, Mapes hoped the low mood would last for a while. In his brooding state, Jason would keep to himself and leave the running of the ship to his first mate.

18.

The captain's mood changed far sooner than Guy Mapes expected. It was the cry from the lookout station at the masthead far above the deck.

"Bloooows! Bloooows! She blooows!"

It was a cry of triumph: the hand who sighted whale was rewarded with tobacco from the slop chest and extra rum, a long-standing custom.

Guy Mapes, standing by the wheel, shouted, "Where away?" and the call came down, "Five points off the larboard bow!" Mapes had hardly turned in that direction when Jason was by his side.

"A humpback or bowhead?" Jason asked. "What the hell. We'll just take it and start filling our barrels. Better than rotting in these doldrums."

It would not be a sperm because that greater prize ranged much farther south in warmer waters. The humpback, a cold water species, yielded less oil than the lush sperms and of lower quality, while the bowhead's huge body was almost one-third bone.

At first sound from the lookout station, the ship had gone on alert. When the captain's glass verified the sighting—"A bowhead, maybe twenty barrels . . ."—all hands sprang into action. Most ran midships and waited for the master to assign boat crews. Some turned to already assigned duties at the try-works where the bulk of the catch would be rendered into oil. They busied themselves with starting the fire in the brickwork furnace below the try-pots, where the oil would eventually be lowered into the hold. Of course there was no guarantee there would be oil to refine, but it was considered bad luck to await the outcome of the hunt. A positive attitude always prevailed.

The *Gray Ghost* carried five boats, two each larboard and starboard and one stowed forward near the bowsprit. Jason sighted again through his glass. The weather was not quite in doldrum as he had described it, though the breeze *was* gentle. Only the topsails bellied. The bowhead was loafing off some thousand yards, half visible on a lacy surface.

"The larboard boats," Jason ordered. "Take the aft, Mr. Mapes, and crew both boats."

Young Peter Wells looked hopefully at Jason until it became obvious that the master of the vessel was going to handle the other boat himself. That would put Peter in ship command, true, but it was small reward for being again barred from the kill.

With the two boats crewed and off the davits, a single sail was raised in each to add to the oarsmen's rhythmic pull. The pursuit of a whale was a highly stylized operation. Jason and Mapes took to the sterns as steerers, manipulating twenty-foot steering oars. The harpooner in the bow pulled the forward oar until time for him to use his iron, the harpoon being the first metal driven into the quarry.

The two boats angled across the chop to engage the whale from behind where the great beast was most vulnerable, its vision cut off by its own bulk.

As the boats approached, Mapes judged it to be a young cow of perhaps twenty barrels—no great prize, but better than wallowing in idleness. Experience told him that the animal should be fairly docile with no great risk, but it also dictated that one could never tell. Even a whale of that size could stove a boat and kill a crew if sufficiently infuriated.

Gauging his approach to that of Jason's, Mapes brought his boat in on the starboard side. Then, just as he was about to signal his harpooner to switch from oar to iron, an unmistakable signal from Jason stayed him.

"Damn!" Mapes exploded as he scowled at the other boat. The young fool was waving Mapes away. He planned to take the whale alone.

It was contrary to all rules of protocol, safety, and common sense. Whaling was not a game of derring-do in which sporting daredevils proved their mettle. Still, one never knew what to expect of Jason Steele.

His boat moved on in; the mast was lowered for action and Jason's oarsmen bent their backs. Mapes' crew rested sullenly on their oars and awaited orders; they were not happy at being deprived of their share of the kill.

Jason's harpooner had taken up the barbed iron and was braced in the bow awaiting the approach. The bowhead cow, evidently well fed, rested half submerged, an occasional lazy spout fountaining from her head. Like an athlete hurling the javelin, the harpooner drew back his arm and threw straight and true to sink the weapon deep in the high shoulder.

Without waiting to weather the first shock of the animal's pain, Jason came forward to handle the killing iron from the bow while his harpooner would become the boatsteerer in the stern. This was established practice—the officer of a boat coming to make the kill—but the officer usually waited a bit to discover the temper of the whale and to handle the steering oar in case things did not go smoothly. Jason was scorning this precaution, just as he had scorned others.

The cow remained motionless for perhaps ten seconds, then she heaved upward at the head, tilting her forty-foot body, and sounded. The tow line followed her down and Jason waited alertly for the course the whale would take. There were several possibilities: Whales had sounded to the very depths, taking the boats down with them if the tow line was not cut in time; the cow could turn in her pain and come up under the boat, dumping the crew into the sea; or she could rise and fight and stove the boat to splinters.

This bowhead chose another alternative. She surfaced, spouted a red fountain, and ran. Mapes sensed the tow line—fine, three-quarter-inch hemp—singing out the tub. If the run continued, Jason had to use his judgment. He could cut the tow, which he would not do. He could let it run its length and possibly be jerked into the whale's wake at sudden high speed, which might founder the boat. Or he could fall in behind with all the speed his oarsmen could muster, while slowing the flow of the rope in order to ease the jerk and achieve the same speed as the whale in a less violent manner.

Jason handled the transition well. When the jerk came, the hundred-yard length of tow line snapped against the surface like a rubber band and the prow of the boat dipped to take in water, but then it leveled away.

Now Mapes's crew was really unhappy. They were being deprived of a Nantucket sleigh ride, the exhilarating experience of being towed at high speed by a running whale; a dangerous procedure, without a doubt, but hardly matched for sheer thrills. The main danger lay in the whale stopping the run to sound. The animal might then turn and attack. The most uncertain point in the taking of the whale was after a sounding, with the tow line limp and giving no signal from below the surface.

In this case the bowhead, in pain and panic, continued to run, Jason's boat cutting a white trough at its stern as it rocketed along behind.

Mapes stared morosely after it. Pursuit with feeble oar and sail was pointless. Perhaps the whale would turn and circle, thus giving Mapes's boat a chance to go in and help with the kill, or assist in towing if Jason made his kill alone. There was nothing to do but wait.

Participation became less probable as the whale continued to run, Jason's boat finally disappearing in the horizon haze.

19.

There was a tapping on Kate's door. She opened it to find Peter Wells in the companionway.

"You may come out now," he said.

"Good heavens, Captain Steele is being most gracious."

"Captain Steele has nothing to do with it," Peter replied. "I am now in command. The invitation is mine."

"Has there been a mutiny?"

"No. Both Captain Steele and Mr. Mapes are off after whale. That makes me the officer in command."

Kate hesitated, laying a hand on his arm. "Peter, are you sure it's all right? I wouldn't want to get you in trouble."

He reddened. "If you feel I do not have the authority—"

"I'm sorry. It's just that—well, you are about the only friend I have on this ship and I don't want to make trouble for you. Of course I want to come out."

"No one wishes you any harm. I'm sure everyone admires your courage."

"Well, I certainly haven't felt very courageous. I've been scared most of the time."

"If Mr. Mapes seemed cold it was just the circumstances—your coming aboard as a stowaway."

"Are stowaways rare?"

"On whaling ships, at any rate. And then your being a girl . . ."

"That does make me a little exceptional, doesn't it?"

"Unusual, I'd say."

Kate laughed. "And the way I looked! Peter, I hope you won't always think of me as a half-drowned bilge rat."

"Oh, Kate, don't say a thing like that! I think you're lovely!"

Kate was feeling better. Peter was good for her spirits.

He was saying, "I'm sure that when Mr. Mapes and Captain Steele get to know you—" His voice trailed off, its tone one of distinct regret.

His obvious fear of dropping to third place on Kate's list of friends brought him the reward of a kiss. It was quick, spontaneous, and full of gratitude rather than passion.

"Peter—you're very sweet. And I promise you that you'll always remain my dearest friend."

She stepped into the companionway. "And now maybe you really can show me around the ship."

"I think it best that we stay aft," he replied and followed her to the deck.

Kate's position as a girl on a shipful of men was now brought home rather forcibly. And it was in no way frightening.

It was all so different here on the ship than

109

it had been in Lucas Peavey's tavern. Kate's fear of men who regarded her with desire was disappearing. In the tavern it had symbolized her helplessness; now it had somehow become an asset. A girl with what it took to make men want her was not at a disadvantage. Quite the contrary ... and so Kate was enjoying the romantic interest of an attractive young man.

For a few daring moments, she allowed her imagination to wander. What would the act of passion be like with handsome Peter Wells ... ?

The young man in question would have been astounded had he been able to read Kate's mind at that moment. All the decent young ladies he had ever known demanded hours of attention, total adoration and yearning in exchange for a single kiss. As to Kate, he did not yet have any clear impression of her. One thing he was sure of: She was a beauty. And no girl he'd ever met had made him feel the ineffectual fool he was around Kate.

In truth, he was seeing an emergence: the first phase of her blooming out into the woman she would become.

He observed, "It must have been wonderful riding about in a wagon over the countryside without having to be at any special place at a given time. Your father must have been a wonderful man."

"He was."

"A painter, you said."

"Yes, all I have left in the world are those canvases."

"Was he a landscape artist or a portrait painter?"

"Daddy was versatile. He did both. I'm in

110

many of his works—I was the only model he had."

It was on the tip of Peter's tongue to ask if she were nude but he caught himself.

Kate pressed his arm in both her hands and said, "Peter, you haven't told me a word about you. Where are you from? What was your childhood like?"

"I was born in New York City. We had a house on Gramercy Park—still have, in fact, but my parents moved uptown. I went to a private school up at Murray Hill and my sister went to a boarding school."

"You have a sister—"

"Yes. There are only two children. Tess is— well, she is out on her own. She never married." There was something in his tone—a certain hesitancy. Kate let it pass.

"You come from a wealthy family I take it."

"Yes. We have always been rich. My grandfather made quite a fortune as an importer." The inflection on the last word amounted to nothing less than a sneer. Kate decided not to let that one pass.

"Did he do something illegal?"

"Oh, no! There were no laws on it then. Of course, there is some moral question about bringing in slaves—trafficking in human misery. And of course my father wouldn't break the law either. He is a financier. He buys up mortgages, and lends money to sweat shops."

Peter's bitterness was making Kate uncomfortable. She was sorry she had asked him about his background.

"I gather that you like the sea."

111

"I plan to devote my life to it. Someday I'll have a ship of my own."

"With your father's backing I'm sure it won't be very long, Peter."

Even as the words were spoken, Kate realized it was the wrong thing to say.

"My father will have nothing to do with it. I'll do it my own way. I'll be a master and command a ship."

Kate pressed closer and looked up at him. "Please don't be angry with me. I think your independence is wonderful."

Their eyes met and held for a breathless moment. When he drew her lips to his she did not resist.

The kiss was firm, possessive, but it was that of a gentleman who would not forget his manners; it was a kiss which went just so far. Did that indicate disappointment? Kate wondered.

The kiss ended with Peter drawing away abruptly.

"I'm sorry, Kate! Please forgive me. I had no right to take advantage of you."

"It's all right, Peter. There is nothing to forgive. I was as much at fault as you."

"It's just that you're so wonderful!"

He looked embarrassed at having uttered such an extravagant compliment.

"I must leave you, I'm afraid. I've been shirking my duties," he said with regret.

"That puts me more at fault for detaining you."

"Oh, no! I did not mean it that way."

Kate turned her eyes to the empty sea. "When do you expect Captain Steele back?"

"It's difficult to say."

112

"Do the boats usually go so far from the ship?"

"It depends on the size and quality of the catch—what the whale does on the harpoon end of the line."

"It can be dangerous, can't it?"

"It often is. Why don't you stay here and enjoy the sea while I go down and put some of those idlers to work. . . ."

Peter Wells hurried away toward midships and Kate smiled after him, her expression more sisterly than mournful. She looked out across the sea and took a deep breath. She was inhaling her new freedom as much as the crisp, salty air: freedom from the drudgery of the tap room at the *Blue Mermaid*; the cold, angry regard of Clara Peavey; the physical abuse of Lucas Peavey. Happily, there were no misgivings whatever on the precarious path upon which she now found herself.

Her mind wandered back to Peter's kiss. She laughed as she visualized Peter's probable reaction if she had deliberately taken his hand and slipped it into her rough sailor's shirt over her bare breast. Of course she would do no such thing, but she wondered just how a loose woman would go about stirring a proper gentleman like Peter into action.

The image of Jason Steele intruded, pushing Peter aside. She recalled the strong physical response the mere sight of him on the Stonington dock had inflicted upon her.

Kate McCrae, back at the tavern you were called a tart, a loose woman, and worse. Is it turning out to be true?

Kate found herself in the narrow confines of

the lower companionway. She passed the door to Guy Mapes's cabin, where she'd had her first interview. On the opposite side, next to her own cabin, was Peter Wells's. She came to her door, but instead of going in she continued to where the companionway widened, to the door of the master cabin, within which Jason Steele spent his private hours.

What did he do in solitude? Did he read? Did he have a musical instrument he played?

Then she was in his cabin with the door closed behind her.

It was low-ceilinged but it spanned the stern width of the ship, giving it considerable size. In the center was a table which Kate decided was for both work and dining, rather narrow but quite substantial. It had probably been brought in through one of the ports in the stern bulkhead, the legs attached later. There was a large chart on the table filled with confusing lines and numbers, also an instrument somewhat like a clumsy telescope. She wondered at its purpose.

Jason's sleeping quarters were on the starboard side, a single bunk with no tiers, carelessly made up with fine linen, _J. S._ monogrammed on the sheets and pillow cases. Kate noted with some satisfaction that they no doubt predated the towels he had thrown to her so carelessly in her own cabin.

The larboard side was furnished with a huge easy chair, a side table, a book shelf, and closed storage space—several drawers and a sizable closet. Snooping shamelessly in the drawers, Kate found a good supply of expensive men's clothing. When she opened the closet, she was intrigued by a small, metal-banded trunk on the floor at one end. It was black, with a cumbersome but unfastened lock. What intrigued her was the bright red ribbon hanging out at one end.

The lid lifted quite easily and Kate gasped at the tightly packed collection of brightly colored female clothing that burst forth. There was a red satin dinner gown of floor-sweeping length which should not have been rolled carelessly into a ball. A creamy-hued Spanish mantilla of fine lace was wadded up in a corner. The tell-tale crimson ribbon turned out to be a wide sash of pure silk which would not have been out of place in the wardrobe of a New York City millionaire's wife. On the other hand, there was a wide-brimmed purple hat with a ridiculous pink ribbon that would certainly draw the stares of passers-by anywhere—and perhaps some laughter.

But the sensational items were still to come. As Kate lifted them from the trunk, her eyes widened with each garment. There was a brassiere of filmy silk net. It consisted of two small half moons which would expose rather than cover. Kate held it to her bosom and could visualize herself in it. She put it down quickly. Next she fingered an obscene pair of pantalettes, proper enough from mid-thigh down, but above they consisted solely of transparent mesh.

No decent woman would wear these clothes. Finding them in Jason Steele's cabin . . . !

The reason was all too clear. Jason was a roué of the basest kind who consorted with the loosest kind of women. No wonder his intended bride had turned from him. She could not have kept her self-respect and done otherwise! And this was the man who had beheld Kate naked in her cabin. The thoughts that must have gone through his mind . . . !

To have the nerve to keep this disgraceful assortment in his cabin!

In his cabin . . .

After all, she'd entered the cabin uninvited, a sneaky little snoop, and the garments had hardly been spread out on the bunk for inspection. But she brushed that aside in her indignation. What sort of depraved man was this Captain Jason Steele?

Kate's anger stayed strong as she jammed the clothes back into the trunk, slammed it shut, closed the closet door, and practically ran out of the cabin.

For reasons she neither understood nor questioned, when she reached her own cabin she flung herself on her bunk and burst into tears.

After the weeping had spent itself, she was able to consider the situation somewhat more calmly. After all, Jason Steele's standards of conduct were of no importance to *her*.

It didn't matter to her what kind of women he chose to share his bed. . . .

20.

Not wanting to stay alone in her cabin any longer, Kate changed into her frock and decided to use what time might be left of her freedom before the whaling boats returned to explore the rest of the ship.

She left the after area and wandered forward. There seemed no harm in it. Most of the hands were either in the forecastle resting up in the event the whalers came back with a catch, or puttering around the try-works arranging and rearranging the equipment.

She walked on, encountering no interference, until she found herself in a secluded area where aft and midships were cut off by the bulk of the forecastle entrance. A young sailor sat inspecting a coil of rope, checking for broken strands.

Kate greeted him with a smile. "I see you keep busy," she said.

He gulped at her sudden presence. "Yes, Miss. A weak spot in the hemp could lose us a whale."

Kate stepped closer to see what he was doing. She did not notice the sudden trembling of his hands as they almost brushed her skirt.

Avoiding her eyes, he said, "My name is Simon. I am from Stonington."

"I worked in Stonington—at the *Blue Mermaid* tavern."

Kate immediately regretted identifying herself as a former bar maid. She realized later that may have given the boy the justification to do what he did. However, there was more to it than that—the excitement of her sudden appearance, and her friendly manner. The attack was totally unexpected and it was surprising that Kate had the presence of mind not to cry out.

She would always remember the look of anguish on his face as he suddenly leaped up and pressed her hard against the sheltering bulkhead. Then his hands were under her skirt, desperately reaching.

"Please! Oh, please!" he implored. He could have been begging for a cup of water or a piece of bread. Even while his hands were sure and decisive, his eyes kept pleading, *Please forgive me.*

So strange was it, Kate did not even start to resist until seconds later when her legs had been forced into a V and one of the boy's hands was pressing into the softness between. But she was pinned to the bulkhead by the desperate lad's weight and superior strength.

Even then, Kate did not cry out, for reason of her own welfare. She had disobeyed orders by coming forward. Wise men had feared this very thing. Now she had brought it on through her own disobedience and heaven only knew what the penalty would be if it came to light.

Her hesitancy was, in truth, also based on an

entirely different reason: a reluctance to fight off the attack. For Kate had begun to respond to the sex-starved boy's fumbling, and once again her body dominated her head.

He was now fondling her breast and Kate sensed a trembling reverence in his touch as the nipple hardened and rose under his fingers.

The effect of what his other hand was doing was similar but infinitely more so. Searching gently among the delicate nerve ends below, it caused a soft, low moan to escape Kate's lips.

"No—no! You mustn't!"

She heard those whispered words—her own—and suddenly she began to struggle. It was to no avail.

"Stop it! You *must* be sensible—do you realize what they could do to you?"

There was still a blank, pleading look in his eyes. Kate understood the problem. Driven to this point by overpowering passion, he could neither retreat nor go forward; fright and inexperience blocked him in both directions. It was curious that at this moment, Kate most strongly sensed an inherent decency in the boy. He, not she, was in truth the victim.

It was obvious that he did not recognize her own sexual response for what it was. She continued to struggle, but not beyond a safe extreme. Not yet. Not when her body was near to exploding and her own silent voice screamed: *Get on with it! Stop fumbling, for heaven's sake! Get it over with!*

Then came flaming fulfillment, and immediately Kate found the strength to free herself. Tears welled in the boy's eyes. "I'm sorry! Oh God, I'm so sorry!"

119

Kate was most forgiving. "I understand," she whispered. "It's all right. I understand and I won't report you. We must both forget this happened."

His expression revealed hope and open adoration. He seized her hand and pressed it to his lips.

Kate allowed him the gesture "I *do* forgive you," she said, and then hurried aft.

Kate McCrae, you're a hypocrite and a shameless woman!

But her spirits refused to cower. There was a singing in her ears, a heady sense of power swept over her.

You ought to be ashamed of yourself!

Thus her better self scolded until she reached her cabin. Then a certain apprehension took over. Her apple-cheeked attacker was so young in the ways of the world; so sincere, so decent. What if he did the manly thing and confessed?

It was a possibility.

She changed back into her cabin boy togs as though that in some way negated the whole experience.

21.

Late that afternoon there came a glad cry from the mainmast: "Boats ahoy! Ten points off the starboard bow!"

Every man on the ship strained joyfully to see and Kate, hearing the news through her open ports, went topside.

Peter Wells was shouting orders from amidship: "Get your pans and go to the cook house. There will be night work and no time for mess."

One of the hands hurried into the forecastle and returned with a stack of metal dishes which were then distributed, and Kate watched as the men lined up at the cook house door, each to emerge with a heaping plateful. The food was unidentifiable, a dark stewlike mixture. She could only wonder if it was dog's body. It did not have that color but perhaps the stuff took on a more disagreeable appearance as it aged.

She could just make out the returning whaleboats on the horizon. It was a good two hours later, with dusk lowering, that the laboring oarsmen pulled the dead whale to the larboard stays.

Kate watched nervously from the starboard

gangway as the whalers came aboard, all the activity on the larboard side. The oarsmen were tired but happy with the pleasure of a job well done. Kate did not miss the tension between the master and his first mate. Mapes had adopted a cold, impersonal attitude which was as far as he ever went in showing displeasure, but Jason caught it. Jason apparently tried to placate Mapes, a friendly hand on his shoulder and a persuasive manner, but Mapes's attitude did not seem to change.

As the rattle and grind of the davits ceased, Kate could make out the conversation. Mapes said, "You're completely exhausted. You'd better go to your cabin."

"You deserve a rest yourself."

"I'll stay on deck. We're shorthanded. I'll have to work all the men."

Jason did not object. As he gained the aft stairway, Kate saw him holding his side with pain evident in his expression.

She was not able to generate much sympathy for the captain, what with her hostility about the trunk in his cabin, and the advantage his condition gave her; seeking only rest, he would not discover her release and order her confined again.

With sudden decision, she rounded the cook house and approached the door. So far in the voyage, she had not seen the cook, having been brought her meals.

Each of the hands in the chow line had stepped just inside the cook house to receive his portion and while she knew *someone* was in there, she had no idea what to expect. Still, she was somewhat surprised to find a short rotund

Chinese. He wore a pigtail and had a moon face built to smile. He was evidently one to take all things in stride because he greeted her with a wide grin, as though female stowaways were not unusual in his tiny kingdom.

"I'd like to help you," Kate said. "I have had experience."

He pointed a finger at her chest. "Who you?"

"My name is Kate. Kate McCrae."

He pointed to himself. "Walter."

The name hardly seemed right for a Chinese.

"Walter Woo," he added, then burst into laughter. "Walter Woo great lover."

The belly-shaking laugh continued, but Kate realized that from the moment she had entered the cook house, Walter Woo had hardly missed a stroke.

The galley was a rectangle with passage down the middle and every available inch on either side utilized. The stove, a four-burner range with an oven, was at the far end opposite a length of worktable. A narrow opening, curtained with canvas, led center aft to where the food was stored.

"You cabin boy?" Woo asked.

"Yes—cabin boy."

He extended the knife he had been using and indicated the bucket from which he had been taking potatoes.

"You peel," he ordered.

Kate was surprised to find potatoes on a whaling ship although she did not see why she should be. She took the knife from Woo and he moved further to starboard where he began scooping flour into a pan.

123

"The men are just back from killing a whale," he said. "And when they're through working it they will be hungry as horses."

Astonished, Kate looked up. The voice, the diction, had completely changed. It was now as occidental as any on the ship. Even the smile the cook threw her way was different. It no longer looked like a full moon.

"You—you speak English very well," Kate faltered.

"Fooled you, huh?"

"Yes."

"It's simple. Everybody expects Chinese to be some kind of a clown along with being a cook, so I worked at it. I didn't want to disappoint them."

"Have you been a cook for a long time?"

"Long enough. I came over with my father a hell of a long time ago. He died in Frisco and I went to work building the Southern Pacific Railroad when I was little more than a kid."

"Where did you learn to cook?"

"From an old western rawhider who was feeding the line in Colorado. I couldn't swing a pick fast enough to suit them so they sent me to the cook shack."

Walter Woo evidently enjoyed reliving the old memories. "That Coot Morhead, he was a wild one. And pretty well educated too. He knew how to cook everything from fried Indian to—"

"*Fried Indian?*"

Walter was now working his dough. He looked at it affectionately and said, "That was his claim. He said that once on the Washoe he couldn't find a bite for love or money so he caught a stray Indian and fried him for dinner. Said he gained ten pounds from the dishes he invented that summer. Fricasseed Indian—Indian on toasted hard tack—"

"Please!" Kate begged.

"Sure, kid, sure," he chuckled. He turned his head to make a more critical inspection of his new helper. "You're the drowned rat they found down in the bilge, huh?"

"I guess so. I was hiding there until I couldn't stand it anymore and came out."

"When the St. Elmo fire hit."

"Yes. It was—well, I never saw anything like it."

"Nothing, nothing at all—you should see a Chinese New Year celebration. Why did you stow away? Who were you running away from?"

"The place where I was working in Stonington when my father died."

"With some horny bastard chasing you, I'll bet. You're probably pretty smooth under those rags. And plenty old enough. You say your papa died?"

"Very suddenly."

"No mama?"

"Not since I was very small."

"Hard luck, youngster, but don't worry. You'll make it. Did you ever read Bret Harte?"

"No, I don't think so."

"A damn good poet.

"Never a tear bedins the eye
That time and patience will not dry
Never a lip is curved with pain
That can't be kissed into smiles again . . ."

125

"That's beautiful," Kate said. She had noticed half a dozen books on a rack above the worktable. "You must read a lot."

"I like poetry. Old Coot Morhead, he used to read it to me and I kind of took to it."

Anxious to keep the conversation away from herself, Kate asked, "Who are your favorite poets?"

"I met Bret Harte once. At least I saw him walking by. He didn't look like a poet but he has a way with words."

A figure appeared in the doorway. Guy Mapes. Kate thought he looked older, craggier, more deeply wrinkled than before.

"Walt, send a pot of hot tea down to the captain, will you?"

"Sure, boss," the cook replied.

Mapes' eye held on Kate for a long moment but he said nothing and his expression did not change. Then he was gone.

Walter stood facing Kate with a large, gray, enamel coffeepot. "Can you carry this?"

"I think so."

She hefted the pot by its wire handle. "This isn't tea."

"Coffee. The men come first."

"But Mr. Mapes said—"

"I know what he said. You take this pot out and make the rounds."

"But won't Mr. Mapes be mad?"

"Officers get crusty sometimes but salt instead of sugar on the plum duff brings them around quick enough. Now shake your stern and spread that brew."

"How about cups?"

"Anybody forgot his cup'll know better next

time. Scamper." With that the cook whacked the seat of Kate's pants in friendly fashion and went on kneading his dough.

Kate stepped out of the cook house and stopped dead. While inside, the expanse of deck before her had been transformed into Dante's vision of hell. Lanterns were hung about the deck and along the starboard side, where a section of bulwark had been removed to make way for the cutting platform against which the bowhead had been securely lashed. Everywhere she looked there was red, the bowhead having stained the sea waters, and sharks miles away would already be streaking toward the *Gray Ghost* for the feast to come. Sea birds awaiting their share were circling in the darkness, screaming in anticipation. The try-works fire threw up a crimson glare, adding to the eeriness.

But fancy could be deceptive. This was merely the routine rendering of a whale on a typical whaling ship. The head of the great sea beast had already been removed and winched aboard. The case would be bailed out for its rich content, after which the head would be thrown back into the sea. The *Gray Ghost* would not harvest the baleen—the whalebone.

The work of stripping the thick overcoat of blubber from the whale's carcass had already begun, and a great sheet of the foot-thick fat was hanging from blubber hooks to be lifted aboard and chopped into pieces small enough for the try-pots. There the malodorous rendering would take place.

Remembering her duty, Kate pushed forward, finding herself welcomed wherever she went. All along the cutting stage, bloody hands thrust out cups for the black, bitter liquid she brought. The hands showed no interest in the fact it was a female who carried the pot.

The mood was cheerful. A whale so soon after putting out to sea foreshadowed a prosperous voyage and money in all pockets. It was only when Kate reached the aftwinch over the cutting stage that she encountered someone whose spirit was markedly different. A great slab of whale flesh hanging on the blubber hooks was being lifted as a tall, handsome man extended his cup. He was an arresting figure, bearded, with long, flowing hair and the stern profile of an ancient prophet. The lantern light reflected the fire in his eyes although he did not look at Kate directly. His gaze, rather, was upon the great slab of flesh being raised. Kate sensed something frightening in his mien, something she could not define. For some reason she thought vaguely of madness as she filled his cup.

Just then the man on the forewinch called out, "Stir yourself, Saipan. Give me an even strain."

Saipan paid no attention. He laid a hand on the wall of whale flesh and Kate could hear the strange words he spoke:

"Rest ye in peace, oh gentle child of the sea. Thou shalt be avenged a thousandfold."

She watched him pour his cup on the cutting stage and then haul viciously upon the winch-line.

Kate returned to the cook house to refill the pot. Again she made the rounds until it was

128

empty. When she came back this time, Walter said, "You look worn."

"I'm all right."

"It's probably the stink of that goddamn rendering. It's a good thing in a way, though."

"What's good about it?"

He winked an eye. "Are you hungry?"

"Ugh! I'll never eat again."

"That's what's good about the stink. Those sea rats out there don't know it but the rendering is what holds their appetites down while they're working. Otherwise they'd all be wanting to stop for chow."

"You know a lot about the sea and people and—well, a lot of things, don't you?"

He ignored that. "You're all whipped out. Sit for a spell. Climb on the table there and let your legs dangle."

Kate accepted the invitation gratefully and inhaled deeply of the bread now baking in the oven.

"What about the captain's tea. Won't he be mad?"

"Maybe," Walter replied indifferently. "But don't worry about it."

"Do you know all the men on the ship?" Kate persisted.

He threw her a smile somewhere between the Chinese clown grimace and his natural one. "Well, I'll tell you. He's a good boy but he's got a lot to learn."

"Who are you talking about?"

"Pete Wells, the second mate. He's the one you're interested in, isn't he? Or is it the high mogul himself, Jason Steele?"

"Neither. I was thinking of one of the men

129

working out there. He was helping lift a big piece of the whale onto the ship."

"One of the winchmen?"

"Someone called him Saipan."

"You stay away from that one."

"I hadn't planned—"

"See that you don't. He's crazy as a locoed roadrunner. Damned if I know why Mapes signed him on."

"He said something very strange. He called the whale a child of the sea."

"He's a crazy coot. You just stay away from him."

"All right, if you say so. Hadn't I better take the captain his tea now?"

"I guess so. And when you get your appetite back, come on up and I'll feed you."

"Thank you. You've been very kind."

"Make the most of it. Wait 'til you see me on one of my bad days. I can throw a pot from one end of this scow to the other."

Kate laughed.

22.

Kate did not deliver the captain's tea. At the head of the stairs to the companionway, as she was wondering if she could make the descent without tipping everything off the tray, she was approached by Second Mate Peter Wells. She had not seen him since their awkward kiss, but he'd obviously been hard at his duties, whatever they were, because his face was streaked with oily dirt and his jacket ready for the wash.

"Kate," he said. "Are you all right? I'm afraid I've had to neglect you."

"Not at all. I found work to do in the galley. Mr. Woo let me peel potatoes and serve coffee to the men."

"He should not have done that. I'll speak to him about it."

"I wouldn't. You might get salt instead of sugar on your plum duff."

Peter was a serious young man with only a thin humorous streak in his makeup. He frowned and said, "Strange. I don't recall plum duff ever having been served on this ship."

"He was joking, I think."

"That tray goes to the captain?"

"Yes. His tea. It's way overdue."

131

"I'm reporting to him. I'll take it in if you like."

"That's very kind of you."

Peter took the tray and they descended the stairs. He hesitated at the door to Kate's cabin. "Perhaps we could have tea together after you've rested and I've seen to cleaning up the deck."

"I would like that, Peter."

It was a stroke of luck to be relieved of seeing the captain. While Peter seemed confident of his authority to allow her the freedom of the ship, she was unsure that Jason Steele would see it that way.

Weary to the bone, filthy from the soot and fetid smoke of the try-works, and faintly nauseated by the odor of blood and boiling flesh, Kate wanted only a bath and rest.

She went to find the tub Peter had previously brought to her cabin, and was fortunate in locating it quickly. There was another storage cabin on the larboard side toward the stern where she found the buckets that had been used. Risking remonstrance she tugged and rolled the heavy receptacle into her own cabin. She then returned to the cook house to ask for hot water, and the man in the chow line who barred her way at the door was none other than John Saipan of the cold eyes and stern visage.

"Do they make you labor like a slave, lass?" he asked.

"Oh, no, sir. They treat me very well."

Walter Woo interceded, frowning as he filled the pails. "Can you lug them all right, chickie? Wait about a while and I'll help you."

"Thanks. I can manage."

Back in her cabin, her clothes tossed on her bunk, she found the steaming bite of the water heavenly as she splashed it over her tired body. She soaped and scrubbed even while telling herself that this could not continue. A bath—two!—every day on a whaling ship was out of the question.

She leaned over the tub with a headful of suds. She rinsed and sudsed again and was finishing with her last rinse when once more she sensed rather than heard the cabin door open. She straightened and whirled about and there he was once more!

The expression on the captain's handsome face was neither angry nor lustful—just perplexed.

"My God, girl! Do you spend all your time posing nude beside a bathtub?"

This time she went behind the tub rather than into it.

"You beast! Do you always go around preying on defenseless women?"

"I'm not preying on anybody. I came in here to let you out and tell you what your duties will be."

"Well, they certainly won't be catering to you!"

Jason stood in his richly quilted satin robe and refused to show anger at her outburst. He regarded what he could see of Kate with pensive interest as he advanced casually further into the cabin. She circled the tub in a corresponding motion. He sat down on the edge of the bunk and said, "Why on earth don't you quit acting the outraged maiden?"

"Because I *am* the outraged maiden!"

"Who outraged you? Certainly not I. You'd think I was the intruder on this ship, not you."

"That's beside the point. I may be a stowaway but I'm entitled to decent treatment."

"Who's treating you indecently?"

"You are. Barging in here as though—as though—"

"I think it's just the opposite. I think you're mad because the sight of your naked body doesn't stir my blood in the least."

Kate glared at him.

"I've hardly led a cloistered life, you see. Women do attract me, and I've seen quite a few of them undressed and otherwise. So I'm not inclined to start panting at the sight of an unclad female."

Kate chose to ignore that. "A gentleman would at least hand me my cloak so I wouldn't have to crouch here shivering."

Jason rose and reached for the cloak in which Kate had fled from the *Blue Mermaid*. Instead of tossing it to her, however, he held it up and advanced toward the tub, positioning the garment so that she could reach up her arms and draw it around her with her back to him.

Turning her face to the ports, Kate lifted her arms.

But as she stepped backward toward the cloak it wasn't there. She turned to see Jason staring at it in distaste.

"This thing is filthy," he said. "Put it on and you'll have to take another bath."

Kate stood with one arm over her breast and

the other across her middle. "Well for heaven's sake, give me *something!* A towel."

"Here, take my robe."

He stripped it off to reveal a loose yellow shirt with balloon sleeves caught at the wrist over black silk trousers broadly banded at the waist and tight over his hips. His feet were shod in soft black slippers.

The robe swamped her, but she drew it around her and said, "You look like an Oriental something or other. A mandarin?"

"A rickshaw boy on his day off, maybe. Now why don't you sit down and quit acting like a canary that wants to get out of its cage?"

Kate huddled down into the only chair in the cabin while Jason went back to the bunk. "That shirt is beautiful," she said admiringly. "You must have bought it in the Far East."

Jason stretched out in the bunk as though he planned to stay a while. "No," he replied. "As a matter of fact, I got it at Wanamaker's in New York City."

"But you've been in the Far East—all over the world. . . ."

"A great deal of it."

"How exciting . . . men have so many more opportunities than women."

"Perhaps. But there are many opportunities women can take advantage of."

"If they are opportunists, I suppose."

"Are you an opportunist?"

Kate laughed. "I refuse to be trapped into declaring myself one way or another."

As the conversation continued, part of Kate's mind wondered about this new person she had become. From cringing and whimpering as a

135

slavey in the *Blue Mermaid*, where she'd hardly dared open her mouth, here she was holding her own with the master of a ship on the high seas.

In addition, she was now boldly testing herself in Jason Steele's presence. What was there about him that had set her juices flowing that day on the Stonington quay? She was no longer entering into the marketplace a penniless beggar. She had proved she was very appealing to men. . . .

". . . so little about you, Kate."

"I'm sorry, I didn't hear you. I'm afraid I was woolgathering."

"I mean you certainly didn't just hatch out of an egg there at the tavern. You came from some place."

"My father and I traveled. He was a painter."

There was a tap on the door. When Kate hesitated, Jason got up and opened it and she could see Peter Wells in the companionway.

In response to Jason's questioning look, Peter said, "I heard voices, sir."

"So—?"

"I—I'm sorry."

While Peter's tongue stumbled over itself, his eyes were busy. They took in Kate's borrowed robe. His lips trembled.

As he turned away, Jason said, "Has the deck cleanup been finished?"

"Almost, sir. It is being washed down now."

"See that it's finished properly."

"Yes, sir."

Jason closed the door. The intrusion had changed the atmosphere, making it less per-

136

sonal, more official. He turned to Kate. "As to your status here on board—I was talking to Mr. Mapes, and we thought you should have some kind of duty."

"I am perfectly willing to work."

"You can help the cook."

"Of course, Captain," Kate replied. "I'll do whatever is ordered." There was no reason to mention that she had already helped the cook.

"Our cook is a prize indeed. He could work in any of the country's fine restaurants. I wouldn't want to lose him so I let him run the galley as he sees fit. Fortunately he has a good heart. I am sure you will like him."

"I'm sure I'll like him too." Kate smiled.

"I'll have Mr. Wells take you to Walter." He regarded Kate intently for a moment and then he turned toward the door. "You can return my robe when you no longer need it."

"Thank you."

"One more thing," he added. "You will remain aft and not mix with the crew."

"Of course," she replied.

Jason left, and Kate, alone, emitted an explosive, unladylike, "Damn!"

Her anger was directed at Peter Wells. He was a dear but why did he have to blunder in just when things had been going so well?

23.

If Jason Steele learned of Kate's premature release, he said nothing. In fact, he said nothing at all to her, and neither did Second Mate Peter Wells. Jason merely ignored her while Peter, when they met, was icily formal. The attitude of Guy Mapes did not change but it had been basically impersonal from the first. He relayed the captain's instructions: Kate was to work directly under Walter Woo. She would also see to the housekeeping, straightening up the captain's quarters once a day. In addition she served the captain's table.

It would seem that such duties would necessitate contact with the captain, but this was not the case. Usually Peter Wells and Guy Mapes took their meals with him, and as there was always one or the other present, Jason did not direct any conversation to Kate. As to the housekeeping chores, Kate was instructed to enter Jason's cabin only when he was absent.

Thus she found herself now with a single friend aboard—Walter Woo—and he became a rather bizarre though effective father substitute. The rotund Chinese was open and frank at all times. He was a person in whom she was able to confide.

"Walter, why are they treating me as though I had leprosy?"

"Who's that, chickie?"

"Jason and Peter."

"Do you mean the captain and the second mate?"

"If you must be so formal—yes."

"How are they supposed to treat the cabin boy, like an old friend?"

"They could at least be civil."

"Have they been uncivil?"

"Well—no—but—"

"What do you want? Do you want the captain to take you to bed the way he did the last female on this ship?"

"Of course not! You're being insulting!"

"All right, we'll drop it. Get busy with those potatoes."

"I've already peeled enough for tonight."

"I mean sprout them."

"I don't understand."

"That's why I've got two bins in there. Potatoes'll keep for a year if the sprouts are rubbed off. So every month or so you sprout them—rub the sprouts off and throw the spuds into the other bin."

Kate went into the larder and began rubbing potatoes as the cook ordered. She was out again in a few minutes, an unsprouted potato in her hand.

"Walter, you said something about another female on the ship. What was she, a passenger?"

"You might say so. She did some work; served meals and tidied up the captain's cabin. She wasn't much help to me, though."

"But she did pretty much what I'm doing, right?"

"More than you're doing. Her main job was sleeping with the captain."

"Do you mean she allowed herself to be *used*?"

"You could put it that way."

"Then she was a harlot!"

"Hmmm, I haven't heard that word in years. Her name was Marita. She was a cute little Jamaican and Jason treated her pretty generously—he bought her clothes and took her ashore with him. She didn't come out on the short end."

"But Jason was betrothed to a girl in Stonington."

Walter Woo chuckled. "I understand he isn't betrothed anymore."

So that was the cause of it all: the fight—the Stonington trouble.

"Marita was a nice kid," the cook mused. "Always bright and cheerful and laughing."

"Are you saying you liked her—you *respected* her?"

"Sure."

"But a prostitute—"

"That's only your point of view. Marita just saw things differently than you do. She lived for today; you live for tomorrow."

"What do you mean by that?"

"I mean we all do what's best for us."

"But you're telling me her way was best."

"For her—yes."

"But not for me?"

"Of course not. It's all a matter of living the life that satisfies you, chickie. Life's made to

140

enjoy and people enjoy different things. Marita enjoyed it her way. You have the satisfaction of keeping your virtue."

"But you're saying I'm a fool!"

"Damn it all! Don't put words in my mouth. I don't judge people. I take them for what they are and wish them good luck."

Kate went back to sprouting potatoes. A few minutes later she came out again and said, "But you wouldn't respect me if I slept with Jason."

"Has he asked you?"

"No!"

"Then what difference does it make?"

"Are you telling me I'm not attractive enough to sleep with a man?"

Walter slammed a pot down in exasperation. "There you go again! I told you what I told you and nothing more. Get back to those goddamn spuds."

Certainly, in addition to completely confusing her, Walter gave Kate a lot to think about, and she tried to face the issues squarely. As nearly as she could figure it, the Jamaican girl did what appealed to her without concern for moral scruples. And she managed to do it without being looked down upon. Well, Kate McCrae had that kind of nature too. Where would it lead her?

The point is, she thought, how would I feel the next morning after sleeping with Jason Steele? Would I feel guilty and miserable, or is wanting people to think the best of you merely being prudish?

It was a good question to ask Walter so she went back into the galley. But before she

141

could speak, he said, "What happened between you and Pete Wells?"

"What makes you think anything happened?"

"It had to. The captain ignoring you is one thing; Pete giving you the go-by is another. You had to offend him in some way."

Without thinking twice, Kate told Walter about the second bathtub incident. He stopped mashing squash to stare at her.

"So there you were in the captain's bathrobe and Pete saw you?"

"But nothing had happened."

"Of course nothing happened—"

"What do you mean *of course* nothing happened? Are you saying I'm so ugly the captain would not want me after seeing me naked?"

"Will you stick to the point? I'm saying that Pete Wells could only draw the natural conclusion—that you belonged to the captain just as Marita did. So he's keeping hands off."

"Do you really think so?"

"I know so."

"I knew something was wrong, but—"

"Don't flatter yourself," he said with good-natured disgust. "I don't think you know enough to blow on hot soup. Get back at those spuds before the sprouts eat them up."

Kate went back to work thankful for the first real friend she had ever had.

24.

Kate was not the only one aboard who found Walter Woo a man worth cultivating. Guy Mapes, after several voyages with the Chinese, had come to know him as a friend, someone who could be depended upon. A man of wise counsel in times of doubt. They met now and again in Mapes' cabin to sip from the first mate's private stock of rice wine, a drink Walter had taught him to enjoy.

On this occasion, after several weeks out, the perceptive cook said, "What's bothering you, Guy. Your jowls are drooping."

"I don't like this voyage, Walter. It's bad. Something hangs over it."

"What's the complaint? Out a month with a bowhead and two sperms. I'd call that happy fishing."

"Things aren't right."

"I know. So exactly what's biting you?"

"Jason, for one thing."

"What's the matter? Isn't he taking his nursing bottle on schedule?"

Mapes scowled. He regretted having opened his heart to Walter on that subject. His vow to William Steele had come pouring out one night after a particularly frustrating day, and that

143

gave Woo the right to air his own views upon the relationship; which he often did: A captain should be a captain; if he was something less, he rated loss of respect.

"That wasn't necessary!" Mapes growled.

"Sorry," Walter replied contritely. "I like the captain. I'm not saying I'd die for him but then I wouldn't die for anybody. I think what you're trying to say is that the captain isn't himself."

"You've noticed?"

"Of course. If the captain of a ship is off-color everybody feels it."

"That's true. Jason is moody, depressed."

"He's always been moody."

"This is different. The only time he comes out of it is when we raise a whale. Then he goes after it as though—as though—"

"As though it was his mortal enemy," Walter finished for him.

"That's about it."

"Reckless. And you're afraid he'll do something crazy."

Mapes nodded. "He made out that losing Elizabeth Penn meant little to him. But I think that may be it. Maybe he wasn't in love with her, but he has his pride."

"And you see danger? You think maybe if Captain Ahab bumps into Moby Dick there may be trouble?"

Never having read *Moby Dick* or heard of Captain Ahab, Mapes did not know what Walter was talking about, but he did not bother to ask.

"It could be that girl on board," Walter suggested.

"There have been women on board before."

144

Immediately the cook sensed Mapes' blind spot. "But not one like Kate," he said.

"What's the difference? A woman is a woman."

"But this one could be bothering Jason. He's left her alone."

"True, but if Jason wanted a woman—any woman—he'd take her. That's his nature."

Walter poured some more wine. "You may be worrying about nothing. Let things ride. The ship's still afloat. . . ."

With little else he could do, Mapes agreed and they let the subject drop. Thus, Walter did not expand on what his experience and perceptions told him: that there is no moralist like a loose-living man suddenly touched by love for a moral woman. It was like a reformed drunkard shouting the praises of abstinence. Jason's problem was clear: He was in love with that little sprite but had never learned how to court an innocent girl. The gay Marita had been a different proposition. She had caused Jason no loss of sleep, but Walter felt certain that Jason was tossing on his pillow over the confusing little bilge rat who had crawled out of the hold.

It was not that any of the foregoing greatly bothered the cook. He was inclined to watch the human drama rather than to participate, and the occasional contributions he made to its progress were whimsical rather than of serious intent.

25.

The next afternoon, during Kate's absence from the galley and a lull in his own duties, Peter Wells called on Walter Woo. The latter had been waiting for Wells to show up, mildly surprised it had taken so long.

"You look like a father hen that's lost its chick. Have you lost a chick by any chance?"

Peter's reply to the garbled comparison was simple and to the point. "I don't know what you're talking about."

"Well, you've been moping about the ship for quite a while. There must be something wrong."

"I never mope. To do so is childish."

Walter shrugged. "So I made a mistake. It happens. How are you getting along with our stowaway?"

"You are referring to Miss McCrae?"

"Has another baggage popped up?"

Woo watched closely for Peter's reaction to the term *baggage* and thought he saw a slight wince.

Peter said, "I cannot understand why Captain Steele does not turn to port and put her ashore." Then his expression darkened and he muttered, "Or perhaps I can."

"What does that mean?"

"He could have his own reasons."

"Because he likes to have a female aboard?"

"Hasn't that been proven on other voyages?"

"I guess so. But you weren't upset when he had the little Jamaican around."

"I'm not upset now, either!" Peter exclaimed.

"I think you are, Pete. You see the captain imposing on Kate against her will."

"Hardly that—hardly against her will."

"I haven't seen anything to put Kate in Marita's class."

"Oh, haven't you? Well I have."

The episode in Kate's cabin poured out quickly after that and Walter listened politely. He emitted a philosophical "Hmmm," then said, "In the captain's bathrobe . . . so you saw that and asked her about it and she admitted the awful truth."

"Of course not! I've hardly spoken to her since."

"You didn't ask her?"

"Of course not," Peter repeated. "It was none of my business."

"I suppose it wasn't. But I was just thinking . . ."

"Thinking what?"

"Nothing important."

"Thinking *what*, man?"

"All right, I was thinking that a young fellow in love with a girl could make a hell of a mistake by blundering along like a stubborn ass."

"You are referring to me?"

"If the noose fits . . . But if it were me, I wouldn't go kicking the chair out from under my feet before I was sure I had reason."

"So I *am* in love with her! There, does that make you happy?"

"Me? It's no hair out of my pigtail one way, or the other."

"But I saw what I saw," Peter insisted.

"Could be. Anything is possible. But there also could be other reasons for the bathrobe. Maybe not a lot, but certainly a few. And you could be losing a fine girl by not finding out for sure."

"Thank you for your advice," Peter replied sarcastically.

"Don't thank me. I haven't given you any advice. I'm willing to, though. In a few words, quite acting like a child and grow up. Now get the hell out of here and let me cook . . ."

Peter left and Walter went on with his work. He may or may not have helped the young second mate; he'd learned from experience that the only people who really listen are those who come to have their opinions changed.

"Love," he grunted. "A waste of time!"

He'd had only one set-to with the enervating emotion, in San Francisco where he'd fallen hard for the madam in a Chinese whorehouse. And he would be forever grateful to the three tong members who chased him out of Chinatown with hatchets.

The reconciliation between Kate and Peter occurred shortly after the latter's talk with Walter; obviously Peter *had* come to have his opinions changed. After the evening meal that same day, he manfully approached Kate by the afterrail. "Kate—please. I've come to apologize."

"Apologize? You have no reason to."

"But I do. And I've got to be truthful. When I saw the captain in your cabin with you, I was deeply hurt, although I had no right to be. I acted like a child. Can you ever forgive me?"

"But Peter, it wasn't what you think."

"I had no right to think anything. And I am dreadfully sorry."

Kate was touched. She knew how hard this must be for him. "What happened was—"

He placed a finger over her lips. "Please don't explain. Just listen to me." He paused and took a deep breath before going on. "I love you, Kate. I've loved you since the first moment we met."

"Oh, Peter! You couldn't possibly have—"

"But I did. I know it now. That is why I made such a fool of myself."

"Don't say that—you are not a fool!"

"Kate dearest—I adore you. I want you to be my wife."

If she had ever fantasized Peter Wells proposing marriage to her, she could not have visualized the shock with which she reacted.

"But Peter, after—"

He assumed she was going to allude to the cabin episode and he cut her off.

"Kate! I know in my heart that you would never do anything to be ashamed of. And even if you did it would make no difference. . . ." He realized he sounded like a smitten school boy tripping over his tongue.

Kate came to his rescue. "Peter, darling, I understand."

"I want you, Kate. I want you to share my life."

They were close together, eyes locked, and the kiss was inevitable. As their lips met a dozen thoughts raced through Kate's mind. Here was the absolute proof that she was desirable, a woman to be loved as well as lusted after—although she might have welcomed more passion and less adoration. Unexpectedly the magnetic figure of Jason Steele came to mind. How would Jason react if Peter became openly possessive? Would he care one way or the other?

Should she accept Peter's proposal? Then, in spite of her best efforts to keep her mind on Peter, the image of Jason Steele flooded her being. She felt his body, not Peter's, pressed against her. It was Jason who had asked her to marry him. . . . She drew back, shivering.

"Are you cold, darling?"

"No . . . no."

"Take my jacket."

"Truly, I don't need it."

She turned to the rail. She had to think of something to say to Peter. After all, he had just proposed to her.

"Peter," Kate murmured. "We scarcely know each other. You know so little about me."

His answer was full of sincerity, scant of caution. "I know all I need to know, dearest. You are wonderful and I love you and want you to be my wife."

The ship's bell interrupted them, stroking off the time of night. Before it finished a figure loomed out of the darkness. Guy Mapes said, "The captain wants to see you in his cabin, Mr. Wells."

Peter whispered to Kate, "We'll talk later," and to Mapes, "Is anything wrong?"

"Not that I know of," Mapes replied as they walked away together. "I think he wants a game of chess . . ."

The interruption was providential: it saved Kate from having to respond. In truth, she was too confused to answer either way. The proposal should have been a dream come true. Peter was handsome enough to be a prince. But there was a joker in fate's deck—an equally handsome knight who consorted with loose women and looked upon the princess with mocking eyes.

Peter represented security and protection in an uncertain, hostile world, while Jason was nothing more than a sweet recklessness. And, she reminded herself, Jason had not evidenced any interest in her whatsoever.

Suddenly Kate saw herself standing before Jason clad in the outrageous brassiere and revealing pantalettes she had seen in the chest, while his passion for her knew no bounds.

The image was so vivid it was several moments before Kate became aware that she was gripping the rail hard, her fingers aching.

Peter was a fine, decent man. He had professed his love for her. The wife he chose would live like a queen. Jason offered nothing . . . nothing—

The tall form of John Saipan, who had come up as silently as a shadow, was beside her.

"What are you doing out here alone, girl?" For some reason he seemed to be accusing her, his eyes filled with judgment.

"I—I was merely taking the air."

Kate knew sudden fear, although there seemed no reason other than the bizarre manner of the man standing next to her.

"In any case, my being here is no concern of yours. I see no reason to account to you," she said loudly in an effort to bolster her courage.

"Be not hostile, girl. I speak only for your good. I am God's emissary doing His will."

"I don't understand you. Please step aside, as I'd like to return to my cabin."

Saipan remained where he was. He was a man burdened with the troubles of the world. "Perhaps it is His will that you are aboard this doomed ship. Do you also have transgressions for which you must answer to Him?"

"Why do you say the ship is doomed?"

"You saw God's signal—the green fire."

"There was a rational explanation for that. It was a phenomenon of the weather, the men said."

"God is the weather. God is the sea and the land and the sky and all things."

Kate wondered what to say to this madman who had her trapped against the rail. Certainly it would not be wise to anger him.

"A sorrowful thing," he was saying, "that one so young and innocent should be condemned to fiery justice."

"Please—I'm quite tired."

"Or perhaps not so innocent as she appears?"

"I don't think that is for you to judge."

"I do not judge. I only carry out the will of the Divine."

"And how do you know what that will might be?" Kate spoke in an even tone, choosing her

152

words with care. She could only hope that this self-styled prophet would leave before she was forced to call for help.

"He tells me," Saipan replied. "We speak as servant and Master. And He has told me His will where it concerns this ship. I am here to carry it out."

"But don't you think that God could do whatever He desires with the *Gray Ghost* without calling on you?"

"Are you mocking me, girl?"

"No—no. I don't mean to. I think it was a logical question in the light of God's power."

"He moves in marvelous and mysterious ways. You cannot conceive the splendor—the glory of His presence!"

Saipan tensed as though in pain. Kate gripped the rail. Did this madman plan to hurl her into the sea? A sacrifice to the greatness of his God?

But then a sharp voice called, "Saipan, what are you doing here?"

The speaker approached. He was broad shouldered, with a rough face, and he spoke as though he had authority. Kate had seen him about but had never been introduced to him. Other than the fact that he had a heavy Scottish brogue and stood at the wheel quite often, she knew nothing about him.

"I asked you a question, mister. You belong forward. The afterdeck is out of bounds to forecastle hands when they are not on duty."

"I *am* on duty. My Master directs me and I obey."

"Go forward where you belong and stay there."

Saipan retreated in silence but hardly after the manner of a chastised forecastle hand. There was an innate dignity about the man through which he was able to radiate contempt.

Kate also detected an undertone of uncertainty in the order given Saipan to leave. The Scot appeared relieved when Saipan left without trouble.

He touched his forelock and said, "Pardon, Miss. I am the boatswain, Cater MacRoy. I'll be so bold as to give you some advice. Stay away from that man. He's not for the likes of any decent lass to be talking to."

"It happened quite by accident. I didn't seek him out," she hastened to add. "I was taking the air and he appeared from nowhere."

"Saipan is strange one, all right."

He nodded to her. Kate bid him good night and walked away in the direction of her cabin.

If she had any further curiosity concerning God's self-styled servant, it would have been heightened had she overheard a later conversation. Upon leaving the afterdeck, Saipan encountered two of the ship's hands in the prow. They were the Jamaicans, Antone Salas and Leon Ramos. Neither had a good grasp of English, so their contact with the balance of the crew remained minimal. They stayed pretty much together during their off-duty hours, and when Saipan came upon them they greeted him with respectful silence.

Saipan said, "You are two of God's neglected children but He has not forgotten you."

Antone Salas replied, "We pray each to God," hoping, no doubt, that was the proper response.

154

"I speak with God and obey His orders and He tells me you must not be harmed. He tells me that your sins against His sea children are sins of ignorance and He forgives you."

"We ask pardon for sins," Leon Ramos said as he crossed himself.

"He decrees that you jump ship at the next port of call because His vengeance is to fall upon all who remain. They will go down into the waters upon which they offend God each day."

The two men, only half understanding, nodded in unison.

"Sí, sí," Salas agreed.

"God is with us," Ramos murmured.

The two took their leave of Saipan with apologetic bows as they backed away. It was likely that Saipan forgot their existence before they were even out of sight. . . .

It could well have been that John Saipan's fanaticism was sparked in his early childhood. He was born and grew up on a farm outside Bennington, Vermont. It was a lonely life for a boy, with few near neighbors, and his only companion a dog—a magnificent St. Bernard.

That was a time of unrest, with renegades abroad in the land. It was young John's misfortune one day to be trapped in the forest by a pair of the most vicious kind. They did not harm the boy but quite casually they shot the dog.

Johnny Saipan's resulting trauma was of stunning proportions. He remained in a daze for weeks. Throughout human history, however, others have suffered such catastrophes and been healed by passing time. From outward appearances that seemed to be true in Johnny's case. Perhaps there was latent madness in the boy that responded to the savagery of the tragedy. In any case, he turned more silent and introverted, but as he had been of that nature before, his parents barely noticed the change.

There were two other contributing incidents in his later years. At seventeen, while riding through the forest in near darkness, his horse bolted and ran under a heavy tree limb. John was knocked unconscious to the ground. He remained motionless for hours after which he arose and wandered lost and in pain for some time. He recovered after a manner, but there was a further change in him. According to his mother: "John came home like a stranger, asking for a piece of bread."

He remained in good health, though, and during the next years gained the reputation of an eccentric. His parents died, and he deserted the land they had tilled, wandering here and there. He seemed a man in search of he knew not what. Then, in his fortieth year, he appeared to find what he had been seeking when he wandered in upon a tent meeting. A "fire and brimstone" revivalist, one Jeremy Gath, was raging against the blazing sins indulged in by mankind and demanding repentance by his listeners.

John Saipan was the first to come forward to be saved, the religious experience changing him more drastically than any which had come before.

A short time later, Saipan was arrested in Massachusetts for the theft of a horse he had stolen, and put away for ten years. The sentence was severe, meted out on the basis of his reputation as an undesirable rather than the seriousness of the crime.

It was in the solitude of prison that God began talking to John Saipan. The guards enjoyed listening outside the cell to his side of the conversation, now and again, but as the voice of the Lord was audible only to John Saipan, there was talk of sending him to an institution for the insane. But nothing ever came of it and when his time was up, he was released.

Again he was at loose ends. While God's sponsorship was absolute, there was nothing in their conversations by way of direction, so Saipan remained a rebel without a cause until he went to sea on a whaling ship. There the divine directive came to him. He was to be the champion of the sea children, the great friendly beasts that were being slaughtered by the ungodly.

But Guy Mapes's brush with Saipan came during the first year of the latter's ocean career, before Saipan got his call, clear and unmistakable, from above. He was a harpooner at the time and his flogging on the *Mary Kane* resulted from a fight in the forecastle. Saipan attacked a hand who had killed a rat in a cruel manner. He accepted his punishment contemptuously and, in truth, Guy Mapes regretted his order.

And now the troubled first mate had God's zealot to cope with anew on that last voyage of the *Gray Ghost.*

26.

Shortly after Kate McCrae's conversation with John Saipan, the lookout reported a pod of sperm playing nearby. Guy Mapes hove the ship to and waited, and at dawn the whaleboats were afloat. Over the next three days four whales were taken; activity remained at fever pitch with no time for other than hard work. But there were a few interludes unrelated to the main business of the ship.

Kate met Jason in the companionway outside her cabin. He was carrying the red velvet dress from the trunk in his closet.

He tossed it to her and said, "Have the cook steam this gown out. I'm tired of seeing you in that getup. Maybe later you'll have a little time to wear this."

Kate was happily surprised but she had no time to thank Jason as he plunged on toward the deck. She took the dress to the galley where Walter put on his Chinese grin and said, "Boss-man making lady out of bilge rat?"

"Stop calling me a bilge rat! I'm quite attractive with decent clothes on."

"Makee silk purse out of sow's ear?"

"I'll have you know that Peter Wells asked me to marry him!"

That brought Walter out of his act. "He's been topping the rum keg!"

"Why do you say that? I'm old enough to get married."

The cook eyed her thoughtfully. "Sure, chickie. And he wouldn't be getting a bad bargain, either."

"Thanks for the compliment. Is the coffee ready?"

While Kate was serving out the coffee, Jason and Guy Mapes were in deep conversation near the forward whaling boat davit.

Mapes was reporting what he saw as unfavorable developments.

"The hand Saipan," he was saying. "There has been talk. . . ."

"What kind of talk?"

"The two Jamaicans. One of them went to Walter Woo with a story that Saipan told them to jump ship or they would be killed."

"What does he have against them?"

"It seemed to be the other way around. He didn't want them dead along with the rest of us."

"That damned St. Elmo fire, probably. He must take it as a bad omen—that the ship will go down."

"Maybe, but a lot of the hands are leery of him. And more to the point, he brought only two things aboard—his chest and a tube of some kind—and one of them has disappeared. The tube isn't in the forecastle."

"So it was something private and he hid it."

Guy Mapes pulled at his chin. "All of this is through Woo but it's worth thinking about. Saipan has enemies among the crew, hands who are afraid and watch him. There are those who confide in Woo. It comes by way of the forecastle that he's planning to blow up the ship."

"Does Woo take it seriously?"

"I think he does or he wouldn't have passed it on to me. They think Saipan brought dynamite aboard and plans to use it."

"Forecastle scuttlebutt!" Jason exclaimed. "I'm disappointed in you, Guy. You've heard that kind of talk before from men out on voyages. They get bored; they have to have something to occupy their minds. They invent their own fairy tales."

"Yes," Mapes admitted. "But never this early. A year out—two years. But we've hardly begun the cruise."

"Right. And we're having fantastic luck. At this rate we'll fill the holds in record time and make a mark for them to shoot at. This Saipan—is he shirking?"

"No, he pulls an even strain. No complaint there," Mapes admitted.

"Well, that's what he's aboard for, so let's not look for trouble."

Mapes nodded but he didn't look satisfied. Jason swung down the line into the whaleboat. At least the captain had come out of his dumps with a vengeance. He was now hell-bent on the objective of the voyage: Take whale; fill the barrels. Mapes suspected that Jason was hitting back at the Penn clique with the only weapon he now had: his whaling ship.

Perhaps Jason was right. Why set such high store on unsubstantiated scuttlebutt? Maybe I'm just getting old, Mapes told himself.

160

27.

There was much of the showman in Jason
Steele; but this did not spring from a particularly overblown ego. Jason was simply too generously endowed by nature. He started life as a
"beautiful" baby, developed into an "angeli-
cly" lovely child, and even escaped the gawky
stage of the adolescent. In his late teens, all the
early promise was fulfilled and he was as handsome and masculine as any smitten maid could
desire. Thus, admiration and praise became a
way of life for him and, in a sense, he tried to
live up to it through spectacular performances.
More was expected of him than of ordinary sons
and he strove to please.

As his grandfather had said in his defense,
there was no meanness in Jason, and no great
flaw other than his Steele temper. His antics
were always on the lighthearted side, springing
from an enthusiastic love of life and geared to
produce laughter. Even when he settled dif-
ferences with his fists there were usually
apologies afterward; if he had remained in
Stonington after the vicious fight with Chester
Manson there would probably have been a
reconciliation.

With women available to him wherever he

went it had always been simply a choice of which one he wanted. He had not greatly wanted Elizabeth Penn on an emotional level. However, the spectacular aspects of the betrothal appealed to him: the handsomest couple in town; the gold-plated children of the local aristocracy—a royal pairing, so to speak. And it was time for him to take a wife—a man could not remain a carefree bachelor forever—time to say farewell to all the beauties he had loved fiercely and treated well.

But now, on this present voyage of the *Gray Ghost*, he was to learn something about himself. The puritan strains of his New England line lay quietly dormant waiting to be stirred by a deeper, more worthwhile emotion such as he had never before experienced—the truer love which transcends that of mere physical attraction.

In fact, through lack of experience in such realms, Jason did not know that this was the situation in which he was enmeshed. He only knew that Kate McCrae was an abrasive element newly introduced into his life. She irritated him, and she kept him awake.

And while in this new quandry, a second characteristic would be revealed. Jason was a snob. While not able to take Kate in the manner of Marita or other women he had casually known, neither could he think of her in the same terms as Elizabeth Penn. A girl to be cultivated with an eye toward marriage? Impossible! No *lady* would have crouched for two days in the bilge of a seagoing ship. But Kate McCrae had done exactly that—and made no apologies for it.

Well, there was no harm in a friendly gesture. The gift of the red velvet gown changed Kate's status somewhat. It made her more of a guest and less of a stowaway. However, the motivation was more simple than that. He was curious to see what Kate would look like in civilized garb. . . .

28.

The post-rendering lull, with the whale catch reduced to oil and stored safely in the hold, brought some respite in the galley; time for Kate to make certain inquiries of Walter.

"Walter, you must know a lot about Peter Wells."

"You ought to know more if he asked you to marry him."

"No, we haven't talked much about backgrounds. There hasn't been time. I know he comes from a wealthy family and that he has a sister—"

"A rich father, sure, but Pete's got money of his own. A lot of it. His grandfather was quite a guy."

"I know. A slave runner. Peter hated him."

"Maybe, maybe not. But the old gentleman liked his two grandchildren while maybe he didn't think so much of his own son."

"What do you mean?"

"Pete's dad turned out to be a stuffed shirt, while Pete's granddad was a real freebooter who kept a couple of mastiffs in the dining room and threw them beef bones after he got through gnawing his own dinner off of them. He wanted his grandchildren to be free of their father's influence so he left them both very well off. So well off that Pete's dad tried to break the will—but he got nowhere."

"Peter didn't tell me much about his sister except that she lives in New York City and isn't married."

Walter grinned. "Uh-huh. That little wench must be something. She sure embarrasses her parents by howling around town for women's rights."

"Then maybe Peter is ashamed of her too."

"He makes out that way but I doubt it. I think he admires her, and wishes he had her guts."

"There is a lot to be admired in Peter, too."

"Pete's had a tough time most of his life trying to figure things out. He's full of guilt. There's a lot of his grandfather in him and his folks taught him to be ashamed of the old pirate. So he's deserted both sides and tried to find his own philosophy."

"I get the feeling he really doesn't belong on the sea. Do you think he is just here until he finds the right place for himself?"

"Maybe. But I'll tell you one thing: Nobody could find a better friend. Pete's the kind of man they made up that saying about."

"What saying?"

"That a friend is a person who knows all your faults but likes you anyhow. Pete would go to hell for anybody he calls a friend. Now if he called that person his wife—"

"Walter! Are you saying I've done something in my past that I ought to be ashamed of?"

Woo contrived to look Orientally inscrutable. "I don't know anything about what you've done, chickie, but I know Pete wouldn't be ashamed of it."

"You—oh, you—I don't know what! You always answer a question by making things more confusing!"

"What you're saying is you think you'd be passing up a good thing by not marrying Pete but you've got the crazy notion you ought to be in love with him and you're not."

Kate was silent for a moment.

"How do you know? Maybe I'm very deeply in love with him."

"And maybe those spuds'll peel themselves if you wait long enough."

"Walter, you're a slave driver! When I get rich I'm going to hire you to cook for me and make you peel potatoes until your fingers are as sore as mine!"

"When you marry Pete? No chance."

"Do you mean he really doesn't want to marry me?"

"I'm saying you couldn't afford to hire me. I come too expensive for even Pete's poke."

Kate sighed. "I wish you'd stop grinning like a Chinese Cheshire cat. It doesn't become you. . . ."

29.

That evening after dinner, Peter Wells returned to the captain's cabin. He entered and saluted, a gesture which annoyed Jason.

"Cut it out, man! Go over and set up the chess board while I pour us some brandy."

Peter relaxed, but not completely. "I'd rather not if you don't mind."

"What is it, then—you've got something to say?"

"Yes."

"Well, sit you down and out with it."

"I don't know any way to say it except direct. I mean, I'm speaking to you as the captain of this vessel."

"You have a complaint?"

"No, not at all," Peter said hastily.

"You're hardly being direct, Peter."

"Very well, here it is: I am in love with Kate McCrae and I want to ask if you'll marry us if she accepts me," he said in a rush.

Jason's brandy glass was halfway to his lips. His arm might as well have suddenly frozen.

"Kate McCrae—the stowaway who hid in our hold?"

They were just words—meaningless chatter to puncture the silence which followed the announcement. When Peter did not reply, Jason said, "*If* she accepts you? Are you telling me she has not agreed?"

"Nor refused. I proposed to her but there has not been time for her answer."

"But you are sure she will accept." Was there a hint of resignation in his statement?

"I am far from sure."

"Then why come to me at this stage?"

Peter hesitated, not knowing quite how to put his reason into words, though it was really quite simple. As things had been, there was an aura of the clandestine about his love for Kate. He wanted it out in the open—and he particularly wanted Jason to know how he felt.

"I wanted you to know," he said simply.

"I appreciate your confidence. As to a wedding ceremony, I could not refuse. You are both of age—Kate *is* of age, is she not?"

"I am sure of it."

As captain of the ship Jason *could* refuse to marry them if Kate was unable to produce proof of her age. However, his thinking had not really gone that far. He was still in the grip of the amazement he felt at what Peter had told him.

"You are sure you know what you're doing?"

Peter stiffened. "I am quite certain of how I feel about Kate. I can only hope her feeling for me is as strong."

"But you don't think it is?"

"I have no way of knowing." Peter paused, a wry smile on his face. "If she refuses me I'll be better able to answer your question."

"Then I can only wish you good luck," Jason said.

It was all polite enough, even pleasant, but there was none of the hearty spirit of warmth and congratulation which usually prevails when one good friend tells another that he has finally found the right girl. Jason was too concerned with trying to evaluate his own reaction to the news. In a curious way, he felt that he was being left behind, that he had lost a contest he had not even entered.

But he managed a certain graciousness. "Oh, by the way, I gave Kate one of Marita's dresses. Actually, Marita never wore it. And I don't think we should have Kate serving us in light of what's happened, so the two of you must be my guests for dinner tomorrow night."

"You are very kind." Peter bowed slightly.

"That is unless we strike a pod, of course."

"Of course."

There was no chess game that night. Peter left Jason pondering why he had extended the invitation. It wasn't from any enthusiasm for the marriage. Well, he had given Kate the dress out of curiosity as to how she would look in it. The dinner would give him an opportunity to find out. . . .

Half an hour later on the afterdeck Peter got his answer.

"I'm sorry, Peter dear, but I have to refuse you."

He took the rejection bravely, leaning out over the rail, lifting his eyes to look across the moonlit sea. "I can only respect you for your honesty. I had no right to think you loved me. Only my own love for you was in my mind."

"Peter, it isn't that—it isn't that I don't love you. But saying yes to you would not be fair.

You are out here alone, away from your friends and your family. You are naturally attracted to me because I'm lonely too—"

His eyes showed compassion.

"So in your case you may be misjudging your feeling for me, and in mine—"

"Yes?"

"In mine I would perhaps be looking for someone to take my father's place and that would be terribly unfair to you."

He glanced at her hopefully. "Then perhaps you are not giving me a final no?"

Kate hesitated. Up to the moment of coming on deck she had made no decision, her words chosen as she went along, and she had a feeling that her answer could as easily have been yes.

Then why did I say no? she asked herself.

"Perhaps it is not a final answer. You are not angry with me for asking for more time?"

"Of course not, dearest. I wouldn't want you to accept unless you were sure."

The compromise seemed to justify a kiss and Kate went into his arms. This time there was more passion in the embrace but Peter still held her as if she might break and Kate could only wonder whether that would change if and when she said yes.

30.

"You're an idiot," Walter said.

"And you're a fat Chinaman who ought to mind his own business," Kate snapped.

Of course they both knew she had wandered down to the galley the next morning to get her friend's opinion on how things had turned out.

Walter was not offended. "Chickie, when you're an old woman with creaky bones and a worn-out face you're going to regret turning down that nice boy."

"Are you saying no other man will ever ask for my hand?"

"When you get ashore and run into the competition for good men you'll find things a little different."

"That's the very reason I refused Peter. It isn't fair to take advantage of him."

"Kate, there's a lesson you've got to learn and that is to grab what you can get when you can get it. But you'll probably learn it too late."

"Didn't your parents ever teach you about honor and that sort of thing?"

"I educated myself and one of the first things I learned is that there's plenty of time to be honorable after you've taken care of number one."

"That may be true, but I'm not sure I love Peter."

"What you're saying is you don't want to close the door on Jason. Stupid; plain stupid. Pass up Pete and you trade a solid future for a stall in the captain's stable. And when the voyage is over he'll turn you out to pasture and look for another filly."

"That's a terrible thing to say!"

"Look, Kate, I'll be frank. Little Marita had you beat a mile in ways to make a man happy, and where is she after a ride on the sea with Jason? Out looking for another man."

"Well, I still haven't given Peter my final answer."

"I know. But you go on playing little girl games with the big boys, you'll find yourself sitting on your rump wondering how it all passed you by."

"You're impossible!"

"Sure. Want a cold potato?"

"No, thank you. And by the way, Jason has invited Peter and me to dinner in his cabin tonight. And I won't be *serving* it. I'll be wearing the red gown Jason gave me and sitting at the table like a lady."

Peter had informed her of the invitation before escorting her back to her cabin.

"Then I suppose I'll have to serve," Walter grumbled.

"And do try to cook something decent for a change. Dog's body would hardly be appropriate for a candlelight dinner in the captain's cabin."

"Listen to her! A few weeks out of the bilge and now she's ordering people around. How

172

would you like to go over my knee and take a few whacks on your rear?"

Kate felt devilishly gay, and with Walter the only person aboard upon whom she could vent her glee, she replied, "Ha! You wouldn't do it. That belly of yours would push me right off your lap."

He grinned down at his stomach. "I'd manage. But here's something to remember, Kate. You can sit at a table like a lady but that's not the same as being one."

Kate took a potato from the pot on the shelf and hurled it, missing his head by inches.

31.

Jason Steele regretted extending the dinner invitation as soon as Peter left his cabin. What had been the point of it? The idea of exalting Kate from the status of stowaway up to that of a guest was foolhardy; now it bothered him.

In the main, Jason was bored, restless. He'd been waiting too long for that cry from the lookout—*She blows!*—and needed the action the signal would initiate. Thus he had too much time to ponder, the wheels of his mind going around and around.

He turned to his book rack for relief, ran over the list of volumes he'd acquired in various ports, and took down the new Oscar Wilde he'd picked up. Jason liked poetry. Coleridge, Wilde, Kipling especially.

After a time he put the book aside, paced his cabin, and resolutely drove thoughts of Kate from his mind. He had two brandies, considered calling Peter in for a game of chess, then changed his mind and went to bed.

The dinner was a great success, mostly due to Walter Woo's efforts. He had embarked from Stonington with something a bit unusual for a rough sailing ship—half a dozen live fowl penned in a corner of the storage section of the galley. He killed two for the occasion and stuffed them with a fine, aromatic dressing which drew compliments from the diners.

Jason, with less effort than he'd expected it would take, was a gracious host, and if Peter Wells was downcast over Kate's tentative refusal to marry him, he hid it like a gentleman. Kate thoroughly enjoyed the meal and the company.

When dinner was over, Peter and Kate left, much as though they were all ashore and the couple was departing their host's home for their own.

Half an hour later, Guy Mapes tapped on Jason's door. His first mate appeared troubled. Jason poured him a brandy and wondered fleetingly if it was because he had not been invited to dinner. But he had not slighted Mapes intentionally.

"I talked to John Saipan about the rumor he brought dynamite aboard."

"What did he say?"

"He denied it, but not directly."

"What do you mean?"

"Well, sir, he rambled—I mean, he went into his mission on God's business again. He's a hard man to pin down."

"Have you searched for the dynamite?"

"As thoroughly as possible. But on a ship this size with all the possible hiding places . . ."

"What do you recommend, Guy?"

"I think we ought to put him in irons. That way if there is dynamite aboard he won't be able to get to it."

Jason frowned. "If we lock him up on what

we've got we'll probably be defending ourselves in a Maritime Court of Inquiry when we put in to shore."

"That may be true, but I'd rather that than the ship blown up."

Jason did not comment.

Mapes added, "For another thing, the crew is getting nervous about him. It was a mistake, my signing the man on."

"Don't blame yourself," Jason said. "Let's just let it go for a few days. A man like Saipan is not secretive; he craves attention. I think we're better off to wait. He might give us solid grounds on which to put him in irons."

"Yes, sir."

Mapes' formality was an indication of his continued anxiety and Jason sought to reassure him further. "We'll put in soon, and then we'll just get rid of him."

"It will be a load off my mind, sir. . . ."

After Mapes left, Jason considered all the aspects of the situation. Had he made the right decision or should he have taken his first mate's advice? Time would tell. . . . His thoughts drifted back to the dinner—and Kate. Jason suddenly recalled that curious roll of goods he'd seen in Kate's cabin—a tube some three feet long. Could it be . . . ? Perhaps Saipan had asked her to keep it for him.

Jason went to Kate's cabin and knocked. There was no answer. He entered and saw the object in question on the shelf next to the wardrobe. Something about it was different. When he'd noticed it originally the tube had been wrapped in some sort of cloth. Now a jacket of heavy oilskin had been sewn around it. He hefted it, shook it gently. It was certainly a handy place to hide a few sticks of dynamite.

Without further thought, Jason returned to his cabin, taking the cylinder with him.

32.

After leaving Jason's cabin, Kate and Peter went up on deck and stood by the afterrail. The sky was clear, the moon showing brightly, the setting ideal for romance. However, Peter made no motion in Kate's direction, his passion still held in check by his inherent sense of nobility which told him it would be wrong to try to influence Kate.

They remained there for quite some time, each lost to his own inner stirrings.

"I have to go on watch," Peter said finally.

"What is there to watch?" Kate asked. "Everything is so quiet, so peaceful."

"I know, but an officer must be on watch at all times to see that it stays that way. Allow me to take you back to your cabin."

"No, Peter dear. You do what you have to do. I'll see you in the morning."

He received a kiss, a light brushing of Kate's lips, and then she was gone, leaving him feeling like an idiot for making no move toward her. The next time it would be different, he told himself sternly. Kate was going to be his wife!

Then he went forward to check the forecastle.

Kate had gone below wondering if she would

get even a wink of sleep that night. There was so much to think about! She went to her cabin but almost immediately there was a tapping on her door. A quick thrill ran through her. It was Peter to say good night again, and now she would tell him yes. He was so good, so decent—so worthy! Why should she hesitate to be his wife?

She opened the door to Jason Steele.

"Will you come into my cabin for a few moments?"

His manner was cool—Kate automatically reacted in kind. "Of course, Captain."

Jason wore a dressing gown but as she followed behind him she noted that his ankles were bare. The bizarre Oriental lounging outfit was not under it. At the door to his cabin he stumbled, but so slightly that Kate could not tell whether or not it was from too much brandy. He held the door for her, then closed it after himself, and as he passed her she caught the strong smell of drink. He was not noticeably drunk; only cold, distant, impersonal.

"You may sit down," he said.

"I prefer to stand if you don't mind."

He shrugged. "Suit yourself."

She saw her role of canvases on his desk. It had been opened. Her anger was instantaneous.

"What are you doing with my paintings?"

"May I remind you that I am the captain of this ship?"

"I don't care if you are admiral of the fleet! You have no right to take my property and rip it open!"

"I had ample reason. To be perfectly frank with you, I was looking for dynamite."

179

"For *dynamite!*" Kate gasped. "Have you gone out of your mind?"

"As I said, my reasons for the search were sufficient. There were reports from my men that there may be explosives concealed aboard. I was told that—"

"I don't care *what* you were told! You didn't find any dynamite, did you?"

"No, I did not."

"Then why was I called in here?"

One canvas had been laid aside. Jason unrolled it and held it forth. "This nude painting of you," he said. "It is you, isn't it?"

"Obviously," Kate said warily.

Jason turned it and regarded it with a grim smile. It was Kate, without doubt. She was lying in the grass with the gypsy wagon in the background. Her hand was extended toward a hovering butterfly which appeared about to light.

"From the first you have made yourself out an innocent, put-upon child—a cringing virgin. And you have been most convincing. You deceived me completely."

"Just what are you implying?" Kate demanded.

"That should be obvious. This painting speaks for itself."

"There is nothing indecent or obscene about that painting. My father did it."

"A girl who habitually appears nude before her father—"

"It is a work of art! My father was a fine man!"

"With a fine daughter?"

180

"Why are you doing this? What are you saying?" Kate's voice had risen sharply.

"My point is that I have a responsibility to Peter Wells, not only as an officer on my ship but as a friend. I know his family, his father and mother. I am certainly not going to let him be trapped into marriage by a tart who came from God knows where and is interested only in what she can get!"

"How *dare* you!"

He stepped closer. "That gown—"

"You *gave* it to me!"

"Not to be worn with so much of your breasts exposed."

"But the dress is too small—"

Kate did not get to finish. Jason grasped the top of the bodice and jerked. The hooks on the back gave and she stood before him exposed to the waist, her chest heaving. But her rage and indignation only made her more desirable.

With Kate momentarily stunned into immobility, Jason seized her around the waist and bent her to the floor. He held her there with the weight of his knee while he tore at the lower part of the gown. Kate was now naked, what was left of the gown bunched raggedly below her breasts. He loomed over her, straddling her body, silent in his ferocity of purpose.

He had already brushed his robe aside to reveal his own nakedness. Now he pushed brutally against her inner thighs to force them apart.

Kate found her voice. "You filthy—rotten—*bastard!*"

And as Jason drove himself deep into her body, her fury was let loose. Her nails clawed

181

at his naked back, her invaded body struggled in protest.

But Jason only thrust deeper, and suddenly her body began to respond—so much so that she sobbed at the unwanted pleasure inflicted upon her.

The delight rose higher, and she surrendered to it. . . .

When it was over, Jason remained on top of her. In his eyes there was a look of triumph. Then he rolled away from her and rose to a sitting position, his hand over his face. The triumphant expression had disappeared. It was the pose of one defeated.

None of that mattered to Kate, however. She stumbled to her feet and staggered toward the door. As she grasped the knob, she turned.

"You filthy beast—!"

Back in her own cabin, after tearing off the remnants of the red gown, she got into her robe—*Jason's* robe—and sat huddled in her chair, still sobbing.

He knew! Oh God, he knew I enjoyed it!

There was a knock on her door. She dragged herself up to answer it. Peter stood there, his expression concerned.

"Kate, I heard you cry out. What is it? Were you having a bad dream?"

"Yes, Peter—oh, darling—a bad dream."

She went gratefully into his arms.

"I'm so sorry, dearest," Peter whispered as he held her. "I wish there was something I could do."

"There is—marry me. If you still love me—"

"Love you? Kate—I love you more than my own life!"

182

Even as she clung to him, to his clean, honest strength, she wondered how he could possibly love her.

"I'm sorry I was such a child, Peter, such a fool. What if you had changed your mind?"

"I'd never change my mind. Jason can marry us in the morning."

"So soon?"

"Why not? We have no reason to wait."

Jason just raped me! It wasn't a dream! If Peter tells him he wants to marry me—

What would he do?

Kate could only bury her face against Peter's chest and try to control her sobs.

Peter moved her toward her bunk and sat her down. "Darling, everything is all right now. Go back to sleep. There will be no more bad dreams, I promise. You go to bed and I'll see you in the morning." He kissed her and left.

He had changed. With her promise giving him the right to do so, he was taking over: Kate's welfare was now in his hands.

But Kate knew it was too late. When Jason told Peter the truth there would be no marriage, only contempt and what Kate dreaded most of all—the deep hurt in Peter's eyes.

Lying there in her bunk, she considered going to Jason and throwing herself on his mercy. He would, of course, never admit to raping her—only to a mutually desired tryst. *No!* Even with her chance of a decent life with Peter Wells hanging in the balance, she could not bend her knee to Jason Steele.

Finally, Kate slept.

33.

Jason did not.

He sipped brandy and, somewhat like a detached observer, examined the thoughts which ran through his mind. Any notion of personal guilt was rejected out of hand. Experience led him to believe that innocence was invariably a pose women assumed in order to gain their ends. He recalled his pre-engagement affair with Elizabeth Penn. So reserved, so sheltered, such a stranger to passion—until that night at the Penn summer place. He had always treated her with the respect to which he felt she was entitled, and then, quite suddenly, she had become the aggressor, a naked princess he could only now compare with Marita in terms of wild, hungry passion. After that weekend she returned to her public masquerade of sterile dignity. Obviously a totally calculated performance.

Still, Kate McCrae was another matter. This was the first time Jason had ever felt cheap after taking a woman. But why? he asked himself. Kate was no different from the others, except that her masquerade of innocence had been more skillful.

Damn! For God's sake quit puling like a smitten schoolboy!

But it *had* been different, and now Jason allowed himself a direct question. Had he degraded Kate McCrae because he knew of no other way to reach her?

Something else became clear. He did not want Peter Wells to marry Kate. He experienced a strong sense of loss; no semblance whatever to his feeling of having escaped a trap when Elizabeth Penn went back on her promise. He needed time to sort out his confusion into some sort of order: time—with Kate remaining out of Peter Wells' bed.

Thus the night slipped by and Jason was in a sullen, hostile mood when Peter knocked on his door the following morning.

"What is it?" Jason demanded.

The sharp question checked Peter's smile. He turned formal, saluting uncertainly.

"Captain, that matter I brought to your attention—"

"What matter?"

"My marriage to Kate McCrae. She has accepted me. As captain of this ship you stated you would perform the ceremony—"

Jason's scowl caused Peter to react with uncertainty.

Jason got up from his chair. "Have you lost your mind?"

"Captain—I don't understand."

Jason caught himself. Now he approached his second mate and laid a hand on his shoulder in what might have seemed a fatherly gesture.

"Peter, while you are on this ship I have a responsibility toward you. You are more than

185

just one of my officers. You are a personal friend. I know your mother and father—"

It was Peter's turn to frown. "Jason, they have nothing to do with this."

"Perhaps not, but I'm sure they would expect me to keep you from making a mistake."

"I suppose you mean well, but—"

"Let's look at this thing sensibly. You are at a disadvantage here on the ship. It's a celibate life with rare breaks ashore to find female company."

"Sir, I've never gone ashore for that purpose."

"But you *are* in a position to be unduly influenced by an attractive girl to make a mistake you might regret."

"I think that is my personal affair. I did not come in here to discuss it. I came to ask you—"

"I'd hoped not to have to go into detail. But I must tell you that Kate is not the kind of girl a man would want to spend the rest of his life with."

Peter's face darkened to a degree that Jason had never before seen. "Sir, I am not interested in your personal opinion of the girl I plan to marry. Only your position as the captain of this ship keeps me from making you answer for your insult."

"Look at this—it ought to prove something to you." With that, Jason picked up the nude painting and spread it open.

"Her father was an artist."

Jason sighed.

"I didn't want to have it come to this. But now I'm going to tell you what happened—"

The balance of what Jason planned to say

186

was lost. Peter's fist dove straight against his mouth. Jason dropped the painting and stumbled up against the table.

Peter kept pace with him. Jason slipped the next punch and used the flat of his foot to push the enraged man backward.

The latter now bore little resemblance to the pleasant, docile young man who had served under Jason and taken his orders. "You filthy-minded bastard! You aren't capable of recognizing a decent woman when you see one!"

That speech cost him, for it gave Jason time to step forward and knock Peter back against the door with a single blow.

Jason won a respite as a result, but it was scanty. Peter shook his head and came on again as Jason marveled at his own misjudgment of his second mate. Instead of being totally quiescent, Peter merely had a strong spring on his trigger. But once that trigger was pulled, heaven help the target! All Peter lacked was a brawler's experience, and this was in Jason's favor. He avoided the clumsy thrusts and coolly planned his attack. Then he braced himself, waited, and laid Peter to the floor with a fist to his middle. It was a telling blow which would have stopped a stronger man. Jason was on him, his fist drawn back to strike.

But with no personal hatred for Peter, the madness of it all came home to him. He might have won Kate easily if he had competed fairly. As things stood, his own stupidity had defeated him. He experienced the same sense of failure as when he had beaten Manson bloody.

Jason got to his feet. He held up a restraining hand. "All right! All right! If you want to play the fool I won't stand in your way. Bring the girl in. I'll do as you ask."

The promise cooled Peter down, that and the nausea from Jason's blow. He, too, stood up. "That's very decent of you," he replied acidly. "When Kate awakens—"

"No. Now—immediately. Fetch her in here before I change my mind. Then after you are married I'll put the pair of you ashore and you can go where you will."

"That will be entirely satisfactory. We have no desire to remain on this ship."

Peter staggered out of the master cabin, took a few moments to quiet his stomach, and knocked on Kate's door.

A few moments later, Kate opened her eyes to see Peter bending over her. But this was a different man from the one to whom she had become betrothed. No gentle smile; no small-boy uncertainty. He was in disarray, and there was a bruise on his face, but the main change was in his manner. It was now that of a man who expected to be obeyed.

"Get up, Kate. We are to be married immediately."

She blinked herself more awake. "But Peter . . ."

"There is no time, darling." He threw back the blanket. Kate's embarrassment at her nakedness was lost on him. He took her hand and drew her out of bed.

"You must get dressed quickly."

"But why are we rushing so?"

"There is good reason. Do you have that frock you brought aboard with you?"

"It's in the closet."

He opened the wardrobe and got the dress out. Only now there was a sign of tenderness. He smiled. "Your wedding dress, darling. When we get ashore we shall pack it in rose petals and store it away."

He helped her into it, fastened the back while she stood, dazed and uncertain, then took her hand and urged her toward the door.

It was no doubt as curious a wedding as ever took place on the high seas, and perhaps anywhere else; two men who entered into the rite with the grimness of warriors ready for battle, even while showing marks of recent combat.

Jason was holding a Bible, but with no great show of the spirit of the occasion. He stepped past them and looked out into the companionway. "We will need a witness," he said. "I called for Mr. Mapes."

Footsteps sounded and Mapes appeared, his expression a question mark.

"You're to witness the mistake these two fools are making," Jason explained—no explanation whatsoever in reality.

The discipline deeply ingrained in the first mate became apparent. He remained silent, and aside from that first look of surprise, he acted as though this sort of thing happened every morning.

Officiating as a joiner of two lives was something Jason had never done before. He turned the pages of the Bible in search of guidance and found none, so he spoke extemporaneously, beginning with the question: "Is it true, Kate McCrae and Peter Wells, that you wish to be joined in matrimony?" Upon being assured

189

that it was, he came swiftly to the point. "In that case, I now pronounce you man and wife."

There were no congratulations. Jason turned immediately to the open log on his desk. "Sit down and write," he ordered Peter. The latter obeyed and Jason, hands clasped behind his back, his face turned away from Kate, began to dictate:

"I, Jason Steele, the master of the *Gray Ghost*, with the authority therein granted to me, have this day married the second mate, Peter Wells, to—" He hesitated and looked at Kate. ". . . to a passenger aboard this ship, Kate McCrae."

There was dead silence broken only by the scratching in the log. No sense of joy prevailed. The atmosphere was electric with hostility and it seemed more an armed truce than the noting of a marriage.

When he finished with the entry, Peter tore a sheet from the back of the book and continued to write.

"What are you doing?" Jason demanded.

"I want a copy—something that will pass for a certificate of marriage. Do you object?"

"Why should I?"

With the second document completed, Peter pushed the log book and the torn sheet forward. "The signatures of the captain and the witness are required," he said.

Perhaps that was the strangest moment of all—when Peter Wells, the second mate of the *Gray Ghost*, sat in the captain's chair and took command of the proceedings.

The newly wedded couple left in silence, and

Guy Mapes a short time later in the same fashion.

At Kate's door, Peter said, "Darling, you go back to bed. I'm sure you didn't get much sleep what with your nightmare, and you were so rudely awakened. I'll come to you later."

"Aren't you going to get some rest, Peter?"

Peter waited until Guy Mapes passed with a nod to them in the companionway before replying.

"I'm too wide awake, and there are things to be done on deck. I shall occupy myself for a while."

He bent down to kiss his wife. Kate went into his arms.

She murmured, "Oh, Peter darling, I do love you. I *do*."

If the inflection sounded more like an effort to convince herself and him, Peter did not pick up on it. He left Kate standing in her doorway looking after him.

It was the last time she was to see the man she had married. . . .

34.

Less than an hour later Guy Mapes returned to Jason's cabin with grave news:

"We have trouble, Jason. John Saipan has barricaded himself in the forecastle and refuses to come out."

"Good God! How did that happen?"

"I brought it about," Mapes said frankly. "I ordered him aloft to trim sail and he refused. His disobedience was so open I could not back down in sight of the hands and I arrested him. He took it calmly enough and asked to go to his chest for some necessities before being put in irons. I allowed it, sending two of the hands with him. It was then that he barricaded himself inside the forecastle. I imagine he overpowered his two guards, for they never came out either."

Jason cursed. "What a stinking mess! All we've had is trouble with that maniac. I hope you realize the mistake you made and the black mark it will cost us."

Perhaps out of anger at himself for doing nothing about Saipan when Mapes had first brought it to his attention, he lashed out unfairly at his first mate.

But still he continued to shirk his responsibility and leave the difficulty to the faithful Mapes. "All right, don't stand there chattering about it! Get the maniac out of there and put him in the brig. When that's done we will head for the nearest landfall and a port to put him ashore."

Guy Mapes left without a word in his own defense.

It must be said of Jason that he realized his duty as captain and followed Guy aft just a short time later.

It was too late, but the same tardiness saved his life. He could see the crowd at the forecastle companionway—most of the crew, with Guy Mapes and Peter Wells in command. When Jason was just past midship, John Saipan executed the *Gray Ghost* and most of those aboard for crimes against God. . . .

The dynamite charge blew a great hole in the forecastle bulkhead. Saipan was himself killed instantly, along with the two crewmen inside, if he had not already murdered them.

The explosion blew out the heavy door to the forecastle and hurled it up the companionway, a deadly missile that cut down those in its path.

The forward end of the ship was thrown upward, to starboard, and chaos was everywhere. The whaleboat aft on the starboard side was smashed against the bulkhead and splintered into uselessness, while the forward boat became hopelessly entangled in its davit lines. The two larboard boats remained functional but panic among the hands worked against any orderly retreat from the disaster. The cry, "Abandon ship!" went up.

The mainmast snapped close to deck level

bringing savage death to two more hands, who were knocked from the shrouds and hurled down into a tangle of equipment below. Another was more fortunate in that the tilt of the ship sent him into the sea.

There were two sources of fire aboard, the galley stove and the flame used by the smithy, who had been straightening a bent harpoon when the explosion came. Flaming fuel and hot embers were hurled toward open holds aft where the covers had been torn away; where barrels, now smashed, floated in the oil they had contained.

In a catastrophe of this sort there are often a few small miracles, and Guy Mapes was the beneficiary of one of these. When the forecastle door blew out and became a lethally aimed missile, the first mate was not touched though men died on all sides of him. He pulled himself clear and made his way forward, progressing as best he could on the tilted deck.

Jason Steele was knocked backward by the forward lift of the deck. Flailing helplessly he hit his head on the edge of an iron mast ring. Blood gushed from his scalp and he was unconscious for a few moments, after which he staggered to his feet. He struggled forward like a man on an aimless, drunken quest.

He met Guy Mapes at the forward companionway just as flame burst from the afterhold.

"The bow boat . . ." he gasped. "The bow boat looks to be shaken loose. Find some hands and try to launch it. I'll go down and get Kate."

Mapes nodded and looked about. He got the attention of three dazed hands and they went on forward to find that the boat in the bow had broken loose from its lashing and lay on its side parallel with the rail. They tugged and hauled and managed to point the prow overside.

When the explosion occurred, Kate was thrown clear across her cabin to land hard against the doorsill. She was not injured though the breath was knocked out of her. She staggered to her feet, gasping, just as the return tilt of the ship sent her in the opposite direction. She found herself against the closed port and she struggled to open it, but the lock was jammed. She made her way back to the door and fought to open it.

Seconds later, three driving blows of Jason's shoulder smashed it open. An abrupt roll of the ship at that moment sent him headlong into the cabin.

"Are you hurt?" he asked Kate when he righted himself.

"I don't think so. What happened?"

"We're in trouble," Jason replied with no further explanation. "Come with me. We have a boat topside."

He pulled Kate into the companionway and up the stairs while the *Gray Ghost* rolled and gyrated not unlike a great whale with a killing iron sunk deep in its vitals.

There was now a group of six at the bow whaling boat, but getting the vessel into the water without capsizing it seemed improbable. Then the *Gray Ghost* in death throes, from a forty-five-degree angle stern down, heaved in final agony to dip the prow into the water. It was a providential act: The whaling boat slipped gently into the sea.

Jason pushed Kate into Guy Mapes's waiting arms. He shoved both of them into the boat, then yelled to the hands, "Get to the oars! Get this boat clear!"

The pendulum action of the ship helped again. The stern rose once more, washing the whaling boat yards off to larboard.

Jason braced himself against the rail and screamed at the top of his lungs, "Get it off! Get it off!" before he slipped away forward down the deck.

Later, at the investigation into the sinking of the *Gray Ghost*, Guy Mapes sought to explain his reactions at that moment. Deserting his ship was agony—all his background, all his training demanded that he stand by Jason Steele's side—but he had been ordered away. Also, there were those men still alive floundering in the sea. So Mapes, who would have preferred the flaming deck of the dying ship, stayed in the boat and went about the less dangerous business of salvaging what human life he could.

Only one other boat remained undamaged but it was so badly tangled on its davits that launching it was impossible.

The *Gray Ghost* now stood perpendicular to the sea, fire rising toward the bow. Many men had died and others were dying; panic and disorganization were complete. The ship did not go down immediately; with the forecastle still above water, some interaction of flame, gases, and buoyancy within the submerged hold held her afloat. Guy Mapes, directing the oarsmen, circled the ship twice but was able to pick up only three survivors.

Then a fourth man, made grotesque by a mask of black oil covering his head and face, struggled toward the boat. He grasped an oar lock and pulled himself up, but then resisted efforts to lift him aboard.

"Wipe my eyes!" he demanded, his voice a croak. "I want to see who's here!"

Kate leaned out and wiped the man's face with her skirt. The features of Jason Steele were revealed. He had obviously gone into the water in an effort to aid possible survivors. He scanned the passengers in the whale boat.

"My God! The rest! Where are the rest?"

It was a rhetorical question; a cry of desperate hope.

"Here," Guy Mapes yelled, "I'll pull you up."

"Go to hell!" Jason gasped. "My ship is going down! There still may be others!"

He pushed away from the boat's side and began swimming back toward the flaming torch, a once proud member of the Steele whaling fleet.

Guy Mapes did not hesitate. He dived in after Jason and there was a fierce struggle. Jason fought him with all the strength he had left. The demands made by mind upon body had lifted him to remarkable heights but now he had reached his limit. He went limp in Mapes's arms and the men hauled them both into the boat. Jason had lost much blood through the slash in his head and now he lay unconscious.

Kate knelt in the boat peering into the smoke and the haze. "Peter!" she was crying. "Where is Peter? He's out there somewhere! We must find him!"

Mapes answered her silently, with a negative shake of his head.

"No! No! You're wrong! He surely got away!" she screamed.

This brought another denial from Mapes and an effort to be comforting. "In the forecastle companionway. The door blew off. He did not suffer. He was killed instantly. . . ."

At that moment those in the lone whaleboat saw what Jason's fate would have been had Mapes allowed him to return to the ship. The oil that had escaped from the smashed barrels in the hold to spread a black smear over the sea now went up in flames. The result was like hissing demons dancing in triumph around the funeral pyre of the once proud ship. Men still fighting for life in the water were caught in the spreading fire to become sudden and horrible torches. Their screams were mercifully faint in Kate's ears, muted by the roar of fire from the dying ship which also drew her gaze.

The major barrier blocking Guy Mapes's rescue efforts was the smoke pall; a thick black cloud rising over the horror. One struggling crewman was fortunate in that he had escaped beyond the oil slick and was staying afloat. Some sixty feet separated him from the boat as Mapes yelled encouragement.

"Hold on, mate, we're coming!"

The rescuers bent grimly to the oars. Then, with the boat only some twenty feet away, there was a swirl of water and a flash of curving, pale belly. Rows of multiple-decked teeth flashed for an instant—hardly long enough to register on the human eye—then the shark vanished.

"My God!" Jason screamed, conscious again. "A Great White! Not here! No Great Whites so far north!"

He rose up but Mapes dragged him down. Jason fought with the superhuman strength that comes with near madness. "Those devils can take half a man in a single gulp! We've got to save him!"

Near to losing the struggle, Guy Mapes smashed his fist full on Jason's jaw. "Suicide, man!" Mapes gasped as Jason went down.

The hideous scene was played out before their eyes. The doomed man lifted his chest high above the water, swimming furiously, then he vanished. Moments later, a hand appeared, reaching toward the boat. Hope flared in those who watched, only to be destroyed by a rising bloody froth.

Patches of human blood now stained the water beyond the perimeter of the flaming oil and the black smoke pall rising into the sky. Darting fins broke the surface as less docile children of the sea rushed in from far and wide for the feast.

The *Gray Ghost* did not go down in blazing glory. She died slowly, hidden by the choking black cloud as the spurts of flame lessened and vanished.

"Pull out and circle," Guy Mapes ordered, his voice now a raw croak.

The men went to it valiantly but it was no use. The drama had finished save for a brief epilogue: Submerged weight hit the whaleboat, tilting it and causing it to shudder; beneath it two sharks were fighting for the remains of a seaman now mercifully dead.

"Pull out!" Mapes ordered. "For God's sake, pull out . . ."

Kate was mercifully spared the sight of the Great White's kill. Huddled in the bow of the whaleboat, she had fainted.

Ironically, she still wore only the frock in which she had escaped from the *Blue Mermaid*; still without underclothing. And again she apparently had no future, a widow before she became a wife.

However, her unflagging determination to survive was marked by her last act before being taken from her cabin by Jason Steele.

She had snatched up the marriage certificate and, waterlogged or not, it was now safely stowed in the bosom of her dress.

Part Two:

NOTORIOUS WOMAN

New York City, 1903–1904

35.

The sinking of the *Gray Ghost* first reached public attention through the enterprise of an *Evening Post* reporter, Dean Cabot. When young William Hearst, fresh from publishing triumphs in San Francisco, brought his new brand of "yellow journalism" to the East Coast, he tried to hire Cabot away from the *Post*; the attempt was unsuccessful, but it was indicative of Cabot's reputation as a journalist. Called "the bulldog in the bowler hat," Cabot had a talent for creating sensational headlines, although his uncovering of the *Gray Ghost* tragedy came about indirectly—as a result of Cabot's interest in the private life of Sarah Bernhardt. The "Divine Sarah," probably the most celebrated actress of her time, was on her way to the United States aboard a Dutch steamer, the *Reinholdt*. Cabot took his idea to publisher Ephram Hager, who was struggling to match Hearst's paper with lurid headlines of his own.

"If I could use your yacht, sir, I could reach the *Reinholdt* on the high seas, get my interview, and still beat the steamer into port in time to get extras on the street before she docks. I have checked the times and the relative speeds very carefully. I could have three hours with Bernhardt and still make it comfortably."

"I'll grant you that," Hager replied, "but what makes you think you can get Bernhardt to talk about her personal life?"

"I am sure I can, sir."

"It has never been done before."

"I am quite confident, sir."

"All right, see what you can do. I'll put the *Ocean Queen* at your disposal. . . ."

Cabot plunged into the assignment with his usual energy. But as things transpired, Cabot did not interview Sarah Bernhardt; while waiting to speak with her a far more exciting story came to his attention. The steamer *Reinholdt* had picked up eight survivors from a sunken whaler, the *Gray Ghost*, and that was a story that was fairly bursting with sensationalism. . . .

There were the embittered forecastle hands, five in all, who accused the surviving captain of the whaler, one Jason Steele, of allowing a madman to roam the decks unchallenged. The captain, incidentally, was the scion of one of New England's powerful whaling families of Stonington, Connecticut. And there was more. . . . The son of one of New York City's most prominent financiers had died when the ship went down in flames. And a young stowaway—a beautiful female—one Kate McCrae, had been married on board to the financier's son shortly before his death.

Who would give a fig for a story on Sarah

Bernhardt with material like that to drool over?

Cabot interviewed furiously, filling two thick notebooks, then reboarded the *Ocean Queen* and raced back to port with his story.

36.

"Yes, my dear, the ship was lost but that is hardly important. Jason is among the survivors and is quite well." Thus William Steele informed Rebecca of the disaster after the call from a New York City reporter named Cabot. "I must pack immediately."

"The survivors? How many?"

"We really cannot say. One boat has arrived. I am sure there will be others." He was sure of no such thing.

The elder Steele had taken the news quietly, to the degree that Cabot had judged him a cold fish however, those New England whalers were a stern lot.

William's lack of surface emotion was but an outward show. Inwardly, he was stunned. In all aspects other than Jason's survival this was a catastrophe beyond measure; signaled as such by that damned reporter's hedging, his equivocation, relaying only enough information to indicate the scope of the disaster with but the skimpiest of detail. Cabot had said little concerning Jason other than the fact that he had been rescued and was well, but that was far from reassuring.

My God! What has the boy done now? A sinking without even the log book saved!

Rebecca was now carefully laying her husband's shirt into his portmanteau, gently pressing down the starched jabot. Packing for William's trips was a ritual they had performed together since their marriage so long ago.

"That fine young man Peter Wells . . . he was lost, you said."

"I did *not* say that, only that he was not in the boat with Jason. There may be other boats waiting to be picked up."

Rebecca maintained her composure, also outward. Within, she was shaking.

He is not telling me all he knows. But enough . . . enough. It has finally happened. A lifetime of indulgence and turning away has borne rotten fruit.

"There will be an inquiry of course."

William was strapping his portmanteau. Not until he was quite finished did he nod. "Most certainly. And until that time we must draw no conclusions."

No conclusions! The ship catching fire on a calm sea. A handful rescued. And we must draw no conclusions!

A touch of Rebecca's inner turmoil surfaced. "William, please don't spare me—"

He turned on her in gentle reprimand. "My dear, when have I ever barred you from my confidences?"

When have you not!

"We raised our family together—"

On your terms! Oh, you hypocrite!

"—and now with Jason in some trouble we

207

go to his aid with every resource at our command."

A worthy declaration, of course. But certain changes were obvious; from the lifelong *I, me, mine,* to *we, us, ours.* Fear and confusion in the mind of a tired old man.

As he watched Rebecca straighten the disorder of the room, William considered possible local reactions to the tragedy. From Jethro Penn . . . In William's bleak appraisal any sympathetic words from the Penn tycoon would be without substance. Jethro Penn's mind worked at all times on a competitive basis. Therefore there would only be unspoken satisfaction.

Rebecca seemingly read his mind. "Elizabeth Penn . . ." she said now. "Do you think the girl went to New York City?"

"I have no idea," William replied.

But the reference was somehow comforting. It brought to his mind a counter-satisfaction—the failure of the Penn-manipulated marriage of Elizabeth to Chester Manson. With the *Gray Ghost* at sea scarcely a week, Elizabeth had scandalized the whole area by deserting her husband and fleeing to heaven knew where. Or perhaps her whereabouts was known, but the Penns were not talking.

The sensational breakup led William to decide that the spurning of his grandson had been a stroke of good luck. It would have been unfortunate to bring such a flighty, immature female into the family.

William made a final check of the straps and stays on the portmanteau, then turned to kiss Rebecca on the cheek.

"I must hurry now, my dear. The train is due. . . ."

Then Rebecca was standing in the front portal watching his departure, as she had so many times in the past. But this one was different—Jason was in trouble. At least his defense would be of the very best; there was strength in the name of Steele, and all the power built up through generations would be brought to bear. Money drew clever minds like a magnet, and clever minds could do clever things.

As Rebecca watched her husband's carriage circle the drive and head north toward the station, she thought again of young Peter Wells. She prayed he had not died at sea. But others had, and Jason was the master who would be held accountable.

And suddenly there came to Rebecca a premonition that she had seen her husband for the last time. . . .

37.

Only a crisis could bring what was left of the Wells family together, and the probable death of Peter qualified. Tess Wells left her bicycle at her Washington Square flat, driving a hired span north to where her parents lived at Fifth Avenue and Fifty-third Street in a mansion every bit as imposing as that of William K. Vanderbilt's just a block south. Both dwellings were rated magnificent by those who admired the accepted architectural values of the time and stood in awe of the wealth which made them manifest.

Tess's description was somewhat different. She saw her parents living in "ridiculous and snobbish seclusion—rattling about in forty-two rooms with an absurd coterie of twelve servants to create an illusion that serfdom is still in flower."

By the time Tess arrived, Godfrey and Beatrice Wells had discussed the tragedy, this discussion being mainly a presentation of Godfrey's conclusions. Beatrice always waited for her husband's guidance before forming her own ideas.

Godfrey said now, "Bea, it is better to accept

the worst; then we have leeway to be thankful if it is proved wrong."

"Do you mean—?"

"I am afraid so, from what I have been told. We have to assume Peter died on that ship."

Beatrice emitted a dry sob into her handkerchief.

Godfrey Wells was a rotund little man with a round, plump face to match. His sparse blond hair could be fancifully likened to pale straw glued to a bowling ball upon which a face had been fashioned: small, deep-set eyes, a button nose, and pink cheeks. It was Godfrey's mouth that set him apart; full-lipped, remarkably facile, it was the only clue to the mind housed in the deceptively soft body. It could reflect a gamut of emotions from gentle regard to vicious contempt. At the moment it gave forth a wistful sadness.

"That Steele person—the captain of the ship. Isn't the captain always responsible for what happens?"

"I think, Bea, accepting that premise—that Peter is dead—we still cannot place blame. There are acts of God beyond human control, and Jason Steele was of good blood. The Steeles are a fine old whaling family. William Steele, his grandfather, is a charter member of the Union Club. Their whaling enterprises are family-owned and they are solid as granite financially—people one must respect. I am sure we will receive their condolences shortly."

"I'm sure," Beatrice agreed. "But the reporter said Peter had married some trollop of a girl aboard the ship. It is all so confusing—I just don't understand. It *can't* be true!"

Dean Cabot had said nothing about Peter marrying a trollop; that had been the Wells's conclusion concerning any female alone on a ship with a crew of men. Cabot had given the term *some* support by mentioning that the girl had been a stowaway.

"If the marriage was a fact, and I can only conclude that it was, we will have no trouble disposing of the girl. On the face of it she has to be an opportunist who hoped to gain financially by trapping Peter into marriage. That would not have been too difficult under the circumstances—a virile young man tempted by the touch and smell of a willing female—"

"Godfrey!"

"I'm sorry, Bea. I should not have been so frank in your presence. What I meant to say is, well, I am sure I can scowl the wench down. If necessary a few dollars will be well used in getting rid of her. Once she realizes Peter's fortune is beyond her reach—"

"Why?"

It was a sharp voice from the entrance to the room. The two turned to see Tess standing in the doorway.

"Tess! You shouldn't just barge in," Beatrice chided. "Laura did not announce you."

"Don't blame the poor girl. I 'scowled her down.' "

Godfrey's mouth formed into a harsh line.

"How long have you been standing there?"

"A while. But you didn't answer my question."

"What question?"

"I asked why."

"Why what?"

"Why Peter's widow is not entitled to his estate."

"We have no *absolute* proof that Peter married her. True, there may have been some kind of a mock ceremony, but weddings on the high sea—and certainly under *those* conditions—are automatically suspect."

"I don't agree."

"Tess," Beatrice Wells interjected in her same complaining voice, "we aren't even sure that Peter is dead—absolutely, I mean."

"My dear mother, death is like pregnancy. You can't be partly dead or partly pregnant."

Beatrice cringed. "I meant absolutely *sure*. I didn't mean—"

"Never mind, Bea," Godfrey cut in, his mobile lips plainly disapproving. "It is what we expect from Tess. She does it deliberately."

Tess advanced into the room, and with the battle lines thus immediately drawn it was surprising to realize that her last visit to the Wells mansion had been some eighteen months earlier.

Beatrice was regarding her daughter with an unhappy eye, picking out minor flaws in her image while dismissing the major ones as being too difficult for her scope and capacity.

The daughter was not unlike the mother in size and features, but at the same time, she was far different. Tess was handsome in a militant sort of way, her dress as well as her manner reflecting defiance, even contempt. Her skirt was inches too short to be fashionable—ankle length, revealing high-button shoes, at a time when most women's dresses revealed only the toe of their slipper. Nor did Tess care about

213

other aspects of style. Her black voile dress was not cinched at the waist by a corset: "Women who crowd their organs into unnatural shapes with brutal corsets invite later distress from malformed bodies."

Any form of restraint was onerous to Tess. She made no apology for her Amazon image—the "Valkyrie look," as Dean Cabot had once put it when covering one of Tess's women's rights rallies.

All in contrast to her mother, a softly fleshed woman who was in essence an extension of her husband—a mirror reflecting his attitudes, his mores, his personality, but in only one dimension, as a mirror would. She was an exaggerated example of what her daughter fought against so bitterly in the social order—a mere unit of the household. "More important than the plumbing and the furniture, but essentially in the same category."

Possibly Tess exaggerated somewhat for effect.

Beatrice accepted her lot with a vague sadness and a strong sense of the inevitable, dominated as she had always been by stronger, more determined people. The youngest of five daughters, the number she drew in the marriage lottery was considered a godsend. Iron-willed Grandfather Noah Wells had selected her as the wife for Godfrey, his considered judgment Beatrice overheard from the terrace one evening shortly before the engagement:

That Nelson girl is well-boned and healthy. She'll be a good breeder and you'll have no trouble with her.

A good breeder. That had cut deeply, but a

worried father blessed with a plethora of daughters gave Beatrice to understand that she could only be grateful for the opportunity to trade her good bones for the good life the Wells money would guarantee. One down and four to go, Keir Nelson had grimly told himself.

The present dispute in the drawing room continued to sift shallowly into Beatrice's ears:

"I can't follow your reasoning, Godfrey."

Tess! Do not address your father by his first name. There should be respect.

"It's quite simple," Godfrey retorted.

"But how do you expect to buy the girl off when she stands legally to gain Peter's entire fortune?"

"The courts may not agree to the legality. I can drag the thing out until she starves to death. Do you think for a minute I'd let the Wells's name be sullied by some dockside trollop? What do you know about her? Have you by chance talked to that reporter on the *Post*?"

"I've talked to no one. I didn't give the girl a thought until I got here and found that she is *your* first concern."

"Why shouldn't she be? Peter made many mistakes, God knows, but never one like this."

"Godfrey, when did you weep for your lost son—*before* I arrived?"

"Don't be insulting!"

"I'm sorry," Tess mocked. "It's just that all the tears seem to have dried."

"Damn it! Of course I weep for Peter!"

Beatrice cut in desperately. "But we don't *know*. We aren't sure. *I* think Peter survived. We shall hear from him soon."

215

Tess threw her mother a quick glance and turned back to her father.

"On what status will you attack the poor girl—as a wife or a widow?"

"I don't understand you, Theresa. Does the dignity of your name mean nothing to you?"

Fighting, fighting, always fighting! "Tess! Why did you come here now," Beatrice asked. "After all the months and months—"

"Yes," Godfrey took up, "after all your *years* of disgracing the Wells name?"

"I think I've brought the name more respect than you ever did."

"Notoriety and contempt. Your absurd parades and silly meetings—!"

Beatrice's voice verged on hysteria. "Oh, please! Please stop it! Must you always fight? Can there never be any love?"

Godfrey looked strangely triumphant. "Now see what you've done to your mother! Keep it up and you'll have her in the hospital!"

Tess caught back her sharp retort. She turned impulsively to her mother, then thought better of it.

"I'm sorry. I should not have come."

With that she hurried from the room.

Never any love in the Wells family. On the way downtown Tess decided it all traced back to Noah, of course, when the old pirate came off the seas with his great fortune and refused to let go. All Godfrey had really tried to do was take charge of his own family, but Noah would have none of it. Poor Beatrice's plaint about hatred, always hatred, was not an idle one, but it traced back to Noah. Godfrey had tried standing up to his father early in the game but

216

to the old savage that was equivalent to a declaration of war, and Noah's weapon was his money. As a final gesture, he made his grandchildren independent of their father by settling fortunes upon them individually.

The carriage hit a deep rut, jarring Tess out of her somber reverie.

Like her grandfather, Tess apologized to no one and asked pardon for nothing. Down deep she secretly admired old Noah's courage. Steeped in sin to the eyeballs he had not whimpered before whatever gods he believed in when they got around to taking him away.

What was the girl's name? Kate—Kate McCrae. Kate *Wells* now, and Tess would see that she did not go unchampioned.

She entered Washington Square, and automatically glanced up to where Peggy would be looking out between the curtains.

Sweet Peggy! Tess got out of the carriage and hurried up the stairs.

The day had been overcast, the weather chill, Tess' spirits bleak. But soon there would be warmth, Peggy's gentle hands soothing her tense body; then bed with passion rising and the release Tess had never found in masculine arms. She could not be possessed; like her grandfather, she too had to be the possessor.

As Tess opened the door, she bid her brother farewell.

Good-bye, Peter. I did love you . . . !

38.

Calvin Gentry had a comfortable fortune, an excellent education, and a club foot. The fortune had come down to him so long ago that money was as commonplace a part of his life as breathing. The education had done little other than to turn him into a polished dandy.

The club foot, however, was a different matter. It had had much to do with shaping his life. It was the malformed foot that kindled his interest in George Gordon (Lord) Byron, the celebrated English poet and roisterer. Calvin studied Lord Byron with zeal, and emulated him with such attention to detail that his college nickname quickly became the same—Lord Byron. Calvin even tried his hand at writing poetry, but there the similarity ceased. This did not distress him greatly, however, as there were so many other facets of his idol to be copied.

In truth, Gentry was more interested in Byron's scandalous escapades—his formation of the Hell Fire Club in London and the dissolute life it symbolized. Gentry did achieve one dubious service through the club he himself formed: Among his followers—or rather, his hangers-on, he instituted readings of the more controversial poets such as Byron, Oscar Wilde, and the more ribald writing of Robert Burns. However, most of the activities of the club were of a different nature.

After college, Gentry found no direction for his life other than to follow it day after day in idleness and what could have been superficially called pleasure. There was one aspect missing: One of his main satisfactions had been to influence others, but his school followers, after graduation, went their own ways, and he found himself pretty much alone or in the company of transients who came and went as their fortunes rose and fell; he had no true friends.

Thus, at the time of the *Gray Ghost* tragedy, Gentry was living rather fretfully in luxurious digs in New York City. His apartment was in the Granada unit of the splendid Spanish Flats complex on Central Park South, and his mistress of the moment was a blonde beauty named Bella Cantrell, a soubrette known in and around various supper clubs in the city.

The morning the *Post* screamed out the sinking of the whaler in bold headlines, Gentry was in his breakfast room with its serene view of the Central Park Reservoir and the surrounding greenery.

Minutes later, Bella Cantrell appeared. There was a queenly poise about the woman as she crossed from the living room, but few genuine queens would have agreed with the propriety of her gown for even the intimacy of the morning meal. It was pale lavender, of expensive watered silk, the front of which was daringly designed. The two piped edgings of the bodice were cut from far out on the shoulders to curve

219

downward, revealing generous portions of her well-formed breasts. The edgings met at a point just above her navel to again curve outward at mid-thigh. Thus, each step revealed a fine, nude leg almost, but not quite, to the hip.

The gown was not necessarily to Bella's taste but it was the sort of display Gentry liked. Bella had always been fair with her men. She was a woman for all seasons, a glittering social hostess, a seductive bedroom companion, a sympathetic shoulder, all with remarkable objectivity and a steady eye on her goal.

As she approached the table, she noted Gentry's far-off gaze. She kissed him on the top of his head. "Daydreaming so early, darling?"

"An old friend has popped up," he replied.

"Really?" Bella seated herself and gave her attention to the iced melon. "Anyone I know?"

"I think not, though I've possibly mentioned him—Jason Steele."

"I don't recall."

"It seems old Jason is in a spot of trouble."

"Nothing serious, I hope."

"Could well be. He's a seagoing fellow. Captain of a ship. The craft blew up and sank. It's there in the press."

Gentry waved a languid hand at the paper on the table. Bella picked it up and read:

TRAGEDY AT SEA
Whaling Ship Goes Down In Flames
Many Die

As she scanned the article, Gentry commented, "Fine old New England family, the Steeles. Whalers from way back."

"Are they blaming your friend for the sinking?"

"Probably. When a vessel goes down the captain is often held accountable. And old Jason didn't go down with the ship. They may also hold that against him."

"Now *that* seems a little drastic."

"There is an interesting angle, as you can see. There was a female stowaway aboard."

Bella frowned at the article. "A woman on a whaling ship?"

Gentry smiled. "Adds spice, does it not? I can see Jason neglecting his work for a pretty piece. Not his fault, of course. Jason drew women like blossoms draw bees. The girl probably climbed aboard to be near him."

"It says here that the girl married another man while on board—a Peter Wells, who died in the fire. Did you know him?"

"Never met the chap. Hardly a nobody, though. If there was any negligence his pater will raise the roof. Old Godfrey Wells, no small fry, that bloke. Big in Wall Street, money to swing about like a club."

"How long since you've seen your friend Jason Steele?"

"Oh, not since college days." Gentry paused to smile. "Old Jason and I were a team. We smote them hip and thigh by the ivy walls."

"There is nothing here specifically blaming him."

"True. Only some mouthings of a few hairy hands before the mast. But those journalist fellows are careful of what they say. The libel laws, you know."

"I'm sure he will be vindicated."

"No doubt, but he could certainly use a friend. I'll just trot down to the berthing and clap him on the shoulder for old time's sake. Decent thing to do."

"I'm sure he will appreciate it."

"By the way, my dear, I've gotten you an engagement at the International Club."

"Oh, darling—!" Jason Steele and his troubles were instantly forgotten as Bella sprang up and kissed her benefactor with grateful passion.

"Thought you'd be pleased," Gentry murmured, obviously pleased himself. "You're to run down and see a bloke named Spencer—manager of the bistro—make arrangements, you know."

Bella's gratitude was not phony. The possessor of a fine mezzo-soprano voice, her dream was to scale the heights to grand opera. She had discovered early on that ability and talent were not enough: Sponsorship was vital. Hence her calculated move from one man to another, rungs of a ladder in her climb to success. She left them one after another, to move up, always to their regret and sometimes to her own; but none could claim in the end that he had been cheated. And now the International Club—not the shining goal of her dreams, to be sure, but definitely a leg up; and as far as Gentry could take her.

There was no other man in sight at the moment, and time was important. While she was fond of Gentry, his reputation was not of the best, and if she tarried too long on his premises her own future chances could be tarnished through the association.

So it was time to start looking around.

Bella was not cruel, only practical.

39.

"You are to come with me, my dear . . ."

The firm but kindly directive was most welcome at a time when the paths open to Kate McCrae seemed bleak and uncertain.

With two hundred immigrants in its steerage, the *Reinholdt* had docked at Castle Gardens, the alien's gateway to the promise of America. There, the Seaman's Protective Association representatives were on hand to aid the rescued forecastle hands—and so was Dean Cabot. Foreseeing this possibility, Cabot had brought along a brace of the *Post*'s bully boys—husky brutes used in circulation struggles with other dailies. Cabot had plans for the crewmen, including luxurious treatment at the expense of the paper. But the Protective Seaman's group was made up of retired stalwarts who had brought along souvenir belaying pins and were not averse to using them. Cabot wisely backed off when he learned that the men would be taken to Bellevue Hospital for examination and possible treatment: He would still have access to them there.

There had been one rebel among the forecastle hands—old Cater MacRoy would have none of the "nursery room nonsense . . . I shall leave for my home and my wife and my bairn in Stonington and whatever man tries to stop me will see a sorry day." He was allowed to leave with some regret although Dean Cabot was not greatly disturbed. MacRoy had remained a stubborn witness, refusing to fault his captain in any manner, which didn't make good press.

The other survivors—Jason Steele, Guy Mapes, and Kate McCrae—had been taken off the *Reinholdt* by the pilot boat and delivered to the harbor master. He allowed them sanctuary in his office against a horde of reporters seeking to gain ground on Dean Cabot, who had the whole thing virtually in his pocket.

During the days of passage on the *Reinholdt,* Jason had ignored Kate, and even prior to the rescue there had been a space between them, a gap filled by Guy Mapes who had been the soul of kindness and consideration for all. Kate thought it was due to what had happened between them on the *Gray Ghost*. And, of course, Jason had been stunned by the disaster, shocked by the sinking itself and probably the realization of his guilt in the tragic affair. He remained grim and mostly silent, dealing with the others through Mapes. Even in her own distress and confusion, and—yes, and even with the memory of the ship, Kate yearned to reach out to him, to comfort him and render what courage and understanding she could. But he had come forward only once, when seaman Jacob Tane had died in Kate's arms. As Jason watched helplessly, Kate could see the agony in his soul, but he remained silent even as he held the dying man's hand in his own. When it was over, he lowered his head and breathed a silent prayer. And she knew at that moment that Jason was ashamed of having been saved.

And now, in the harbor master's office, Kate was again pretty much ignored, politely seated in a corner by an official who did not seem to know quite what to do with her.

So she watched the comings and goings and the reunions and she waited. First came a strikingly handsome young dandy in fashionable attire, rich gray trousers molded to his figure with a bulge at the crotch which was attractive or distasteful, according to one's point of view. A frothy jabot of white lace graced his shirt front to compliment a gray, black-trimmed jacket. A tall, gray, furred hat topped a proudly tilted head, over light brown curled hair styled with long sideburns.

The man advanced, smiling, upon Jason. "Old chap! You do recall, don't you, the finer days we knew?"

Kate was temporarily fascinated into forgetting her own troubles. There was something most *outré* about the young man. She had never seen such finery on a male.

Jason stared, frowning. Then his face lit up.

"Calvin Gentry! For God's sake! Where did you come from?"

Gentry beamed. "Quite, old friend. Heard you'd come a cropper so I dropped by to extend the fraternal hand."

"Of all people—" Jason marveled.

With his arm across Jason's shoulders, Gentry led him across the room in fine theatrical manner. "You wound me, Jason," he chided. "You should have known that the dark clouds would bring me. What are old friends for?"

Jason shook his head in wonder. "Whatever brought you, Cal, you are like a ray of sunshine at midnight."

"I've come to offer you my digs for rest and contemplation. I've a little place in Spanish Flats, not a palace but remote enough from the common herd."

"It sounds fabulous. Just what I need."

"Then let's have at it. Are there any formalities here—chits to be signed or whatnot?"

Jason glanced toward the harbor master, who seemed perplexed.

"I have to remain available," Jason said.

"No problem at all. I vow to produce you at a moment's notice. Let's go."

It was not to be. Two gentlemen entered the office, older men, whose attire was in sharp contrast to that of Gentry's; severe black of a stern, no-nonsense cut that gave them an aura of authority. One of them addressed Jason.

"You are Jason Steele, I believe."

"Correct."

"Permit me to introduce myself. I am Cletus Wing, of Gordon, Wing, and Stillwater. I represent your grandfather, William Steele. He is hurrying toward the city but has been unable to arrive in time to greet you personally."

At the mention of his grandfather, Jason's expression turned grim. He stepped away from Gentry and nodded.

"It is your grandfather's wish that you come with us to the Union Club and await his arrival there. He should be in the city by late afternoon or early evening."

Jason appeared to have forgotten Gentry's existence. His change of manner was eloquent

227

even in his silence. He stood erect, like a prisoner waiting to receive sentence.

The lawyer now turned to Guy Mapes who stood patiently by. Wing's impersonal but commanding manner was akin to that of a schoolmaster ticking off a list of duties in their order of importance.

"And you are the first mate of the Steele ship in question? Mr. Guy Mapes?"

"Yes, sir."

"Mr. Steele wishes you to accompany us to the Union Club as his guest."

Kate sensed a condemnation of Jason in the words used. It seemed to her that Jason was being *ordered* to await his grandfather's pleasure at the Union Club while Guy Mapes was invited as a guest.

Calvin Gentry perceived the situation quickly. He knew where the power lay and backed off gracefully.

"Old chap, you'll of course concede to your grandfather's wishes. But my invitation still stands. Whenever you can come you will be received with great joy."

Jason squeezed his hand. "Thanks, Cal. You've no idea how happy I am to see you again."

"Until later, old man."

With that, Jason, Mapes, and the two lawyers left without a glance in Kate's direction. Gentry regarded her with some speculation. But if he formed any ideas concerning her, he made no gesture, simply turned and left in the same grand manner in which he had entered.

There was a single flaw in the performance. Gentry's exit was blocked by a new entrant, a woman who shouldered him aside with an imperiousness of a more genuine quality even than Gentry's. She paused just inside the room, surveyed the harbor master as though he had just brought in the laundry, and spotted Kate.

"My dear, I am so sorry to be late."

Kate could only stare. The unbecoming dress of black voile revealed high shoes with white buttons. The blond hair was caught in an uncaring knot under a too-small hat.

"I am Theresa Wells, child. Peter's sister. You *are* the girl he married before his death?"

"Kate McCrae."

The smile was as patronizing as the *child* in Tess's greeting. But Kate was too grateful at being received at all to take offense.

Tess said, "As Peter's bride and widow, that name is hardly appropriate. Kate Wells sounds much better."

"I'm sorry. Things have—"

"I know, I know. You are to come with me, my dear. My home is open to you." Tess frowned and added, "You *do* have proof of your marriage with you, I hope?"

"I have it here. It's a copy of the page from the ship's log. Peter did it when we were married."

"In his handwriting! Excellent. The reason I asked is the newspapers reported that the log was lost when the ship sank. I thought there might be some trouble proving . . ."

As Tess talked, ignoring the harbor master completely, she steered Kate toward the door and out onto the cobbled street. Shouldering reporters and onlookers out of the way, she deposited Kate inside the waiting carriage and climbed in after her.

"How are you feeling, child? You must be exhausted."

"No, I feel quite well. The rest on the steamer was long enough."

"Good. That dress—most becoming—"

Kate managed a smile. "It is something *I* could never afford. A kind lady gave it to me when we were rescued. The passengers were very nice."

"You said you have a copy of the marriage certificate from the log. . . ."

Kate drew the folded page from her bodice and handed it to Tess. The latter scanned it carefully, then nodded. "Yes. Peter's handwriting." She gave it back. "Tell me—are you certain that Peter is dead?"

The question was strange only in that Tess had waited until then to ask it.

"Yes," Kate replied. "Peter was killed by the explosion."

Tess regarded her intently. "I imagine you find me abrupt—too much so, perhaps?"

"Miss Wells, I am happy to find *anyone*—under any conditions."

"I'm glad you feel that way. It will make things easier. I am not one to agonize over things past and done with which cannot be changed. Only the future is important—and that you understand the situation, and what you are up against. Do you agree?"

"I could hardly do otherwise."

"To begin with, you will find the Wells family somewhat unique in that we have never greatly cared for one another."

"I know that Peter was bitter about his family. There wasn't time for me to learn much more."

"Neither of us could stand our parents, and we both left home as soon as we were legally allowed to do so." Tess paused. "I won't ask you why you married him. I am the only one, my dear, who is not surprised by Peter's marriage. I knew Peter better than anyone else: When he found the girl of his choice—whoever she was—that would be it. And he was certainly ready for a wife."

Too much was being said too quickly! Seeking to change the subject, Kate asked, "Where are we going?"

"To my flat on Washington Square. You will stay with me for the time being—until your affairs are straightened out."

"That is most kind of you."

"You may as well know the truth. My parents will not accept you. My father may try to have the marriage annulled. There will be a fight, you can be sure of that."

"But why should they resent me?"

"It is quite simple. They are snobs: my father is a pillar in the financial community; and social climbing is my mother's sole occupation."

"I admit that I—"

"Child, you are a nobody. Also, the circumstances of your marriage to Peter are highly suspect. There have been so many rumors in the papers since the sinking."

Kate never quite knew why she reacted as she did. Perhaps the guilt had become too much and she thought confession would ease the burden.

"Their attitude does have some foundation, Miss Wells. I was not in love with Peter."

"But he was in love with you."

"So deeply that he was willing to take me on any terms."

"See, I was right about Peter. I told you that I knew him better than anyone else did."

"He was a fine person."

"We aren't debating that point. Were you in love with someone else?"

The long pause was most eloquent, as was Kate's sharp, hostile, "No!"

"The captain perhaps? He has the reputation of being a lady's man—"

"I said no. Please leave it at that."

"Of course." But it was obvious that Tess had formed her opinion to the contrary.

"Miss Wells," Kate continued, "I feel you are entitled to an explanation. In some measure your parents are right about me. In comparison to their position in life, I *am* a nobody. My father was a fine man from my point of view but I am sure not from theirs. He was a painter, and I've led a gypsy existence from the time I was a small child. When he died I was left with nothing but his memory and a few of his canvases, but the paintings were lost with the ship."

"Bravo," said Tess.

"I don't know what you mean by that, but there is more. It is not my plan to apologize to your father or mother or you or anyone else and then slink away like a thief. I plan to survive, and as Peter's widow I will have a far better chance than otherwise. In short, Miss Wells, I shall fight any attempt to change my status."

"As I said, bravo! Your frankness is refreshing and your attitude even more so. Why do you think I came down here and took you in?"

"Curiosity as to what manner of person Peter married?"

"To some extent, yes. But let me be just as frank. When the news of Peter's death and his marriage reached me, I did not give you a second thought; you did not exist for me. And if things had stayed that way we would probably have never met."

"What changed?"

"I visited my parents' home and heard what my father had to say. We will get to know each other, of course, but my decision to help you is hardly personal. You are a woman about to be stripped naked by the male power structure, and I will not have that. We shall fight my father tooth and nail. And we shall win."

Kate was not required to reply. At that moment the carriage stopped before a series of three-story flats, each section marked by a narrow, pillared entrance with steps rising between carved balustrades. "I am on the third level," Tess said. "Up where a person can breath. The smell of horses and drays is turning this city into a garbage heap."

Kate, thankful for a haven under any circumstances, would not have minded if the flat were on the street.

40.

Cletus Wing addressed William Steele with dignified deference. "Sir, I am happy to report that I have procured the services of Benjamin Stein."

"He is Jewish, I believe."

"Yes, but he is the very best. Ben Stein does not go into court to lose."

Finding a trial lawyer had been a matter of vital importance. Wing's firm specialized in civil matters only. They were hardly in a position to furnish expert defense in a criminal case and in Jason Steele's case there would be criminal action or none at all.

"Has Stein been given the details?"

"Exhaustively."

William Steele had arrived in the city some four hours after the docking of the *Reinholdt* to find his grandson safely deposited in the exclusive Union Club. Their meeting was restrained. Jason rose from the table at which he sat in the bar and advanced toward his grandfather. He was struck by the change in him. William Steele had aged greatly in such a comparatively short time, Jason thought.

"My boy, how are you?"

"I'm well, Grandfather."

They embraced in a formal manner.

"Would you care for a drink?" Jason asked.

"A little sherry, perhaps."

When they reached Jason's table, Cletus Wing, who had accompanied William Steele and remained hovering in the background during the reunion, now joined them.

"Grandma Becky," Jason said. "Is she well?"

"As well as could be expected," was the reply.

It was as close to a reprimand as William Steele would come.

His examination of his grandson was veiled but keen. Jason was changed, yet not. The handsome, magnetic features were the same, though clouded by a new remoteness, a somber mien that gave depth to his image rather than transformed it. He appeared to have lost his irresponsible boyishness.

"Mr. Wing has informed you of developments, has he not?"

Jason nodded. "You have made plans for my defense?"

"Please do not misunderstand, Jason. There may be no need of a defense, but I deem it wise to be ready. The newspapers, particularly the morning *Post,* have been feeding the tragedy to the public as fast as their presses can turn out extras. Much is no doubt rumor and hearsay but, as I said, it is best to be prepared. We have retained a fine criminal lawyer, Benjamin Stein. I understand he is to arrive shortly to speak with you. You will of course be frank with him."

"Of course."

It was Jason's manner that troubled him. He was so remote, he gave no sign whatever of his thoughts. William would almost have welcomed

235

a rejection of his plans; at least that would have given him a basis for argument and persuasion. As things stood, it was like watching a cat on a fence waiting to see which way it would jump.

"Until Stein has spoken with you there is nothing we can do. I think I'll go to my room and rest. It has been a tiresome journey."

"Please do, Grandfather."

The three of them rose together. Jason's gesture to be of assistance was brushed aside and William slowly left the bar, his sherry untouched, the ever-solicitous Cletus Wing by his side. Jason sat down again and lifted his brandy glass. . . .

Two hours later there was a conference held in one of the private rooms with William Steele, Cletus Wing, and the renowned Ben Stein. Stein was a man of average height and girth with a shock of carelessly combed black hair. He wore a plain gray business suit, his only affectation a flowing black tie which added a somewhat artistic touch. A wide-brimmed slouch hat would have completed the effect but Stein sported a plain black derby.

His manner was brisk. "I've talked to the young man," he said, "and while he was not uncooperative, he nonetheless volunteered little."

"Jason promised me he would be frank with you."

"Oh, he was—frank enough. In fact he denied nothing, rather tended to agree with everything in the papers. He offered no defense."

"In your opinion," Wing asked, "what will happen now?"

"It isn't a matter of opinion. There will be a hearing. I'm sure a Federal judge will preside."

"But there must be a charge," Wing put in. "Something more concrete than a lot of newspaper headlines."

"There will be." He turned to William. "I believe you were covered by International Surety . . . ?"

William nodded.

"They will bring charges that will justify the hearing. With what they have—what has been made public, true or not—they will fight payment."

"Suppose I waive payment of the insurance?"

"It must be a large figure."

"Quite large."

Stein regarded the other man with heightened respect. His willingness to accept such a loss indicated what the old gentleman would sacrifice for his grandson.

"That would be most unwise," Stein said gently. "It could be interpreted as an acceptance of Jason's guilt."

"The future looks to be most difficult," William replied. "Those damning statements from the forecastle . . ."

"Don't be too discouraged. They were taken by a scandal sheet reporter in search of sensation. No doubt he influenced the men—might even have put words in their mouths. When those men face a judge under oath, the stories could change."

"Assuming the worst is put forward, what do you think the charges will be?"

Stein shrugged. "At the worst? Criminal

237

negligence. Possibly even second-degree murder on numerous counts."

"Prison offenses," Wing muttered.

"Yes, there are precedents: second-degree murder on the high seas on ships under United States registry. Conviction brought a life sentence in one case, but every case is different. This one has some unique aspects. A great deal will depend on what can be uncovered about the madman who blew up the ship—whether or not there was true cause for the captain to see him as dangerous."

"What sort of a defense do you plan, sir?"

Stein smiled. "Delay—delay—and more delay."

There was a tap on the door, and Jason entered. He stopped just inside the room and regarded the three men somberly.

William said, "Come sit with us, Jason."

Jason turned and made his way to a chair in a corner of the room. "Go on with it. Don't let me interrupt."

After a moment, Stein turned back to the others. "Delay—delay—and more delay," he repeated. "We start from the very beginning to keep things from moving, with Jason in seclusion recovering from the ordeal he has gone through. I'm sure we can get a doctor to vouch for his not being able to appear at a hearing. That tactic will eventually wear thin. The hearing *will* take place and then perhaps nothing will come of it."

"But you don't believe that," Jason cut in.

"Frankly, no. But then we really go to work. There is the adverse newspaper publicity. We are entitled to a postponement until it dies down. After that, we request a change of venue, trying to get the case moved to your ship's port of embarkation. I think all the petitions will fail but time will be passing. During that time, we work to gain Jason a good public image. This must not seem forced. He will appear here at the Union Club. He will attend church. There will be the better entertainments, opera, concerts, always in the company of the best people. Then, when the case comes to trial—"

"And you are sure it *will* come to trial," Jason pursued.

"I think it quite likely. Then there are other methods—"

"Legal tricks?"

"I beg your pardon?"

"I said, legal tricks. Shabby shyster evasions."

Stein did not rise to the bait. "Young man, it is the duty of any attorney to use every legal means possible in defense of his client."

Jason got to his feet and approached the table. "I won't have it! I will not cringe and dodge and hide. The consequences must be faced without hiding behind technicalities."

William felt a chill in his bones. The cat had jumped—in the wrong direction. This *was* the old Jason but his grandfather had hoped his more volatile side would have remained submerged until this terrible affair was over.

Jason went on, "Grandfather, please don't think me an ingrate. I am more grateful for your love and trust than I can ever express. But I am an adult with the responsibilities of an adult and if I proceeded as Mr. Stein has outlined I couldn't live with myself, whatever the outcome."

Ben Stein remained calm but he was thoughtful. "Are you saying, Jason, that you will plead guilty to whatever charge?"

"I am not a fool, but I will do nothing to circumvent the law."

"You are saying that you will not help us."

"I will not be a puppet to be pushed here and there in order to create a false image! I will not continue to hide in this marble mausoleum."

"But you will not work against us."

Jason turned to his grandfather. "I am more sorry than I can say, but I think we understand each other. I do not think you would be very proud of me if I became a part of Mr. Stein's plans, however laudable in his own eyes."

As Jason strode from the room, Stein's pensive gaze followed him. "The prisoner stands mute," he murmured to no one in particular, then he turned to William Steele.

"Tell me, sir, does what just happened change your personal attitude toward your grandson?"

The answer was prompt. "Not in the least."

"Then it is settled. We defend the young man—" He paused to select his words carefully. "—vigorously—as though he wished to be defended. . . ."

When Stein and Wing left, William sat alone in the conference room.

He should have known that no man could put a ring in Jason's nose. Jason was a Steele and Steeles were men of sterling worth.

41.

Striker's Cottages had once been quite grand. Eight two-story homes in a single structure at Fifty-second Street between Tenth and Eleventh Avenues, they were ambitiously advertised by General Striker in 1850 as each having "four bedrooms, two parlors and kitchen . . . with cornice and centerpiece." The ad extolled piazzas and verandah fronts, elegant forest trees, and the fact that the stagecoach line passed near the premises.

But fifty years can bring many changes and when Kate's carriage drew up to Number Five, she found a depressing row of neglected, run-down frames that had lost the battle with time.

Two youngsters, surprisingly clean in contrast to the rags they wore, clung to the dead stump of the cottage's "elegant forest tree," and stared in silence. Kate smiled. Their expressions of solemn wonder did not change.

As she advanced up the tilted wooden walkway, two older children appeared in the doorway. The eldest looked to be eight or so.

"Is your mother home?" she asked.

The girl turned and called back into the cottage, "Maw, there's a lady!"

The woman who appeared had never been

beautiful, perhaps not even pretty, and though she was still young,—surely not past her middle twenties, Kate thought—the bloom of youth was long gone, worn away by worry, poverty, and too frequent childbirth.

"You are Mrs. Jacob Tane?"

The woman nodded a little warily.

"I am Kate McCrae. I have come to offer my condolences in your bereavement."

"You mean Jacob."

"May I come in?"

There was a threadbare rug on the floor, a sofa with towels covering burst upholstery, a breakfront containing a mixed display of dishes, and a corner table upon which there was a gilt-framed photograph of a man Kate recognized.

"Sit down, please. My husband is dead. But you must know that or you wouldn't have come."

"I was on the *Gray Ghost* also. I was with him when he died."

Whatever grief the woman had suffered was over. Now there was only the sadness of having accepted what had happened, and the strength to bear it.

"I would like to know," she said. "All they told me was that Jake died in the rescue boat. Did he suffer a lot?"

"No, I think not." Kate's thoughts returned to the two days of Tane's slow dying, the pain from the burns so excruciating that death had been welcome.

"His last thoughts were of you. He said, 'Tally—Tally and the tots.'" A kindly lie. He had been hardly conscious at the end.

"Jake was a good man. I didn't see him very often because he was a sailing man. It was all he knew so he had to be away."

"Raising four children under those circumstances must have been difficult."

That brought the woman's gaze to her children, clustered at the door watching in silence. "Go and play," she said gently. They obeyed without protest.

"Mrs. Tane—"

"I'd rather you call me Tally. It's really Talliaferro but they pronounce it Tolliver in the South. A terrible name to give a girl but it was my grandfather's and they gave it to me."

"You are from the South, Tally?"

"New Orleans. Jake worked on shrimp boats. Then we were married and we came north because he saw a chance of getting a lot of money if he could sail on a ship that made a big catch. He'd heard about ambergris. That's the stuff they make perfume out of, you know. Whales spit it up, I think. Anyhow, a big lump of ambergris, if it's big enough, can add up to a common seaman's share on a whaler."

"There isn't any whaling out of New York City. I mean, I would expect you to have lived farther north."

"Jake was going to give up whaling after his last trip. I mean the one before the one that killed him. That was what he said. I don't know why he went out again. I guess he thought he could make a little more money." She lowered her head into her hands. "The years—the terrible long years—"

She did not cry. But her anguish was just as apparent.

243

Kate opened her purse and took out the five hundred dollars she had borrowed from Tess Wells. "Tally, I want you to have this. . . ."

Tally looked at the money then shook her head. "Thank you, but—"

There was the sound of another carriage stopping in front of the house.

"Please don't think of it as charity. I want you to take it—from one friend to another."

Laughter could be heard from the porch, and Kate looked to see Jason with the children clustered about him; he was giving them candy. Then he good-naturedly shooed them away, tapped on the open door, and entered.

For a moment he simply stared at Kate, as though coming in out of the bright sun had dimmed his vision. Then he cried, "Kate! It's good to see you!" As if the past that stood between them had never happened . . .

Kate extended her hand. "Jason, you are looking well." It was an automatic reply, but he did not look well at all. His dandyish attire—dark, form-fitting trousers, gray waistcoat and ascot—was fashionable enough, but Kate's scrutiny went deeper. There were shadows under his eyes, and his cheeks were hollow, and he had lost weight. It detracted not a whit from his ability to arouse emotion in her. She wanted to reach out, to console him. The barrier of arrogance, as she remembered it, was gone.

Turning to Tally he got to the business at hand. "Everything is arranged," he said. "I found a cottage in the country, well away from town. It is out near the house Alexander Hamilton lived in—Harlem Heights, Hamilton's old country home. It will be much better for the children there. They can run free, and you can plant a garden. . . ."

"You are so very kind."

"Not at all. Your husband more than earned what I am giving you. A dray will come tomorrow morning to move you if that is convenient."

"We will be waiting."

"Now, is there anything else? Your ready cash—"

"What you gave me is quite enough."

"There will be a regular monthly allowance from now on."

"How can I ever thank you?"

"There is no need for thanks."

"We are forever grateful to you."

Jason said, "I'll take my leave then."

On impulse, Kate stood up. "I must be off too. I have friends waiting."

When they had reached the unpaved street, she extended her hand. Jason took it, then said, "We both go in the same direction. Why not ride with me?"

Kate tried hard to look as though she were debating the invitation. "But I have my own carriage," and she pointed.

Jason approached the carriage she had hired, said a few words to the driver, and returned. He handed her into his carriage and then climbed in next to her.

"It was most generous of you, what you did for Tally Tane and her family."

"I hardly see it that way. It was no more than they are entitled to." He smiled faintly and added, "It was my good fortune to get there ahead of my grandfather."

Kate let that go, whatever it meant. "Is Mr. Mapes well?"

"You couldn't kill him with *ten* sinkings. He went back to Stonington, where he is supposed to be resting. I'll vow that he is busy fitting out another ship."

"Will you be returning to sea?"

"Not in the foreseeable future. There are things to be looked into—formalities to be gone through."

Why can't we reach out to each other?

While her demeanor did not change she trembled inside. She laid her hand on Jason's arm.

"Jason, you are not blaming yourself for the sinking of the ship, are you?"

"Kate, when a ship goes down the blame is placed where it belongs—on the captain's shoulders."

"That can't be true! Suppose it went down in a great storm?"

"The *Gray Ghost* stood in fine weather. There was no act of God involved."

"But in a way there was. How could anyone know a man like John Saipan was aboard? I mean, how could you have known what he had in mind?"

"There were warnings."

"But you *did* investigate. My paintings—"

She stopped. Reference to the paintings brought them close to a subject they were both studiously avoiding.

Jason said, "You are very kind to defend me.

The authorities will be less sympathetic, and rightfully so."

"What *will* they do, Jason? What will happen now?"

"There will be an inquiry."

"Soon?"

"As soon as the attorney for the insurance people can arrange it. A heavy indemnity was placed on the ship and if they can prove certain facts, the contract would be canceled and they would not have to pay for the loss."

Feeling then that the subject should be changed, Kate asked, "Will you be staying in the city?"

"Mostly. I plan to go to Stonington to visit my grandmother. My grandfather is here in New York now."

"You are staying with him?"

"No, I have a friend, Calvin Gentry, who lives in the Spanish Flats off Central Park. I'm staying with him."

There was silence until Jason asked, "Are you well situated with Tess Wells?"

He knew where she was staying!

"I am quite comfortable. Tess has tried to make me feel at home."

He was frowning. "Frankly, I thought it a little strange, Tess offering you her hospitality. But I suppose not: She and her parents are not on good terms."

"Tess hates her parents and they hate me. That was what put her on my side. I'm not sure what will come of it but I had no other place to go."

Kate instantly wished that she had not made

that last remark. It sounded as though she were chiding Jason for having neglected her.

He did hesitate for a moment, then said, "If Godfrey Wells tries to cheat you, please let me know. I have a good attorney . . ."

The carriage stopped in front of the Washington Square flats. Jason got down and helped Kate to descend. He accompanied her to the stairs.

"Won't you come in? I am sure Tess would be most happy to see you."

"I'm sorry, but I must be running along."

"Thank you for bringing me home." Kate looked straight into his eyes. She touched his hand. "Jason—take care of yourself."

"You too, Kate."

On the way upstairs she realized that no word had been said between them about Peter. It did not really matter. Peter was gone, sweet, devoted Peter who had loved her.

She mounted the porch and entered the flat and Tess was upon her like a high wind.

"Darling, I have wonderful news!"

"I could certainly use some. Let me get my things off and then tell me . . ."

Kate removed her hat, and went through into her bedroom. She sat down on the bed and laid her head against the wall.

What on earth was wrong? A sudden weakness. While Tess was speaking to her the faintness had increased to a point where she had feared that she would swoon.

She forced deep breaths into her lungs and her strength seeped back. Soon she felt better.

Never in her life had such a weakness over-taken her. The outdoor life she had lived with her father had been healthy. The only exhaustion she had ever felt was at times during her gypsy life when youthful vitality overflowed and she would run like a deer through woods or over fields until her lungs fairly burst and she would drop to the ground in a state of satisfying collapse.

Her thoughts went of their own volition to Jason Steele. Could strong physical yearning for a man bring on the fainting symptom?

She shook her head, sighed, and got to her feet. Everything was all right now; no point in mentioning it to Tess. Kate returned to the living room where Tess was waiting.

"A glass of sherry, dear?"

"Thank you."

"Sit there by the window. I'll bring it."

Kate obeyed. She looked out at the vacant curb. Jason had left. It was ridiculous to hope the carriage still stood there, and feel disappointment when it was not.

Idle thoughts . . .

Tess brought the sherry, loomed over Kate and raised her own glass. "To your good luck, darling."

"You said you had some good news."

"I talked with Godfrey."

"Godfrey?"

"My father."

"Oh, your father—of course. What did he say?"

"He backed down."

"Backed down?"

"It was his intention to fight your marriage. I expected him to question it, to make things very difficult for you and deprive you of Peter's fortune."

"Your father changed his mind?"

"I changed it for him. You see, I know his weakness and that is where I hit him. The family name. He is deathly afraid of losing stature in the community. Both he and Beatrice battle twenty-four hours a day to rise in society."

"That seems such a waste of time."

"From our point of view, yes, but not from theirs. Godfrey is a member of the Union Club and just recently another member was dropped because of bad publicity. It would kill Godfrey if he was ever asked to resign."

"Is there any danger of that?"

"I convinced him there might be. I told him that we would fight him right up to the Supreme Court and he would be in the position of persecuting a helpless girl who had lost her beloved husband in a tragic fire."

Beloved? A lie as tragic as the fire. Do I deserve the reward?

"He took me at my word and he withdrew his objections. My lawyers are hurrying Peter's estate through probate. You will be a wealthy young woman very shortly."

Kate could scarcely react. It was too sudden, too unfamiliar. Instead she asked, "Tess, why do you hate your father so?"

"I don't hate Godfrey. I only hate what I would have become if I had not rebelled and started to lead my own life at the first opportunity." She shuddered, half comically. "You've never met my mother, but if you ever do, you'll understand. To become the person she is—what she has become under Godfrey's domination—would be a terrible fate."

"Your father can't be as bad as you paint him."

"Unless you meet him head-on, strength for strength, he will wear you down and defeat you. Peter realized that also. The poor dear had no personal goals in mind; he only knew that he had to get beyond Godfrey's reach or he would have become what Godfrey wanted him to be."

"But Peter was very lonely on the ship."

"I'm sure. But he chose that loneliness rather than submit to the molding of his character by his father." Tess set down her glass and reached out to smooth Kate's hair. "You look so tired, my dear."

Kate's reaction was spontaneous warmth. "Tess, oh Tess, why are you so good to me?"

Tess drew Kate up and folded her gently into her arms. "Because you are such a lovely little girl, darling. I can understand why Peter loved you and I feel that I must protect you now that he is gone."

Tess' firm lips were pressed against her cheek. "Kate, what you need is a nice warm bath, a bite to eat in bed, and a good night's sleep. I think a sleeping powder would be in order. Come, I'll draw the water while you undress."

"Tess, you mustn't pamper me!"

"I don't mind, darling. Honestly I don't."

This was a new side of Tess, a softer, gentler side; sensitive, considerate, compassionate. As Kate lazed in the warm, soapy tub with Tess insisting upon administering to her even there, it occurred to her that perhaps she brought out Tess' mothering instinct. By the time she was bundled into bed and kissed tenderly upon the lips, however, Kate was beginning to feel a little ridiculous with all the attention.

Alone finally, she drowsed. The image of Jason Steele returned, and she was reliving that tempestuous mating in the master cabin of the *Gray Ghost*. In her half-dreaming state she smiled and felt the weight of his body on hers, when she had ceased to fight, when they rose to the heights together. . . .

Kate slept and Jason returned again and again.

But he was different; softer, more gentle, pleading rather than demanding. Far different . . . what pressed against her now was not a hard, hairy, satisfying chest but two soft breasts . . . the breasts shifted and the seeking mouth—

This was no dream!

Kate's reaction was curious, her thoughts running from the shocking revelation of finding Tess' warm body on hers to the fact that without Tess she would have been lost, stripped of all gains, and turned out into the streets. She owed Tess a great deal—her very precious survival. Was this too large a price to pay—?

Tess' eager mouth sought hers, pressed for admittance.

She gently pushed Tess away and sat up.

"No—no, Tess. I'm sorry. You misjudged me. I couldn't . . . I couldn't possibly . . ."

Tess, too, sat up.

"I had to find out. I had to know. Do you condemn me for that?"

"To be perfectly honest with you, I wish that I could be what you want, to pay you to some extent for all you have done for me. But I can't."

Tess forced a smile, she picked her robe up from the floor and put it on. "At least you will not be so naive anymore. That will be a help to you."

"Naive?"

"Of course. Else you would have known from the beginning. You would have seen Peggy for what she is—my lover. You would have understood me without having to be shown." Tess paused. "Does learning the truth about me bother you so much?"

Kate was silent.

"What will you do now?"

"Leave. It's the only thing I can do."

Tess took a deep breath. "It is your decision to make, but it is not necessary for you to leave."

"After what happened, would you want me to stay?"

"As I said, I had to find out. I'll confess I did not expect you to respond. But I might have been wrong and so much between us would have been lost."

"What I have done—taken everything and given nothing. I married your brother when I was not in love with him; he gained nothing from the marriage. I came ashore and accepted your help and you have gained nothing. . . ."

"I'm sure Peter knew how you felt. I think that you would have been true to him had he lived, which is all he would have asked. I told you in the beginning that I had an ulterior mo-

253

tive in befriending you, that I would get much personal satisfaction from facing my father and defeating him. I did—and something more."

Tess went on, "You, Kate, as a friend. You may not believe it, but I never had a friend before. I am a difficult person."

"No friends? But Peggy—"

"Peggy is a dear little helpless chattle. I found her and I nourish her and she blooms under my attentions, but a friend? Hardly."

"Tess, I'm so confused . . ."

"The decision is yours, Kate. Whether or not you can forget this incident—pretend it never happened, and go on as we were."

"Can *you* forget?"

"Honestly, no. But I can accept."

When Kate did not say anything further, Tess turned away and moved toward the door. "As I said—your decision."

Alone, Kate's mind raced. *If I leave, where would I go? What would I do?* The fact that she would soon have enough money to go anywhere she wanted was temporarily forgotten.

The memory of Tess's eager mouth on hers caused her to grimace with distaste. If there was that side to the strange woman who was legally her sister-in-law, there was also much about her to be admired. She had courage and dedication, she was a force for betterment in the world, and she had been good to Kate.

When Kate entered the living room to find Tess, their eyes met for a brief moment.

"Kate dear, have you ever ridden on a bicycle?"

Kate blinked in surprise and accepted the

small brandy Tess had poured and brought to her. "A bicycle? Why, yes . . ."

"I'm glad. We are having a march next week—or as soon as I can possibly organize it. We will form in front of the Liberty Shirtwaist Company at Coenties Slip and parade to Madison Square, possibly clear to Central Park."

"On bicycles?"

"Yes. It is most important that we keep our cause in front of the public. The trouble we get into will be advantageous. It should put our story on the front pages of every newspaper in town."

"Why should we get into trouble?"

"For one, I'm sure that I will be arrested."

"For whatever reason?"

"I will do whatever is necessary to bring it about. I will be arrested and hauled off to jail, and reporters will flock about."

"Do you think being arrested will really help?"

"It will be a step. We must win our victories inch by inch. We cannot open the gates of male dominance without the way we must travel being slow and difficult. But little by little we gain sympathy. Sympathizers become allies. Gradually public resentment fades."

"But how long does all that take?"

"Years," Tess murmured. "Generations. A lifetime passes and we make a little progress. . . ."

And so they put the past behind them by mutual consent and looked to the future.

42.

Kebble, Smith, & Morningside, the law firm retained by International Surety, entered the *Gray Ghost* fray at somewhat of a disadvantage: They were unaware of William Steele's covert willingness to forego half a million dollars of insurance money in order to protect his grandson. Expecting the claim to be lodged at any moment, Victor Kebble took the offensive by going straight to the Federal District Court to request a hearing. On the basis of Dean Cabot's newspaper reports and his own interviews with the survivors, he felt little apprehension as to the outcome. The three-week delay due to illness of principals in the case did not bother him greatly; in the history of legal delays, this was but a moment. But when the time had elapsed and he and Cletus Wing were to appear before Judge Henry Holt, Kebble arrived in court grim and furious.

Standing before the bench, Kebble said, "Your Honor, I request a postponement and a conference in your chambers."

Judge Holt was not averse. He preferred the comfort of his easy chair to the hard bench. Moments later, his robe discarded, savoring a fine cigar, he asked, "What's on your mind, Counselor?"

Kebble had red hair. He was now red of face, and "seeing red." He said grimly, "I bring grave matters to your attention; possible contempt of this court."

"You might explain that."

"My witnesses, my *prime* witnesses, have gone beyond immediate reach. But fortunately not beyond the jurisdiction of this court."

"Go on."

"Five of the common seamen rescued from the *Gray Ghost,* the vessel in question, were taken to Bellevue Hospital for examination and treatment."

"I am aware of that."

"But two days ago, on the tenth instant, when I went to the hospital to inform them that they were due to appear at the scheduled hearing, I found that three of them had left the hospital. A further check, your Honor, revealed that they have also left the country aboard a whaling ship, the *Constance B. Haggerty,* and are now somewhere in the Atlantic Ocean."

Kebble turned now to glare at Cletus Wing. Judge Holt also looked in that direction. "Are you saying," the judge asked, "that the witnesses were forced onto a ship and carried out to sea?"

"Not directly, your Honor."

"Mr. Wing, were you aware of this wholesale exodus?"

Cletus Wing nodded. "Yes, your Honor."

"Then let us hear something further from you."

"I was aware, your Honor—"

Judge Holt frowned. "Let's have done with this 'your Honor' business. We are not before the bench." He drew on his cigar. "Proceed."

"Well, Judge, the three witnesses in question were and are free agents. I heard indirectly that they became restless from the hospital confinement and yearned again for the open sea."

"The open sea," Judge Holt murmured reflectively. "So they signed on a whaler and went beyond our immediate reach."

"Yes, Judge, I am afraid they did."

"And you felt no obligation to inform Mr. Kebble of this?"

"None, Judge."

"Or the Court?"

Wing paused before answering that one. "No, Judge, I did not. It seemed to me that if my distinguished adversary in this case was so neglectful of his duty to his client as to withhold the subpoenas which would have restrained his witnesses from leaving, then it was not my place to assist him."

"You arranged the whole thing!" Kebble shouted.

"Careful, Counselor," Wing murmured. "Don't say anything you might regret."

Judge Holt asked, "The ship they sailed on, the *Constance B.* something—"

"*Haggerty,* Judge."

"The *Constance B. Haggerty.* Is she a Steele ship?"

Wing's smile might well have been saying, *Do you think Ben Stein would be that stupid?* He shook his head. "No, Judge Holt. Definitely not."

"Who is the owner?"

"I don't know. I only ascertained that it was not owned by the Steeles."

"But very likely a friend of the Steeles?"

"That is quite possible. Many of the New England whalers are friends."

Judge Holt puffed thoughtfully on his cigar as he gave the situation proper judicial attention.

Kebble said, "I shall ask for a contempt citation naming—"

"Come now, you know better than that, Counselor. Where are your grounds?" Judge Holt said rather gently.

"Conspiracy to disrupt the workings of your court."

"Would you care to go into court to prove it?"

Kebble looked miffed. Finally he said, "At least I should be able to obtain subpoenas."

"Of course." He turned to Wing. "What is that ship's first port of call?"

"That is difficult to say. It may well not be established as yet—the fortunes of the sea, you know. A whaler can stay out for some months. And what with the location of whaling grounds, the ship would probably put in at some South American port when supplies run low."

"I see. It is an unfortunate situation, but the dignity of this court must not be flouted." To Kebble he said, "Get me a list of the most likely ports. We will deliver subpoenas through our embassies requesting those governments to return the material witnesses." He shrugged. "That may work—it may not."

"An unconscionable time will pass," Kebble wailed.

"That does seem likely."

Wing said, "I do have some comforting news for Mr. Kebble. The ship, I was told, will eventually dock at San Francisco to unload her cargo of oil. That port, of course, is within Federal jurisdiction and the witnesses could be returned overland by Federal marshals."

"I guess that is the best we can do," Judge Holt said. "Unless, Mr. Kebble, you choose to go to trial with what you have."

"That is a possibility but it will take time to reshape my case. Also, I demand that all witnesses for both sides be put at my convenient disposal."

"Mr. Kebble," Wing cut in indignantly, "are you saying that I would conspire to keep you away from *my* witnesses?"

"In plain words—yes!"

"Judge Holt! I protest—!"

"Stop it, both of you. Mr. Kebble, I'll grant a sixty-day postponement after which time you will come to the bench and report your progress and your inclinations. We will then consider any further delay of the hearing."

Kebble was the first to leave, almost running in his haste. When they were alone, Judge Holt asked Wing, "The old gentleman—William Steele—is he bearing up under the tragedy?"

"Yes, as well as could be expected, Judge."

"I never met him but we have nodded to each other in passing at the Union Club. A fine man."

"May I inform him of your sympathy?"

"You may not . . ."

All in all, Cletus Wing was happy with what had transpired in chambers. Judge Holt could have been far more severe in his questioning; the sympathetic slant of the conference indicated the leeway he would be given in the future. He had known of Holt's membership in the Union Club, of course, but had not expected the judge to make mention of it; that in itself was a strong plus.

Wing felt a little sorry for the hapless Kebble, whom he rather liked.

43.

After breakfast in the suite at Spanish Flats, Calvin Gentry was lounging in the morning room clad elegantly in a purple gentleman's robe fresh from a fashionable London tailor's workroom. Jason Steele sat nearby finishing his second cup of coffee.

Gentry yawned and brushed at the waxed ends of his mustache. "What are your plans for the day, old chap?"

"Nothing in particular. I've got to pack later. I'm going north to see my grandmother tomorrow morning."

"This pottering about the museums the way you've been doing. Doesn't seem quite your forte, Jason—at least not the Jason I used to know."

This may have been a subtle hint that Gentry was disappointed in his guest—no longer the gay, reckless fellow he had known in college.

"Only one museum, really," Jason replied. "The American Museum of Natural History. I've been going to see the native precious stones."

"Native? Do you mean from American soil?"

"That's right."

"But Jason, there aren't any. A few old Indian arrow heads—a piece of quartz or two—"

"On the contrary, some remarkable stones have been unearthed."

"Fancy that! But why your interest? You were never one to go beyond the counters at Tiffany's for your precious stones. Why the interest in museum pieces?"

"Frankly, I think it comes from a sudden feeling of uselessness."

"You speak in riddles. Clarify."

"I can't, really. I suppose it's more restlessness than anything else. After this mess is cleared up, I've decided to go west."

"You don't plan to go back to sea?"

"No. I have to be realistic about the situation. As it stands, I could go to prison, but there is no doubt whatever happens that my master's license will be permanently revoked."

"Come, now, perhaps not. One cannot accurately predict one's future."

"There are great opportunities in the west. The nation doesn't stop at the Hudson River. Mining; development. San Francisco is fairly bursting with opportunity."

"Old man, I think it's still a rum go out there. Until Delmonico's opens a branch establishment west of Jersey, I'd recommend staying here."

Gentry had definitely been disappointed in Jason's sojourn. He was delighted to have him, of course, but Jason had not entered into the spirit of things. He'd actually moped in solitude instead of joining in to pursue the happy hours. There was always hope, however.

"Jason," Gentry said now, "what you need is

a touch of fresh activity. Fortunately, my group is gathering tonight."

"Your group?"

"The Brimstone Club." Gentry shrugged. "That's what the prudes call us from behind their fans so we let it stand. I think you ought to join us. You might find it amusing."

The implication was that it was Jason's obligation; that he owed his host something more than the role of the remote guest.

"All right, Cal. What time and where?"

"Around ten—after the general herd is bedded down for the night—" He winked cozily, "—and the constabulary is reluctant to stir about."

"I have a dinner engagement with my grandfather's representative, but I can drop around about that time."

"On Hudson Street just off Bank, old chum. You'll find a sinister little bistro called the Straight Flush—where the good folk never go. We have the basement. Drop in when you get clear . . ."

At a quiet dinner in Fraunces Tavern, Cletus Wing used all his persuasive powers to convince Jason that he should be more cooperative.

"Your grandfather is most disappointed, Jason."

"I'm sorry, more sorry than you can possibly know. I wish I could explain. Maybe it has come too late, but suddenly I've got to take charge of my own life."

"But if you could just postpone that worthy resolution for a time, until all this is over. Off by yourself—all alone—"

"Oh, but I'm not alone—far from it. The ghosts of a few dozen dead men go everywhere with me."

"Jason, for heaven's sake! That's morbid! In that state of mind a man can easily make mistakes."

Jason laughed. "Making mistakes has always been quite easy for me."

Probing about for another approach, Wing said, "We never really got into it, the two of us, as to what happened on the ship. It would help me a great deal if I knew. About that madman, Saipan. Did you honestly not see him as dangerous?"

"If I admitted otherwise, Cletus, could Ben Stein honestly defend me in a murder trial?"

"Defending you under all circumstances is his job. Of course he could. We're checking into Saipan as exhaustively as possible—he is the key to the whole thing—but you must help."

"What did Guy Mapes tell you?"

"Poor Guy. He would give his life for you but being dishonest is painful to him. He stands between the devil and the deep."

"He warned me about Saipan. He urged me to put him in irons."

"He told us that—most reluctantly."

"Did he say anything about Kate McCrae?"

"Very little. He called her a decent young woman. He said her presence on the ship, a lone unattached female, was unfortunate."

"An understatement," Jason murmured with some bitterness.

"Tell me this, Jason. Was there, ah, competition between you and Peter Wells for her favors?"

"I did not compete for her hand in marriage, if that is what you mean."

"I don't *mean* anything, Jason; I am only trying to determine the facts as they were. The girl is not under our control as a witness. And a curious situation has arisen on that score. Godfrey Wells hates the girl. He would like to destroy her as an opportunistic little trollop—"

"She is far from that!"

"I'm sure. But from what I understand the Wells' daughter, Theresa, has taken charge and is protecting the young woman's claim."

"You haven't talked to Kate?"

"I haven't been able to reach her. She may be a hostile witness, for all I know."

"I met her once since we got back. I'm sure she's not hostile."

"Do you have access to her?"

"I think I probably have."

"Then for God's sake see her! Talk to her. Get her to meet with Ben Stein, if you can."

"I'll try."

"What are your immediate plans, Jason? Are you going to stay with Calvin Gentry?"

"Not permanently. Tomorrow I'm going up to pay my respects to my grandmother. It's high time."

"That's good. That's very good. I never met the lady but I admire her greatly."

"When is Grandfather returning to Stonington?"

"I don't know. He has said nothing about it. His sole interest in life right now is to protect you. To be perfectly frank, Jason, there is almost something unhealthy in his compulsion. It is as though in saving you he is saving himself.

266

He bears a tremendous guilt, and he bears it alone."

"I love my grandfather and I know he loves me, but a barrier has come up. I suppose I've built it myself. I wish I could tear it down."

"He feels that if he doesn't save you from a murder conviction he is himself lost."

"That seems to be the wall between us. And yet I am sure that if I cower and cringe behind the safeguard of his power and your legal expertise, *I* will be lost. Oh hell, I don't know! Cletus, I've got to get out of here. I have an appointment."

"Of course. I understand."

As Wing watched Jason stride from the table, he wished in heaven's name that he *did* understand.

The streets were as empty as though a signal had been given and everyone had fled the city. The neighborhood into which Jason's carriage bore him had the benefit of Mr. Edison's new invention, electric street lamps. Gas lights still predominated elsewhere and Jason found their softer radiance more satisfactory. The comparative glare of electricity seemed to violate the night as he had known it. The shabbiness of daytime streets, previously hidden by the shadows of gaslight, now remained to abuse the eye.

The entrance to the building Gentry had specified was dark. Jason dismissed the carriage and approached to find a man standing in the gloom of the basement stairs.

"Looking for someone, guv'ner?"

"A friend of mine, Calvin Gentry."

"Oh yes, guv'ner. Mr. Gentry told me to watch for you special. Right this way."

The man led Jason into a pitchy blackness suddenly broken by a rectangle of dim light as he opened a door. He did not enter but gestured on ahead.

"That there's a curtain, guv'ner. Just push it aside and you'll be where you're aimin' to go." He chuckled, closed the door, and Jason was on his own.

He pushed the curtain gently aside and surveyed the interior through a narrow slit. It was circular, centering down to a round, sunken stage with benches on three sides for spectators. The illumination was mixed. An electric lamp hung over the stage while subdued gaslights ringed the outer walls.

The club members, some two dozen fashionably dressed dandies of the Gentry ilk, clustered all to one side as though for mutual protection, eyes on the stage, where two naked women were wrestling. Jason slipped in through the curtain and found a seat on the near end of a vacant bench. He scanned the faces of the club members and picked Cal Gentry out of the lot. Cal sat in the center, his eyes fixed avidly on the contestants below.

A peculiar mood held Jason in a sort of frozen posture, as though he were in a museum, viewing an obscene animated wax reproduction of something from the ancient past.

He studied Cal Gentry. Was the man deriving true joy from what he watched, or was his expression of pleasure also calculated? Jason knew that Gentry's main satisfaction came from the group around him, moneyed lackeys he had recruited as followers, thus making himself the leader he yearned to be.

But Gentry was Gentry. Jason found it impossible to sever their friendship. He genuinely liked the man, despite his pretensions.

He turned his attention to the women in the ring. They were evenly matched, a buxom duo, and in deadly earnest about winning whatever prize was at stake. One of them had flung the other to the mat, using her brick-red hair as a lever—hair artificially colored, as proved by the black swatch of pubic growth widely revealed.

Jason's reaction to what he was seeing was quick. In his wildest days of womanizing he would have turned from this sort of thing in disgust, and he did so now, slipping quietly out of the grubby basement and into the clean night air.

The doorman was gone. Jason began walking north through the quiet, deserted streets. He kept his eye out for a cab but when one rattled by, he let it go and continued to walk. It was a long hike from the Greenwich section to the lower edge of Central Park and the Spanish Flats, but Jason was enjoying it.

He arrived at his destination, entered the suite, and found that while Gentry had not yet returned, he was not alone. A lovely figure, framed in the soft glow of an oil lamp, appeared in the foyer as he closed the door.

"Cal, is that you?"

"No. Cal is not with me."

"Oh, Jason. I'm so glad you came home. I was getting lonely."

Jason was on formal speaking terms with

Bella Cantrell. He knew her status, of course. She was Gentry's mistress of the moment, Jason ascribing no permanency to her tenure because he well knew Cal's reputation for fickleness.

Jason could not help being impressed. by Bella. She had a grace and dignity about her that put her somewhat above what he had come to expect in other women of free morals. Her personal grooming was impeccable. She had never appeared anywhere in the suite with a hair out of place. Even at breakfast, which the three often shared, she came as though prepared to go on stage at any moment.

That was another aspect that interested Jason. From what he had learned, Bella, a mezzo-soprano, often appeared in many of the city's best supper clubs and had a long list of musical credits. Thus she should have been quite able to support herself. Could she, he wondered, possibly be in love with his peacock friend?

She was especially attractive at the moment, in a gold lamé salon gown, her blonde hair a halo of soft light.

As he removed his topcoat, Jason's reply was spontaneous. "I'm glad you're here, Bella. I've been lonely too."

Her laugh was silvery, controlled. "Marvelous, two lonely people who can tell their sad stories to each other. How opportune. Let's try the den. It is quite a companionable place." He followed her and found that the gaslights had been turned off in favor of a pair of candelabra which threw quite enough light for the occasion.

Bella said, "What would you like to drink?"

"It doesn't matter. Whatever is handy."

"I was just pouring my own nightcap of hot chocolate when I heard you come in."

"Chocolate will be fine."

Seating herself, Bella poured his drink, and Jason thought a print of the scene would not have been out of place in *Harper's Bazaar* or *Godey's Ladies' Book*. He leaned forward to look more closely at the silver service.

"My grandmother has a service almost identical to this one," he said. "It came from Tiffany's, I believe."

"This one is from the continent. I bought it in Paris. One of my few treasures. It's a tea service, of course, but it does quite nicely for chocolate, although chocolate should be served from something Dutch—a lovely blue delft pot."

Jason sipped from fine china. "It doesn't matter. Your chocolate is delicious."

"I can't take credit, I'm afraid. Fellows made it for me before he left for the night."

Fellows and his wife were Gentry's sleep-out servants. They moved silently and efficiently through their duties. Jason had never discovered Mrs. Fellows in his room, yet the bed was always made to store-window perfection, the bath always perfect to the smallest detail. He'd wondered idly what became of the pair each night when they slipped out into oblivion, to reappear in darkness early the next morning.

"Did you spend your evening pleasantly?" Bella asked.

"More or less. I had dinner with my lawyer."

She regarded him thoughtfully.

She said softly, "Jason, you *are* in bad trouble, aren't you?"

"Oh, really, now—nothing I can't handle. Tell me about Bella Cantrell. Who is she? Where does she come from?"

"She comes from a long line of buskers," she said, after a pause.

"Buskers are actors, aren't they?"

"Sidewalk performers outside the London theaters. We entertained the people waiting to go in. I learned to sing and dance almost before I could walk."

"A romantic background."

"Not to me. It is hardly romantic, living on coins people throw at your feet. My father wanted all his life to be a Shakespearean actor and failed. My mother had a fine voice but never got a chance to really use it. I was more fortunate. When I was sixteen I looked twenty and ran away to the States with a young composer from Chicago whose father had given him two years in Europe as a graduation present."

Bella was off on a nostalgic journey. "That was romantic, I suppose, at least for a time. We lived here in New York but then the boy's father finally closed his checkbook and told his wandering son to get back home and learn the hardware business. I waved good-bye at Grand Central Station and—well, that was that."

"You were left stranded?"

"Hardly. I have never been one to turn tail and run. I formed various attachments and lived fairly well." She brightened as a thought struck her. "You know, Jason, Theresa Wells, from what I've heard, and I are much the same."

"I'm afraid I don't see the comparison."

"In relation to men, and to women's rights. It is just that our methods are different. Tess Wells uses her head as a battering ram. I use what's inside—my brains—and I am mainly interested in the rights of *one* woman—myself. I find that honey is a better weapon than public demonstrations."

"I see."

Jason now had a better understanding of Bella. He saw her as a courtesan who put a high value on herself and dealt only with men who were able to pay. He wondered how many "business" transactions she had made in order to reach her present position.

"Do you plan to marry Cal?"

"No."

"But you could if you so desired."

"I suppose so. But by marrying, one acknowledges defeat. To me, marriage is a hole card of last resort."

Jason laughed. "Bella, you *are* amazing. To you!" He lifted his cup.

"All right, I've been candid, so now how about you? You're in love with the girl in the headlines—the stowaway on your ship—right?"

"Why on earth would you think that?"

"It was a shot in the dark."

"Well, you missed by a wide margin. Kate McCrae does not interest me."

"I'm glad to hear that. Otherwise you might have a problem. Tess Wells is a lesbian, you know."

"A lesbian!"

Bella examined a flawless fingernail with a certain smugness. Her shot in the dark *had* paid off. "And she doesn't try to hide it, either. Not that she shouts it in the streets, but it is an open secret."

Jason concealed his inner reaction well. Only his hand gave him away. His cup stopped halfway to his lips, and he set it down very slowly. Bella, knowing she had scored, gave him no leeway.

"Tell me, Jason—I only know what I read in the papers, but—why did you let her marry Peter Wells?"

"I don't wish to be rude, but you're prying into private matters."

"Private for the moment perhaps, but you know very well it will all have to come out."

Damn! This woman was too smart!

Bella lifted the silver pitcher and sweetly asked, "More chocolate?"

"No thank you. If you'll excuse me—"

"Jason, sit down! I'm your friend. Can't you understand that? I'm on *your* side."

A certain caution prevailed. Jason would have preferred to stride away in anger, but Bella might be a good friend to have. Her *savoir-faire* was obvious and she certainly seemed sincere.

He eased back into his chair and Bella poured more of the rich, dark chocolate into his cup anyway.

"As I was saying, I might be of some help."

"In what way?"

"I am a snoopy person at heart; I enjoy intruding into other people's affairs. It occurred to me that I might visit your Kate McCrae as an interested friend—your friend—your surrogate, so to speak. You have a legitimate interest in the girl, as captain of the ship upon which she was a passenger—or was she really a stowaway . . . ? Anyhow, I could go down there and report the situation to you."

"God damn it, woman! Are you toying with me?"

"Jason, wouldn't you like to know what's going on?"

"You're just too damned smart for your own good."

Bella's silvery laugh rang out. "All right. It's agreed. I'll drop in at Washington Square tomorrow, and come back with what I find."

Jason was not required to suffer the humiliation of actually commissioning Bella to the task. There were sounds in the foyer and Calvin Gentry appeared. He swept off his cape with its red satin lining and removed his opera hat. "Hi ho, you cozy pair. Whose reputation are you shredding?"

Bella replied, "We are trying to decide who to vote for—William McKinley or William Jennings Bryan."

"Bryan will make it this time. No doubt about it."

"Did you have a nice evening?"

"So-so. Only a trifle less boring than usual."

He ignored Jason, probably as a reprimand for not appearing at the stag. Gentry obviously did not know he had come and gone. He came over and sniffed at the silver service.

"What are you drinking? Chocolate? Great

gods, how disgusting! Bring me a brandy when you come up."

With that, Gentry limped off, leaving Jason to ponder that his friend was proud of his limp. The club foot made him different; it lifted him above the "common herd."

Bella rose from her chair. "The master calls," she said. "Sleep well, Jason . . ."

Jason wondered if Gentry really thought he was Bella's master. If he did, it definitely proved him an arrogant fool.

44.

There were three hacks at the station when Jason's train pulled into Stonington. He chose the one with a driver he knew, Henny Sarno, somewhat of a character, and the patriarch of Stonington transportation.

"Hello, Henny," Jason greeted. "Run me up to the house, will you?"

Henny was middle aged and had worn out three spans of horses in his career as a hackie; Jason noted that he now had a pair of matched sorrels.

"Not today."

"I beg pardon?"

"Not in *my* hack."

With that Henny clipped the gee sorrel with his whip and pulled away.

It was a shock, but Jason understood immediately. The town had lost many men when the *Gray Ghost* went down.

The other hackies seemed willing to carry him but instead he picked up his bag and began walking. The trip to the Steele mansion told him little more than he had already learned. Some of those he passed nodded, others looked straight ahead. The town had not yet reached the tar-and-feather stage, however, and that at least was encouraging.

He found his grandmother in her morning room although it was late afternoon. She was exactly as he had left her and the curious thought came to him that she had not moved since then.

He crossed to her and kissed her gently upon the cheek, then sat down opposite. Grandma Becky's blue eyes took him in, up and down.

"You have lost weight."

"Some. It's good for me. I was getting fat and soft."

"Did you see your grandfather in the city?"

As if there was any doubt. Jason kept it going: "We met several times at the Union Club."

"When that reporter called him he left immediately . . ."

"Grandma Becky, Henny Sarno refused to drive me up here. Are things that bad in town?"

"The sentiment is mixed. Henny's nephew Simon was on your ship."

"I didn't know."

"Is all hope gone or is there still a chance?"

"No chance, I'm afraid. All but those in a single boat went down."

"Was it your fault, Jason?"

"Yes, it was my fault."

"I wanted to know for sure. Are *you* sure."

"I am. I let things drift when I should have taken charge. Guy Mapes warned me."

"Guy is heartbroken. He came here to pay his respects. He had little to say but you could see it in his eyes."

"I understand that Cater MacRoy came home also."

"Yes. He stayed two days with his family and then went to sea again on a ship out of Nantucket. Have you seen Elizabeth?"

"No. Do you really think I should?"

"Not here in town. In New York City. She deserted Chester and left. I understand she went to the city."

"Elizabeth left Chester? I didn't know that!"

"I thought perhaps William would have told you."

"What happened? What went wrong?"

"I don't know. The Penns do not come here to talk over their troubles."

"Did the fight Chester and I had have anything to do with it?"

"I doubt it. I think that after being swept into the marriage by Jethro, Elizabeth had time to think. Perhaps she panicked—perhaps she is still in love with you. Anyhow, I hear that Jethro, to save face, has blamed the break-up on Chester and is making an effort to have the marriage annulled."

"Poor Chester. God, what a fool I was!"

"That is some progress at least, Jason. A step in the right direction. You are still young enough to profit. With me it is too late."

Jason desperately wanted to do something; to touch her, to take her in his arms, to banish the sadness from her face.

"You're talking nonsense, Grandmother," he said gently.

"You know what I mean—I goaded you into that fight."

"Ridiculous! What do you think I am—a child with no mind of my own?"

"You would have obeyed your grandfather and gone straight to sea."

"I don't agree, but what difference does it make? I'm going to apologize to Chester for my stupidity. If he doesn't accept I'll give him a free swing at my jaw."

"I forbid that, Jason. It would give Jethro Penn too much pleasure."

Jason was relieved. He'd made the offer in an effort to please his grandmother; even though he regretted the fight, apologizing would have been a painful ordeal. His reaction to the news of the broken marriage was not as clear, except for one aspect: He took no joy in Chester's humiliation.

"Are you staying over, Jason?"

"For the night. I'll have to go back tomorrow."

"Then I'll see you at dinner."

"Of course."

With some hours to kill, Jason felt the urge to go into the streets and further test the atmosphere; to count friends and enemies and hope for a favorable ratio. It was three blocks down on Front Street that he came face to face with Chester Manson.

The two men looked at each other in silence, each wary, each trying to read the other's mind. Jason was the first to speak.

"Chester—how are you?"

"Well enough—and you?"

"I could be better. I'm sure you've heard."

"About the *Gray Ghost*? Yes, I'm sorry."

"Thank you. Would you let me buy you a rum?"

"I don't mind if I do."

The King's Pine Tavern was convenient and quite deserted. They took a booth and sat self-consciously for a time, neither having anything to say. The rum was served and again it was Jason who spoke first.

"I heard about you and Elizabeth. I'm sorry."

"It was probably for the best."

"To be perfectly honest, Chester, I made a fool of myself. I look back now and wonder how I could have been such an idiot."

"You weren't the only one."

Jason felt an urge to make himself understood; a need to retrieve a friendship he now valued highly. "I just talked with my grandmother," he said. "I told her I'd find you and apologize, and if you didn't accept I'd give you a free shot at my jaw."

Manson smiled. "I think it would be more appropriate if I gave someone a swing at mine. I was a damned fool, Jason. You see, I thought I was using old Jethro Penn, but he was using me. And—well, in a way, we were both using Elizabeth." He stopped and scowled into his mug of rum, then raised his eyes. "Jason, did you really know Elizabeth? I mean *really* know her?"

Jason's mind flashed back to that memorable weekend with Elizabeth wanton as an unbred filly in heat.

"I thought I knew her," he said simply.

"Well, what it added up to was—Christ, how

can I put it?—she needed a full-time stallion and I'm a plain, old-fashioned work horse."

"I understand."

"There were secrets in her past nobody knew—Jethro paid off a couple of blackmailers. It can't be proved but I know damned well he sent one of them to sea and the poor devil didn't come back."

"How did it end, Chet?"

"It was damned strange. I actually felt sorry for the poor girl. She was browbeaten into the marriage by her grandfather. Afterward, she felt trapped."

"Somehow I had that feeling about her."

"Anyhow, I'll say this for her: She tried—with me, that is. And I made a stupid mistake—I refused to cooperate—I couldn't; I didn't know how. I went into a tirade about how my wife had to be decent, had to be—I don't remember all that was said, but she screamed at me, called me a—a *eunuch,* for God's sake!"

"Easy, Chet. It's over. Forget it. I owe you a hell of a debt. You saved me from going through the same thing."

"Anyhow," Manson went on wearily, "she left, and Jethro piled it all on my head. I'd abused her—I'd been cruel and frightened the poor girl away."

Jason could visualize the proud Jethro Penn accusing Chester Manson of such conduct.

"Chet, he took that way out because he knows what kind of a man you are—that you wouldn't fight back to defend yourself by blackening Elizabeth's name."

"I don't know what he thinks. In any case he offered me a fat payment to leave Stonington."

Loyalty to the family: It was bred in the bone. While Jason condemned Jethro Penn for his unfairness, he could not help but compare him to his own grandfather. Defend the family name at all costs.

"You turned the money down, right?"

"Of course."

"You shouldn't have. You should have taken what you could get. You earned it."

"I got what I deserved. I wanted some of the Penn power. That's why I wanted Elizabeth. I got what I deserved," he repeated.

"You haven't left town."

"I'm going to, but in my own time."

"Do you have any plans?"

"I was thinking of San Francisco."

"No more sea duty?"

"I'm through with the sea."

"So am I, but not by choice." Jason smiled ruefully.

"Then you think they'll pull your license?"

"They're sure to do that; maybe a lot more." Jason lifted his mug to signal for more rum. "Maybe it *is* by choice," he reflected. "I left a lot of dead men out there. . . . But why Frisco? Have you something in mind?"

"I'd like to get into ship building," Chet said earnestly. "I think I'd be good at it, Jason. I know I'm through in this part of the country. Jethro has seen to that."

"Don't be too sure. The old son-of-a-bitch has a lot of enemies. If you went to Nantucket, New Bedford—places right here in this area— I'll wager you could find plenty of work."

"No, I want to get clear away."

It suddenly dawned on Jason that perhaps Chet *had* been deeply in love with Elizabeth, in spite of her nature.

"Chet," he said impulsively, "why don't you come on down to New York with me? I've got some problems there, as you know, but when they're cleared up I'll be making new plans, and I need somebody I can trust. I've been thinking of going west, too. Mining . . ."

With three mugs of rum under his bridge, the difficulties lying ahead for Jason were all leveled out. Optimism bloomed bright in his foggy mind. He didn't give the other a chance to answer.

"Where are you staying, Chet?"

Manson blinked at his freshly filled mug. "Up the road. Around the corner. Don't wanna go there. Wanna go to San-Fran-cis-co." He was in the same condition as Jason.

"I know a place we can go and have a nice long talk. Come on, old man—"

They left the bar arm in arm.

A few minutes later, Clara Peavey answered a pounding on the back door of the *Blue Mermaid*. She stared in amazement.

"You two! My God!"

"A room for the night, tavernkeeperess. The attic will do fine. . . ."

The following morning, Jason slipped into the Steele mansion and out again. When Rebecca Steele awoke, she found his note:

Dear Grandma Becky,

Forgive me for missing dinner. I met a friend. We talked and got sidetracked.

All my love and God bless you,

Jason

As he waited for his train, Jason tried to remember what he and Chester Manson had planned. He was not sure of the details but it had been all to the good. He hadn't realized how much he had missed Chester's friendship; one that had not seemed nearly that close in the days before they clashed.

Jason's spirits were high. He felt strong and resourceful once again.

45.

Kate was practicing with her knitting needles, a craft she was mastering under Tess' supervision. Tess was off somewhere and would be back for dinner. The silence in the flat on Washington Square was suddenly broken by the faint sound of sobbing. Kate got up and went to investigate.

She found Peggy Dale on Tess' bed, her head in her arms, crying as if her heart would break.

Kate laid a hand on her shoulder. "Peggy dear, what on earth is the matter?"

Peggy whirled on her. "*You* are the matter! Why did you come here? Tess loves *me*, not you. Why did you have to come here and ruin our lives?"

Kate drew back, stunned by the onslaught. This could be Clara Peavey hurling accusations at her back at the *Blue Mermaid*.

Please, Mrs. Peavey! I have tried to avoid your husband. . . .

Two different women. Two different kinds of love. But the same desperate need to fight off the intruder. And this time, a different Kate McCrae.

She seized the still-hysterical Peggy by the shoulders and shook her.

"Peggy! Stop it! You're acting like a child! Sit up and listen to me!"

Peggy caught her breath in a sob.

"What you are saying is utter nonsense. I am not in love with Tess. She is my friend and she has helped me, but for other reasons entirely."

"That's a lie! She sent me away so you two could—"

"Stop being a baby! Nothing has changed. I'll be here for a while and then I'll leave and your life will go on as it did before. There is nothing—*nothing*—between Tess and me."

Kate had seated herself beside Peggy with an arm around her shoulders. The physical contact appeared to quiet the distraught girl more than the assurances. She looked tremulously into Kate's eyes, her throat still working.

"Kate, I—oh, Kate, I'm so confused!"

"There is nothing to be confused about."

In a spasm of remorse Peggy tried to twist more deeply into Kate's arms.

"Kate—"

Kate disengaged herself and stood up. "Now stop your crying. Wash your face and comb your hair. You wouldn't want Tess to come home and find you like this—"

There was the sound of the doorbell.

"I'll go see who it is."

Kate left the bedroom with a light step, feeling that she had handled the situation well. With maturity came assurance and self-confidence.

She opened the front door and all vagrant musing ended. A woman stood there, a golden

287

blonde wearing a lovely blue silk gown hour-glassed at the waist. It draped from the left, sweeping down to a raised hemline on the right. Expensive, no doubt the latest Paris mode. Kate was impressed.

The woman's poise was also impressive. "Good afternoon. I am Bella Cantrell. I hope I'm not intruding."

"Not at all."

"You are Kate McCrae?"

"I am Miss McCrae, yes."

"I am a friend of Jason Steele. If I may come in for a few minutes—"

"Of course," Kate managed to say, somewhat puzzled.

Bella Cantrell swept past her, lifting the draped skirt in a graceful gesture as she stepped over the threshold. Kate led her into the parlor, where Bella seated herself and looked out upon the square.

"A lovely view. You must be quite comfortable here."

"Most comfortable, Miss Cantrell . . ."

"Bella—please. And may I call you Kate? I do feel that I know you. Jason has spoken of you so often."

"Are you from Stonington, Miss Cantrell? Did you know Jason there?"

"No, I met him here in New York. He is staying with a friend of mine—Calvin Gentry."

Kate was on the verge of asking why Jason had not come himself. Instead, she said, "I saw Jason just a short time ago, and he mentioned that he was staying at Spanish Flats."

"Just now he is in Stonington with his grandmother. I am not quite sure when he will be back. As the captain of the ship from which you were rescued he feels a certain responsibility and he wanted me to inquire as to whether you needed anything—if you are being well taken care of."

Bella was not an actress for nothing; there was a note of genuine concern in the query; enough to keep Kate from openly resenting what might otherwise have been a patronizing attitude.

"Is Jason well? He seemed tired when I saw him."

"Quite well, I think. I find him to be a wonderful person, so easy to talk to. The sinking of his ship affected him deeply. He is a lonely man. He needed someone to talk to."

But why this woman? There was no reticence in Kate's admission to herself that she was more than willing to be Jason's confidant. Why *this* woman, whom he'd known for only a short time, earned the role was something Kate could not understand.

"It was gracious of Jason to send you to inquire into my welfare. But as I said, I'm managing quite well."

"He will be glad to hear that."

"Is there anything—I mean, have you gotten any news as to how serious Jason's trouble is?"

"Quite serious, I'm afraid. But that does not necessarily mean that his punishment will be drastic. It is a legal matter and he has very good attorneys. The prosecutor may find it very difficult to convict him."

"Then he will be tried?"

"We have to assume so."

What did she mean by *we?* Where did she fit

in? Kate tried to tell herself that she wanted Jason's innocence established by any means, and so any help given him was to be welcomed. Still, she found it difficult to accept that Bella was part of his defense.

"I had been hoping to meet Theresa Wells," Bella was saying. "Is she home?"

"I'm sorry, she will not be in until later."

"A pity. I am one of her admirers and wanted to express my appreciation for her efforts on the behalf of all women."

Tess would no doubt be gratified by Miss Cantrell's moral support, but so far as Kate could see, Miss Cantrell herself needed no champion. She seemed to be doing quite well on her own.

"If I may be so bold, Miss Cantrell, what do you do? I mean, do you have a profession?"

"I am an entertainer—"

I'll bet you are!

"—a singer. Beginning Monday I am to appear at the International Club. It's a supper restaurant on Madison Avenue near Twenty-third Street. I'd be flattered if you and Theresa would drop in to hear me."

"I'm sure we would enjoy it, but two unescorted ladies . . ."

"That will be no problem. Just telephone me at the Flats when you can make it and I'll see that you are admitted."

"That is very kind of you."

"Not at all. And now I must be running along." She rose gracefully from her chair. "You have been most gracious to receive me."

"The pleasure has been mine."

As they approached the door, a key rattled

in the lock and Tess came flying in the door in her usual manner—as though she were hurrying to an important appointment.

"Tess, I'm so glad you got back in time. We have a visitor. This is Miss Bella Cantrell."

Tess extended her hand in masculine fashion and Bella took it without hesitation.

Kate went on, "Miss Cantrell is a singer of note. She has invited us to her performance at the International Club."

Bella laughed, totally at ease. "That's quite true but I did not make this visit entirely for that purpose. Kate and I have a mutual acquaintance—Jason Steele. Kate having been aboard the *Gray Ghost*, Jason wanted me to check that Kate's needs are being taken care of . . ."

Kate was close to gritting her teeth. This damned, patronizing female! Why didn't she go on about her business?

To the contrary, Bella was making no effort to depart. Stiffly Tess said, "You may tell Mr. Steele that Kate is doing quite nicely."

"I certainly shall," Bella replied cheerfully. "Miss Wells, I am so happy to meet you. I am one of your most ardent admirers. I fully appreciate what you are doing for our sex."

Tess swallowed the bait instantly, if bait it was. "Won't you sit down, Miss Cantrell. I'm sure you don't have to rush off." She gestured back to the parlor.

"You are so very kind."

Kate, left standing, said, "I have some things to do so I'll leave you ladies to your conversation. It was delightful meeting you, Miss Cantrell."

"I'm sure we'll meet again, dear. And it *has* been delightful."

Kate left with the uncomfortable feeling that she had been dismissed.

46.

Whoever and whatever was lost in the sinking of the *Gray Ghost* under Jason Steele's command, the legal profession gained and prospered. There was, first of all, Gordon, Wing & Stillwater, brought swiftly into action by William Steele on his grandson's behalf. And Benjamin Stein, the ace criminal lawyer they had retained. Along with Kebble, Smith & Morningside, commissioned to see that International Surety did not come to financial harm, the cream of the nation's legal profession was present.

The most beleaguered of the counselors was Victor Kebble. Stymied by the wily Ben Stein, he'd caused subpoenas to be flung like confetti up and down both seaboards. Kebble had appeared before Judge Henry Holt after the specified time period to beg further delay and obtained it. Thus, two full months passed before Kebble decided to go ahead, using what he had. Ben Stein pondered the wisdom of seeking further postponement of the hearing and decided not to. It could still be a long time before a trial date was set, with any number of postponement possibilities popping up. Secondly, he wanted to find out exactly what Kebble had come up with by way of damaging evidence. It was possible—but highly improbable—that Judge Holt would find no reason to send the case on to a grand jury.

Ben Stein's last conference with Jason prior to the hearing disturbed the attorney. In an effort to reassure Jason, he had said, "We are not going to overlook Guy Mapes' culpability in this affair."

Jason frowned. "What culpability?"

"I'm sure you're aware of it. You recall your order to Mapes when he came to you that final time to report Saipan's refusal to obey a command?"

"I recall the occasion but I see no culpability—"

"You ordered Mapes clearly and without hesitation to put Saipan in irons. Correct?"

"Correct."

"Mapes failed to obey you."

"Good God, man! What are you saying?"

"I'm saying that Mapes was lax in his duty. Even while knowing Saipan was dangerous and having your direct order, he allowed the maniac to retire to the forecastle literally by himself—"

"He was *not* by himself—"

"The laxity on Mapes's part will weigh heavily in your favor. You recognized the situation for what it was; you gave the logical order and—"

Jason's face darkened. His glare would have intimidated a man of lesser stomach than Stein. As it was, it stopped the lawyer in midsentence.

"I won't have it!"

"But Jason—"

"Understand me, sir. You will under no circumstances state or imply that Guy Mapes was other than a conscientious, loyal, able officer aboard the *Gray Ghost*. If you plan to do otherwise I will repudiate you as counsel regardless of my grandfather or anyone else!"

Stein seethed. If this misguided young fool wanted to wear a halo far too big for him he could accept the consequences and to hell with him!

Still, down deep, there was grudging respect. Idealism, however impractical, revealed admirable moral fiber.

They were in the bar at the Standard Club. Stein shrugged and raised his brandy glass.

"Very well, Jason. Let's drink to the diminishing hope of keeping you out of jail. . . ."

The hearing was held in Judge Holt's court. Holt explained:

"This is a hearing, not a trial. It is an attempt to ascertain the facts concerning the case in question, therefore the strict rules of trial procedure will not necessarily hold. Although the witnesses will be under oath, they are not required to answer any questions which they think might be self-incriminating. Is that clearly understood?"

Assistant United States Attorney David Griffen called the first witness—Guy Mapes. The first mate of the *Gray Ghost* was sworn in. Griffen said, "Mr. Mapes, the roster of the *Gray Ghost*, of which I have a copy, shows that a man named John Saipan was signed on as a common seaman. Is that correct?"

"It is correct."

"You signed John Saipan on personally?"

"I did."

Using information dug up by Victor Kebble and Dean Cabot, Griffen asked, "Had you had any previous experience with Saipan on the high seas?"

"Yes."

"Would you please explain?"

"He was under me during a voyage on the *Martha Kane*. He attacked another seaman and I had him flogged."

"You are saying that you found him an unsatisfactory hand."

"To the extent of that particular incident—yes."

"Yet you signed him on again when the *Gray Ghost* set sail."

"I did."

"Was that not bad judgment?"

"As things turned out, it was. But we needed hands and aside from that one time, John Saipan obeyed orders and was a good seaman."

"Did you discuss signing on Saipan with the captain of the *Gray Ghost*—Jason Steele?"

"I did."

"You had various conversations with Captain Steele about John Saipan?"

"Yes."

"At one time you recommended putting Saipan in irons?"

His replies now most reluctant, Guy Mapes said, "That is true, but it had to be the captain's decision and his opinion of the situation was that I was being too hasty. He had every right to that opinion."

"But there are strong indications that John Saipan blew up the ship."

It was a statement, not a question, and Guy Mapes did not reply.

With the attorneys for the principals given leave to cross-examine, Victor Kebble stepped in.

"Mr. Mapes, in your opinion, was Captain Steele derelict in his duty as commander of the vessel by not heeding your warnings regarding John Saipan?"

"In my opinion he was not."

"Even in the face of rumors that Saipan had smuggled dynamite aboard the ship and planned to blow it up?"

"I questioned Saipan on that. He denied it. He was carrying out his duties in a satisfactory manner. The captain was correct in not restricting a man on the basis of rumors."

Kebble, knowing Mapes to be a hostile witness, did not question him further. Ben Stein sat quietly, waiting. Having established Saipan on the ship, Griffen called Antone Salas, the surviving Jamaican seaman.

"Mr. Salas, would you like an interpreter?"

"I know English pretty good."

"Very well. Mr. Salas, did you know a seaman on the *Gray Ghost* named John Saipan?"

"We know him."

"Did he ever speak to you?"

"He tell us get off ship. He say God not want us killed."

"He suggested that you jump ship?"

Salas nodded vigorously. *"Sí, sí."*

"You said *we*. To whom else are you referring?"

"My friend, Leon Ramos. He with me when the man tell us."

"Your friend was killed in the explosion?"

Salas lowered his head and nodded sadly. "*Sí*," he whispered.

"Did you tell anyone else on the ship what Saipan had said to you?"

"We tell Woo."

"You are referring to the cook aboard the ship, Walter Woo?"

"*Sí*. China fellow."

"Why did you talk to Walter Woo? Why did you not report to one of the ship's officers?"

"Woo good fellow—listen to sailors."

"You told him you thought John Saipan was dangerous?"

"We tell him what man tell us—get off ship."

Salas was dismissed and Griffen called Guy Mapes back briefly. "Mr. Mapes," he said, "you have heard Mr. Salas' testimony. Did the cook, Walter Woo, relay the conversation in question to you?"

"He did."

"Did you do anything about it?"

"I questioned Saipan. He admitted talking to Salas and Ramos but he denied encouraging them to jump ship."

"Did you proceed any further?"

"I passed the information on to the captain."

"Thank you. . . ."

Again Ben Stein had no questions.

At this point, Kate McCrae was called to the stand, and Ben Stein came alert. From the very first he had considered that Kate McCrae, a lone girl on a ship full of men, would be a crucial element in the case. His own investigators had been thorough. Stein had Kate's background, including her stay in Stonington and before, carefully documented, and he was not encouraged. A tavern wench, more or less; the daughter of an itinerant, and no mother on the scene. The tavern people, Lucas Peavey and his wife, could probably tear Kate McCrae's reputation to shreds, and even the implication that Jason had brought a doxie aboard ship would hurt his case immeasurably if it came to trial. Therefore, much hinged on how thorough Kebble's own pre-hearing investigation had been.

Griffen's questions were put to her gently but firmly worded nonetheless.

"Miss McCrae, what was your status on the *Gray Ghost*?"

"I was a stowaway."

"For what reason did you board the vessel?"

"To escape from an untenable situation ashore."

"Will you please go into some detail as to that situation?"

"I was working in the *Blue Mermaid* tavern in Stonington, Connecticut. The proprietor, Lucas Peavey, made my stay there unendurable. I had to get away, and I had no place to go."

"Miss McCrae—after you were discovered as a stowaway, how were you treated by the men and officers on the ship?"

"They were all very kind to me."

"Now Miss McCrae, this is a very important question. Prior to your stowing away on the *Gray Ghost* were you acquainted with the man named John Saipan?"

"No, sir. Even after I was aboard it was some time before I so much as knew of his existence."

"Did you speak with him at all?"

"I became aware of him while I was serving coffee to the men during the whaling operations. Later, he approached me and we exchanged some words."

"Were you in any way involved in his plan to destroy the ship?"

"Absolutely not!"

Griffen caught Judge Holt's frown, hesitated briefly, then dismissed the witness.

Victor Kebble objected. "Just a moment—I have some questions to put to this witness."

He approached the chair and eyed Kate sternly. "Miss McCrae, during the voyage, you, a stowaway, were involved with, and subsequently married to, one of the officers—the second mate, Peter Wells. Is that not true?"

Ben Stein came half out of his seat but objection was not necessary. Judge Holt rapped his gavel.

"Mr. Kebble. I don't like the phrasing of that question. Just what are you trying to bring out?"

"I intend to bring a most unusual situation to light, your Honor. There were some exceptional happenings aboard that ship."

"I agree with you on that point. But does what you are trying to uncover bear directly upon that sinking—upon the actions of John Saipan?"

"Only indirectly, but—"

"Mr. Kebble, there will be no browbeating of witnesses in this hearing. Unless you are very sure of yourself I would suggest that you desist."

"I apologize, your Honor."

"Please," Kate cut in, turning to the judge, "there is something I would like to say."

"Very well, you may do so, Miss McCrae."

"I think I *was* at least partly responsible for the sinking."

"In what way?"

"I said that I had spoken with John Saipan. One night he approached me when I was taking some air, and he talked to me."

"What did he say?"

"I cannot recall his exact words but he said it was a sorrowful thing that one so young and innocent—meaning me—should be condemned by God to suffer a fiery death."

"Did he say he was going to blow up the ship?"

"He did not say that directly but he did say that he was there to carry out God's will—to exact God's vengeance. In the light of what happened, he *was* telling me he planned to sink us."

"Why do you feel you were partly responsible?"

"In not telling the captain or any of the officers what he said, I *was* responsible. If I had told Captain Steele of our conversation, he would certainly have locked the man up and the tragedy would have been avoided."

Kate had turned pale.

"Miss McCrae—are you ill?"

"No—no, your honor. I am quite all right."

"This witness is excused," Judge Holt said.

Tess Wells, who had come to the hearing

with Kate, hurried forward and escorted her out of the courtroom. Jason Steele's eyes followed her. He started to rise but at that moment he was called to the stand.

Ben Stein pulled him back down and whispered rapidly, "Jason, for God's sake don't go up there and start confessing everything. Remember your grandfather. Don't destroy him!"

As Jason approached the witness stand, Stein's worried gaze followed. A dangerous moment; this could well be it. The weakest link in Stein's proposed defense was, ironically enough, the man he was trying to protect.

Griffen accorded Jason the same deference with which he had treated the other witnesses. There was no indication that he saw Jason as a prospective defendant. Through his questioning, Jason corroborated the testimony of the preceding witnesses. He then was asked, "But you did not feel that the evidence against Saipan was strong enough to put him under restraint?"

"Obviously not or I would have done so."

As Griffen turned away, Kebble came to his feet. "I have some questions, your Honor."

He advanced to Jason in an attitude of overt hostility. In a prosecuting attorney's voice he said, "Mr. Steele, is it not true that you were so preoccupied with your own personal matters aboard that ship—with romantic entanglements—that you—"

Judge Holt's gavel came down with a bang. "Mr. Kebble—I warned you there will be no browbeating of witnesses in this courtroom. If I have to remind you again that this is a hearing and not a trial, the penalty may be severe."

Kebble lifted his hands in resignation. "I apologize, your Honor. I have no further questions of this witness."

Ben Stein grinned behind his handkerchief. It was encouraging to have Kebble admonished.

As Jason rose from the witness chair, Stein addressed the bench. "Your Honor, a question or two of the witness."

Jason sat back down and Stein came forward briskly. "Mr. Steele, were there reports that John Saipan was suspected of smuggling dynamite onto the ship?"

"The rumors were called to my attention."

"What did you do?"

"I had the ship searched."

"Did you participate in this search yourself?"

"I did."

"What was the result?"

"No explosive of any sort was found."

"Mr. Steele, were there any actual witnesses to the explosion which sank the *Gray Ghost?*"

"No actual witnesses. The explosion took place in the forecastle where Mr. Saipan had barricaded himself with two men."

"Then it cannot be stated definitely that John Saipan deliberately detonated an explosive of whatever nature. It could have been an accident."

Victor Kebble sprang to his feet. Braving Judge Holt's frown, he cried, "Your Honor, Mr. Stein is one of Mr. Steele's legal representatives at this hearing. I protest his efforts to exonerate his client before he has been accused of anything."

Judge Holt turned to Stein. "Can you deny that, Counselor?"

"Of course. I am merely bringing out the facts. My questions could as well have been answered by other witnesses close to the scene of the explosion."

Judge Holt banged his gavel. "This hearing is adjourned until two o'clock." He rose and left the bench.

Outside, an aide asked Ben Stein, "Is it about over, sir?"

"Like hell," the lawyer replied. "It's just started. . . ."

47.

It was Tess who insisted they go to see Bella
Cantrell perform at the International Club.
"Kate, Bella Cantrell is a woman prominent in
her field. I'm anxious to know her better. She
may be of help to us."

Tess had begun to include Kate in her activities and while Kate had never been able to generate any great enthusiasm for the cause she
felt that it would be ungrateful of her to object.
And Tess did not impose on her too often.
There had been two lectures in shabby halls,
where Tess strove to stir up the women who
came to hear her. While the crowds were not
overflowing, they were of a respectable size.
There was a sprinkling of women of the upper
class and the donations in support of Tess's efforts kept coming in.

Tess's efforts were now largely geared to
the bicycle protest. It would be of impressive
size, she said, and would certainly make the
male opponents to women's rights sit up and
take notice.

"The bastards . . ." as Tess referred to them.

In response to Tess's urging, Kate got in
touch with Bella Cantrell through use of the
telephone, lately installed in the Washington

Square flat. The device, a mystery to Kate up to that time, was gaining acceptance. It was used mainly by business and industrial firms but was being extended into the residences of the wealthier citizens.

Bella received the call with obvious pleasure. She told Kate that word would be left at the door of the club that evening, and she and Tess would be her honored guests.

The International Club was well filled when they arrived. There was an intimately decorated dining room aglow with red velvet and gold trim and crystal chandeliers. It spoke of wealth and the comfort of those who could afford the best.

The *maître d'* was most cordial, obviously having been alerted to their arrival. "In accordance with Miss Cantrell's instructions, I am to inform you that there are two gentlemen who wish the honor of your company."

Tess frowned but Kate had caught sight of Jason Steele at a table with another gentleman. Jason had risen from his chair and was looking in their direction.

Kate said quickly, "Why, yes, we would be delighted. You may escort us to the gentlemen's table."

As they crossed the room, Kate was aware that both she and Tess looked their best. It had been a pleasant surprise to discover that Tess had gowns other than her shapeless black frocks—and knew how to wear them when the occasion demanded. Tess had chosen a lime green dress of a style recently made popular by the glamorous Lillian Russell. It swept the floor and had the faintest suggestion of a bustle below its hourglass waist. A Princess Eugenie hat with a rakishly swept brim added flair. Jason's stunned expression as he beheld Tess was proof of how splendid she looked.

But the other gentleman had eyes only for Kate. Kate recognized him as the dandy who had come to claim Jason at the harbor master's office.

"Jason Steele, Tess Wells."

Jason nodded respectfully. "Allow me to introduce Calvin Gentry. Truthfully I'm sorry now that I brought him along. I would love to have both you lovely ladies to myself."

Gentry acknowledged the introduction with a nod to Tess, then held a chair for Kate. She had done some shopping at Tess's insistence and was wearing a gown described at Wanamaker's as "autumn tan." It was simple in design, a fine silk crepe, actually of an off-white cream, the delicate shading in sharp contrast to Tess's brilliant lime. A pink cameo borrowed from the collection kept carelessly in Tess's bureau drawer was the only touch of color, other than Kate's flushed cheeks.

The dinner and Bella Cantrell's talents were served up simultaneously. The four dined variously upon pheasant under glass, a thick, robust bear steak, and veal in a French wine sauce, with Gentry totally ignoring his dishes but often raising his wineglass.

A dark red curtain opened to reveal violin, bass viola, and piano. After the overture, Bella entered to generous applause. Her gown was yellow satin. From her generously revealed bust, the heavy material swept downward to curve around her lower body in diminishing swirls until it ended close around her ankles. Kate was once again impressed by the other woman's attractiveness.

Bella's presence dominated the dining room, her manner self assured and her smile warm. She sang four arias, all well received. The curtain closed and opened several times in response to the applause, quite hearty for a genteel crowd not usually given to demonstrativeness.

A few minutes later, Bella appeared at her guests' table. Gentry and Jason stood up, and after the well-deserved "Marvelous!—Magnificent!" Bella accepted the chair brought by the waiter and the men sat down. She refused wine, saying, "Thank you, but I have another performance."

Tess was most effusive with her compliments. ". . . Places like this do not deserve your talent, Miss Cantrell."

"Thank you so much. And please call me Bella."

"Of course. As I was saying, you should be on the opera stage."

"You are much too kind." With that, Bella turned to Kate. "You look lovely, my dear."

Kate smiled her thanks. She was adjusting her earlier opinion of the statuesque soubrette. Her cattiness had been unjustified, the result of jealousy concerning her possible relationship with Jason.

Turning back to Tess, Bella said, "I sincerely enjoyed our talk at your flat and would like to inquire further into your efforts in behalf of women's rights. We need a champion of your ability."

Jason laughed. "Now wait just a minute. . . . Are we males such monsters?"

Tess's answering laugh was not quite as merry. "Now don't get me started on that subject or no one will enjoy the rest of the evening."

Bella excused herself a short time later to go backstage. It was Gentry who noticed Kate's sudden pallor. "Miss McCrae, you are ill!"

She tried to smile. "It's nothing, really. The air in here is rather heavy."

"We will correct that immediately."

Ignoring the others, he helped her from her chair, snatched up her wrap, and guided her toward the exit without a backward glance. Jason stared after them helplessly, then he, too, stood up.

He and Tess arrived outside to find Gentry's carriage gone.

"He outmaneuvered you beautifully," Tess commented drily.

Jason frowned. "I don't know what you're talking about."

"Don't mind me, I often speak out of turn. He probably took her home."

"The way he acted, he might have rushed her to a hospital."

"He did seem quite smitten with my little houseguest."

Jason signaled for a hack and as they were riding south, he said, "You have been very good to Kate, and for that you have my gratitude."

"Does she mean that much to you?"

"She was aboard the *Gray Ghost*," Jason replied stiffly, "and therefore she is important to me."

"Kate is a wonderful person. My brother loved her and I find myself greatly attached to her too."

What sort of a personal relationship had developed between them? Jason wondered. He found no words to open the subject, however, so he had to let it pass.

"You seem quite taken with Bella," he said.

"An attractive woman. She has trouble with her upper register but she fakes it very well."

Jason laughed. "Tess, you're a hypocrite. All that guff about her appearing in the opera."

"Not a hypocrite—a diplomat. I think Bella can be important to me. Her interest in my work seems sincere and having a woman with her prestige on my side could be valuable."

Jason nodded. "What about Kate? Has she been ill?"

"Not to my knowledge. But after all, she went through a terrible experience. She must get her strength back."

When they reached the square, Gentry's carriage was nowhere in sight. "My God," Tess muttered. "Maybe he kidnapped her."

When they reached the flat, Peggy met them at the door. "A gentleman brought Kate home," she reported.

"Is he still here?" Tess asked.

"I assured him she would be all right and he left."

"*Is* she all right?"

"Oh yes. She went right to sleep."

310

Jason refused a nightcap and took his leave.

"It was a lovely evening," Tess said.

"Most enjoyable," he responded. "We must do it again sometime."

48.

The faintness passed, relaxed and sleepy in her warm bed, Kate allowed herself to dwell upon the evening: Jason sitting there so close to her; the tenderness and concern she'd had to hide under a cool exterior while she longed to touch him, to smooth the tiny furrows in his forehead with her fingertips.

I love him.... she thought, in the last moment before she fell asleep.

49.

When Jason left Tess he gave the address of Spanish Flats, but after a couple of blocks he changed his mind.

"Take me to the Union Club."

He was admitted on personal recognition—non-members were barred unless they were guests of a member—and went directly to the bar. He ordered whiskey straight, then consulted his watch. It was not terribly late—the evening at the International Club had been quite short considering all that had happened—perhaps his grandfather had not yet retired.

Jason called a page. "William Steele, is he in the club?"

"He left the dining room half an hour ago, sir. I am sure he went to his chambers."

"Take him a message, then. Tell him his grandson is here in the bar."

The page hurried away. Jason looked at himself in the mirror behind the bar and felt good at his decision. A true reconciliation with no reservations on his part; his grandfather deserved that much. He had given him so much. . . .

"Mr. Steele! How lucky to find you here!"

Jason turned and was looking into a florid, unhandsome face; a face he knew.

313

"Cabot—what are *you* doing here?" If Jason's tone was hostile, he'd meant it to be.

Dean Cabot stood by with just the right amount of silent deference.

"Are you a member?" Jason pressed.

"Oh no, hardly that. I am here by appointment to interview a city official. I just happened to catch sight of you. A happy circumstance."

"I'm afraid I don't share your enthusiasm."

Cabot's bulldog face eased into a wistful smile. "A reporter's life is hard, Mr. Steele. We are used to being unwelcome but we learn to live with it."

"Well, what do you want?"

"A favor, if you would be so kind. I have not been able to reach Miss McCrae for an interview."

"What do you expect me to do about it?"

"I thought perhaps you might see your way clear to helping me contact her."

"What makes you think I could do that?"

"Of course you could if you chose to. After your intimacy with her on your ship—"

Jason was relieved. From the first moment he'd set eyes on Cabot he had hoped for *some-thing*—anything—as an excuse to hit him, but he had not expected it to come so soon.

He turned and punched Cabot with all the strength his anger lent him.

Cabot clutched at the bar, staggered backward, and lost his hold. The floor of the bar was polished to icy smoothness. The reporter slid across it on his back, the derby hat, so closely identified with him, rolling after.

The barkeep was not a bouncer; an establish-

314

ment of the caliber of the Union Club did not need one. Nevertheless, he was over the bar in a single leap to lay restraining hands upon Jason. "Now, now, Mr. Steele. We can have none of this. Not in the club, sir—not in the club."

The barkeep seemed to be implying that it would be perfectly all right out in the street, but Jason was not looking for a brawl. He was satisfied with things as they were.

He took his hat and cape from a nearby chair. "Never mind. I'm leaving."

The page he had previously hailed had just returned to the bar. "Please give my grandfather my regrets," Jason said as he walked out.

He was too keyed up to consider the possible disgrace he had brought down on his grandfather by this most recent incident. He felt wonderful, his spirits feather-light as he hailed a hack and headed for Spanish Flats. As he fumbled with his key, the door was opened from within.

"Fellows! Isn't it a little late for you?"

"There is a visitor, sir. I could not leave until someone arrived."

"Mr. Gentry isn't home yet?"

"No, sir. Nor Miss Cantrell."

"Well, you can run along now. I'll take over for them."

"The visitor came to see *you,* sir. She's in the library."

She?

Jason threw his hat and cape at Fellows and hurried toward the library. He stopped just inside the doorway and gaped.

"Elizabeth! What in God's name are you doing here? How did you know where to find me?"

"Darling, you're more famous than you think. A simple inquiry to the *Post*—a little man with a bowler hat was very helpful. But aren't you glad to see me?"

"I'm—well, I'm certainly *surprised.*"

"I don't know why you should be. You must have known in your heart that I would come back to you."

Jason had never felt so confused. The wild idea flashed into his mind that his world had reversed and was spinning backward. God in heaven, didn't he already have enough troubles?

"It is always nice to see you, Elizabeth. Is Chester here in town with you?" A feeble try. He knew Chet was in Stonington.

"Jason! You certainly must have heard what happened. I haven't the faintest idea where Chester is, and I don't give a damn anyway."

She was as lovely as ever. Her beauty had once glowed like an unreachable star behind the propriety of the Penn name and Elizabeth's own illusion of maidenly innocence.

She was even more alluring now that the false image had been stripped away.

Elizabeth came forward. Suddenly her arms were around him and her sensual warmth flooded his being. But there was an urgency about her which puzzled Jason greatly.

He literally had to pry her off him. He held her at arm's length.

"Liz—for God's sake! I'm flattered that you've missed me so much but let's not lose our heads. You're a married woman."

She seemed not to take offense.

"Jason, why should a piece of paper bother us? What happened in Stonington was only an interruption. Now we can take up where we left off."

"It's not as simple as that, Liz."

"It is as simple as we want to make it. You have a lovely place here. I'm sure you were thinking of me when—"

"It isn't mine. It belongs to a friend. I'm only here as a guest."

"Then I'll be a guest too. I won't take up much room. Only the other side of your bed."

Jason was disturbed by her behavior. Even with the details Chet had given him, he had not imagined *this*. But his first thought was to get her out of the apartment. "That isn't possible. You must leave, Liz. You can't stay here."

"Not even for one little night?"

"Not even for that."

"But you can't just throw me out into the street."

Her attitude was so strange. There was no anger, no resentment. She remained gay, unoffended, as though all this was really of no consequence. But now was not the time to try and figure it out.

"Of course I won't throw you into the street," he said. "I'll get you a hotel room."

"Do you know of a place where they will take an unescorted lady? There can't be very many."

"I'll find one. Excuse me."

Jason left his unwanted guest seated in a chair with her shapely legs thrown over the arm. She blew him a kiss as he departed.

He cursed under his breath. Where the hell was Gentry?

Bella entered at that moment.

"Jason—what is it? You look positively ill."

"Tell me, do you know of a decent hotel where I can put up an unexpected guest? A *female* guest?"

"What is this, Jason? What's happened? Is Kate—?"

"Not *Kate!* Don't ask questions. Just help me."

"All right—calm down. The Algonquin, perhaps . . . I know—I have a friend with an apartment on Madison near Gramercy Park."

"Will she take my friend in?"

"Why not keep her here?"

"Damn it, answer me!"

"Good heavens, Jason, you *are* worked up. It's a man, a musician. He's away—New Orleans. I have a key to his place, as I promised to collect his mail. You can put her there if you wish. But she'll have to be out in a week."

"She will be. You're an angel. Give me the key and stand by."

"Just who is this guest of yours? I certainly have a right to know."

"Elizabeth Penn—or rather, Elizabeth Manson."

Bella's eyes widened. "The girl you were going to marry? What's she doing here?"

"I found her here when I got home."

"Where is her husband?"

"God only knows," Jason said impatiently. "Just give me that address and call a hack."

"Of course. Anything else I can do?"

"Stay close. I may have to drag her out by her heels."

But Elizabeth treated the whole thing as a lark. Bella, though highly intrigued, watched from the shadows of the dining room as Jason escorted Elizabeth through the foyer and out into the waiting hack.

After they were gone she tried to make some sense out of the incident in particular, and Jason in general. From what she had been given to understand about Jason in the past, his frenzy to rid himself of an attractive woman—and whatever else she was, Elizabeth Penn Manson was certainly that—married or not, was definitely out of character.

Bella shook her head and prepared to retire. One thing was certain: Jason had changed.

50.

The following morning Kate began getting telephone calls. The first voice, thrown off pitch by the instrument, was still recognizable.

"Mr. Gentry!"

"Miss McCrae. I am taking the liberty of calling to inquire about your health."

"You're very kind! I am quite well, thank you. And please call me Kate. We are not exactly strangers, you know."

"You honor me—Kate. I am so glad to hear that there are no aftereffects from last evening."

"You were very sweet, Mr.—ah, Calvin?"

"My friends call me Cal."

"Then I shall too."

"Assisting you was my privilege. I was wondering if, perhaps, when you are completely recovered, I might have the honor of calling upon you. Perhaps we could have dinner together."

Kate hesitated. He was so nice, so polite, and he had been very kind to her. "I would be delighted," she replied. "Some evening when I am up to it."

"Of course. I wouldn't dream of allowing you to tax your strength."

"Perhaps you would be so good as to call me next week?"

"I shall. And thank you so much."

"Good-bye—Cal . . ."

Why had she been so hesitant? she wondered. Calvin Gentry was certainly an eligible young man in every way; a little foppishly dressed, perhaps, but that was quite unimportant.

A second call almost immediately made her catch her breath. Perhaps *this* was Jason.

"Miss McCrae, this is Dean Cabot. I would like very much to talk to you."

"I see no point in that, Mr. Cabot. I have nothing to say to you."

"I am sorry to hear that, Miss McCrae. It would really be to your advantage. Some of the things you read in the papers were in error. If I could see you in person I am sure I could straighten you out on some of the misinformation."

"The misinformation, I believe, was *your* doing, Mr. Cabot."

"A reporter can be misquoted even in his own newspaper. One thing I did want to get from you, Miss McCrae, were your comments on Jason Steele's reconciliation with his former fiancée."

Kate gripped the receiver so hard her hand hurt.

"I don't know what you're talking about."

"Then you haven't heard? Elizabeth Manson came to the city and Mr. Steele installed her in an apartment on Gramercy Park, a very fashionable place."

"And why should I be interested?"

"I thought possibly you might, seeing as how you and the captain were so close on the ship and—"

"You are insulting!" Kate cried, and slammed the receiver into its hook. She viciously cranked the handle on the side of the box to signal the end of the call and stormed into the living room.

That disgusting man! And Jason Steele, too, for that matter. So he and Elizabeth were together once more! She never wanted to lay eyes on him again.

A fine resolution—except that she was in love with him.

Her anger resurfaced, but this time it was not directed at Jason. Was she going to let that snob from Stonington worm her way back into Jason's affections without a fight? So Jason had seen her; obviously, if he had installed her in an apartment. Jason had also entertained that girl Marita on the *Gray Ghost*, and Kate had forgiven him that. Or had she? Well, at least she had learned to live with it.

What it added up to was that if she wanted Jason, she had to be willing to go into the arena again and fight for him.

Curiously enough, Kate experienced a sense of elation, a relish for the coming battle. If the physical was the appropriate weapon, so be it! The next time they met, Jason would be in for a few surprises.

That left only one problem: the approach . . . a call to Bella Cantrell!

She telephoned the Spanish Flats, but got no answer. Then she spent the rest of the day trying to figure out how she was going to compete for Jason's attentions against a former fiancée obviously far ahead.

The right telephone call finally came the next morning. Tess tapped on her bedroom door. "Jason Steele is on the phone, dear . . ."

After taking the call, Kate came to the breakfast table, striving for calm, as though the call were a commonplace occurrence.

Tess, with her usual bluntness, asked, "What did he want?"

"To drop around this afternoon."

"Hmmm. Then it was not a dinner invitation?"

"Hardly."

"Then it could be something important."

Kate replied offhand, "I think he probably wants to inquire as to my health after what happened at the International Club."

"He could have done that over the phone."

She managed a noncommittal shrug. "I'll know what he wants when he gets here." But she hardly touched her food.

Tess was most accommodating. She and Peggy disappeared for the afternoon so that Kate could be alone with Jason. He arrived a little after two o'clock.

The early minutes of his visit were strained. Kate had difficulty with small talk; she was all aflutter inside, waiting for the reason for Jason's visit.

"Kate, there is something I want to say."

"Yes, Jason?"

In spite of her resolve to play the disinterested sophisticate, Kate moved closer to him and looked up into his face. She saw yearning there akin to her own. A kiss—one quick kiss would

323

not be out of place. She lifted her head and closed her eyes, waiting. It *must* be love that was turning the ever self-confident Jason Steele into a bashful schoolboy.

There was a kiss but somewhat more brief than she had hoped for. "Kate—"

"Yes, Jason?"

"You can't go on living here."

"No? What would you suggest?"

"I'm not sure. We must discuss it. But you can't stay here with Tess. She is . . ."

Kate's smile faded. "She is *what*, Jason?"

"Damn it, she's a lesbian! She makes love to women."

"Are you implying that Tess has made love to me?"

"Has she?"

"Why, you—you *bastard!*"

"I only asked. You must realize my concern for—"

"Your *concern?* Your snooping, prudish, impudence!"

"My God, is it prudish for a man to feel disgust at unnatural practices?"

"I'll have you know that Tess Wells is one of the finest women alive!"

"I didn't say she wasn't. I admire Tess very much."

"Well, you've got a fine way of showing it— walking in here and implying she is some kind of a monster."

"I didn't say that either. But I have every right to—"

"Right to what? To meddle in my life?"

"Kate—!"

324

"Get out! Just get out and leave me alone! I hate you, Jason Steele. I *hate* you!"

Kate turned her back, forcing herself not to cry. She would not reveal by a single tear that this—this *womanizer* had torn her heart to pieces.

After a moment she heard footsteps retreating, then there was the slamming of the front door—then silence.

Kate fled to her room and flung herself on her bed, her face buried in her arms.

Then she let the tears come.

51.

Jason gave the hack driver the address in Gramercy Park. He pounded impatiently on the door of Elizabeth Manson's temporary quarters. When the door opened, however, he was taken aback.

Elizabeth's hair was an uncombed tangle. Her eyes were red and there was a pallor to her cheeks. She wore only a chemise, one breast bare to the nipple. The only appeal in the picture she presented were her slim, beautifully turned legs.

But Jason scarcely noticed.

She eyed him blearily. "Jason—if I'd known you were coming . . ."

He picked her up in his arms and carried her through the small living room into the bedroom. She struggled out of surprise rather than anything else.

"Jason! What are you doing?"

"What you wanted me to do at Spanish Flats!"

"But I'm not in the mood."

"Well I am!"

He threw her on the bed and when she tried to rise he straddled her, jerking off the chemise.

"Stop it! You've gone mad!"

But Elizabeth did not fight him. Rather, she stared in bemusement as Jason grimly stripped off his clothes. Then he was upon her, driving hard with no thought to tenderness or even pleasure—only release. She could do nothing but hang on and endure.

Finally he disengaged himself. He turned from her as though she no longer existed, sitting on the edge of the bed, his face in his hands.

"Jason, I'm in trouble. I need your help."

"You *got* my help. I found you this place to stay—I imposed on my friends in your behalf. What more do you want?"

"I am grateful for that, but now it's different—"

"If you think this means anything, you're mistaken."

"Please *listen* to me!"

"You're married to Chester Manson, for God's sake!"

"I'm not talking about your coming here—it's all right. . . . Oh Jason, please *listen* to me!"

He dressed quickly. He had to get out of there. He had to get outside. . . .

"Stay out of trouble," he mumbled as he fled.

He left her staring after him—desolate, lonely, and terribly afraid. After the door slammed she went to the dresser and lifted up her purse. She dumped the contents onto the bed and pawed among them like a street scavenger. Whatever it was she wanted so desperately, it wasn't there.

She sat back in abject misery.

"Oh my God, my God . . . what will I do?"

52.

Back on the Avenue, Jason walked purposefully until he came to a saloon. There he paused but did not enter, moving on, walking swiftly for a man going nowhere.

The rage was disappearing, and regret seeped in, regret for the mistakes he'd made. He'd handled Kate all wrong. Why in God's name had he behaved like such a complete ass? Snooping—prudish—arrogant. Kate had been absolutely right. Actually, he liked Tess, he admired her. He just did not want Kate associating with her.

Of course Kate had not been completely reasonable either. She could have held her temper and let him explain. But now it was too late—he'd be damned if he'd crawl back like a whipped pup. And the chances of Kate seeking a reconciliation were nil.

Jason turned from mulling over Kate to thinking about Elizabeth. Not with any tinge of regret, however: He'd earned what he'd taken. But there *was* something bothering him—her condition.

He would have to go back; it was the only decent thing to do. But not now. Tomorrow . . .

53.

When Jason returned to the Flats, he found a visitor awaiting him.

"Chester! For God's sake!"

He hadn't seen or heard from Chet since that night in Stonington. Why did he have to turn up *now*—today—when Jason had just finished forcing himself on his wife? My God, did he *know*?

Jason examined him closely. He looked shabby, as though he had walked for hours, days, weeks, without regard for his personal appearance. He moved forward and seized Chester's hand in quick sympathy. "Man, you look as though you've been through hell!"

"Not exactly. Just roaming around, trying to get my thinking straightened out. Then I remembered you had given me your address and I decided to look you up."

As Chester spoke, Jason poured two brandies. Chester certainly looked as if he needed one, and Jason could sure use a drink.

"Well, I'm really glad you did. A bath, a meal, and a night's sleep and you'll be on course again."

Chester's reply was a tired smile. He sipped at his brandy. "To tell you the truth, I've been

329

worried about Elizabeth, not knowing where she is or how she is faring—even though we parted so bitterly. There was no word of her when I left Stonington, and I'm fairly sure the Penns don't know where she is either."

Jason thought quickly. If he was to tell Chester of Elizabeth's whereabouts it had to be right now, and to hell with the consequences.

"Elizabeth was here a short time ago, Chet."

Some of the weariness left Manson's face. "Then she's all right?"

Jason continued hurriedly, "We found her a temporary place to stay down on Gramercy Park. Now what you need is a good meal under your belt and some sleep. Then tomorrow you can go and see her."

"No, Jason. I'd better go now. Give me the address."

Jason saw that further attempts at persuasion would be useless. Obviously he was still in love with Elizabeth, the grandiose plans to go to San Francisco and become a ship builder just a lot of talk.

Poor Chet . . .

54.

Time passed in more or less orderly fashion. After the completion of the hearing, Ben Stein informed Jason that the findings would be presented to a grand jury. Kebble's plea for a special blue ribbon panel was refused; in accordance with normal procedures, there would be a convening of a grand jury in about two months.

Stein attempted to be reassuring. "Nothing to worry about, son. Kebble may not even get a true bill. The grand jury could find insufficient cause."

"But you don't think they will."

"It all depends on the Federal attorney—how hot he is on the case, how much Kebble goads him. But even if we do have to go to trial, there'll be a lot of water under the bridge in the meantime."

Jason had to be content with that.

He had not heard from Chester since directing him to Gramercy Park and Elizabeth. Bella told him that her musician friend would be delayed another week in New Orleans, leaving the apartment clear, and Jason used that as an excuse for not contacting the pair. When he finally went down to find out what was happening, both Elizabeth and Chester were gone. There was no message for him. He wondered if Elizabeth had told Chester what had happened before he showed up. It hardly seemed to matter now. He also wondered if he would ever see either of them again.

One evening when Cal was out, Jason was talking with Bella. Bella said, "I'm leaving here, Jason. I have made other arrangements."

"That *is* news. Have you told Cal?"

"No, but I will shortly."

"I wish you the best, Bella. May I ask where you are going?"

"I'm moving in with Tess Wells and Kate McCrae. Tess has plenty of room and she invited me."

"Good lord! I know you two profess to admire each other, but moving in with her . . ."

"We've gotten together several times, and I think it will work out just fine."

"How do you think Cal will take it?"

Bella frowned. "Honestly I don't think he will mind. He's changed lately, Jason. Have you noticed?"

"Can't say that I have, but we really haven't had much contact."

"He has become quieter, more remote. I think perhaps he has grown tired of me. You know Calvin was never a one-woman man."

"Has he been abusive in any way?"

"Oh, no. To the contrary. Even more gentle, more considerate."

"This is going to be a problem, Bella."

"A problem for you?"

"Partially. You see, I'm planning to change

332

digs also. I've never really belonged here. It was supposed to be just a temporary shelter until I got things straightened out. I've been looking around south of here. I've about decided on one of two places."

"We may be neighbors, then."

"That's possible, but I was thinking of Cal— both of us deserting him at the same time."

"It does seem a little inconsiderate but I think Calvin will survive. Actually I've felt lately that he would rather be alone."

"I hope that's true." Jason had no intention of changing his plans even if it were not.

As it worked out, Jason's fears as to his host's sensibilities were unfounded. When Gentry was told of his plans he said, "I understand, old man. Being up here away from everything is a bit difficult. Anyhow, it's been a nice visit and we mustn't lose track of each other."

"We certainly won't, Cal. You must come to my Washington Square place and let me pay back some of your hospitality."

"I'll look forward to it."

Jason now noted the change in Cal that Bella had mentioned. A remoteness that seemed out of character. Jason gave a mental shrug and turned his mind back to his own affairs.

He made the move into a small furnished flat on Waverly Place off Washington Square. Although the days still dragged slowly by, when Cletus Wing summoned him to announce that Ben Stein's fears had been confirmed, he was surprised to find that two months had passed.

The grand jury had indicted him, the trial set for mid-January, three months hence.

Jason took the news well, almost with a feeling of relief.

At least the other shoe had fallen. . . .

After numerous delays, Tess Wells's bicycle parade was arranged. She managed to assemble some seventy-five enthusiasts.

She gave a fiery speech in front of the shirt-waist factory, while amused passers-by looked on and the owners of the factory, two cigar-chewing men, watched angrily from above. The foreman of the shop walked among the machines, making sure that production did not lag—keeping the women away from the windows.

After the speech the participants mounted the bicycles Tess had rented and the cavalcade started north. Riding the cycles might have caused some difficulty had not all the ladies been clad in bloomers, a daring variation of the garment introduced by Elizabeth Smith Miller some fifty years earlier. The original costume consisted of a short skirt and full trousers; the new female garb was publicized by Amelia Jenks Bloomer in her magazine, *The Lilly*, and thus acquired her name. Now the skirt had been discarded, and the trousers shortened, and the more skimpy knee-length garment became universally known as bloomers. Tess's followers had no trouble straddling the bar extending from handlebars to seat, an established feature of all cycles since they were manufactured solely to be used by men.

They pedaled grimly northward, Tess leading the parade. Kate labored along behind her. She found the ride somewhat less than enjoyable but she handled the bicycle well enough, managing to steer around the pot holes and bulged-up bricks in the cobbled avenue.

When the militants reached Madison Square, a line of policemen was waiting for them.

The spokesman for the law, who identified himself as Captain Leo Barry, pointed his club at Tess and shouted, "In the name of the law, I command you to disperse."

"We refuse!" Tess shouted back.

"Those who refuse will be arrested as law-breakers."

"What law are we breaking?"

"There is a city ordinance forbidding females to ride bicycles built for males."

"Is there also a law forbidding us to breathe?" Tess mocked.

"Riding bicycles inside the city limits is a misdemeanor subjecting you to ten days in jail or a twenty-dollar fine or both. I have now informed you of the law."

"I know of the ordinance. It was passed by male tyrants almost fifty years ago. There is another law which you might bring to bear concerning a female deliberately displaying her legs in public. Did you miss that one?"

Captain Barry's face reddened in anger. "Are you deliberately violating the law?"

Some of the cyclists had dismounted. Others still straddled their bicycles. As Tess hurled her defiance at the law, however, Kate slipped quietly to the ground in a dead faint.

"See what you've done now, you brute?" Tess cried as some of the women ran to Kate's aid. "Is there no limit to the lengths you will go in your persecution?"

Captain Barry was thrown off balance. Quite a few gentlemen of the press were in evidence, with two artists busily sketching the scene.

"Call an ambulance," Barry ordered, and one of his subordinates hurried off to obey.

But an ambulance was not necessary. Although Bella Cantrell had refused to ride in the protest—"Tess, darling, I sympathize with your cause but I don't need *that* sort of publicity." She had come to the Square as an observer.

Kate was stirring feebly when Bella reached her side. Bella signaled to her carriage, and she and the driver lifted Kate inside.

The action had stopped during this scene. Now it resumed.

"I call upon you to disperse," Captain Barry repeated.

"We refuse," Tess answered again. She was obviously quite delighted with the way things had gone. She smiled in triumph as a patrol wagon drove up and she was loaded into it, bike and all.

Tess's followers were not as enthusiastic about jail as their leader. Unnerved by the jeers and insults hurled at them by the sneering males standing about, they listened nervously to Captain Barry's instructions. "I command you all to dismount and take those vehicles back to where you got them. Any of you who disobey will be arrested."

The protest ended with Tess under arrest and the ladies trundling their bikes south to the Paramount Cycle Company where Tess had rented them.

Bella had taken Kate back to the flat.

"You *must* see a doctor, Kate. Something is

336

seriously wrong. You went through so much on that ship—and all those days you spent in an open boat. You probably have some lingering illness."

"I'm not sick," Kate protested. "There's nothing wrong with me."

"You can't be sure. It may be lung fever."

"Tuberculosis? No, Bella, it's not that—my lungs are in excellent shape." She closed her eyes briefly.

"Then what—?"

Kate sighed.

"I'm pregnant, Bella."

55.

Tess's lawyers were prompt and efficient and she was home within two hours.

She found Bella in the parlor, quietly sipping chocolate.

"Well—?" she said sharply.

Bella smiled innocently. "Well, *what*, dear?"

"What would I be inquiring about—the state of the nation? How is Kate?"

"Just fine, just fine."

"You got her home all right then." Tess poured herself a cup of chocolate then scowled at it. "You may not be worried, but frankly, *I am*. This was her second attack. Or is it the third?"

Bella relented. "Tess, I'm sorry. I shouldn't have been so flippant. There is nothing wrong with Kate—unless pregnancy is a disease."

Tess almost dropped her chocolate. "Pregnant! Oh my God!"

Bella laughed. "Darling—don't take it so hard. After all, Kate *was* a married woman."

"I'm not taking it hard. It's just that—well, it's such a surprise. If she had only told us earlier! I would never have allowed her to get on a bicycle. Do you think—?"

"That it injured her in any way? I'm sure it didn't." Bella's teasing manner had changed.

This caused Tess to ask, "But there *is* something?"

"Nothing we can't take care of ourselves. The poor child was frightened—quite depressed, really. I finally got her to sleep."

"Frightened? Doesn't she want the baby?"

"Oh, nothing like that. It's the publicity. Kate has been battered from pillar to post by the press. Those disgusting reporters always sneaking about trying to haul her onto their front pages. She is afraid that when word of this gets out it will be worse. With Jason's trial coming up and all, Kate has had quite enough of being in the public eye."

Tess nodded. "As you say, it's something we can take care of. That is if she will cooperate."

"I'm sure we're thinking along the same lines."

"No doubt. She can vanish from the scene, so to speak. There are places. In fact I know of one where discretion is the watchword. Kate has only to select another name, an alias—"

"What sort of care would she receive?"

"The very best." Tess had set down her cup and was counting on her fingers. "Let's see, she was married to Peter three months ago . . ."

"Closer to four."

"Then we haven't got all the time in the world. We must talk to her."

Bella regarded her new friend with affectionate amusement. "Darling, how will it feel to be an aunt?"

"I'll no doubt survive," Tess answered a little stiffly.

"This place you mentioned—"

"It's in White Plains. The Westmore Clinic. It's run by Dr. Hartman, one of the finest obstetricians in the country."

Bella's fine eyes were twinkling. "Hmm—"

"Hmm *what?*"

"I was just wondering how you happened to know of it. You don't by chance have a little cuddler of your own hidden about somewhere?"

"Bella—!"

Bella enjoyed ruffling Tess's feathers at times. Her friend was so completely dedicated to the cause she needed to be teased out of her seriousness once in a while. Bella now raised a defensive hand.

"Sorry, but you know I have a very devious mind."

"It just so happens that I know of a situation or two. Names I would never mention. But you must realize that even the upper classes get into embarrassing situations once in a while."

"Oh, I can believe that." Bella decided it was time to change the subject. "How did the march go after I left?"

Tess brightened. "It went off perfectly. I was afraid for a time that they would refuse to arrest me but they did. Now I'll demand a jury trial and scream to high heaven about the panel being all male."

"How Machiavellian!" Bella murmured. "Tess, you positively astound me."

56.

Fall came brilliantly to New York State that year and the extensive acreage around the very private sanctuary for soon-to-be mothers were ablaze with flaming poplar, oak, and maple; yellows, reds, and shades of copper turned the grounds into a fairyland. Kate's neat little cottage was so situated that all of the outdoors was at hand just beyond her windows.

There were paths and she walked a great deal, and in her solitude, she reveled at the stirring in her body and dreamed of great futures in store for that eager, kicking little mite of life.

The conspirators—if that was the word—in Kate's disappearance were now three in number. This had been Bella's doing. Tess, the hardy one, always came alone to visit Kate, riding her bicycle over the rough roads beyond the city. Bella, however, demanded an escort, and Calvin Gentry had been selected. This had proved to be a fortunate choice. Tess and Bella, with affairs of their own, could not manage too many visits but Cal Gentry was constancy itself, never coming less than twice a week.

Kate was grateful for the attention, but it did pose problems. With a sure instinct, she knew that Cal was in love with her. Over the weeks, the formality had lessened and his intent had become apparent, an open declaration of love certain to come. And with her lying-in period almost over, she had a strong feeling that this would be the day.

Kate had anguished for many hours over her reply. There was still that old gnawing misery. Jason—Jason—*Jason!* Always there in the back of her mind to surge forward unexpectedly at odd moments and always with the grinning specter of defeat interwoven. That last terrible scene at Washington Square had separated them forever; the wall of pride between them was too great.

So the wheel of Karma had turned and it was just as it had been on the *Gray Ghost*: She yearned for one man while circumstance and common sense directed her into the arms of another.

This time, however, it would be different. There would be no panic, no spur-of-the-moment decisions.

At the proper moment, a firm, quiet *yes*.

She *would* marry Cal Gentry. . . .

"Kate dear—how wonderful you look!"

He took her hands in his as she laughed and replied, "Cal, how can you say that, with my bulging tummy and duck waddle."

"You never looked so lovely. But it is a little chilly out here. Shouldn't you be inside?"

"Perhaps it is time. Would you like a cup of tea?"

"Nothing would please me more."

As they walked slowly toward Kate's cottage, she wondered about the stories she had heard from Bella about Cal's loose women and reputation for fast living. And of course she knew about Bella's relationship with him. Kate had never seen that side of him. He was the kindest, most gentle person she had ever met, this man who had been ever there when she most needed him.

The parlor of her cottage was a large room, sparsely furnished as compared to the over-stuffed decor so popular among the wealthy of the period. Clutter had been avoided in favor of plain but comfortably functional pieces. Hard maple polished to a warm, glowing sheen predominated.

"I have the water on," Kate said. "T'll be but a moment." She took the whistling kettle from its hook over the burning log in the fireplace and retired to the small kitchen, to return with the tea service on a cart. There was silence while she brewed and served the tea.

"The leaves will go soon and the trees will be bare. But with snow on them they will be just as beautiful," she chattered nervously.

Cal ignored both the tea and her comment. He stood up and with two limping steps was beside her on the settee.

"Kate—darling—you must let me speak."

Her look of surprise was a bit of acting that would have done Bella proud.

"You must know by now that I love you."

"Cal, you have been most kind—far more so than I deserve."

"But you must have seen it for more than kindness."

"Yes, Cal, I have."

"And you had to know that when I found the

343

courage I would bring up what is closest to my heart. Darling, I am asking you to marry me."

"Oh, Cal—I don't know what to say—"

"You have been through hell, dearest—I know that. You lost your husband in a tragedy which would have destroyed a weaker woman. Now you will bear his child and put the pieces of your life together, and I want to be a part of it. I want to be close to you and give you my love and protection for the rest of our lives."

When Kate remained silent, he asked, "Is there anyone else? Is there anyone I must compete with for your love?"

Kate gained a curious relief from the question. It gave her the chance to say the words, "No, Cal. There is no one."

When it seemed that Kate would say no more, Cal murmured, "Darling, I have been selfish. While you face this coming ordeal, I thought only of myself, not considering your state of mind, heaping more upon it. But please—don't turn me away."

"Cal! I could never turn you away!"

"Then there is hope—"

He broke off abruptly and got to his feet. "I've overtaxed you," he said gently. "I'll leave now and let you rest."

Kate seized his hand. "But you'll come back, won't you?"

"Of course!" He smiled. "Darling, it would be impossible to keep me away."

Alone, Kate sat for a long time staring at the glowing logs in the fireplace. Her lips moved as she whispered harshly into the silence:

"Damn you, Jason Steele! *Damn you!*"

57.

Jason was not happy. The days dragging by were like leaden boots weighing his feet to the ground. He wondered often about Kate, about what had become of her, but he did not inquire. Their last confrontation had had a final ring to it. He thought she had probably gone into seclusion somewhere and he saw that as a good thing. Public interest in the whole sensational affair had died down because of lack of new material to keep it alive, but the gentlemen of the press were ever alert to revive the story.

With nothing to do but wait, with enforced idleness harder and harder to bear, Jason tried gambling to pass the time. He started frequenting the Casino Club, a rendezvous of the racier set. He played cards, threw the dice, and tried his hand at roulette. He drifted from one game to another. He was not a gambler at heart; the true gambler finds his game and sticks to it. He won and he lost but not enough in either direction to make gambling really interesting as a diversion.

One afternoon, the mystery of Chester and Elizabeth's disappearance was cleared up. He returned to his Washington Square apartment from the Casino Club and found Chester waiting for him.

Chester looked beaten, even worse than that last time. His clothes were seedy, and soiled. He was pale and there were dark circles under his eyes. He said, "I hope you don't mind. I told your landlord I'm an old friend and he let me in."

"That's perfectly all right . . ." Jason began.

Chester glanced down at himself and grimaced. "I know I look like the very devil, but—"

"What happened to you and Elizabeth? I went down to Gramercy Park and you were both gone. I didn't know *what* to think."

"I could apologize, of course, but that would be futile. When I got there, Jason, and saw what kind of shape she was in, I—well, I just got her out of there as quickly as I could."

Jason waited for him to go on, aware of an overlay of embarrassment in his friend.

"I took her to a little flat I found on Thirty-fourth Street. We've been there since then—up to now."

"I see," Jason said, although he didn't. He moved to the liquor cabinet. "Brandy?"

Chester shook his head. "Jason, I came here about Elizabeth."

Jason prepared himself to pay for his sin, for betraying this man he valued as a friend by raping his wife. God, how terrible that sounded now as the thought echoed through his mind! But Chester was in no way belligerent; depressed, rather, his face tense with worry.

"Jason, I'm in a hell of a lot of trouble."

"Anything I can do, old friend—anything."

"I'm broke. I need a loan."

"So far so good. You came to the right place."

"A big loan, Jason. Five thousand dollars."

Jason showed only the briefest flash of surprise before saying, "What you need is up to you, Chet. You know that."

"It's damned fine of you. I need it for Elizabeth."

Jason now understood one thing beyond all doubt: Chester's bitterness during their talk back in Stonington had stemmed from a hurt and anger he had not been able to suppress. He still loved Elizabeth and always had.

"If you need cash we can go right down to the Morgan bank and get it."

"Cash would help. There are some pressing bills. But first I want you to go with me to see Elizabeth. I want you to know exactly what the money is for."

The request was logical, coming from Chet Manson, Jason thought. He was too damned ethical for his own good. "That isn't necessary," he said. "*You* know the situation, whatever it is. I have the feeling it's a collapse of some kind. She did not appear too stable when I saw her."

"It's a collapse all right," Chester replied grimly. "Please come with me, Jason."

Their destination was Bellevue Hospital. This in itself did not surprise Jason, but something else did. A white-coated orderly took them to the door of a room and said, "Don't be too long, gentlemen," before he unlocked the door and hurried off.

Before opening the door, Chester reached

into his pocket. "Did you ever see one of these things?"

Jason stared at the object in Chester's hand. "A hypodermic needle?"

"Right. It's what she was using when I found her."

"I must have been blind!"

"Not your fault. She kept it secret." Chester returned the needle to his pocket.

She had asked for his help—begged for it, and he'd turned away. A little time—a few questions, and he would have known the truth! Jason Steele, you should be horsewhipped, he cried silently.

"We'll go in now," Chester said. "I think seeing you will cheer her up."

But that was not the case. Chester preceded Jason through the doorway into what was more a cell than a room. Jason saw, lying on a cot, the pitiful wreck that had once been a beautiful girl.

Her eyes lit up at sight of Chester, then she saw Jason. Her worn face turned into a mask of rage. The change was so sudden neither of them was prepared for what happened next.

Elizabeth leaped up and crouched on the edge of the cot, her bare feet hard against the uncarpeted floor. "Get that monster out of here! Get him out or I'll kill him! I swear it! I'll scratch his eyes out! That filthy bastard deserves to die!"

Obscenities as foul as any Jason had ever heard on land or sea spewed from her lips as she lunged forward. Chester caught her before she reached Jason. She struggled against his restraint, her fingers curled into claws as she strained toward the object of her hatred.

"You'd better go," Chester said, clearly shocked.

"I'll wait outside." Jason left the room. As he did so, an attendant came running, drawn by Elizabeth's screams. He entered the room and closed the door behind him.

58.

"Bottoms up, old man. You need it."

Chester Manson downed the double bourbon in one gulp. Jason refilled his glass from the bottle on the table and Chester ran a finger moodily over the beads on the rim.

With Elizabeth quieted, Jason had taken Chester directly to the nearest saloon, where they were seated in a booth.

"It began before you two were engaged—back in Stonington. There isn't much heroin around those parts but one of the bastards she met during a regatta she went to had some. She only sniffed the stuff at first but she liked the effect and kept at it. Later she started using the needle. I think that was after Jethro broke up your engagement and before I married her. I don't know why she lashed out at you particularly. I guess anyone in the shape she's in can be expected to do almost anything."

"Chester, there's something you should know. I visited Liz once after finding her that flat. I went there and—well, I forced myself on her. That may have been the reason."

Chester stared across at Jason, his eyes centered on Jason's weskit. "Christ," he muttered.

350

"What am I supposed to do now? Get up and hit you with this bottle?"

There was anguish not anger in the words; a pathetic questioning of fate itself, lamenting this added problem laid on top of all the rest of it.

"Damn it, man! Why didn't you just keep it to yourself?"

"Then Liz didn't tell you."

"Hell, she's been attacked by phantom ghouls and goblins until she can't tell one from the other."

"How could I have been so blind? I walked away and left her there in her own private hell."

"We all make mistakes," Chester said wearily. The subject of Jason's attack upon Elizabeth seemed to be closed.

"I've got to get her out of Bellevue," Chester said. "It's too hard for her the way they do it—cold, off the stuff completely."

"Have you got a place in mind?"

"Yes. There's a Doctor Wendrow with a clinic down on Maiden Lane. It's called a rest home but it's a clinic where dope fiends and alcoholics are helped to break their habits. Some very big-name people are in there."

"Do you think Liz wants to be cured?"

"Christ yes! She's done everything she can to help herself there in Bellevue. All she needs is a little outside help."

"Then let's see that she gets it. Come on, we'll take a walk. . . ."

Half an hour later, Jason put five thousand dollars in cash into Chester Manson's hand.

"You know where I live, Chet. Anything more I can do, just let me know."

Chester turned and left without a word of thanks, but Jason understood. He silently wished him luck.

Jason walked slowly toward the Battery—up Wall Street, and into Trinity churchyard. The weather was chill. Sharp little wind devils stirred dried leaves, sending them against the old headstones. His spirits were as low as they had ever been. He thought of Kate McCrae, her lovely, vibrant little face as he'd seen it aboard his ill-fated ship. He lived again with her anger as it had flared up at him in all its young fury. He did not dare give room to the priceless moments he'd held her naked in his arms. The fire, the answering passion—they were too painful to remember.

At this moment he would gladly have run to her, begged her forgiveness, told her of his love, and reached for her with all the hunger of his heart.

Silly thoughts. He knew very well that even if he could discover where she was he would never reach out to her: Pride would intervene. Jason Steele did not know how to beg. He knew only how to take.

"The hell with it," he muttered as he left the bleak cemetery. "To hell with everything . . ."

59.

The month of February, 1904, brought cruelly cold weather to New York. The poor suffered, most of the very wealthy fled to warmer places, and the middle class huddled into their overcoats and struggled on through the snow and the slush.

There were several events of note.

On February tenth, the long delayed trial— *The People* v. *Jason Steele*—got under way.

On the twelfth, at 3:00 A.M., a young woman, registered at the Westmore Clinic in White Plains under the name of Mary Clinton, gave birth to an eight-pound boy.

On the twenty-ninth, a three-month delay not of Ben Stein's making was granted in the Steele trial when Rebecca Steele died quietly in her chair in the morning room of the Steele mansion in Stonington, Connecticut. The Federal attorney, David Griffen, did not object strenuously to the overlong delay because one of his prime witnesses had been located in San Francisco and arrangements were being made to bring him east.

The most sensational turn of events came on the last day of that month when a front-page story under the byline of Dean Cabot appeared in the *Evening Post*:

HEROINE OF *GRAY GHOST* DISASTER GIVES BIRTH TO SON
Post Reporter Unveils Mystery

As a result of the untiring efforts of this reporter, he is able to reveal to the readers of the Post *that a son has been born to Kate Wells, the widow of Peter Wells, the ill-fated second mate who died a fiery death during the sinking of the whale ship* Gray Ghost *in the late spring of last year.*

A mysterious element of the story was uncovered when this reporter's investigations revealed that Kate Wells went into hiding prior to the birth of her son. She entered the Westmore Clinic, a fashionable medical retreat in White Plains, New York under the assumed name of Mary Clinton. Her reasons remain unexplained as neither this reporter nor any other has been able to reach the new mother for an interview. An attempt to reach prominent financier Godfrey Wells, the grandfather, was also unsuccessful. The public is advised to watch the pages of the Post *for new developments.*

It is of further interest to note that Jason Steele, scion of the illustrious whaling family of Stonington, Connecticut is now on trial for criminal negligence while acting as commander of the vessel upon which Peter Wells met his death. The trial is now in recess due to the demise of

354

Rebecca Steele, grandmother of the defendant.

Around town, other gentlemen of the press groaned in unison. That son-of-a-bitch with the bulldog face had done it again! The bastard would go to any lengths to reveal the pain and suffering of people who in all decency should be left to themselves. He did beat out Hearst, though. You had to give him credit for that. . . .

60.

There were various reactions to Dean Cabot's revelations in the *Post*, and probably that of Godfrey Wells was the most violent. He had retired early on the previous night and at breakfast got the story as picked up by Hearst, who had put out an extra. He then referred back to Dean Cabot's article, snorting his displeasure as he read it.

Throwing both papers to the floor, he glared at his wife. "Did you read it?"

"Yes," Beatrice replied. "Isn't it nice? Now we have a grandson we can cuddle and spoil just like other grandparents. A baby changes everything. We can invite the little mother to come and live with us and—"

"Are you out of your mind? Do you think for one minute I would let my grandson remain in the hands of that kind of a woman?"

"But Godfrey—she's the baby's *mother!*"

"I think you'd better just keep your mouth shut if you've got no more sense than you are now displaying. You could do irreparable damage to my plan."

Beatrice's chin quivered but there was no greater reaction than that. She was used to her husband's abuse.

"Godfrey," she asked after a moment, "are you planning to take the child away from our daughter-in-law?"

"Daughter-in-law? She's no relation of ours! I'm surprised that you don't see the situation in its correct light. Of course I'm going to take our grandchild away from her—a woman like that!"

Always trying to make the best of a situation, Beatrice said, "I suppose having the baby all to ourselves *would* be a good thing. We will turn one of the bedrooms near ours into a nursery and find a nanny with the best of qualifications . . ."

Godfrey was not listening. He was cranking the phone viciously and when the operator came on he barked a number.

In a short while, the operator gave Wells the wire into the home of David Brandt of Quincy, Brandt & Associates.

An hour later, David Brandt was in Wells' living room, the early morning sleep he had been enjoying barely out of his eyes.

Godfrey had never seen any reason to be gracious to underlings, even senior partners of prestigious law firms. He purchased their services, which made them lackeys in his eyes. "Brandt, I don't want any of your legal blunders in this matter. I want it to go through with all possible speed. You will petition the Domestic Court, I presume."

"Quite right, Mr. Wells."

"How long should it take?"

"I'd say about two months."

"Too long. Far too long."

357

"We must prepare our case. Investigate your daughter-in-law's background—"

"For God's sake, don't call her my daughter-in-law. We are only technically related. I was ready to proceed against her when she came ashore but my daughter appealed to my sympathies and I allowed her to do so. It was a mistake."

"We will go ahead with all possible speed but there is the court docket. It may be crowded."

"You certainly have *some* influence."

"We will do our best," Brandt replied with dogged patience, "but I would not want to mislead you. I would say that two months—"

"Oh, very well. But I want periodic reports on your progress. For what I pay you people, that's little enough to ask."

Brandt left, happy to get out of Wells's abrasive presence.

61.

With Dean Cabot's exposé, there was no reason for Kate to remain undercover any longer. As soon as she was cleared by her doctor at the clinic, she returned to Tess Wells's flat preparatory to locating a place of her own. Her son was christened Clinton James Wells, the middle name that of Bella Cantrell's father and given in thanks for Bella's help and loyalty.

The search for a flat went slowly, what with things so comfortable at Tess's and Peggy Dale's slavish devotion to the baby. She hovered over him, proudly wheeling him in Washington Square as if he were her own.

This was the situation when the bombshell fashioned by Godfrey Wells broke over Kate's head. Tess tried to reassure her.

"I'll go and talk to him. I'm sure it's a bluff. I handled him before and I'll handle him again. . . ."

Tess failed. Returning to the flat she conferred with Bella before breaking the news to Kate. "He wouldn't even see me. I lowered myself in that house, I truly did. I fairly got down on my knees to my mother, begging her to plead with him but even she refused."

"How terrible!"

"It is because he is a coward, of course. He was *afraid* to face me. But that's not important. The important thing is that he will go ahead and try to take Kate's baby away from her."

"Can he succeed?"

"I'll be able to tell you better after I talk to my lawyer."

John Haines of Gable and Haines listened attentively to Tess—the whole story as she saw it—before breaking in. "Tess, I sympathize with you. I don't believe any child should be taken from its mother except in the most drastic situations. But I also respect your father's intelligence. Granted he is the cruel, heartless person you describe, he is still no fool and he does not fight for hopeless causes. He must have some telling material against your Kate Wells. I'm afraid your description of her is somewhat biased. If she were as you describe, your father would not have a chance of winning."

"Then you refuse to represent her?"

"I did not say that. What I am saying is that I must have the facts—all the facts—if I am to proceed with any hope at all."

"There *are* some negative aspects in Kate's background but they are things over which she had no control."

"Suppose I talk to the young lady. I would have to do that anyhow if we represent her."

"Of course. I'll speak with her first. As yet I don't think she realizes the odds against her."

"Another thing, Tess. We are corporation lawyers. We have had no experience in criminal cases or in the domestic courts. However, if

360

we take the case, we will find you the best possible man for the job."

"I guess I can ask no more than that," Tess said and returned to Washington Square.

Kate took the news with far less distress than Tess expected. In truth, she was quite calm.

"No one," Kate said, "is going to take my baby away from me."

"Of course not."

"I'll bundle him up and leave New York City."

"No, darling, that is not the thing to do under any circumstances. You don't know my father when he gets the bit in his teeth. He is relentless. He will find you wherever you are and hound you. He will hire private detectives to follow you around. He will make your life miserable. You must stay here and fight."

"You are probably right. I don't want to spend the rest of my life dragging Clinton from one hiding place to another."

"Now you're being sensible."

"Tess, no one is going to take my son away from me."

It was a laudable determination but if Kate could have followed John Haines in his search for a likely attorney she might have begun to have her doubts. In going over the list of those most qualified, he hit upon the name of Ben Stein, a quite logical choice. Stein might be busy, but then he always was. It was worth a try. He just might accept the brief.

Haines and Stein had lunch at Delmonico's and Stein listened as Haines detailed the situation. His reply was disappointing.

"John, I couldn't take the case if I wanted to. I'm handling one already which would constitute a conflict of interest. You corporation fellows keep yourselves so far back in your plush bottom chairs that you miss what goes on around you. I'm representing young Steele in the *Gray Ghost* criminal negligence case. As a result I know quite a lot about Kate Wells."

"Of course. It completely slipped my mind."

"A word of advice, though. If I were you I wouldn't represent her."

"I beg your pardon?"

"Unless you relish losing cases."

"I don't understand."

"What I am saying, John, is that you don't have a prayer. With what Wells can dig up in regard to that girl's background and with his high-powered legal machine, he'll tear her to pieces and have the child out of her arms in a matter of days. A mere law student could win over the telephone."

"You are most encouraging, Ben," Haines said sarcastically.

"Just giving you the facts. Say, this coffee is damned good. I think I'll have another cup. . . ."

On the way back to his office Haines considered the difficulties that lay ahead in the terms Ben Stein had outlined. Haines did not for a moment consider rejecting the case now. But the matter of finding another good lawyer became vital.

62.

In May of that year, the case of the *People* v. *Jason Steele* again got under way. It was over-shadowed in the public press, however, by the Domestic Court confrontation between Kate McCrae Wells and Godfrey Wells. Public interest was higher in the latter case for two reasons: the Jason Steele affair had dragged on for so long that the public was tired of it—a situation Ben Stein had labored deliberately to bring about; while Godfrey Wells's efforts to get custody of his grandson had the gossipy flavor of a family quarrel out in the open, the details spicier by far.

After a thorough search, John Haines settled for a young lawyer, Keith Burns, who was making a name for himself in defense of women's rights. Burns had lately been awarded compensation for an elderly couple whose daughter died of tuberculosis brought about by the hellish conditions in a local garment factory. The judgment caused quite a stir, and generated anger and resentment in the industry. It also earned Burns the reputation as a crack trial lawyer.

Jefferson Keenan, the associate David Brandt had selected to represent Godfrey Wells, was not as spectacular or as brilliant as Burns but he was a plodder and did his pre-trial work exhaustively.

The evidence against Kate was damning from the outset.

Lucas Peavey, brought down from Stonington to testify, stated the following in essence:

He and his wife had taken Kate in off the street out of the goodness of their hearts, and she had proved to be trouble from the start. Customers in his tavern began complaining about her advances. He had reprimanded her several times, and out of fear that her continued presence would give the tavern a bad name, he insisted that she leave.

Clara Peavey added a bit more color to her husband's testimony:

"The girl was no good. She made advances to my husband and tried to supplant me in his affections. I endured it as long as possible, longer than I normally would have because my husband is of good heart and tried to be a father to the girl."

Keith Burns encountered resistance in his cross-questioning: Judge Jacob sustained Keenan's objections on a ratio of three to one. The good judge maintained that he was not going to allow decent people of the Peaveys' ilk to be maligned in his court by a troublemaking lawyer.

Guy Mapes was subpoenaed to testify as to Kate's presence on the *Gray Ghost*, and while he was reluctant to blacken her reputation, his sworn testimony under oath did exactly that.

The trial moved swiftly, and Burns, a man not given to illusions, told Tess, "It looks bad—very bad. Calling Kate to refute the Peavey testimony and accuse that old scoundrel of rape would only prejudice Jacob even further. I think you had better prepare our client for the probability that she is going to lose her child."

Meanwhile, Jason Steele's trial was going well for the defendant. Ben Stein, through skillful legal work, had constructed a strong case: Jason had listened to the rumors about the ship and had *not* ignored them; he had instituted a search for the suspected dynamite but none had been found. To have put John Saipan in irons on the information he actually had would have been infringing upon the seaman's rights as an individual. No one could say with any authority what had happened in the forecastle prior to the explosion. It could have been an accident, or one of the two men sent to guard Saipan could have been the true culprit.

All in all, the trial was going well. "We'll get the right verdict, never fear," Stein told his aides.

Although Jason's trial would drag on, that of Kate as a fit mother was coming to a conclusion. Another day—another two days—and it would be over.

Jefferson Keenan informed Godfrey Wells of the progress and assured him that the verdict in his favor was certain. Godfrey went home and told his wife to start preparing the nursery. "The baby will be here before we know it."

Late that afternoon, he received a call from

a man he'd heard of but did not know personally:

"Mr. Wells, my name is Calvin Gentry. I would like to talk to you."

Calvin Gentry. Oh, yes, that rounder who got his name in the papers now and again. A scandalous young whelp.

"What do you want to talk to me about, Mr. Gentry?"

"About Kate McCrae Wells, sir."

Interesting. Most interesting. If the little tart was mixed up with people of the Gentry ilk, that was another point in Godfrey's favor.

"What about the girl, Gentry?"

"I would rather discuss it when we meet."

Godfrey considered. Nothing that Gentry could tell him would help Kate in the least. The case was already won but anything he could do to further damage the girl would be to his added satisfaction.

"Very well, Mr. Gentry, I'll talk to you. Not here in my home, however. I'll meet you outside."

"Excellent. How about St. Thomas Church? I will be in front, waiting for you."

"An hour?"

"I'll be there. . . ."

At the appointed time, Calvin Gentry limped toward the carriage which pulled up in front of the church. "Mr. Wells?"

"Correct, young man. Get in beside me. We can drive around."

Wells was mildly surprised. He'd heard of Gentry's escapades, his flamboyance, and had not expected a young man so quietly dressed. To all appearances, Gentry could have been one of his own subordinates, or a clerk at Tiffany's or wherever.

Gentry quickly appraised the situation. Wells' coachman was high up and forward, and not in a position to hear a quiet conversation. He climbed in beside Wells and the carriage pulled away.

"Now, young man," Wells said briskly, "what have you to tell me concerning Kate McCrae?"

"Her last name is Wells, I believe."

"I have never recognized the marriage."

"You are taking her baby away from her."

"That's common knowledge. Let's get down to cases. What was your reason for contacting me?"

"To warn you, sir."

"Warn *me?* About what?"

"Your personal safety."

"I don't understand."

"Then I shall make myself plain. If you take Kate's child away from her, I shall kill you."

The statement was made so quietly, with such lack of emotion, that Godfrey did not identify it as a physical threat. Gentry was referring to something else—damage to his reputation? Destruction of his business? The situation was almost amusing.

"And just how do you plan to do that?"

"I shall take a pistol, point it at your head, and pull the trigger."

"Are you saying you would actually *kill* me?"

"I don't know how to put it any plainer, Mr. Wells."

"You are talking like an idiot! What is your interest in my grandson's mother?"

"I have an affection for her. Losing the child would literally destroy her. If that happens I feel it only just that you too be destroyed."

"Then why don't you kill me now? Wouldn't that prevent me from taking the child?"

"You have not yet accomplished your purpose. There is always the chance you may not be able to."

This was most interesting, Godfrey thought; sitting there quietly discussing his possible murder. He marveled at his own courage and self-control, even though Gentry's threat was absurd on the face of it.

"But it is a foregone conclusion that I will win custody."

"In that case, I will kill you."

"You really mean that, don't you?"

"I was never more serious in my life."

The promise was disturbing, but not frightening. It was a desperate threat and nothing else. However, Godfrey now wished that Gentry would show a little more emotion; some indication of being an unbalanced man making a desperate, empty attempt to intimidate him.

And then Gentry took a small derringer from his pocket. "This is the weapon I will use, and there is no way you can escape being killed if that becomes my objective. You cannot hide indefinitely. Bodyguards would be of no value to you because time would be on my side."

"Are you telling me that you would be willing to hang for my murder?"

"I might not hang. But in answer to your question—yes, I am willing to risk hanging."

"You must love the girl very much to be willing to risk your life."

"Mr. Wells," Gentry replied politely, "my feelings about Kate Wells are none of your business."

"I suppose not. . . . Now am I expected to cringe in terror and tell you I will withdraw my claim?"

"That is up to you, sir."

"My answer is quite simple. Get out of my carriage and be on your way."

"I will be happy to if you will tell your man to pull up."

As he returned home, Godfrey was quite proud of himself. He had faced an incident totally new in his experience and carried it off well. He congratulated himself. He had looked at the weapon which Gentry said he would use as a tool of murder, and had scorned it and the man. It was too bad that his stand could not become a part of his public image. It would certainly enhance the respect others had for him.

He had difficulty getting to sleep that night. Not, of course, because of the idle murder threat. Rather, it was due to excitement, the certainty that tomorrow his son's child would be awarded into his custody.

63.

"Kate, it looks bad—very bad."

Even without Burns' gloomy predictions, the prospect of defeat had become more and more certain as Keenan's witnesses testified. Tess's regret now was that she had advised Kate against running away. When she had done so, she had truly believed they would win. And now it was too late for Kate to flee.

Tess was relieved that Kate was taking it so well. The latter remained calm—too calm—and merely reiterated the oft-made declaration:

"Nobody is going to take my baby away from me." This time she added, "Tomorrow I will testify."

"Of course, dear. Mr. Burns plans to put you on the stand." Tess did not add that it was merely a last desperate effort with practically no chance whatever of saving the situation. In fact it could definitely seal baby Clinton's fate when Keenan got his chance to cross-question.

Tess recalled the confused, frightened girl she had found in the harbor master's office that long-ago day, brave enough but the courage only a facade to hide the uncertainty underneath. Now that courage seemed to have become a part of her. The depth of her character stood clearly revealed. Motherhood had done wonderful things for her. Tess could only hope that her new inner strength would be enough to help Kate bear up under the loss of her son.

The following morning in court, Tess was somewhat encouraged. Kate was calm and controlled, with an air of quiet dignity as she took the stand. Tess prayed that the jury would be impressed, this being Burns' last desperate hope. A slim one, however; the young attorney did not believe in miracles. Then, as Burns approached to begin his questioning, Kate turned to Judge Jacob.

"May I make a statement, your Honor?"

"Of course."

Burns paused, frowning. Kate had not consulted him about making a statement. He had no idea what she was going to say.

Kate ignored him, directing her words to Judge Jacob.

"Your Honor, I wish to state that Mr. Godfrey Wells has no legal claim whatever to my son. My deceased husband, Peter Wells, was not the baby's father. Our marriage was never consummated. There was no time. The fire which destroyed the ship came immediately after the marriage ceremony."

Judge Jacob's eyebrows shot up. He waited, then asked, "Is that all you have to say?"

Kate took a deep breath and looked squarely at the judge. "No, your Honor." She paused. "On the night before he married us, Captain Jason Steele raped me in his cabin. Jason Steele is the father of my child."

A heavy, choking silence fell over the courtroom. It was broken by assembled gentlemen of the press falling over each other in a mad dash for the corridor door, as excited buzzing broke out in the courtroom.

Aghast, Keith Burns stared at his client, still on the witness stand. "I have no questions, your Honor," he managed to mutter.

Judge Jacob raised his eyes toward Jefferson Keenan. When the latter, mouth open, seemingly in shock, did not respond, Judge Jacob said, "The witness is excused."

Kate walked, head high, through the courtroom to the door leading out to the corridor. She paused only once, to speak with Calvin Gentry who was seated in the public section. "Cal, will you please come to the flat this afternoon? I would like to talk to you." All eyes still on her, she left the room, her demeanor betraying nothing of the turmoil inside.

After conferring with his stunned client for a few moments, Jefferson Keenan approached the bench. "Your Honor, we request a recess to consider the testimony just given."

"We will recess for an hour," Judge Jacob replied. He hurriedly retired to his chambers.

An hour later, when court reconvened, Keenan again approached the bench.

"Your Honor, my client wishes to withdraw his petition."

"Granted," was the response, and it sounded to some that there was relief in the judge's voice.

In his carriage on his way home, Godfrey Wells reviewed his decision. Doubt as to the child's parentage was ample reason for withdrawal, certainly.

The silent figure of Calvin Gentry seated there in the courtroom had nothing to do with the relief he now felt that the case was over, he told himself.

64.

Calvin Gentry followed Kate to the Washington Square flat, arriving almost on her heels. Kate got the sleeping Clinton from his crib, sent Peggy to the store on an errand, and joined him in the parlor.

"Cal, I shall speak directly because there is little time. Events have transpired so swiftly."

"Whatever you wish to tell me—"

"At the clinic, you asked me to marry you. You said you loved me. Is that still true now?"

"It will never change."

"Cal, I sincerely wish that I did love you," she said sadly, "but I do not—not in the way you would want. I do have a deep affection for you. You are a good man, and I trust you, and possibly I could learn to love you. I want to accept your proposal now, so long as you understand my reasons for doing so."

"Your reasons are undoubtedly worthy."

"I need your protection, Cal. Is that worthy? I need your protection for my baby. In exchange, I would be a good wife to you. I would be faithful and true and in every way as loyal as if I were able to give you my love in the way that you wish."

When he remained silent, Kate went on,

"Another thing, Cal—I want to leave New York City."

"Where do you want to go?"

"As far from this city as I can get. I have been thinking of San Francisco. Would you object to leaving?"

"Not in the least. I have no ties here. Outer Mongolia would be all right if you could find happiness there."

"It is not a question of happiness. The reason is that I do not think that my danger of losing Clinton is over. There is still William Steele. He is every bit as powerful as Godfrey Wells. And Jason himself. Is it not likely he would fight for custody of his son?"

"Perhaps."

"Then what is *your* answer, Cal?"

He walked to the sofa where Clinton was still asleep and stood looking down at the infant. Then he turned to her. "I too must be honest, Kate. I will not marry you."

Kate turned away to hide the impact of his refusal. She had not expected it. Perhaps honesty was a luxury she could not afford. "Then you have changed your mind."

"On that point, yes. I was wrong to propose. It would be unfair to marry you under the present circumstances."

"I understand, Cal."

"However, it is only the marriage that I am refusing."

"What do you mean?"

"The rest of it, I agree to, if you are able to accept *my* terms. I will go with you wherever you choose. I will stand by your side. I will regard Clinton as my own son and give him every protection I can."

Kate went to him. She offered her lips without reservation. He drew her close. Her kiss was warm and genuine, if a spontaneous gesture of gratitude rather than an invitation to passion.

She drew away. "Cal, am I just an opportunist completely without morals?"

"No more than I am," He smiled tenderly at her. "When do you want to leave for San Francisco?"

"Would tomorrow afternoon be too soon?"

"Not for me. I have no ties here. I have only to go to the Bowery Bank and arrange a transfer of funds. That, and make travel arrangements. I'll call for you at three o'clock. . . ."

After he left, Kate remained in the parlor, watching her infant son as he slept, thinking back on her public confession which had enabled her to keep him out of Godfrey Wells's clutches.

In logical sequence, her thoughts went to Jason Steele. Tomorrow she would start on a journey that would put three thousand miles between them. . . .

65.

Ben Stein was in conference in his office.

"She killed us! That scheming little bitch killed us! She sank Jason to save her son!"

"But, Ben," an aide protested. "It wasn't your fault. There was no way you could have known."

"It *is* my fault—at least partly. I was too cocky; I should have had the sense to demand a sequestering of the jury."

"You may be worrying needlessly."

"You're right. There's no point in worrying. We haven't got a prayer now. Worrying is just a waste of energy."

"Damn it, Ben, you can't be sure. It's too late for Dave Griffen to introduce the rape as evidence."

"It doesn't have to be introduced. The jury reads newspapers. They went home and read what happened in that stupid Domestic Court and they will come in tomorrow licking their chops. Just wait 'til you see their faces in that jury box."

"But you can't be positive."

"You're a goddamn fool! What we've established—what we've been riding on—is doubt, the establishment of doubt in their minds. And it worked. They think Jason Steele *might* be guilty of what he's accused of, but we've planted enough doubt to probably bring us in an good verdict. That little whore's accusation of rape is an extra rock on the wrong side of the scale. They'll figure if he did *that*, he did all the other things he's been accused of."

The conference was interrupted. "There is a phone call for you, Mr. Stein."

Stein sighed. "That'll be the grandfather, wanting to know how bad it is. . . ."

When Ben Stein entered court the next morning, the faces of the jurors reflected exactly what he had predicted: a lost cause.

Ben held himself in check as Judge Holt rapped his gavel and court was opened.

Immediately he stood up. "Your Honor, I ask that the defense be allowed to introduce another witness."

David Griffen sprang up. "I object, your Honor."

Judge Holt, who had been up late playing whist at the Union Club, regarded them both with weary resignation. "Will the attorneys approach the bench?"

When the two antagonists were before him, Judge Holt said, "Mr. Stein, you completed the case for the defense yesterday, so what you are asking is most irregular. Who is this witness you refer to?"

"Mrs. Kate Wells, your Honor. She was on the ship in question at the time of the sinking."

"I am aware of that fact from the hearing

378

brief. But if she is important to your case why did you not call her earlier?"

There had been an unspoken but mutual agreement not to call Kate as a witness. When the hearing established that she had no connection with John Saipan, Griffen had refrained from calling her because of her testimony, sympathetic to Jason Steele at the hearing. For his part, Ben Stein had refrained because her influence on the trial was unpredictable. He had preferred to let well enough alone.

In answer to Judge Holt's question, Stein said, "Your Honor, we are here in pursuit of justice, to ascertain all facts, and I feel the testimony of this new witness will be of value in that respect."

Judge Holt looked at the prosecuting attorney. "Mr. Griffen, do you have an objection?"

Griffen had been thinking furiously. He had read the papers, of course, and he was surprised at Stein's bad judgment—surprised and wary.

"Does the defense plan to introduce new evidence?"

"Perhaps," Stein replied. "Perhaps not."

A last, blind, desperate effort on Stein's part, Griffen decided. The old fox was making a bad mistake.

With a smile, Griffen replied generously, "Your Honor, as my distinguished opponent says, we are here to establish facts. I have no objection to a reopening by the defense."

"Very well, let's get on with it."

Moments later, Stein was thoughtfully regarding Kate in the witness chair. There were dark circles under her eyes. She looked even more worn and harrassed than when she had called him to her flat late the previous afternoon. Obviously she had spent an agonizing night. He pitied her, but this was of her own choice.

"Mrs. Wells," he said, "did you testify recently in Domestic Court before Judge Jacob that you were a passenger on the whaling ship *Gray Ghost* just prior to its sinking?"

"I did."

"Did you testify also that on the night before your marriage to Peter Wells, Captain Jason Steele raped you in his cabin?"

"I did."

Griffen gasped in amazement. Stein had actually introduced the damning evidence! He was throwing his client to the wolves! Cross-examination might not even be necessary.

"Now, Mrs. Wells," Stein went on, "was the testimony that you were raped a true statement of fact?"

"No, it was not."

"Then what is the truth, Mrs. Wells?"

"Jason Steele did not rape me. *I submitted willingly.*"

Silence followed. Then, several long seconds later, the courtroom erupted, and Judge Holt was hammering his gavel furiously.

"There will be order in this courtroom or I'll have it cleared!"

Ben Stein stood quietly beside Kate while the noise lessened and died. Then he said, "I have no more questions. Your witness, Counselor."

Griffen stormed to the witness stand. "Mrs. Wells, what kind of a person are you?"

380

"Objection!" Ben Stein shouted. "Mr. Griffen is asking for an opinion from the witness."

"I withdraw the question," Griffen said before Judge Holt could speak. He paused to collect himself after his uncontrollable outburst.

"Mrs. Wells," he said quietly, "when you testified in Domestic Court that Jason Steele raped you, you were under oath, were you not?"

"I was."

"You are under oath now, are you not?"

"I am."

"Then please tell us—in which court have you perjured yourself?"

"I committed perjury in the Domestic Court."

"And why, Mrs. Wells, should the jury be expected to believe that?"

"Because it is true. There is no privacy on a whaling ship. Had I objected to Captain Steele's attentions, I had only to cry out. I did not. The only true statement I made in Domestic Court was that Jason Steele is the father of my son."

"Madam, you astound me! A blatant perjurer—"

"Your Honor! I object to the badgering of this witness!"

Before Judge Holt could rule, Griffen added grimly, "I have no further questions."

As Kate left the stand, Ben Stein turned his eyes to the jury. Had the unbalancing stone been removed? As decent men, the jurors would view rape as a monstrous act. But to take a willing young woman into one's arms? There was probably not one of them, Ben Stein hoped, who would have resisted Kate Wells's charms if she had chosen to bestow them. Even there on the stand, sleepless and anxious, she was beautiful. As things stood, could they blame Jason Steele?

By the time Ben Stein finished with his analysis, Kate had left the courtroom.

66.

Back in the flat, Kate was well aware of her perilous situation; she did not need a lawyer to point it out. She was guilty of perjury. She had to get beyond the jurisdiction of New York State law as soon as possible because they would surely come for her in time.

Kate had other cause for anguish. The newspapers would have a field day with her testimony. Was Calvin now aware of what had happened at Jason's trial? Would he still come for her—would he still be willing to give Clinton his protection?

Kate had said her good-byes. Bella was at an important rehearsal and Tess had taken Peggy to the doctor with a highly inflamed throat, so Kate was alone with the baby as she waited.

Three o'clock crept slowly into being and as the clock struck in the parlor, a carriage drew up in front of the house. Footsteps approached, there was a knock and Kate opened the door. Calvin entered and she searched his face; searched desperately for clues as to what lay behind it.

There were other footsteps. The coachman.

"Fetch the trunk and the bags," Calvin ordered. Then to Kate, "Keep the baby well wrapped. It is breezy out. . . ."

Nothing more was said as they climbed into the carriage and traveled in the direction of Pennsylvania Station.

Part Three:

VERDICT AND JUDGMENT

New York City—San Francisco, 1904–1905

67.

If Kate had happened to be standing at the window on Washington Square to see Jason fling himself from a cab and rush up the steps, she would have been most gratified. Certainly his intent was obvious.

But Kate was already far away when Jason impatiently rattled the bell. He was less than delighted to be received by Bella Cantrell. He had seen Bella on only one occasion since they both left Spanish Flats, and the meeting had been stiff and formal. Something had been lost in the parting that neither particularly cared enough about to replace. Still, Bella was not uncordial in her greeting, though there may have been an inner smugness she did not make too great an effort to hide.

"Jason! What a surprise! So nice of you to drop in."

"Bella, I must see Kate at once!"

His eagerness, the glow in his eyes, told Bella all. He had come for the reconciliation both he and Kate had wanted so desperately and which each had been too proud to initiate. Bella knew a touch of regret, a feeling akin to pity for the man who stood before her, a man she had once called a friend.

"I'm sorry, Jason. Kate is not here."

"She'll be back soon?"

"I'm afraid not. She left for good—baby, baggage, and all."

"But where did she go?"

"She left the city, the state, the East Coast. When she gets settled, I'm sure we will hear from her."

His distress was obvious. "But that can't be! She didn't let me know!"

"My dear friend, was there any reason why she should?" But even as she spoke sharply, Bella's compassion for Jason's predicament was keen. Justified or not, Jason was deeply hurt.

He caught himself up however, and rearranged his features into an expression of less concern. "I see. But you'll let me know when you do hear from her?"

Bella was carefully measuring her next words. She decided that if Kate had wanted Jason to know of her intentions she would have seen to it that he found out. But if Bella had Jason pegged correctly, he would find out on his own. Therefore, it was not necessary to be uncooperative.

"Why of course. I'll be glad to."

"Thanks. I'll keep in touch."

He turned to leave, then said, "Bella, I called Cal yesterday. Fellows answered. He told me Cal was no longer at the Flats."

Bella said only, "I have not seen Calvin for some time."

As Jason walked back to his flat, he considered the situation. He gave little thought to Calvin Gentry, his inquiry merely an afterthought. Without knowledge of his old friend's passionate interest in Kate, he could only attribute the simultaneous disappearances to coincidence.

His thoughts returned to the trial. Ben Stein's reassurances had had a buoying effect. Time had brought some changes in his earlier fatalistic attitude. The martyrdom he had felt—a willingness to make whatever payment the courts decreed—had lessened as the end drew closer. Jason still carried the burden of guilt for those who had died, but a realistic dread of cold prison cell walls also loomed large.

One firm resolution had formed. When the verdict was in, good or bad, he would reestablish the relationship between himself and his grandfather. He thought of William Steele's faith and loyalty—unshakable under all conditions.

The elder Steele had not returned to the city after Grandma Becky's funeral. There was really nothing more to be done but await whatever was to come. If the verdict was favorable, Jason resolved to go immediately to Stonington, put himself under his grandfather once more, and do whatever was asked of him by way of carrying on the family name.

Kate would remain a memory in the back of his mind. Her loveliness, her confession at his trial—he could only guess at the shame and humiliation she had been willing to endure to help him. . . . Most heartbreaking of all was the revelation that he was the father of her baby. And Jason might never set eyes on his son. . . .

68.

The trial ended the following week with the two summations and Judge Holt's instructions to the jury. With the jury out, Ben Stein exuded quiet confidence, even when the day passed and the jury was put up in a hotel for the night.

On the following afternoon, however, Stein appeared more nervous with each passing hour. He paced the room and kept consulting his watch.

When the jury filed in, Jason held his breath. The foreman read the verdict:

Innocent on all counts.

Stein showed no elation whatever. He turned and shook Jason's hand hurriedly, then seized his black leather case and rushed from the courtroom.

An aide hastened to explain to Jason. "Mr. Stein has accepted a brief down in Virginia. He will defend a wife who allegedly killed her husband. In another half hour he would have missed his train."

"I didn't get a chance to thank him."

"Don't worry about it. All the thanks Mr. Stein ever wants is a favorable verdict."

It was over. After so many months it was

difficult to comprehend that he was free, that he could go where he would. To the ends of the earth, if his fancy dictated.

Jason's first urge was to walk. He wanted to stride forth, to feel the cold wind in his face and suck in the icy air until his lungs were numb. He stood on the courthouse steps and inhaled deeply.

There was a tap on his shoulder. He turned. A pink-cheeked boy nodded deferentially. "Mr. Steele, sir, I have a message from Mr. Cletus Wing. He asks that you come to his office at your earliest possible convenience."

"Very well. I'll come immediately."

The boy trotted off. Jason moved to follow and at that moment Chester Manson hurried up the steps.

"Jason! Congratulations!"

"Thanks, Chet." Jason brightened at sight of a friendly face. "How are things going? I was hoping to see you again."

"Jason, when you have a little time I'd like to talk to you—thank you for—"

Jason stopped him with a quick gesture. "Let's talk over a drink. I'll be leaving for Stonington tomorrow but why don't you drop in at my flat this evening? I'm sure to be back by eight."

"I'll be there."

"Good. See you then."

Cletus Wing received Jason in his private office.

"Jason ... so good of you to come. A little brandy?"

"I could use some."

As Wing poured from the carafe, Jason

thought it odd that he had no word of congratulations. In fact, the lawyer's manner was somber, unsmiling, to a point where one would have thought the verdict had gone the other way.

With both of them seated, Wing asked, "Jason, what are your immediate plans?"

"I leave for Stonington tomorrow."

"Then I am glad I was able to catch you before your departure."

"Has anything happened to my grandfather?"

"I am sure he is fine. But there is a matter he asked me to conclude immediately upon termination of the trial."

Wing reached into his desk and brought forth two envelopes. They were both addressed to Jason, each marked with a letter.

"The letters are for my reference," Wing said as he extended one of the envelopes. "I was instructed to give you this one if the verdict was favorable. The other, if it was not."

As Jason took the proffered envelope, Wing struck a match, held the other over his ashtray, and touched it with the flame.

"You're burning it up!" Jason exclaimed.

"Per my instructions."

They watched in silence as the envelope was transformed to ashes. Jason asked, "Did you know what was in it?"

"The burned one—no. The one in your hand, yes."

He rose from his desk. "I have some small matters to attend to, Jason. I will leave you in privacy to read your grandfather's letter." With that, he left the office.

Jason stared at the envelope for several long

moments. Then he tore it open, took the letter out, and unfolded it. It was in his grandfather's precise, legible hand, each line straight across the paper. He settled back to read.

Jason,

This missive is to inform you that I have taken the name of Steele off the seas forever. The liquidation of Steele & Co. now goes swiftly toward completion. The United States Coast Guard is purchasing three of our ships as training vessels. The remaining four will go to Penn Whaling Inc. I think Jethro is experiencing some triumph in the acquisition, but in the main I feel him to be a fool. The days of whaling as we and our forebears knew them are over. Modern methods have destroyed us and in due time they will destroy the great mammals off which we lived and prospered.

This belief influenced me greatly in my decision. But there were other reasons for the liquidation. Your grandmother's death. My advanced age. And no one in the offing with ability to carry on the business and make the necessary transitions. . . .

The hand holding the letter dropped to his lap as Jason raised his eyes to stare blankly at the wall. The implication of that last had cut deep. But it was nothing to what followed.

And now to my final words. You have been exonerated of blame in the Gray

393

Ghost *tragedy. My efforts in behalf of your defense were instinctive. Any other action on my part would have been unthinkable. However, we both know that you were guilty. I also charge you, through your unconscionable actions, to have been at least partially responsible for hastening your grandmother's death.*

Your rightful share of the family assets, a quarter of a million dollars, has been deposited at the Dry Dock Savings Institution in your name. Therefore, it is not required that you and I ever meet again.

William Steele

Had Jason been in a different state of mind, he might have noticed that the last several lines of the letter varied from the others. The handwriting was no longer strong, but became tremulous and uncertain.

After a time, Cletus Wing tapped timidly on the door to his office. When there was no response, he opened it. The sound appeared to startle Jason, as though he had lost track of where he was.

He then rose from the chair and walked past Wing as though the man did not exist, and on out of the office.

Alone on the street, still in shock from the contents of the letter, nevertheless one question stood out clearly among the jumble of confused thoughts racing around in Jason's mind.

What had been in the other letter?

He would never know.

As Jason pondered what had happened to

him there was no hostility, no anger; only the realization that the man he'd thought he knew so well had been a stranger. He had never known his grandfather at all.

69.

The long trip across the Great Plains, down through Utah and Nevada and finally to the Oakland station of the Southern Pacific, was tiring for Kate. Cal Gentry had reserved the best accommodations possible—two private compartments—but dust and cinders made no allowances for wealth.

Kate struck up an acquaintance with a woman who, under other circumstances, would have been diverting—a Mrs. Gay Stafford by name. Perhaps forty-five, Mrs. Stafford was busty, vibrant, and outgoing.

"My dear, you have a lovely baby—just *lovely!* I admire you so much for your courage, setting forth on your own to a new life in a new city. . . ."

Mrs. Stafford had been in New York City on a shopping expedition. Four trunks of fashionable clothes were returning with her, and while in the East she had obviously read everything in the newspapers concerning Kate and her affairs. "You have led such a *romantic* life, my dear. How *thrilling* it must have been!"

One thing was certain: Mrs. Stafford did not condemn Kate in the slightest.

Kate, for her part, found the woman reminded her somewhat of Bella Cantrell. To Gay Stafford, men were creatures to be used by women and she did so without remorse.

"I was slinging hash in Virginia City when I met Frank—he was my first husband, you know. That was when silver mining was still going strong and the town was booming. I just *had* to get out of that hash house. Only three months after we were married, Frank was shot one night during a poker game—a man named Sam Parker killed him. Four months later I married Sam."

"You married the man who killed your husband?"

"I suppose that *does* sound a little strange, but Frank could get very nasty when he was drunk, you see, and he accused Sam of cheating and waited outside to kill him. So Sam was only defending himself—everyone said so. Sam came to me the next day like the man he was and apologized for killing Frank. I would have nothing to do with him at first but he came again, several times. He assured me that he hadn't cheated in the card game. He didn't have to. He had a producing silver mine and only played cards for recreation."

"How interesting," Kate murmured.

They were in Kate's compartment where she had been lulled into lazy immobility by the monotonous *click-click* of the rolling stock and Gay Stafford's cheerful but inexhaustible chatter. The murder episode had brought her alert but now she was ready to lapse back into her semi-dreamy, half-listening state.

"Of course Sam and I were never *really married*," Gay Stafford prattled on, "although we said we were. He paid for everything, my apartment, my clothes, and he gave me a generous allowance—but he was away a lot. We planned to get married later, when he finished up some deals and had more time. I didn't *really* mind. His being away left me with free time of my own. Then poor Sam had an accident. He slipped and fell down a mine shaft. I went to him immediately and he died in my arms. It wasn't until then that I found out he was already married, to a woman over in Steamboat, and had two kids. It was *terrible!* He died in *my* arms and *she* got everything!"

A sympathetic comment seemed called for. "How unfair," Kate murmured.

"Sam had been generous when he was alive, though. I stayed single for a year. Then I met Barney." Gay's flow of words ceased. Kate glanced over. The woman's blue eyes were soft with memory. "He's *such* a dear! So *stable*. So *solid*." Another pause, then she went on dreamily, "Good Lord, that was twenty years ago! How time does fly!"

"Does Barney own a silver mine?" Kate asked.

"Heavens no! Silver petered out *years* ago, my dear. Barney had some interests but he knew when to back off. We went to San Francisco where he made piles in real estate." She glanced brightly at Kate. "Are you planning to invest in San Francisco?"

"Invest? Why I really don't know—"

"If you do you *must* talk with Barney. He's a *wizard* when it comes to real estate deals."

"Thank you. I'll remember that."

There was a quick knock, and Cal entered

the compartment. Kate was unsure how she should present him. Cal came to her rescue. He extended his hand and said, "I am Calvin Gentry. I am traveling with Miss McCrae."

Gay Stafford seized the hand, shook it heartily, and introduced herself. Then Cal left and he and Mrs. Stafford did not meet again until the train reached the Oakland station. Calvin stayed mainly in his own compartment the whole trip.

Nor did Gay Stafford refer to him in her interminable chattering. Kate wondered if this was out of tact on Gay's part or because an unmarried couple traveling with a baby disturbed her sensibilities not a whit. She suspected the latter.

At the station, Kate was introduced to Barney Stafford. He was a huge man with a thick, curved mustache over drooping jowls. He removed his hat and bowed solemnly.

Kate had been dreading their arrival, envisioning hordes of reporters waiting to pounce on her. She was greatly relieved to find this was not the case. There *was* a sizable group of journalists but they were flocking around a flashingly handsome man whom she recognized as John Barrymore, the youngest member of the famous Barrymore family. He had come West for an acting engagement. Kate and baby Clinton remained quite unnoticed.

But there was no getting rid of Gay Stafford. She pressed her Nob Hill address upon Kate and assured her that she would phone the St. Francis Hotel to make sure she was getting the best of service. After all, Barney owned shares in the place.

But there were no problems with the hotel, or any other aspect of their arrival. In his quiet, unobtrusive way, Cal had made all the arrangements, the suite at the St. Francis was reserved, even a private launch instead of the crowded ferry to take them across the bay.

He was considerate as ever, but the change in Cal was a growing puzzle to Kate. She harkened back to his passionate attentions at the clinic, his feverish marriage proposal, then his quiet, firm refusal of her belated acceptance and his counter-proposal. From the ardent suitor, he had turned remote, yet still serving her with 'slavish devotion.

From the moment they had left Tess's flat, he had gone behind a wall of his own making. But it was a wall of velvet, his kindness and gentle regard not diminishing in the least.

Kate was at a loss to deal with the situation. On the train, he had kept to himself, staying in his own compartment with his books and, presumably, his own thoughts. He was not sulking, exactly, nor was he reproachful, and he was always at her elbow when there was need of him. Thus she could find no excuse upon which to question him; no opening through which to approach him.

Had she been alone she would have forced her own opening. But there was Clinton, requiring most of her attention.

He is disappointed in me, she told herself.

70.

"It's nothing but your goddamn pride," Chester said.

"I'd appreciate it if you'd mind your own business."

"Sorry, Jason. I owe you too much and I know you too well."

"Damn it, just leave me alone! I'll make my own decisions in due time."

"Look here, I realize what your grandfather did to you was a hell of a blow. But neither of you can call back the wind. You both made mistakes. He was too damned easy with you and you took advantage of him while you knew all the time you were doing it."

The two men stood on an East River pier under an angry, lowering sky, hands deep in their greatcoat pockets. Chester could see that Jason's fists were clenched and he wondered how soon it would be before Jason slugged him. So far, Jason had held his temper in check.

Chester took a fatalistic view. If it came to a fight, so be it. What he was saying needed to be said and he was not going to mince words.

Since the not-guilty verdict had been handed down, Chester found himself involved with two emotional misfits instead of one, and it spoke well for his character that he accepted both responsibilities.

Jason had not been at his flat that first night when Chester had shown up. Chet located him days later in a saloon, an entirely different man than he had left on the courthouse steps, and Chester's thankless task had begun. By the time of the East River pier meeting, he had made no progress.

"So the old gentleman disowned you. A hard blow. But I doubt if anyone was ever let down so gently."

"What the hell do you mean?"

"For God's sake, Jason, give him *some* credit! Try to visualize the pain and agony he went through. He felt you were guilty from the beginning. Yet he stood by you. He believed that your actions helped to bring on your grandmother's death. Still he stood by you. But when you got clear, he had to salvage what he could of his self-respect. Can't you see that? He had to be true to himself and what he's stood for all his life, and he did even that without injuring you. Jason, the man loves you! You are all he has left. Writing that letter was torture for him!"

Jason's fists came out of his pockets. "Will you get the hell out of my life?"

"If you'd only—"

"Shut your damned mouth! Don't you think I know all that? Are you calling me stupid?"

"I'm calling on you to be at least half the man he is—to follow his example. He has resigned himself to living out the rest of his years without the thing he loves most—you. So why don't you start looking ahead and decide what you're going to do with the rest of *your* life?"

"It's none of your damned business what I do with the rest of my life!"

With that, Jason started to walk away. Then he stopped, and turned back.

"How is Elizabeth?" It was the first time he'd asked.

"Fine—just fine. She's out of the clinic, you know."

"I didn't know. I'm glad."

"Elizabeth is a lot stronger than we gave her credit for. After the struggle, and it was rough, she recovered rapidly."

"Did she go back to Stonington?"

"No, we're together. We kept that flat on Thirty-fourth Street. She cooks and keeps house and goes for walks. It's working out all right. She told me to ask you over for dinner one evening."

Jason ignored that. "What are you doing with yourself?" *Other than following me around town?*

"I'm looking for employment."

"How are your resources? Do you need—?"

Chester waved him off. "We're getting along all right. I'll get work soon and start repaying the money you so generously loaned me—"

Jason brushed that last away with a gesture and hurried off. But the inquiry had altered Chester's thinking, his decision that he had failed in his responsibility to a friend who had helped him without question in his own time of dire need. Maybe, just maybe, Jason was coming out of it.

All right—one more time. One more time before I quit!

The next meeting took place a week later in a saloon where he tracked Jason down. Chester did everything but hit him over the head.

"The trouble with you, Jason, is that you're a selfish bastard. You hang your chin over a glass and brood on the injustices done to you when you're probably one of the world's luckiest men. Do you give any thought at all to those who love you? You're nothing but a baby! You use your pride and stubbornness like a sugar tit. Poor abused me! Ha! Jason, you *enjoy* being an idiot."

"Chester, God damn it—I'm warning you. I've had all the interference I'm going to take!"

"Oh, sure. Babies go into tantrums when they don't get their way."

Thus Chester held his ground, though he tensed instinctively as Jason's hand curled tightly around his glass.

"Have you given a single thought to Kate McCrae? Christ, man! She held herself up to ridicule and contempt. She *perjured* herself to keep you out of jail. Now I suppose you're mad because she ran off to California."

"How do you know Kate is in California?"

"If you bothered to read the papers you'd know too. What do you want her to do now—crawl back on her knees and apologize for helping you?"

Jason said nothing.

"Those are my final words to you. I won't hound you anymore. You can go to hell in your own way."

Then he was gone.

Jason sat staring into his drink.

Perhaps it was the genuine disgust and contempt of a friend. Or maybe it was the loss of that friend who, true to his word, no longer unexpectedly appeared at his elbow. In any case, a few evenings later he knocked on the Mansons' door. Elizabeth opened it and Jason stood mute for a long moment, amazed by the change he saw in her. No longer beautiful—what she had been through had taken its toll—but serene and clear-eyed.

"Hello, Liz. Chester invited me to dinner a while back. Is the invitation still open?"

Later that evening over coffee in the parlor of the shabby little flat, the old Jason took charge.

"It's high time we made some plans," he said. "Do you remember that ship-building idea we talked about?"

71.

Calvin Gentry's refusal to marry Kate did not, as she believed, reflect the nobility of his spirit. Nor did his subsequent remoteness have anything to do with her at all. It was not the case, except possibly in an abstract sense. Now, in the luxurious Nob Hill flat Barney Stafford had found for them, Calvin was like a newly blinded man groping through a lonely and sometimes frightening darkness. A shattering change had taken place within him. He knew the exact point of its beginning. It was the night of his last stag affair to which he had invited Jason Steele.

Seated there in that shabby basement watching two naked women sweat and struggle like animals for the miserable pittance they would be paid, he was struck by a sickening thought.

My God! I arranged this! It was I who brought it about!

Disgusted with the scene, disgusted with himself, an actual feeling of nausea overtaking him, he left without explanation to his followers.

He limped through the silent streets, frightened and terribly confused. By the time he reached the Flats he had somewhat recovered but the attempt to appear himself in front of Bella and Jason was mainly playacting. By the morning, he told himself, the strange feeling would be gone.

But it was not, and as time went on he began to dread his moments of awakening from sleep. Somewhere in the night, a force or entity against which he was helpless ripped and tore at his ego, stripping away whatever defenses he had built up over the years.

These were not dreams. The scathing attacks came from below that level and he was aware of them only through their effects—awakening in bitter despair and hopelessness.

Forced to accept the stag incident as a genuine *something*, he strove to apply common sense. He refused to accept the sword-flung-down-from-outraged-heaven theory. In his solid materialism, he doubted if heaven even knew of his existence. So it had to be a sudden eruption of poison isolated like a boil in his being and finally spewed out by a desperate subconscious.

It was an explanation of sorts and would have to do until a better one came along.

In his searching, he turned to books, to the like experiences of others—St. Augustine; St. Paul's wracking transition from God's enemy to a most dedicated warrior in His then-sparse ranks. He read Thomas De Quincy's *Confessions of an Opium Eater*, and examined what he could find of Sigmund Freud's writings.

He arrived at only one definite conclusion: instantaneous conversions, rakes into saints, the vicious into the gentle, were mainly fictional. If the change in him had been divinely directed, which he doubted in the extreme, the job was sloppy. His previous foundations had been knocked out from under him with no suggestion whatever of an alternate course.

That was his condition when he first set eyes on Kate McCrae at the International Club. There was her simple loveliness, the impact of her youth and perfection in that sophisticated setting. She was like a bright light turned on suddenly in his terrible darkness and he did not see love born in an instant as being unusual.

The fervor with which he pursued her was the entirely sincere actions of a normal lover and his subsequent proposal of marriage was honest in its intent.

It was during the days following her return from the clinic that the realization came to him that he had been put upon a rose-strewn but false trail; that Kate had not been a goal but rather an integral part of his transition.

It was ironic indeed that the day Kate accepted his marriage proposal he had come to the flat intent upon releasing her.

His counter-proposal was not illogical in light of his state of mind nor did he see it as self-sacrificing. In plainest terms, he saw no reason for not protecting and aiding Kate simply because he had changed direction. His genuine affection for her and his wish for her well being and happiness had not diminished.

So there were areas in their relationship that did not mesh: Kate's belief that he was still in love with her but angry for some reason, and his refusal to straighten her out on that matter for fear that in her pride she would refuse to accept the help and protection he felt it his mission to give.

That was where things now stood between them, Cal grateful for each passing day that Kate delayed the fulfillment of one aspect of her promise—that of being a dutiful lover. When she finally came to him he would have to reject her.

What would be her reaction—Shame? Humiliation? Beyond any doubt, it would end the arrangement.

72.

"He's a very nice man," Gay Stafford said.

By her simple standards, this was her verdict on Cal Gentry. If a man took care of his woman, he was a nice person; other characteristics were of no importance.

Gay's attention to Kate's comfort and welfare remained constant. She had located a nurse for Clinton, a thoroughly reliable middle-aged woman; a real gem. "You needn't have a worrisome moment about Clinton from now on."

Biddy's arrival was a blessing but there were other considerations. Kate had used the excuse of continually attending to her child to delay dealing with Cal. Now there was no excuse.

Regrettably—she later realized—she had confided her domestic situation, at least partially, to Gay.

"He stays in his room and reads. You never saw so many books."

Already aware that there was no marriage, Gay asked, "What have you done about it?"

"Well—nothing yet—"

"Tell me, dear, does the gimp foot bother you?"

"Of course not!"

410

Gay smiled. "Personally, I think it makes him more romantic. You should start paying attention, Kate. Otherwise some other woman will snap him up."

At almost any time of the day or evening, Gay would stride into the apartment to innocently snoop, question, and advise. Kate, troubled, uncertain, lonely in her new environment, was grateful for Gay's help and friendship even while trying to keep her at arm's length. But she reckoned without the other woman's talent for boring in without seeming to do so; and now Gay knew practically everything Kate had resolved to keep to herself.

The other side of the coin was that Gay was an experienced woman wise in many ways.

"You've got to do right by your man," she advised. "And what the hell—it should be fun!"

"I know. I fully intend to."

"Is it the other one? The father of your kid?"

"No! I never give Jason a thought!"

Gay said nothing.

"That isn't really true," Kate finally admitted. "I do think of him."

"I knew it!"

"But not in that way," Kate said hastily. "He was exonerated in court, you know. I read it in the paper. I'm scared that now he will come out here after his son."

"How do you know?"

"He'll try to take Clinton away from me just as Godfrey Wells did."

"All right, let him come. We can take his measure. He won't get the tot."

Gay did not entirely understand the problem

411

or Kate's agonizing dilemma—the yearning to see Jason, the veritable reaching out of her whole being—that, against the fear of what would happen when he arrived.

"The thing to do," Gay advised, "is to get Calvin's ring on your finger."

"He refused to marry me."

"And you just sit there? Jesus, sweetie! Do you need lessons? Do you want me to explain exactly how it's done?"

But I don't want to marry Cal!

That at least remained unspoken. However, Kate did realize that she had been unfair in not offering Cal the physical privileges the fulfillment of the pact required. But what if Calvin then changed his mind? What if he renewed his proposal? With the panic, the pressure of that terrible time in New York City removed, Kate knew that no matter how grateful she was, she could not agree to marriage.

Still, her obligation to a sexual relationship remained.

73.

Having convinced herself of the course she must follow, only the opportunity was needed. It did not come quickly. Calvin's quarters were to the rear of the apartment; a bedroom, bath, and parlor with a direct side entrance so that he did not have to pass through the rest of the house. As she recalled, it was that feature that attracted Calvin to the apartment originally. Tapping on the corridor door, she got no response. She entered and found the rooms empty of their occupant.

It was most puzzling—Calvin's comings and goings. He would vanish for a day and a night, for two days perhaps; then quietly return, inquire if Kate needed anything, and retire to his books and meditations. Had he found another woman? She could not quite sort out her reaction to that possibility. There was disappointment, certainly. Keyed to her physical expectations, she felt let down, rejected. There was also a touch of jealousy. *Had* another woman wormed her way into Calvin's affections? Calvin had every right to seek comfort and companionship elsewhere. Still, losing what she had so easily gained did not sit well.

Aside from Gay's words of wisdom regarding

Calvin, she had been most insistent in her advice to Kate to invest her money.

Barney Stafford was of great assistance in this respect.

"Barney *believes* in this city. He sees it growing and growing. One day, he says, it will be greater than New York City or Chicago or even London and Paris. He says there is a pioneer spirit out here. This is frontier, the last frontier of the nation, and fortunes are waiting to be made."

Real estate—that was the key. Barney, in calmer, more specific terms, convinced Kate of that. Barney knew the city top to bottom, end to end, and his analysis seemed sound.

"The thing to do, Mrs. Wells, is to buy improved properties at current cost on the perimeters of the better sections, and always in the direction the city is moving. Away from Nob Hill toward Telegraph Hill, and for long-term development, in the direction of Russian Hill. As things stand, a person need not worry about overinvesting because immediate rental and leasing revenue is available. Then, in less time than one would imagine, the land itself will become valuable. New, modern buildings will be erected. San Francisco will become a city of giants."

Barney was a great help in other respects, too. He handled the details of transferring Kate's assets from the East Coast to the Crocker Bank, and such was her confidence in him that the recommended purchases began at once. Barney's enthusiasm was catching. Also, there was pride in becoming a woman of property.

In addition to setting up her domestic life, Gay drew Kate into the social whirl of San Francisco where, to her surprise and pleasure, she found that people were too busy living to spend time poking at the lives of other people. Gay introduced Kate into circles where, if you had money and had learned to hold a teacup correctly, you were accepted. Nor did the city lack those symbols of social refinement for which eastern and European rivals were famous. Culture invariably follows wealth, thus there was the opera season, plays featuring the world's finest performers, and affairs of glittering splendor. Under Gay's sponsorship, Kate was hurled into the midst of it all. It filled up her hours and her days and the popularity accorded her was heady stuff. If there were twinges of conscience at times—guilt at allowing Calvin to go his mysterious way—she fell back on the dubious belief that it would be straightened out in due time.

She was quite naturally courted by an enormous number of men.

With Gay hovering by as the ever-watchful chaperone, Kate was somewhat needlessly well protected; also, by way of Gay's file cabinet mind, she got data and statistics on every man who caught her attention.

"Jeff Pepper—richer than sin. More millions than he can count."

"Lee Winterhouse. A gambler. Loaded one day and flat on his ass the next."

And so on.

But in Carter Hayden's case, there was no thumbnail description. Kate met Hayden during intermission at *Hamlet*, which starred John

Barrymore. Perhaps the performance primed her for her response to the meeting with Hayden. The slim, attractive Barrymore gave a strong portrayal of the gloomy Dane that afternoon, a portrayal that stirred something in Kate that had been too long dormant.

When Carter Hayden pushed through the crowd in the lobby and insisted upon being introduced, the firm grip of his hand sent a thrill up Kate's spine. Tall and dark, there was an intensity about the man that reminded her of Jason Steele. She drove the thought from her mind.

Gay had performed the introduction, naturally. Later, while Gay was in the ladies' lounge, there was a whisper in Kate's ear.

"Miss Wells—may I call upon you this evening?"

There was no time to think, only to react, and Kate's, "Yes, Mr. Hayden, you may," came from an empty place deep inside her soul.

"Eight o'clock then," he said, and vanished into the crowd.

74.

Coming home to Clinton was always a joy to Kate; a moment when her love flared in fierce delight. Gay's appraisal of the nurse Biddy had been more than accurate. A quiet, mousey, middle-aged woman, Biddy attached herself to Clinton like a loving but firm grandmother. The infant was a godsend to her, canceling out the sadness of a lonely life and making her an important part of a household. A perplexing household, true enough, but it was filled with kindness and Biddy, grateful for what had been given, asked no questions.

She and Clinton were waiting at the door. Hardly an infant anymore, Clinton, now close to his second birthday, was what Biddy happily termed a "real bundle." With inexhaustible energy, his love for Kate was a screaming, roughhousing delight, and already she could see in him the appealing likeness of his father; also, perhaps, something of Jason's erratic nature.

Kate played with Clinton in his nursery for somewhat longer than the standard late-afternoon hour, after which Biddy asserted her authority and took possession.

As she left, Kate said, "By the way, Biddy, I'm having company tonight."

Biddy nodded. The simple statement was enough. On such occasions Biddy remained out of sight and saw to it that Clinton did also, except when Kate ordered him delivered to the front rooms of the apartment to be displayed and admired.

The apartment was of the railroad type, a term used to identify its basic plan: a long central hall with rooms giving off on either side. The overall structure was well built, walls thick to a point of being close to soundproof, the ceilings high, the floors built on cinder blocks.

Kate's domestic staff consisted of a cook, maid, and housekeeper all rolled into one— *rolled* being an inappropriate term. Maria Valdez was a Mexican woman of astonishing girth, with household expertise to match. She occupied a small room off the kitchen and generally kept out of sight when her duties were completed.

Kate sought her out in the kitchen. "Maria, don't bother with my dinner tonight. After you feed Biddy and Clinton you may take the evening off. I'll fix myself a salad if I get hungry."

With her evening thus cleared, Kate headed toward her bedroom for a short nap, excitement at the evening's prospects mounting.

"There is letter for you," Maria called after her.

Kate turned. "A letter? I didn't see any mail."

"No stamp. On table in parlor. A boy bring it."

"A messenger?"

"*Sí*. Uniform, cap."

Kate could only wonder. She'd half-expected

flowers from Carter Hayden before his arrival, but a letter? Perhaps he was canceling. Kate felt a touch of disappointment. She should have felt relieved, she told herself wryly.

The letter was simply addressed to Kate Wells, with no return address or clue to the sender.

She dropped into a nearby chair and opened it. Inside was a single, tightly scripted sheet of heavy, cream-colored stationery.

Dearest Kate,

This letter is most difficult for me, yet I find great joy in knowing that you are reading these words. Much has happened to me since you left New York City without giving me an opportunity to thank you for the courageous, self-sacrificing gesture you made on my behalf....

Kate's hand shook. A feeling like a chilling wind swept over her. A tightness gripped her throat.

A letter from Jason! He was in San Francisco!

Her thoughts were chaotic. The fear she had lived with for so long, of another battle to keep Clinton, hit her like a physical blow. But there was also the deep need to see Jason again. The two opposites collided to erupt in a sob as she lifted the letter to continue reading:

There are no words in my poor vocabulary with which to thank you....

She frowned. It did not sound at all like the

419

Jason Steele she had known. She glanced at the bottom of the page for reassurance. It was there:

> *Yours forever,*
> *Jason*

She lifted her eyes to where she had left off:

> *As you may have heard, I was cleared by the verdict at my trial and thus freed to go on with my life—a life, I sincerely add, which seems empty, desolate, and pointless without you. Your sweet face has haunted my days and nights and the pain of being without you does not lessen with passing time.*
> *I realize that I have much to make up to you—to you and to our son whom I long to see.*

The tears came, so that the words were no longer clear. She squeezed her eyes tightly shut. She could hardly believe what she read, nor the happiness that was rising in her breast.

> *Dearest Kate, there is much I cannot put into words, I fear, even if I am privileged to see you. Please allow me to do so. With this hope, I shall call at your door this evening. If you do not receive me, I will understand.*

Kate pressed the letter to her bosom. Her voice was a choked whisper.

"Oh, Jason, my love—do come! Come to me!"

She sat lost in the rosy haze of pure joy, all time suspended.

Then the doorbell rang; a sudden, jarring reality.

She dashed to the window and peered out.

Carter Hayden stood on the door step.

Forcing her numbed mind to work, Kate rushed to the nursery where Biddy sat placidly beside her sleeping charge.

"Biddy, come quickly! I have a task for you. There is a man at the door. You must tell him I am ill and cannot see him this evening."

But on the way back to the foyer, she realized that feigning illness would be only a temporary solution. Hayden might be back and with the promise of a reunion with Jason she never wanted him coming here again. It had to be final and there was only one way.

"Biddy, forget what I said. I want you to tell the gentleman I do not want to see him now or ever again."

"But if he doesn't understand—?"

"I don't care! You must get rid of him! Tell him—tell him never to come here again. If he does I shall call the police. Do you think you can manage that?"

"I'll try," the poor woman mumbled.

Biddy went to the door. What if Hayden refused to be dismissed? What would she do? She strained her ears but could not hear what was being said. But then she heard the door close. Self-recrimination came right along with relief: How *could* she have used long-suffering Biddy that way?

"Is there anything else, Miss Wells?"

Kate hugged her. "No, Biddy, that was quite enough. You were wonderful!"

"Then I'll go back to Clinton."

"Do that. And by the way, I'm expecting another visitor tonight."

Biddy regarded her dubiously but said nothing. She returned to the nursery.

The expected ring came thirty minutes later—minutes that seemed hours. Kate rose from her chair, smoothed a last trembling hand over her hair, and went to the door.

For all her tension, she appeared calm and self-possessed. Although her lips trembled slightly, she smiled warmly and said, "Jason! So wonderful to see you!"

He hesitated. "My letter was delivered?"

"Yes. Do come in."

She led him into the parlor, turned, and extended her hands. He took them, undisguised hunger in his eyes. "Kate, you look wonderful!"

She remained silent, smiling, trying to decide how *he* looked. There had been a change. He was thinner than before and something of the Jason she had known was missing. The cynicism from his eyes? The amused quirk from his lips? It did not matter. Something else had been added. There was a look about him that spoke of hardships endured, and the boyishness she remembered was gone.

Kate tried to still the pounding of her heart. "You look wonderful too, Jason."

He clung to her hands. "So much has happened," he murmured. "The brave thing you did for me . . ."

He was struggling. Kate said quickly. "Jason, would you like to see your son?"

"Oh, yes. Yes!"

She withdrew her hands and hurried to the nursery. Biddy looked up hesitantly, wondering what strange task was now in store for her.

"Biddy, I must take Clinton for his father to see."

"Oh, has Mr. Gentry returned?"

Kate merely compounded the good lady's confusion. "His *father*, Biddy. Will he stay asleep?"

"Oh, yes. He sleeps the sleep of angels."

Kate extended her arms, then drew back. "You bring him, Biddy. I can't trust myself."

Decidedly perplexed, Biddy lifted her limp charge into her arms and followed Kate to the parlor. There she stood silently and witnessed another strange incident in a long string of them. The man waiting there came forward carefully, as though he were afraid she would turn with the baby and flee. He stared at Clinton with such a look of awe that what she held there for his inspection might have been a verified piece of the true cross. Biddy half expected the man to drop to his knees.

"Would you like to hold him?" Kate asked.

Jason raised his hands, then drew back. "No, I'd better not. He might wake up."

"Put him back to bed now, Biddy," Kate directed.

Alone again with Jason, Kate took refuge in the brisk approach. Taking his hand, she drew him to the settee. "Now tell me about yourself—what you've been doing—why you came west," she said brightly.

423

Jason took the cue. "I was exonerated, you know."

"Yes, I knew. I was delighted."

"I had a very good friend in New York City—Chester Manson. I don't think you ever met him."

"I don't recall . . ."

"He married Elizabeth Penn, the girl I—"

"The girl you were engaged to."

Encouraged by Kate's interest, Jason related the parts of his New York experience Kate would not have known about.

". . . . Elizabeth made a magnificent recovery and Chester and I decided to go into partnership—a ship-building business. We got a contract immediately to build a yacht for a local man, even before we found a place to do the job—an old pier upon the point of the peninsula. We're building a dry dock now. . . ."

Kate was trembling inside, the fire fighting to surface. Jason had taken her hand in his; his thigh was pressed against hers. She could stand it no longer!

Their eyes betrayed them, each to the other. Jason squeezed her hand, drawing her close to him.

"Kate—Kate darling!" Her name on his lips was a desperate plea.

Kate replied with her eyes, her lips—her body. . . .

They rose together and Kate led him to the bedroom, their arms clasping each other tightly, almost floating down the long corridor.

Jason undressed her gently, only his shaking hands giving evidence to his impatience—his anticipation. Stripping off his own clothes, he

424

lay next to her, and the desire so long imprisoned inside them exploded in a fierce coming together. All the longing of the past years surfaced in their hunger to touch, to taste, to feel. . . . They spent themselves finally, their mutual release so great they cried in each other's arms. . . .

Jason slept, the exhaustion of spent passion overtaking him. Kate outlined the beloved features with her fingertips—gently, so as not to awaken him—marveling at his presence beside her, the fantasy of her darkest, loneliest hours made real.

When Jason awoke, he found Kate in a silk dressing gown, setting a silver tea service on the bedside table.

He reached for her and she bent down and kissed him gently, then poured the tea. She put the cup in his hand. "A little refreshment, my love," she said sweetly.

He lifted the cup in a silent toast.

Between sips of her tea, Kate said unthinkingly, "It's too bad Cal isn't home tonight. I know he'd be thrilled to see you."

"Cal?"

Instantly she realized she'd made a terrible mistake. "Calvin Gentry," she said slowly, reluctantly.

Jason's cup was frozen halfway to his lips. Deliberately he set it back in its saucer. "I don't understand."

Her eyes pleaded with him. "Calvin came west with me."

"You two are married?" Jason looked bewildered.

"Of course not!" Kate snapped.

"I lost track of Cal. I had no idea where he went. I didn't try very hard to find out," Jason rambled, as if to keep the truth at bay a little while longer.

"He was such a help when I came west. I don't know what I would have done without him. He came to me before Clinton was born. He comforted me and—and afterward he . . ." Kate tried to explain but it seemed to her that she only made it worse.

"And now you two are living here—together?"

"But it's not what you think—"

The damage was done.

Jason was out of bed. Kate faced him, and it was like old times—the hunger for each other, the need had been satisfied but the understanding, the trust did not exist.

Rage blazed up in Jason's face. "You cheap little whore!"

Kate lashed out with an open palm, but Jason seized her wrist.

"You haven't changed one bit!" she cried. "Cal's a finer man than you'll ever be!"

His face darkened. He still held her wrist. Now he threw her from him with such force that she fell against the bed.

She remained that way for several seconds. Then, "Get out," she said quietly, each word a cold, well-aimed dagger. "I never want to see you again."

Jason tossed on his clothes and strode from the room, his face a mask of barely controlled emotion.

When she heard the front door slam, Kate

426

got slowly to her feet, supporting herself with one hand on the night table where the tea was cooling in the gleaming silver pot. She closed her bedroom door, lay face down on the bed, and began to sob. . . .

The yelling had reached Biddy's ears in the nursery. So this was little Clinton's father! How had dear Kate made such a terrible mistake? As Biddy had told the nice blonde lady in the park, she had never worked in such a peaceful household—Kate was such a loving and devoted mother. Biddy sighed. But she was an ever hopeful soul: Maybe the man would go away and all would be peaceful again.

75.

Mercifully Gay Stafford left town for a week's visit to Los Angeles. A friend of hers there had gotten married and Gay was terribly excited about meeting the new husband and passing judgment. So, after Kate spent that terrible night when Jason left putting locks on her mind, Gay was not immediately around to break in on her privacy.

When there were no more tears, and no possibility of sleeping, Kate got up from the bed and huddled in a chair for the remainder of those dark hours, one dreadful thought predominating: Now Jason would come for his son.

There were things she might have done. She could have taken Clinton and run away again. She could have appealed to Barney Stafford, who was important in the town and might have helped. But a sort of lassitude had come over her. No longer did she seem able to gird up for battle. Instead she sat like a prisoner of her own inaction and waited for the doorbell to ring. There was only one change in the daily routine: She forbade Biddy to take Clinton for his airings. Biddy wondered but obeyed.

The doorbell did ring on the second day after

that night of horror, but it was only Barney Stafford who lumbered in with a business report:

"Kate, you are just about cleaned out of cash but that's no problem. . . ." He paused. "Are you all right, child?"

"Oh, yes. Just a little tired. You were saying I'm about out of money."

"It isn't that I over-bought for you—just that I made cash purchases. That's the best way to operate."

"It's so good of you to do all this for me."

"A pleasure, a real pleasure. You now own seven properties outright: four residential buildings and three small but healthy factory properties. They were all distress sales because of bad management on the part of the previous owners, which made them good buys. I brought a list with me with all the details."

"That is most kind of you. But you say I am out of cash so what would you suggest?"

"I'm coming to that. Now, the deeds to your properties are all in your lock box at Crocker's bank. And on your power of attorney I have appointed Pacific Management, a fine firm, to handle your affairs. They will keep your accounts and collect your rents and deposit the returns in your account at Crocker."

"You have done so much for me," Kate repeated.

Barney's smile was slow and wide. "If you had a wife like Gay, you would understand. But I enjoyed it and you owe me no thanks. Now, as I was saying . . ."

When Barney left, thinking that Kate seemed a little under the weather, she returned to her chair in the parlor. Her wheel of fortune had made a complete circle and there she was again, awaiting disaster. It really did not matter where she did the waiting—on Washington Square or Nob Hill. It was all the same. . . .

The following morning there was again that baleful ring from the porch. Jason—accompanied by the law? Kate went to the window. A man; a stranger, but at least it wasn't Jason. Maybe his representative. She debated, then went to the door. Might as well have it over with, she decided. The waiting had become too terrible.

About the only description Kate could hit on for the stranger on her doorstep was "ordinary." He was stocky, Jason's age or a bit older, with plain features; the sort who *would* bring legal papers.

"Mrs. Kate Wells?" he asked politely.

"I am Mrs. Wells. Are you a process server?"

"My name is Chester Manson. I am a friend of Jason Steele. I wish only to speak to you— for Jason—if you will permit me."

In the parlor, Chester Manson spoke quietly, impersonally, as though he had rehearsed his speech. "Jason has carefully considered his position and yours, Mrs. Wells. He sees any possibility of reconciliation as non-existent, with the child, Clinton, as the only mutual concern between you." He paused to draw a deep breath. "In that respect, he concedes that the infant is no doubt well cared for, and he asks only that he be allowed to see the child at reasonable intervals here on your premises— the visits in no way suggestive of a reconciliation between you and Mr. Steele. Would that arrangement be agreeable to you?"

Chester did not add that the solution was of his creation, not Jason's. He did not mention the hours of debate and persuasion out of which it had come.

"Is this some sort of trick Jason is playing?"

"I assure you, Mrs. Wells, it is not. Jason is totally involved in a full-time project of industrial enterprise. Much hangs on its success. He has no time for games."

"Then I agree. I have no wish to be other than reasonable."

The man seemed in a hurry to leave. Acting as an intermediary was obviously distasteful to him. He rose and bowed. "Then I shall take my leave and inform Jason."

"Please—please thank Jason for me."

"If you wish." He left with another bow.

Kate felt unbounded relief. She no longer needed to fear with Clinton out of her sight. For a time she moved aimlessly about, replacing an antimacassar on the headrest of a chair, moving a fern a few inches from its place on a windowsill, then moving it back. Finally she turned and fled to her bedroom, threw herself down on the bed and wept. Along with true relief was the now-familiar misery of losing Jason.

Chester Manson walked home deep in gloom. He did so well with other people's problems while his own had again begun to mount. The devils of misfortune he was sure he had left on the East Coast had found him in San Francisco and were plaguing him anew.

How pleasant that interim had been! So was he now going to cry foul and give up? Quit the fight? Like hell! He straightened his shoulders and walked on.

76.

Fate, it seemed, was relenting in Kate's instance. Or perhaps she was being saved for later disaster. At any rate, there was that persistent bell again the following afternoon. Kate looked out, then rushed to the door.

"Bella! Oh, Bella! How wonderful to see you!"

The regal figure unbent. Kate was smothered in Bella Cantrell's arms for a frantic reunion while the gentleman Bella had in tow wore a quizzical smile and waited patiently. They forgot him completely and moved on into the parlor, and he could only follow.

"You are a naughty one," Bella accused. "You didn't write."

"Forgive me. I meant to. How did you find me?"

"From the hotel, the St. Francis. They dug out this forwarding address. Oh, Kate, I have so much to tell you!"

The gentleman lifted one gloved hand from the silver head of his walking stick, smoothed his mustache and murmured, "Ahem—"

"Oh, I am so sorry! Kate, this is Señor Carlos Varga y Gonzalez. Kate Wells."

Gonzalez removed his glove, took Kate's

hand and kissed it smoothly. "Señora, an honor. You are most beautiful." He was certainly magnificent. Flawless of feature, figure, and dress—he favored various shades of brown from his stirrup trousers up through fawn-colored weskit, creamy jabot, and darker furred stovepipe—the señor had a warm, friendly manner. The two of them, he and Bella, were an impressive pair indeed.

Kate was fluttering like a bird. "Oh, do sit down! We must have tea. Or would you prefer something stronger, Señor Gonzalez?"

"Please call me Carlo. And tea will be perfect."

Kate pawed at the drape, found the cord, and sent the signal that would bring Maria. When the cook arrived, her eyes brightened at sight of a fellow Mexican and a rattle of conversation followed in their native tongue. Kate was most favorably impressed. An aristocratic gentleman who would converse amiably with a servant was certainly unusual.

Bella's news began spilling out. "Kate, darling, you won't *believe* my reason for being here. I am going to sing with the great Enrico Caruso and Antonio Scotti at the Grand Opera House!"

"You are going to sing *opera?* Oh, Bella! That's marvelous!"

"But with *Caruso!* The greatest! I am to sing the title role in Bizet's *Carmen*. Oh, Kate, how I've worked and studied!"

"You deserve the honor. You have a beautiful voice."

"It was Carlo's doing. He knows so many

people and he is a patron of the arts in Mexico City. That is where we will eventually go when we are married. Kate, you must be with me for our wedding. . . ."

There was so much catching up to be done. Tess Wells?

"Still fighting it out on the streets of New York. And enjoying every minute of it. She sent her love."

Dear Calvin?

"Oh, away on business. He'll be so happy to see you when he returns."

"The child! I can hardly wait to hug him."

"Oh, Bella, I'm so sorry. If I'd only known you were coming. We found a wonderful nurse and she wheels him in the park when the weather is good. But next time you come—"

Bella would return ever so soon.

There was a curious little incident as the visitors departed. A letter had been left in the box, one end exposed through the slot. Bella withdrew it. "Mail for you, dear," she said, but not before she checked the return address. "From Calvin. Is he in the wine business now?"

Without waiting for an answer, she took Carlo's arm and was handed down the steps. Kate waited until they were in their carriage, then retired to the parlor, where she sat down and frowned at the letter for some moments without opening it. The return address read *Peaceful Valley Winery, Doral California,* under Calvin's name.

During the preceding days, with so much happening and so much on her mind, Kate had given Cal scant thought other than to note his absence. It had been two weeks, the longest he had ever stayed away. And now a letter. Somehow it was frightening. She ran a fingernail slowly under the flap.

77.

Jason was troubled even though, by all standards, things were going well. The dry dock had been completed, the laying of the keel begun with eleven good men on the payroll, and the work going forward smoothly.

Going well by all standards except one. The partnership seemed to be tottering. Chester had taken to the bottle.

The situation was somewhat unique, geared as it was to the relationship of the two men. Having seen Chester through the torment and torture of their pre-San Francisco days, Jason could not imagine Chester going to pieces with all the old problems now solved. So he was slow to see it.

Also, Chester's change for the worse was a gradual process: a little more drinking than usual, periods of long silence. Jason invented reasons for the change and excused it.

Chester continued to go about his work but in increasingly disinterested fashion. Still, when Jason began to question the change, he did so gently: "Everything all right, Chet?" And always the reply that everything was. But the assurances were delivered so tersely as to imply resentment of the inquiries.

Jason held back for those reasons, telling himself that whatever it was, Chester would come out of it.

The situation worsened. Chester retreated deeper and deeper into the bottle, until one morning Jason found him at his desk staring at the dregs of an almost-consumed quart.

"Chet! For God's sake! What's wrong?"

Chester looked up dully. "You're early."

"You stayed here all night! You didn't go home!"

"It's my office, isn't it?"

Instantly Jason *knew*—while ruefully admitting to himself that he'd known all the time. It had to be Elizabeth again; nothing else would bring Chester Manson this far down.

A wave of guilt swept him. Immersed in his own affairs, he had neglected Chester and Elizabeth. They'd taken a flat on Chestnut Street off Russian Hill for its convenience to the dock while Jason found rooms practically overlooking it. Especially after his scene with Kate, that small perimeter became his temporary world.

There had been no invitations to dinner and that, coupled with Chester's decline, should have revealed the truth, but Jason had used even that as an excuse. They wanted to be alone—by themselves—to live their lives in privacy.

God, what a false friend he had been! Now, with the truth forced upon him, he realized that he had deliberately blinded himself. He hadn't *wanted* to become involved in their misfortunes. He wanted to build boats and make a name for himself and prosper.

He guessed that Chester was now in a precarious emotional state, and had to be handled very carefully.

Picking up the conversation, he said, "Of course it's your office—"

A sweep of Chester's arm knocked the bottle off the table. "If you want it back, you can have it! I'll walk out. There'll be no need of a settlement. All the money is yours anyhow."

"Chet! For God's sake! Quit talking like that. If you need help, I'm here—"

"I'm not asking you for a damned thing."

"You didn't walk away when I needed *you* to lean on. So I'm not letting—"

Chet laughed without humor. "I may have wanted to."

"But you didn't."

"I didn't have anything else to do at the time."

"God damn it, man! You came to me once before when you were in trouble. Why not now?"

"Repetition can get monotonous," he answered wearily.

"Look, if you think I'm going to let this partnership go to pieces, you'd better do some more thinking. It means too much to me—"

His words trailed off. They were going in the wrong direction. Even now he was still skirting the main issue.

Speaking in a quieter voice, he said, "It's Elizabeth, isn't it?"

The anguish broke through. "You know it is."

Even with the certainty, Jason had hoped against hope to find that it wasn't true. He recalled her brave battle in New York—fighting the monster, beating the demon. Out of the clinic and back with Chester, they had been so hopeful, a gay trio planning for the future. Elizabeth's spirits improved, her vitality returned. Chester's pride had been a glowing thing. Jason, too, had been proud.

Jason shaded his voice carefully. "How bad is it?"

"Damned bad. She's back on the stuff."

"Where does she get it?"

"Who knows? Chinatown? She won't say."

"As bad as before?"

Even though he was grateful for the unburdening, Chester could not tell Jason how bad it really was:

I loathe him! Oh God how I loathe him. He's got that tart living in luxury up on Nob Hill. And where am I? Wallowing in this filth.

This isn't a bad flat, Liz.

It's a pig pen beside what she's got.

But Jason has nothing to do with it. She has her own money. He's never given her a dime.

He put that baby in her belly, didn't he?

Liz, you've got to stop tearing yourself apart.

It should have been my baby. It could have been. It should have been me, not that little whore.

We can have a baby if it would make you happy.

That slut of a nurse wheels the kid out in the park as proud as a hen peacock. She watches over him as if he were some emperor's brat.

You've been up there?

I know all about that bitch. I talk with the stupid nurse.

Liz, you stay away from there....

440

So I'm not good enough to look at his child?

Oh God, Liz! Things were going so well. . . .

Chester grabbed up the glass before him in and slammed it through the window. The men on the dock looked up, then went on with their work.

"Damn it to hell! I can't take anymore! I'm going to have her committed!"

"Easy, man—easy. Maybe that's the answer."

Chet seized Jason's arm, his nails cutting into the flesh. Jason scarcely felt it as he gripped his friend's shoulders against the wracking sobs that issued forth. Then Chet jerked away and buried his face in his hands.

"She tried so hard," he sobbed. "She put up such a fight, and she won! And now hell has her by the throat—"

"Easy, Chet. Falling apart yourself won't help."

"I *love* the woman! God help me, I love her."

That, thought Jason, is the tragedy of it all.

78

Kate read Calvin Gentry's letter for a third time. It said so much: Calvin was not coming back. Yet it said so little; nothing of what he was doing, what he planned.

Dearest Kate,

I fully expected to return and give you the news myself. But as things worked out there seems no need for it. There has been a certainty in my mind for some time that I would find my niche in God's scheme so I made some preparations. Your basic expenses, rent etc., at the apartment are paid for the balance of the year. And with your affairs shaping up so well under Barney Stafford's wise assistance, your financial future will be well taken care of. Therefore my own penniless state will in no way imperil you or the child. . . .

Kate was appalled. Had she really been that thoughtless and inconsiderate? Penniless! It was true that she had assumed Cal's wealth to be limitless; or rather, had given no thought whatever to the matter. Arrangements, expensive ones, were always made; money was never mentioned. Allowing Cal to handle such things had become a way of life. With what justification on her part? Kate grew hot with shame. It had been assumed that she would reimburse him in due time—when she got around to it; that she would deliver to him what he no doubt longed for: herself.

The monstrousness of her stupidity now struck her full force. She had refused to favor the odious Peavey with her body in exchange for sanctuary; she had haughtily deprived Jason Steele on the *Gray Ghost* until he wrested payment by force. But sweet, gentle, patient Calvin Gentry—she had assumed the role of his mistress without qualm of conscience, had taken everything he'd so gallantly offered, and then blatantly cheated him of his due. Of course it had not been a deliberate act on her part but that made no real difference. She was as much a thief as if she had stolen from him and then laughed in his face.

Oh God, how she had hurt him! She reread the first paragraph of the letter. "There seemed no need to return and give her the news." Of course. Why should he even have bothered to write after the way she had treated him?

... *My own penniless state.* She had stolen—yes, *stolen*—his last dollar while he might well have suspected her of laughing behind his back. She forced herself to read the balance of the letter:

And now, Kate, I ask a favor of you. I would be grateful if you would see to it that the books in my quarters at the flat

443

are crated and sent on to me. They can be drayed to the ferry and taken across to the railroad. The Southern Pacific comes in my direction and will stop on signal at Doral for freight and passengers.

Let me thank you in advance, dear Kate. Kiss the child for me and rest assured that you will both live, bright and beautiful, in my heart.

Calvin

79.

The wrinkled oldster had one eye, a shock of untended gray hair, two hollow-hipped bays, and a two-wheeled cart that might well have belonged to the genius who invented the wheel. Each wheel was solid wood, a circular slice of redwood pierced by pegged axles.

"I am from the winery. I came for the box. I get the work because they can't leave. They didn't say nothing about no woman, though."

Kate said, "They did not know I was arriving. I'm sure it will be all right." As she spoke, she wondered. The man had said *they* could not leave. What was the place? A prison? Her mind rushed ahead. If so, she would get in touch with Barney Stafford immediately.

The old man continued to scowl. "No place to sit. Get your skirt all dirty."

"I don't mind, really. These are traveling clothes. See? Dark material."

As the old man considered, Kate had visions of plodding along behind the ancient rig.

He shrugged. "A dollar?"

"Two, if you wish. I want to be fair."

Cheered by her generosity, the drayman pushed the crate forward and seated her on the floor, backwards, with her legs dangling. He juggled the box to balance the load and then left it up to the bays who leaned dejectedly into their collars and plodded off up the slant.

Kate had plenty of time to think. The trip had not been difficult to arrange, no more so than getting the books packed and away. The only inconvenience had been reaching the station at a quarter of five in the morning. It was a four-hour run. The train would return north at seven in the evening. She bought a round-trip ticket and to insure that the train would stop for her told the conductor she would be returning that evening. Actually, she was sure of nothing.

The cart bumped along for some five miles through hot, dusty country. Lush, green hills bordered the two ruts which made up the road. The cart rounded a hill and Kate saw a cluster of white adobe buildings surrounding a taller structure with a bell tower, obviously a church.

Her idea of a prison faded when the cart stopped and two cassock-clad men came forward to unload the box. If the place was a prison to some extent, the imprisonment was self-imposed.

A monastery! What on earth was Calvin doing there?

The two men, middle-aged and undistinguished in appearance save for their sandalled feet and rough monk's cloth cassocks, conversed with the old drayman in what Kate took to be Spanish. Then one of the pair motioned to her and she followed along a path bordered by pale pink roses to a building where a third man stood outside the door. His hands were thrust into his sleeves, Chinese style, his head was tonsured, and his robe was pure white in contrast to the dull gray of the others.

His greeting was civil enough though hardly cordial, and for some reason there flashed into Kate's mind the interview with Guy Mapes on the *Gray Ghost* so long ago.

So long ago? Not really. But with all the changes in her life, it seemed decades.

"Madam, I am Brother Astansia, the director here. You have come with a mission?"

"I am Mrs. Kate Wells. I have come in response to a letter from a—a friend. Mr. Calvin Gentry."

"Was the letter an invitation to visit us?"

"Not exactly. Mr. Gentry asked that I send his books from San Francisco. I took it upon myself to accompany the books, hoping to speak with Mr. Gentry himself. Is he here, or were the books a gift to your monastery?"

"We are not exactly a monastery, Mrs. Wells. We are but simple farmers banded together in God's name."

"I see—but Mr. Gentry—?"

"The day is oppressively warm, Mrs. Wells, and you have had a dusty ride. Allow me to offer you some refreshment and a few moments of rest."

As he spoke, Brother Astansia turned and walked toward a table and several chairs shaded by a tall palm tree. Kate followed.

"Please be seated," her host said. But instead of joining her he turned and disappeared into a nearby odobe. Just then, a second brother appeared bearing a tray which held an earthen jug and a glass. He put them on the table and left immediately.

Kate had hoped to ask some questions of Brother Astansia. Evidently that was not permitted, and if she was being treated ungraciously, she had only herself to blame for coming uninvited. She sipped at the purple wine from the earthen jug.

After what she considered a reasonable lapse of time, Kate rose. She was obviously being watched because Brother Astansia appeared instantly at her side.

Kate said, "The wine was very good. I thank you. But I came all this way to speak to Mr. Gentry. I hope that can be arranged."

Brother Astansia considered the problem with monkish calm. "Such meetings are against the rules of our order except in situations of emergency. But I think perhaps in this case—"

"I appreciate your consideration."

The director lifted his eyes and peered off across row upon row of grapevines which extended over toward the near hills. He pointed to the northeast.

"I believe that is Brother Calvin there—in line with the tool shed beyond. You have permission to visit him."

"Thank you."

The director nodded and returned to the white adobe from where he had first appeared.

Kate plodded off into the blazing sun, wishing that she had worn comfortable walking shoes rather than the modish high heels in which she might sprain an ankle. After a walk of some two hundred yards, she reached the place where Cal, having seen her, was waiting. He wore the same gray robe as the other brothers. His feet were visible and she saw that

448

a special leather shoe supported his misshapen foot. On the other, he wore a thick-soled sandal. He leaned on the handle of the hoe with which he had been chopping at the rich soil and greeted her with a warm smile.

"Kate! You should not have come all the way down here. The dust—the heat. You must be exhausted."

"No, Cal. Not at all. I *had* to talk to you."

"You should have written. If I'd realized it was imperative I would have insisted upon coming to you."

"Then you *are* a sort of prisoner here!"

"Not in the terms you suggest. Our seclusion is self-imposed. I have not as yet taken the final vows, but I shall do so soon."

It was all so impossible! So—so *ridiculous*. Kate searched for words.

"Tell me, Cal, tell me. . . . I just don't understand."

His attitude in no way reflected her concern. He displayed the same calm that Kate had seen in Brother Astansia, but with a difference. There was a touch of humor in Cal's gentle smile.

"How cruel I have been!" Kate murmured. "I've driven you into the priesthood—"

At that he laughed outright. "Not the priesthood, Kate. Far from it. And I was not driven."

"Cal! Help me understand!"

The smile faded. His expression turned thoughtful. "There is much I can't explain because I do not understand it myself. Why I was drawn to this life. It is as mysterious to me as—well, life itself. I was never religious in any sense."

He gazed off across the vineyard as though out there somewhere he might find the right words. Then he lowered his eyes, searching within himself.

"Still, there was that moment I shall never forget."

"A single moment?"

"A time of sudden fright—almost physically terrifying in its severity. I was engaged in a—well, in a most unworthy pursuit, the most charitable way I can describe it. And quite suddenly, I was terrified for my immortal soul." He paused, a small, sad smile on his lips. "Does that sound crazy—unstable?"

When Kate found no quick reply, he went on:

"My immortal soul. It was as though I became aware of its existence for the first time in my aimless, wasted life. And I realized what I had done to it, what a monstrous, diseased thing it had become. After the first shock, I scorned the reaction as a show of weakness. I sought to turn from it. But it would not go away. It remained to plague my waking hours and found hiding places in my sleep. So I began reading, searching. It was as though some force was pulling me—drawing me—and would not let go."

He shook off the near-spell of the mood and spoke with humorous self-deprecation. "I did aspire to the Jesuits—can you imagine? But then I was informed of the requirements. First the study and preparation for admittance into the Church; then fifteen years of further study at the monastery before entering the Order. I may well have come up as the oldest Jesuit ever to be accepted."

He shrugged. "I would not have minded that but the Abbot convinced me that I was still too much of the world to undertake 'the ordeal,' however strong my inclinations.

"You see, Kate, I once promised a man that I would kill him if a certain situation came about. It did not, so I was spared the mark of Cain. But I am sure I would have kept my promise if circumstances had dictated. Therefore, a great stain was left to be washed from my soul."

All that while I never knew! I went on taking, taking, blinded by my greed and selfishness. Oh God, what is there to say?

Cal was still talking. "With my background, I had trouble even entering the faith. Then I was directed here. We are the Brothers of the Crucifixion—laymen to whom the call came too late or who were without the strength to follow Him clear up to Calvary. We work the soil, we harvest the grapes. We worship God."

He spoke so quietly, with such matter-of-fact calm that he could have been describing his work as a teller in a bank. This should have added some reality to the setting, but for Kate it remained a dream. This could not be happening!

"Oh, Cal—" She could find nothing to say, but he sensed the guilt with which she struggled.

"Kate dear, you are blaming yourself for the path I took. Don't burden yourself falsely. You take blame for not giving me the love I begged for, and actually it was the greatest help you

451

could have given. At the time, I was confused and in great error. It would never have worked out. The kind of love I asked of you, Kate, I did not really possess myself. Our marriage would have been a tragic mistake."

"But Cal—all the money you spent ... you said in your letter that you are penniless."

This brought back the half-amused smile. "By my own choosing. Actually, I am not penniless at all. After my obligations, I turned my cash and assets over to the Order. We need new buildings. There is land still to be cleared and put under cultivation. Tools are needed."

"But Cal—you are trapped here!"

"Not trapped, Kate. You must understand that. I was trapped out *there*. Here I have a freedom I could never before have conceived of. Kate darling, you must realize this change of direction did not come upon me overnight."

Kate saw the futility of it. She never *would* understand, no matter how fervently he explained. Still, her burden of guilt had been lifted somewhat although it was not banished.

Cal was looking out over the vineyards. "Kate, do you know the really incredible thing?"

"The incredible thing?"

"Yes. It's the power He has to forgive. It truly surpasses all understanding."

Then, "Kate, I must get back to work. Three more rows must be hoed before vespers. And you have a long journey ahead of you."

"Yes, a long journey," she echoed.

"Good-bye, Kate. God bless you."

"Good-bye—Brother Calvin."

She turned and fled, slowing down only after she had twice turned her ankle.

The oldster with the crude cart had waited, possibly detained by Brother Astansia's foreknowledge of what would happen out there in the vineyards.

"You go back now, lady?"

"Yes, I go back now."

No one came forth to bid her farewell.

Huddled in her seat as the train labored northward, Kate tried to accept as reality the unreal day through which she had passed. It was difficult. With her mind centered upon Calvin Gentry's departure from her life, it became symbolic of all the departures which had gone before. Her thoughts went back to Walter Woo, her fat Chinese father of sorts, a man of sterling worth; dead in the holocaust of the *Gray Ghost*. She had not been allowed even to say good-bye to him. Sweet Peter Wells, the boy she had treated so badly; gone forever. Tess Wells—not dead but past just the same. Precious relationships along her road to survival. Bitterness welled up. So *this* was survival! The heap of dross at rainbow's end.

Deliberately, no doubt, she saved the most difficult for last, Jason Steele. She had pushed him out of her thoughts as she climbed memory's ladder from her father's sudden death in Stonington. It was that eternal image in her mind's eye that hurt the most. She would have to harden herself and stop indulging in those childish dreams of what would never be. She and Jason had come together at intervals like two orbiting bodies, to clash and

453

spark and veer off again. Now they had clashed for the last time; two tamed and chastened comets, so to speak, but set on separate courses that would never merge again.

Her own future was easily forecast. Thank God she had Clinton! There would never really be loneliness in her life with Clinton to love and care for.

She closed her eyes and, in a sense, left her past back in the vineyards of the Crucifixion Brotherhood.

80.

That was September of 1905, and life did go on.

Jason Steele's affairs were going well so far as she knew; at least there were no reports to the contrary. He came to Nob Hill at intervals to see Clinton and she tactfully arranged to be out of sight on those occasions. It was Biddy who maintained a watchful eye from a respectful distance.

The days passed with Kate now paying more attention to her investments, visiting the sites, speaking with tenants, planning improvements. She was becoming a competent businesswoman.

But the old pattern went on—friends kept dropping out of her life.

There was Barney Stafford's ridiculous accident. Descending his front stairs one night in the dark, he miscounted and missed the last one. He did not fall but as he was a big man of great weight, he sank to the ground, the jarring effect having dislocated a disc in his spine. To all intents and purposes he was rendered helpless.

The result was that Gay took him south, locked like a mummy into a body cast. There would be at least a year's recuperation in the sun and if that did not work, a trip east for an operation.

The parting with Gay was tearful, with promises to write often but Kate knew it would not be. Friends who dropped out of her orbit always went on to other things.

Bella Cantrell's exodus was sad too, but in another way.

She had arrived in triumph at the crest of her mountain: a performance of *Carmen* with Caruso! Kate attended with great anticipation, sitting with the distinguished Señor Gonzalez in his box. But as the production progressed, it was clear that Bella was no match for the great tenor.

After the last curtain they hurried to Bella's dressing room and found her in tears. She wept in Kate's arms while Gonzalez raged and pronounced maledictions on the audience.

"Asnos estupidos! Bobos! Peons!"

Kate tried to console her friend. "Bella, stop crying. It wasn't as bad as all that."

"But it was! They laughed. They *laughed*, Kate. Oh, I want to die!"

There had been some laughter from the more heartless, but mainly it was an overall lack of attention. The buzz of conversation filled the auditorium, bored patrons leaning across their seats to converse with others.

"What made me think I was ready for opera? The Maestro was furious!"

Caruso *had* been less than tactful. Afterward he'd strode past Bella with a ferocious Italian glare.

"But things went so well in rehearsal," Kate said, genuinely puzzled.

Bella shrugged. "I was adequate there. But the performance itself . . . something happened. Somehow I was back on the London streets, a little girl singing for coins!"

Carlo turned to her fiercely, as though to deny it. Bella smiled and took his hand, pressing it to her cheek.

She said, "And there was my Carlo—his belief and his faith in me." Lifting her eyes to his, she added, "And your huge donation to the opera company, my darling!"

Reconciled, or at least resigned to the situation, Bella seemed to cheer up.

"We're leaving on Friday, Kate. We will be married in Mexico City."

"Wonderful, Bella! I know you two will be very happy."

"He is a fine man—more than I deserve—and he loves me."

Kate was surprised. Bella—the old Bella—was never self-deprecating. The opera humiliation seemed to have humbled her.

"I'll miss you so much, Kate."

"And I'll miss you."

"We'll write. We must not lose each other."

"Why, of course, we'll stay close. . . ."

Christmas was a pleasant interlude. Kate released Maria for the holidays so that she could go home to her village to the south. She would return after New Year's Day.

She gave Biddy the holidays off too, so she had Clinton completely to herself, and his pleasure in the first Christmas he could really understand filled her with joy.

Jason came bearing gifts. Kate did not feel

457

that she could rightly hide from him on the occasion of Christmas. His visit was most pleasant; they were both restrained and polite, like two people who knew each other but had never been very close.

Kate stilled the yearning in her heart with stern discipline but the visit was somewhat disturbing because it proved to her that the longing had not been extinguished. It was still there waiting to flare up with the least encouragement. Fortunately that encouragement was not forthcoming.

The new year was born and began aging immediately. January turned to February and February blended into March. Kate made plans to improve and expand one of her factory buildings as soon as her steadily growing bank account would permit.

One morning in late March when Jason came to see Clinton, he told Kate he was returning east for a while. William Steele had died, and Jason had some business to take care of. He was somber and seemingly depressed by his grandfather's demise, but Kate thought it odd that the business to be dealt with should be mentioned almost in the same breath. Jason took his leave with a polite, restrained goodbye. He would return, of course. Kate could not help equating the farewell with so many others through the years. However, with their parallel orbits now set and unyielding, the yearning for his arms was under control.

Some days later, Biddy rushed home from the park in an hysterical state. She practically fell through the door screaming, "Call the police! Clinton's gone! The blonde lady took him!"

Kate fought to keep herself under control. One hysteric was enough. She quieted Biddy sternly and demanded details.

"The blonde lady was always so nice. She came to talk with me and play with Clinton. Today I went for a drink at the fountain and came back and the lady was gone, and so was Clinton!"

Kate called the police and two detectives responded. They took down descriptions from Biddy and told Kate not to worry. The woman could not have gone far—they would have the child back before nightfall.

The day wore on. Kate's suffering increased by the hour. She was tempted to go out hunting herself but the police had told her to remain at home and wait: Perhaps there would be a communication from the kidnapper.

And then, in the late afternoon, a man came to the apartment with Clinton in his arms. Kate held the child to her breast for long minutes, relief flooding through her. When she finally gave her attention to the man standing quietly before her, she was shocked to realize it was the same one who had come to speak for Jason many months ago.

Chester Manson assured her firmly that Jason, still in the east, had had nothing to do with it.

"I throw myself on your mercy," he said now. "It was my wife Elizabeth who took the child. Elizabeth is not well. She has been ill for many months. But there was no evil intent: She brought your son straight to our apartment under some sort of an illusion that he was her own. I know she would not have harmed him but I also realize that you may not agree with me on that point. It was kidnapping and you have a right to legal redress. I can only beg that you be charitable. I can assure you that it will never, never happen again."

Clinton was back, safe in her arms. The man before her was a good man. It was not hard for Kate to forgive.

"Mr. Manson, I understand. You have grievous problems and I sympathize with you. There will be no charges. If there is anything I can do to help you—"

Were there tears in his eyes? "God bless you, Mrs. Wells." He laid a slip of paper on the table. "If, after thinking things over, you change your mind, this is our address."

"I will not change my mind, Mr. Manson. Thank you for bringing my son back safe and sound."

Alone, Kate's heart went out to the man who had left. She knew more about his situation through Jason, than she had revealed, and that knowledge increased her thankfulness for her own lot. Compared to so many others, fate had been gentle with her indeed.

Part Four:

THE ANGRY LAND

San Francisco, 1906

81.

The animals knew before the people. From the northern reaches of the California coast, horses pawed the ground and whinnied fearfully; cows rattled their stanchions and held back their milk; poultry fluttered about and fussed at each other while high up on the San Andreas fault a herd of donkeys brayed a requiem into the night.

The Earth itself became angry with the ubiquitous upstarts who had piled weight after weight upon its crippled spine, and was now driven to shrug their ridiculous burdens off.

The earthquake began on the ocean floor. Forty fathoms below the steamer *Argo,* it ripped the Earth's crust like paper. The impact hurled unnumbered tons of water upward. On a calm, windless sea, the *Argo*'s steel plates buckled, its bolts torn off like badly sewn buttons.

Heading inland, the quake whimsically selected targets along its way.

Like a giant tiptoeing down the coast, it stepped here and there with bewildering daintiness. It turned the Russian Church at Fort Ross into matchwood with a single touch of its foot. It ground a heel into the Skinner farm, moving the vegetable garden to where a giant eucalyptus tree had been, and placing the tree, still erect, into a berry patch. It split some pasture land, dropped a cow upside down into the crevasse and closed it up again, leaving the tail above ground as though the poor beast were growing from the soil.

As the giant headed south, redwood forests were reduced to kindling in the flash of a footfall.

South, ever south, where San Francisco lay beyond.

82.

Kate did not go home to the apartment that night. Since plunging wholeheartedly into managing her business affairs, she had opened a small office in the Palace Hotel lower down in the city. The Nob Hill apartment was a place to live; falling out of bed into an office chair was in her view a slovenly procedure.

On the morning of April seventeenth, she arrived late at the office and worked until evening. After dinner in the hotel dining room, she called home to find that Clinton was asleep and Biddy listening to music on the new Berliner disc phonograph Kate had bought her for Christmas. So Kate returned to her office and worked until well after midnight, then retired to the room she held on semiannual lease in the hotel.

The Palace: It had been built to last forever. A foundation of bedrock, eighteen-inch-thick walls—a hostel to symbolize, in strength and luxury, the very town itself. The Paris of the Pacific: All the great names had enjoyed and added to the elegance and the grandeur. Kipling, Oscar Wilde, Ellen Terry, Lillie Langtry, the Barrymores, even the great Sarah Bernhardt with her pet baby tiger had signed the register. On that day of reckoning, Enrico Caruso was ensconced in his lavish, eight-room suite. The Palace: It would not bow to a typhoon, earthquake, or the day of judgment.

Kate's quarters, a single room and bath, were, in terms of other accommodations, modest but adequate enough. As she drowsed on that fatal night, she thought of Tess Wells. Tess would have been proud of her; of the strides she had made toward her own emancipation if not that of all womanhood. Of course, attitudes on the West Coast had had a great deal to do with it; Kate could not visualize achieving such success in New York City. Though San Francisco was dominated and controlled by men, of course, they were too busy garnering their own riches to bother censuring a lone female going in the same direction. Yes, Tess would have lauded her. She smiled and drifted off into a dreamless sleep, so deep that she missed the first shock that came with the dawn.

A milkman leaving the dairy in preparation for his rounds heard the earth beneath his wagon roar as though in pain. The street broke up and began undulating like the tail of a Chinese dragon on high holiday. His horse screamed in terror and went down, and the man, too stunned to cry out or to pray, followed. In a matter of seconds, the iron piping system from the reservoir had been ground into twisted metal, cutting off the water supply which would be so sorely needed in light of what was to come.

A mailman crossing to his station stood bemused, doubting the veracity of his eyes as a tall, narrow building nearby began dancing, weaving from side to side as though to the beat of soundless music. As the building collapsed, the man was lifted and carried some fifty feet. Still on his feet, he staggered back against a brick wall and whimpered in fear.

From that moment on, the destruction was widespread, and fires bloomed across the doomed city almost immediately.

Kate woke to the trembling of the bed upon which she had slept. Coming slowly awake, she did not associate the vibration with any disaster in the making.

Nor did any awareness of what was occurring come to her immediately. The Palace Hotel had merely shuddered; it was not in the path of the first devastating shock.

Uptown, however, along the first wound that ripped through the city, buildings continued to tumble into ruins, jerry-built structures on the perimeter coming down so swiftly it was as though they were tired of standing, and grateful for the excuse.

Kate yawned, called room service, and ordered a light breakfast that would never arrive. But such was the caliber of the Palace staff, the devotion to duty, that room service politely answered, "Yes, Ma'am. Ten minutes. . . ."

A second pulsation followed the after-shock of the first. Again the structure trembled and when Kate's comb rattled and slid off the dresser, she knew something was wrong. Concerned but in no way frightened, she finished dressing and went out into the corridor where she found other guests in various states of dress and undress.

The five beautiful redwood-lined elevators were still functioning smoothly, the elevator boys as alert and polite as though an earthquake outside the hotel was something to read about in the evening paper.

The hotel's policy of courtesy and service to its guests was somewhat strained but still in effect. Apologies had already been made to Enrico Caruso for allowing the hotel to shake, thus causing his breakfast plate to skitter off the table. They promised him that it would not happen again.

In the lobby and elsewhere, assurances were delivered automatically. Everything was all right, the disturbances of a minor nature. It was not until hours later that the hotel ordered the guest rooms cleared, and then only after the death and destruction closing in on that last sanctuary forced the upper-floor evacuation upon the reluctant hotel officials.

Kate had been lulled by the early assurances. Although she went immediately to her office to telephone Nob Hill and found the phone line was dead, inquiry to the hotel switchboard elicited the response that the trouble lay in the trunks outside the hotel and would soon be repaired. It was in keeping with a fixed hotel policy that anything could be taken care of for the comfort of the guests, and not of deliberate intent to deceive. And to some extent it was wise. It kept guests from running panic-stricken into the streets where there was far more danger than within the hotel's thick walls.

However, when Kate began seeing the destruction from her windows—flames rising from the buildings, other buildings collapsing, the very streets themselves buckling into grotesque heaps of convulsed rubble—she no longer paid attention to the reassurance. She rushed out with the intention of hailing a hack to take her to her son.

A quick check beyond the Palace perimeter revealed the futility of acquiring transportation. There were no hacks in service and in many cases no streets for them to traverse even if they had been available. Already wagons and carts loaded with household goods blocked the available thoroughfares as aimless, terror-stricken people fled to they knew not where.

Kate began pushing north. As a pedestrian, the blocks from the Palace to Nob Hill now stretched an impressive distance. Obstacles other than disorganized traffic dogged her path. The heat from burning buildings—still nowhere near the searing temperatures to come—sent hot drafts up into the sky, the gale force hurling people to the ground. Maddened horses tore loose from carts, adding their panic to the terror around them.

Kate had managed three choked blocks when the next shock hit. Chance put the damage on the opposite side of the street where the walk buckled and split, spilling people about like chaff, killing and maiming. A building collapsed, the cement front breaking into blocks as the structure tilted forward. People scattered, a few not escaping, others climbing and leaping over the fallen bodies.

Kate was thrown to the ground, where she lay stunned. When she tried to rise, she found herself trapped, a jagged cement block sitting on a length of her skirt. That her leg had not been smashed seemed truly remarkable. She tugged at her dress to no avail. A man with dazed eyes bent to push the block aside, then straightened and moved on, unaware, it appeared, of his action.

Kate rose, one side of her skirt in shreds. After taking a single step, she stopped and stripped away the remaining material. Two crinolines went with it, leaving her in pantalettes and a short petticoat which extended from the camisole. None of the passers-by even looked. Around here there were women in nightdresses, men in long underwear. . . .

Kate pushed on northward. There were dead and dying all around her now, and out of her memory came flashes of dying, screaming sailors and the flaming pyre of a ship.

The traffic thinned somewhat and she began making better progress, but it was close to noon when she reached her destination, the sight of heavy black smoke rising from Nob Hill, a frightening omen.

Once there, she was a stranger seeking an unfamiliar address. The street had changed. To traverse it one had to climb over piles of rubble—the giant had stepped hard upon this block. Kate refused to believe it at first: that pile of rubble, that impenetrable mass of wood and mortar could not have been her home. She screamed and seized the arm of a man hurrying by. "Help me! Please! My child is in there! You must help me!"

The man paused. "Lady, there's nobody alive in there! Use your head!" With that, he pulled loose and hurried on.

There was a curious sight at the lower end of the street where the punishment had not been quite so severe. Three houses still stood, one of them afire. A fire wagon had arrived from somewhere and while one fireman held the frightened horses, six others fought the blaze. Why they bothered was not clear. The whole city was in flames.

Kate hurried toward the fire wagon. As she approached, the stream from the hose dribbled away; the pumpers stopped work. There was no more water.

Kate repeated her plea for aid and was again rebuffed. "Lady, we got to report in. Nothing's afire up there and we couldn't do nothing about it if it was."

With that, they climbed on the rig and drove off in a zig-zag course along the damaged street.

Kate's mind began playing tricks, offering impractical suggestions. She had to have help, and there was that nice man who brought Clinton home. He might even know where Jason was. Jason would know what to do.

Thus Kate turned in the direction of Russian Hill and the address Chester Manson had given her. The route led downhill but otherwise the going was difficult, forcing her to call upon her last strength.

The area between Russian Hill and the bay, a potential tinder box, had been one of the first sections to go up in flames. Kate found Chestnut Street but was not allowed to approach the address she wanted. It was merely another smoldering example of indiscriminate destruction.

Grim-faced men with red arm bands were loading death wagons while others were giving whatever aid they could to the survivors. A row of bodies had been laid out. Some recognizable as human; others shapeless heaps under blankets.

The man Kate approached carried a notebook under his arm and had a handful of white, stringed tags. His tone was sympathetic. "Are you looking for relatives, lady?"

"For friends—"

"You probably won't find them."

"Mr. Chester Manson and his wife."

He pointed to the row of bodies, then to the quickly erected first aid station. "They're either down there or over there, or maybe they've left. They could have gone to the emergency station at City Hall or the big one in the Palace Hotel."

"I just came from the Palace Hotel."

The man was incredulous. "Alone?"

"I walked."

His look said it all. The poor creature was out of her mind, obviously. He said, "We've got some identified. You can look if you want to." With that he hurried off.

Kate bent to the grisly task. Feet protruded from beneath blankets. White tags had been attached here and there along the line.

She knelt and went down the line until she came to two tags reading: *C. Manson; E. Manson.* Feverishly Kate went on down the line of bodies. She had to know if there was one lettered *J. Steele.*

There was no tag with that name but there were still the unidentified bodies. She had to find Jason. She could not let him lie there on the ground under a dirty blanket. She went back up the line, lifting the coverings off, looking at the faces, coming again to Chester and Elizabeth Manson. There she paused. At least they had died together. . . .

Someone took Kate by the arm and lifted her to her feet. It was the man to whom she had originally spoken.

"Lady, you've got a lot of courage looking at those bodies. Did you find your friends?"

"I'm looking for Jason Steele. I must find him!"

The man lifted a hand. "Just a minute." He ran down the names on his list. They covered two pages. "No Jason Steele," he said, "and we've got them all identified but three females. He either left the section or he was never here."

Thus did he lie mercifully. Very few identifications made, Jason Steele could well have been one of the covered heaps of human debris.

"I think he returned from the east just recently," Kate persisted irrationally.

He steered her gently away.

83.

Those were Kate's lost hours, her lost days, as she moved with other stricken souls through the stricken city.

Her purpose had remained fixed until she got back to Nob Hill. On the way, she told herself over and over that everything would be all right. Any other thought would have been unbearable. There would be people waiting to get Clinton and Biddy out of the collapsed building; they would be all right. She would take them to safety. Jason would come to them. . . .

Dusk was falling when she arrived back at Nob Hill. She looked about for the people who were going to help her reach Biddy and her son. They were not there. Nor was the street the same as when she had left it. There was no longer the rubble she remembered. Now the building was a small black heap barely visible in the vanishing daylight. She could have walked among the dying embers. The same fate had befallen the other buildings along the block.

There was no reaction of horror to this new development. Kate's emotional well was empty: It has been drained to a point where the dead, rising to walk again, would not have stirred her.

Darkness had now come, with Kate close to complete exhaustion. It all seemed so unimportant. With Clinton gone, nothing else mattered. She continued to walk purposelessly through the ruins of the once-proud city but finally total exhaustion took over and she crept into a sheltered space to rest. There were others there too but she was aware of them only vaguely. A child cried and fretted somewhere in the darkness. A woman sobbed. A man cursed in a low, steady monotone.

Dawn came but Kate slept on until a hand on her shoulder brought her awake. A woman was bending over her. She wore a bonnet and had a kindly face. A man with her was carrying a container with a spigot at the bottom. The woman held forth a steaming cup.

"Here, my dear. Drink this. It will give you strength."

Some sort of thick soup steamed in the cup. Kate drank it all.

"Are you injured, my dear? Can you walk?"

Kate nodded and the woman took that to be an answer to her last question. "Go two blocks west and turn north for one block. Our rescue station is there. People are waiting to take care of you."

Kate murmured her thanks, and the pair moved on.

She lay where she was for a time, then stumbled to her feet and headed toward the rescue station.

But not having listened carefully to the

directions, she was soon lost amid the waste and the rubble.

An effort to begin the cleanup had been undertaken. A two-wheeled cart manned by three men passed Kate. There were bodies in the cart and half a block beyond one of the men spied another under a fallen beam. Two of the men lifted the beam while the third pulled the body out. It was tossed into the cart and the unit moved on. It didn't occur to Kate's benumbed brain to ask them to direct her.

She walked; aimlessly and without a conscious destination. Several blocks further on, a shouted "Halt!" stopped her. She looked about and saw that it had come from a man on the other side of the street. The order was directed at another man further down who had just emerged from a wrecked building with his arms full. He turned at the command, panicked, and began to run. The challenger raised his rifle and fired. The man fell, his loot flying in all directions.

A block further on, Kate saw a poster nailed to a wall. *Looters will be shot.*

She walked on. The heat in her body was getting more oppressive, rising into her head.

Some distance further on, she stopped. Beyond, she could see the waters of the bay. What now? Mentally as well as physically exhausted, Kate continued to walk, the Palace Hotel having become her goal in a sudden clear flash. There was no real reason to select that as her destination, but it was enough to keep her struggling forward.

Soon she came upon a different aspect of the catastrophe.

Utter desolation.

This was no doubt a temporary pocket in the vast pattern of a destroyed city; a small segment illustrating what it would have been like if total evacuation had been ordered and successfully carried out. No living thing in sight. Or so it appeared.

However, two scraps of human refuse had remained. Two bearded ghouls waited for prey. They were crouching in a niche formed by a pile of debris and a wall which had stood against the quake, and as Kate came within range she was seized and dragged into the makeshift den.

There was no great fear on her part. Previous shock and too much horror had dulled her ability to panic. She was capable only of murmured protests as she realized that they were stripping off her clothing.

They were impervious to her pleas. Kate felt herself lifted and turned and then there was the sound of a savage ripping down her back. A knife blade had sliced through the laces of her corset, and the garment thrown aside. Grotesquely this brought Tess Wells's militant figure to mind. Tess, who had orated against the unhealthy restrictions of corsets. Kate almost laughed, the absurdity overtaking her in her hysterical but numb state. On her back, her body exposed from breasts to ankles, she waited for what was surely to come with no strength left with which to protest further, even the men themselves vague in her vision.

She watched as one of the men fingered her nipples. They remained flaccid. At this point, the second brute became annoyed at the delay.

He shouldered his companion roughly, pushing him aside. The man lashed out with the knife he'd used to expose Kate, ripping the other's sleeve. They stood warily, measuring each other.

Kate lay watching, without the strength or will to take this opportunity to escape. It was like two dogs fighting over a bitch, she thought. The attacker with the knife dropped to his knees, and Kate felt the weight of his body. There was some clumsy thrusting before the other man's impatience again asserted itself and the first man was jerked off her.

Kate was vaguely thankful for the respite, however brief it would be. She was struck by the fact that there had been no conversation between the two. They functioned in a weird silence as though they had all been hurled back through time to an era when grunts and snarls served as communication. ... The shadow of a third man intruded into her mental ramblings.

A third man?

He was tall and broad. He stood there quietly, only his eyes active, a double-barreled shotgun in the crook of his arm.

The two antagonists froze in silent question. Was the new man a vigilante, a thief, or a possible participant?

The man with the shotgun searched Kate's face for an answer to his own question: Were the two men rapists or were the three of them engaged in a desperate pursuit of pleasure amid the destruction around them?

The decision went against the pair. The man raised his shotgun and fired. The far man, his chest blown away, fell dead against the wall.

The second man resembled a cornered rat as he poised himself to spring past the gunman to freedom. But there was no opportunity. Another blast, and he fell away, his life's blood splashing over Kate where she lay.

The killings had been carried out totally without emotion; an execution rather than a murder. The man's expression did not change as his eyes brooded upon Kate.

She got to her feet and pulled what clothing remained over her bloodied legs and belly. She moved slowly past the man and out into the street. He remained where he was, staring down at the bodies. Kate could neither condemn her attackers nor laud her rescuer. To call the killer good and the rapists bad seemed trivial and of no consequence under the circumstances.

She moved on. After an interminable length of time, with the sun lowering in the west, and with her body curiously disassociated from her mind and moving of its own volition, she arrived at the Palace Hotel.

Its sturdy bulk still held out against the destruction all around it, but its future was uncertain. Fires were spreading everywhere. Dynamite had been used to stay the flaming onrush but had only strewn more flammable debris in its path. Soon, the devastation would be complete.

Kate entered the Palace lobby with only a portion of her awareness intact. It was a strange scene. The lobby was filled with people, many of them apparently in the same condition as she. A most curious scene: there was a whole wall given over to messages tacked up in haphazard fashion. Kate studied the board, peering with glazed, half-closed eyes:

Clarence Blaney,
We were here, leaving for Los Angeles,
will wait for you there.

Jenny and Mae

Dazed humanity trying to sort itself out and regroup. Pathetic obituaries: a note scrawled in a childish hand—*My daddy is dead*—with no signature.

Other unfortunates were wandering here and there, looking into faces. Some wore placards on their chests with names inscribed; either their own or those of the ones they were seeking.

Kate slipped quietly to the floor.

So this was death. Not painful. Not frightening. A gentle taking over from the world beyond. A beautiful place, with loved ones waiting, concerned faces all around her. Biddy and Maria and Clinton, and a handsome young face she did not recognize. One of God's angels, no doubt.

And there was Jason's dear face close to hers. He carried her into darkness, but it was all right, for Jason knew the way. "Oh my darling! Thank God! *Thank God!*" came his fervent whisper.

With no effort whatever, she left the trap of the flesh and looked down from above. She could see them all, Jason and God's young angel more clearly than the rest. Clinton with his hand tight in that of the faithful Biddy; Maria, moving like a small balloon. Tess and Bella too. They did not belong in San Francisco, but somehow even the dimmer figure of Calvin in his gray monk's robe was not surprising.

Jason, his strong arms holding her spiritless body so protectively . . . they would be together until the end of time. . . .

84.

Kate heard voices.

"The delirium took most of her strength but the fever is broken. Now she will need a lot of rest—a lot of sleep."

"Thank God—!"

"To be honest with you, I don't know how she is still alive."

The voice had a heavy south-of-the-border accent.

"Señor Steele, you must get some rest. Three days you have not left the bedside."

"I'm staying, Maria. Where is the boy?"

"He plays outside with Miguel."

"Keep him close. She will want to see him when she opens her eyes."

Kate drowsed. She planned to open her eyes but she was so cool and comfortable, so pleasantly secure, that she did not get around to lifting her eyelids. Sleep came too quickly.

She surfaced again. "She needs food now. The soup. You must feed her."

"Asleep?"

"She is awake now. Open your eyes, child."

Kate obeyed. A great grizzled man was looking down at her; a man all gray until her eyes adjusted. She found him solemn of mien and smelling of antiseptics; or perhaps that was the room. A strange, low-ceilinged room: brown adobe walls; a crucifix framed in fresh roses hanging opposite her bed; an open window with red geraniums on the sill; the *baa* of a goat outside, and an answering *baa*. Two goats.

Maria stood at her bedside with a bowl and a spoon.

"Where—?"

"Do not speak," the gray man said. "Eat and rest. I must leave now. I will come back."

The soup was thick and bland. Kate thought of the woman in the bonnet with the kind face. She never did find the rescue center.

Maria spooned soup into her and said, "Doctor Angel Cadiz, he take care of our people. He take care of you when you come here."

"Clinton and Jason?"

"The boy plays with Miguel. Señor Steele sleeps like dead man."

All seemed well, Kate thought dreamily. She closed her eyes. Maria took the bowl away, and she slept.

Her vitality returned with surprising speed. Doctor Cadiz shrugged. "Young body, strong mind. Not ready to die."

Kate now knew she was at the home of the Valdez clan in Concepción, the village from which Maria had gone forth to supplement the income of her people, sustenance taken mainly from the soil. In essence, it was a native Mexican village transplanted to northern soil. The inhabitants were looked down on as crop-harvesting *peons* by the surrounding landowners in the lush valley.

That morning Kate saw Jason clearly for the first time. His eyes were like burnt holes, his cheeks were shadowed and unshaven. He was beautiful.

They brought Clinton to her bedside. He had not changed nor did he quite understand the momentous events through which Kate had passed. He suffered himself to be kissed but with his eyes on the window. "Miguel has two goats of his very own, Mama. He is going to give me one."

Kate let him go back to his play, with a silent prayer for all the children who had not been so fortunate.

With her crisis past, Jason left for the city. Maria remained by her side to answer her questions.

"I knew it come before it happen. Horse in street rear up and tear away from cart. Horse know and he tell me—like dogs running scared up and down and growling. They tell me too. I tell Biddy, but she no believe me. First shake come. Biddy freeze, will not go. I take boy away from her and come here."

"Biddy—?"

"I think maybe she die when house fall. All houses fall. We hear. We see from hill. You want taco? Good for you."

"No, Maria, thank you. I'm stuffed with tacos. Tell me—I was there at the Palace Hotel—"

"We hear how it was. I send grandson Jose into city to hotel with name on chest: Kate Wells. He walk around. Señor Steele looking too. He find Jose. They find you."

How simple! How lovely! Kate sought words

of thanks and could not find them. Women like Maria, the great rocks no disaster could budge. Kate seized her hand and squeezed it in silence, her throat working. Maria remained unperturbed.

In due course, Jason returned from the city with two casualties of the terrible earthquake—Chester and Elizabeth. They were buried in the Concepción cemetery amid redwood crosses and fresh flowers on lovingly tended graves.

Kate arose to attend the simple ceremony but found her strength had not yet fully returned, and left the others to mourn her friends while she went sadly back to bed.

Jason remained alone at the graveside when the services were over. Kate could see him from her window, first against the blue sky, and then against the sunset.

He went back to the city a few days later, from which he returned to report:

"Almost completely burned out. The fires were worse than the quake. Even the Palace went down. The fools used dynamite without knowing how."

"How fortunate we were," Kate murmured.

Jason smiled wryly. "Others too. Mr. Caruso, ever the artist, came away without a scratch. He was found on Nob Hill when it was all over, with his paints and brushes, doing a landscape of the shattered city."

That was all for the moment, nor did Kate have any questions. What had happened in San Francisco seemed long ago and far away; it was as though she had stepped across a threshold into another life. It was all so different there in Concepción; truly another world.

Kate had gone to meet Jason at the stage stop. Walking back to the village hand in hand, listening to his report from the city, musing on their good fortune in surviving the disaster, she was shaken out of her reverie to hear him say speculatively, "I'm sure there must be a padre somewhere around."

"At the church, wouldn't you think?" she replied quietly.

There were no apologies for the past, no petitions for forgiveness. The bond was there, solid, unbreakable, accepted without a need for words. The pride and the bitterness had been drained away, leaving only the enduring love which, in truth, had been the cause of it all.

Later, with the sun quartering in the west, they left the village and climbed a slope to a high grassy ledge overlooking the valley. As they walked, Kate said, "You haven't told me all of it. What's left of the city?"

He shrugged. "There was that whole bayfront. The fire reached it at one point only; at the tip of the peninsula where I built our dry dock. All that's left are four stumps burned down to water level. I'm broke—I haven't got a dime."

Kate had never felt so wonderful. "You don't have to sound so proud—as though you were the only one! I have a few dollars in the Crocker Bank—if it's still there. I'm sure all my property has been leveled. The lots are still mine, I suppose; that is, if the deeds aren't in ashes. Otherwise, I'm as penniless as you are."

The valley stretched out before them, fading off into a soft, green, shadowed haze.

Jason looked out over the pastoral scene. "I like this place." He pointed. "Those sections over there—government-owned. Rough and rugged but the soil is rich."

"I like it here too."

"Open to homestead. You sign some papers, put up a hut. If you remain in residence for six months, it's yours."

Kate nodded. "Let's go down by the water."

They descended to the valley floor. Some beavers had built a dam in the creek. The result was a sylvan pool that glowed like a bright silver medallion in the slanting sun.

Jason murmured, "Yes, I like this place."

Kate thought her heart would swell to bursting with happiness.

"How about a swim?" she said. Without waiting for a reply, she stripped off her clothing. Clad only in the gold band newly put on her finger, she knew she would never be truly naked again.

She ran to the water's edge, then turned and waited for the man she had been destined to love for all time.

Preview

MADELAINA

Michaela Morgan

The following pages are excerpts edited from the first chapters of this new novel scheduled for publication in October, 1977.

Madelaina Obregon awakened this morning prepared for hat she anticipated would be the most exciting day of her ung life. Never did she dream that by nightfall she'd be a anged woman ... or that she might never learn of the cir-mstances which brought about the changes.

A burst of crackling sunshine spread a vast comfort of eer over the hills of Sanlucar de Barramedas. The Spanish untryside had never looked as colorful and appealing to r. Throngs of gaily dressed people had milled excitedly in d about the ancient city for days having traveled from the arby villages and hill country to this mecca just to witness e skilled perfection of Joselito Barrancas, the finest matador all Spain.

Time passed swiftly on this day and Madelaina had hardly ough time to see all that her eager, impressionable eyes anted to devour. She'd arrived the day before in the com-ny of her uncle, Don Diego Obregon, Don Felipe Cortez, d his son Armando Cortez, her truest friend.

Now, finally, they were at the Plaza de Toros, seated in eir private box witnessing the colorful pagentry of the *Cor-da.* Leaning forward in her seat, her eyes feasting on the spectacular pomp and ceremony, Madelaina felt as if her heart would burst with excitement. Then, suddenly the arena had been cleared as the rumbling sounds of kettledrums echoed throughout the ring and a lone trumpeteer held up his horn to sound the prelude of the contest between man and beast. All heads turned expectantly, their voices subdued as the sound of thundering hooves seemed to shatter the very earth around them. Two thousand pounds of black dynamite came sliding down the chute and crashing through the gate only to come to a full halt when the glaring sun blinded the bull. Clouds of gray dust burst all around him at the sudden stop and *el toro* tossed his powerful head to the right and left of him until he caught sight of his enemy. Standing a short distance away, Joselito Barrancas, in a glittering suit of gold embroidery, stood in a formidible pose eyeing *his* enemy before he moved in to divert the beast.

Then—like all exciting things must, the *Corrida* came to an end. Madelaina, a true *aficionada*, still saturated with youth's exuberance glanced about the immediate area of dispersing crowds eager to locate the young man most responsible for this most marvelous day in her life; Manuelito Perez.

She raised herself on the toes of her leather slippers, craned her neck, and stretched her small, lithe form to see over the heads of the endless hordes. Her uncle, Don Diego and the father of Armando, Don Cortez, both dressed in their elegant black suits of wealthy *hacendados*, were engaged in animated conversation with ring officials. She could hear them reconstruct the *Corrida*, play by play, raving over the merits of Joselito Barrancas.

Observing Madelaina from a short distance, with a frown of annoyance on his handsome face, Armando Cortez, simultaneously gave passing *señoritas* a careful once-over with roving eyes as he fingered the lapels of his well-cut suit with its flared bottom trousers, bolero jacket, and white silk ruffle shirt. He could feel the rising excitement as visions of the next several hours filled him with eager anticipation.

Madelaina wouldn't back out now—not now. She'd promised. She wasn't the kind to break a promise, he told himself. He supposed she was looking for Manuelito, by the look on her pretty, but anxious face. Damn! If that *peon* wasn't such a good friend he'd have put him in his place long ago. Going around with calf eyes, love sick over Madelaina. But, without Manuelito's help this day might never have come to pass—at least not as soon. Madelaina, such a child in matters of the heart, hadn't sat still enough for him to make overtures to her. Where could Manuelito have gone to? Why hadn't he remained as he'd promised? She paused to tu down the jacket of her trim-fitting traveling suit and reluctantly removed the blood-red rose from behind her ear where she'd tucked it when Manuelito had given it to her earlier. She began to twirl the blossom in her fingers as her dark, vibrant, brown eyes flickered in rising annoyance. She tapped the toe of her right slipper in total vexation. Manuelito was nowhere. He had vanished. *Very well, señor matador, spoil the best day of my life by being petulant and surly. See if I care!*

She felt uncomfortable in this new hairstyle which made her look so grown up. Even Armando's eyes had widened with desire when he caught sight of her dressed like this. Her thick shock of coal-black hair, waist length, and usually hanging free had been lifted off her neck and dressed into two satiny coils. Even the suit to her was a farce. She'd have been more content to wear her *torerra* suit, men's trousers, shirt and bolero, boots, and a flat-crowned sombrero.

It wasn't an easy task for Madelaina to submit to maternal supervision. She was constantly at odds with her aunt due to the fact that her formative years had been spent under the haphazard parental guidance of her father, General Alvaro Obregon, who'd left her to roam the forts of Mexico where he was stationed, under the casual supervision of countless *duenas* unable to cope with her strong-willed, headstrong, tomboy attitudes. This motherless girl-child had become an army brat very early in her young life right under the nose of her father without an awareness of the metamorphosis occurring in her. He was unable to handle the tedious ritual of raising such a defiant child who emulated the men of authority she saw each day. And when complaints reached him from the various wives and mothers in the military compounds that he was too permissive, too lax, and too easily won over by this tomboy child who wrapped him around her little finger, he was forced to take some remedial action. He sent her off packing to Spain to become a lady.

"Madelaina!" the sound of her name being called interrupted her reverie. "*Vamenos, querida.* Let's go my dear." It was Armando Cortez. Sweet, handsome, and patient Armando, her dearest friend in the whole world.

Madelaina nodded her head and stepped down off the wooden seats where she'd climbed earlier to gain a better view of the area in search for Manuelito. *Very well, Manuelito, go off by yourself and sulk,* she told herself stormily. *It isn't all my fault that things got so mixed up today!* Worse, she didn't understand this strange feeling of consternation gripping her, nor did she comprehend this feeling of attachment she suddenly experienced for Manuelito. Emotions shot through Madelaina, the kind she had never come to grips with before. Her stomach felt fluttery, she chilled with a rising excitement, then, alternately she experienced a glow of perspiration popping on her face and forehead. She fanned herself with a lace handkerchief.

"I'm coming, Armando," she called to him glancing soulfully at the blood-red rose before wistfully tossing it into the bull ring below her. She forced a light smile on her face as she gazed up into Armando's suggestive eyes. Damn! Why had she made him that stupid promise? She'd have much rather gone to meet Joselito Barrancas as Manuelito suggested earlier to her. For some unearthly reason she'd promised Armando the rest of the afternoon. And he, in turn, had promised her the most glorious surprise of her young life. Now she centered her attention on what this might possibly be.

It's true. Her curiosity had been heightened by the mystery and suspense Armando projected. He refused to speak of the surprise except to say it was the one way she could pay him back for providing her with many glorious hours spent in learning the art of bullfighting. After all it *was* Armando who had encroached upon Manuelito to teach Madelaina the art of the *Corrida*. She owed him something—didn't she?

* * *

Madelaina Obregon had turned sixteen on this fifteenth day in May, 1909. So her excitement was tenfold since she'd been able to spend it in the manner most pleasing to her.

Now, two hours after the *Corrida*, scintillating thoughts of what had transpired earlier dimmed temporarily by the opulence and magnificent splendor that greeted her when she and Armando entered the old palace, purported to have been the country estate of Queen Isabella, one of her ancestors. The sprawling estate stood high in the hills overlooking Sanlucar de Barramedas and the open sea of sapphire water in majestic dignity. From this very port Columbus set sail for the New World! Imagine, she thought, as she passed the foyer of elegance.

She allowed her dark, impressionable eyes to roam in every direction past the marbled floors of the circular foyer. Wherever she looked, something unique and astonishing commanded her attention. She followed Armando to the top of the spiraling staircase with its graceful rail of gilded wood and turned left through a corridor on the second floor of the palace into a very special room.

Armando closed the door behind them and taking her hand

shered her through the unusual salon. The walls and ceiling were painted in a continuous fresco of a bawdy life depicted n the ancient Greek and Roman eras, the likes of which he'd never seen or heard of before. Men and women—in ome cases gods and goddesses, and in others men only were ngaged in what was described to her as forbidden sexual leasures.

* * *

She had no real concept of what was about to happen, although admittedly Armando continued to pique her interest hrough hints of something so marvelous it was beyond the ealm of description. Even on the ride to the palace, he re-ained enigmatic and would only roll his eyes skyward when he eagerly questioned him about the surprise. Now, in this rand old palace as she gazed about her at the visual and ex-licit scenes, her curiosity was heightened and her expecta-ons provoked.

"What are they all doing?" she asked Armando, her eyes xed on the continuum of frescoes.

"Making love, silly goose." He helped her remove her gar-et-red velvet jacket. "Exactly what we intend doing today."

"It seems so complicated." She took off her feathered bon-et and shook out her raven-black hair until it cascaded over ae shoulders of her nude-colored alençon lace camisole ouse. She expressed her naïvete glibly. "Do we have to get ndressed as they are?" Observing the countless frescoes of otica, she smiled at the seeming foolishness of it all. Even e bedposts were carved into male and female figures doing hat to Madelaina seemed the most foolish things she'd ever en. Madelaina giggled openly and moved on to the next ene, painted on one side of the bed upon the wall. Her eyes idened like saucers and her face turned a berry-red.

Armando with a certain measure of pretended worldliness ughed at her discomfort. "This, *querida*, is called Forbidden ove. You see? Already progress has been made. Notice in is picture there are no little demons—little devils lurking in e background of the painting. Only cupids waiting to scend upon the lovers, *chiquita*. Not Satan with his fiery l tongs."

Madelaina, highly impressionable over many things exam-ed the highly erotic pictures and scenes in her stride, cer-nly with no overbearing desire to emulate their contents d not in the least titillated by their explicit frankness. She ped Armando would hurry up and do what it was he was ing to do and be done with it. His preamble had been long enough and drawn out over a period of three months. He kept playing games with her; innocent games bent on provoking her curiosity and which to her seemed so pointless. Why couldn't he have asked her straight out?

One day, not long ago, following a two hour exhilarating workout with Manuelito and the bulls, she had mastered a somewhat difficult *veronica*. Flushed with excitement and inflated with pride, she smiled dazzlingly at the spectators who clapped their hands and shouted *"Olé!"* to her. She hadn't seen the dark-eyed scowling glance of her sullen teacher Manuelito. What she noticed was that Armando held her tighter than usual with a marked degree of possessiveness, in a manner totally different than ever before. Their eyes met in a tender most affectionate moment, bringing a blush to her cheeks. She hadn't fully understood the flush of pleasure she experienced, only that when it happened, she moved instinctively out of his embrace and busied herself brushing off imaginary dust and dirt from her shirt and trousers.

Armando had moved in closer to her that day and whispered softly, "You really appreciate all I've done to coax Manuelito to tutor you in bullfighting?"

"Of course," she'd replied. "How many times must I tell you to convince you how happy you've made me?"

"Then, you'll do me a favor—as I've done for you?"

Madelaina had chided him. "You have to ask?"

That's how all this had begun—as a reciprocal favor.

Now Armando devoured her with his eyes as they lay side by side on the four-poster bed in total nudity, in this unusual setting of erotica. Madelaina thought, what a beautiful man Armando. She loved the feel of his thick, light-brown curly hair as she ran her fingers through it. His eyes, the color of turbulent green sea had a hypnotic effect on her. Though he was a bit overly impassioned at times and inclined toward the melodramatic, she listened politely as he spouted verse and sweet nonsensical tidbits in her ears.

"Oh, my sweet, I am enchanted with you," he whispered seductively. "I need you desperately. My heart swells in your presence. Can't you see how consumed I am with your very being—your body—your soul? If we don't express our love the way a man does with a woman, my heart will wither and die."

Madelaina suppressed the desire to laugh. Deep inside her she felt all this was a bit naughty and wicked, but how in sense of decency and love could she permit Armando's heart to wither and die? How? He was her very best friend.

She lay back on the feathery mattress of the bed thinking of all that had happened to her on this special day, as A mando's overly-heated body covered her and he made several motions to penetrate her body. Very well, she thought, do what you must, Armando, dear.

What a day! Her sixteenth birthday. An exquisite diamond ring; twin stones ten carat diamonds each, perfectly matched handed down from Queen Isabella had arrived two days ago as a gift from her father, General Alvaro Obregon, from Mexico. The ring, a stunning piece of artistry, too overpowering for her small hands, had been placed away in her jewel case. She had read the letter from her loving Papa and placed it in the case with the ring.

Armando groaned and moaned over her and she tried to accommodate his movements as he whispered what she must do.

Her thoughts wandered back to a far more exciting and rapturous event, the *Corrida* earlier that afternoon. Joselito Barrancas! The greatest matador in all Spain. *Dios Mios*, such excitement. At four o'clock in the afternoon she'd seen the splendor of contest between man and beast. Imagine— Barrancas had dedicated the bull to her. And all because he was the friend of Manuelito Perez. It had all been too much—a day of firsts for her. Her first diamond ring—her first *Corrida*—and her first—her first—?

* * *

No question Madelaina felt terribly let down. She'd felt more excitement at the bullfights than she had with Armando in their acts of forbidden pleasures. She turned her head toward him and watched as his hand stole upward toward her fully rounded breasts. She felt a strange tingling, a murmur, something she hadn't felt earlier and tried with difficulty to understand what was happening.

"A woman," whispered Armando, "a woman. There's nothing like a woman. The passion of a woman is like a rare, exotic fruit. Gather her beauty while you can, release the passion in her many treasures for in it is the power of Eros, greater than the power of Zeus. Eros, the creation of flowers and trees is the power that makes rivers flow and winds blow. Nothing in man is greater, more divine than the strapping powers of Eros girded in his loins."

"How beautiful, Armando," she whispered. "Did you write this?" She loved his voice. It thrilled her more to hear him speak than it did for him to go through these outlandish gyrations.

He continued, spurred on by her compliments. "You who are beautiful of face shall lie on your back where I can feast upon you. If your back is a thing of divine beauty, then let my eyes devour you. Ride me, you small thing of perfection as lover rides lover in unbroken rhythm and let me devour you in all your splendor."

* * *

Madelaina listened dutifully to all he told her. It all seemed so very important to him, how could she let him know how truly disappointed she was? She wouldn't hurt Armando Cortez for anything in the whole world. She closed her eyes and listened as Armando worked himself up again into a state of frenzy.

She considered all his machinations a bit much and concluded Armando to be a love sick, calf-eyed Lothario. His words, beautiful and inspiring, however a bit foolish at times, effected her deeply. Nonetheless, he was her best friend, her truest. She made a solemn vow that whenever he wanted to exchange his love with her, she'd let him take his pleasure, but never, ever, would she tell him she felt none of the enjoyment he seemed to get from coupling. Why she didn't enjoy it was something she didn't give much thought to until later, much later.

* * *

She began to write in her delicate calligraphy.

"*Querido* Armando: It is with a mixture of sadness and exquisite happiness that I write this to you. On Monday, God willing, I shall depart for my home in Mexico to reside with and keep house for my father, one of the duties to which a woman is resigned. It happened quite by a strange coincidence and quite hastily, I might add. I received a letter from Manuelito today! Thank the Blessed Virgin he is fine—and in Madrid someplace, although he didn't elaborate on what he was doing. Feeling somewhat despondent over the revelation of his love for me, contained in the letter, I felt the urge to handle the bulls.

Well, need I tell you what happened? My *tia* saw me—she was very upset that I had disgraced myself to do such a terrible thing as fight the bulls. One thing led to another and I have been given permission to return to my country.

As exuberant as I am to be leaving, I entertain mixed feelings of despair to be leaving you. Truly, *querido* you've been more than just a friend and superb lover—" Madelaina hesitated over this word, shrugged and wrote it anyway. "The many moments we shared together are imprinted upon my heart and soul until I die. In your heart I'll know you'll cherish me more than any other since it was you who plucked my virginity. I wish I loved you as you claim to love me. One day you'll find true love, and I shall become the faded dream of your youth. *Querido* you will always be welcome at the *hacienda* of my father and should you need further enticement, the most desirous maidens reside in Mexico. The idea should titillate your senses, and allow for a speedy visit to our shores. Fondly in affection . . ."

Before she sealed the letter, she added a postscript.

"Please, Armando if you ever find Manuelito Perez, tell him for me how terribly disappointed I was that he should have left us without a farewell. Tell him that I will always love him as I've loved you, and that I wish him happiness and peace wherever he is. I know one day, if he dedicates himself to his art he will be better than any matador in all of Spain. Confide to him how miserable we've all felt that he should have disappeared from our lives without thinking how much he'd hurt us. But it's all in the past and I only have good thoughts for him. More important tell him all is forgiven. He'll understand.

Madelaina Obregon."

Madelaina would have to smuggle herself out of Spain . . . a near impossible feat. And then, somehow, get to Mexico. It is then that we meet the irrepressible and charmingly rugged Peter Duprez. He, indeed, had a way to bring Madelaina to Mexico.

* * *

"The only possible way we can get you aboard the *Mozambique* is as Mrs. Peter Duprez, my wife."

Madelaina stared at him. "But, this is incredible. No—it is impossible! I am Catholic. I would have to be married by a priest."

"All the more reason to get it annulled when I get you home safely in Mexico."

"This is the only way, Mister Duprez?"

"Afraid so, l'il girl." He explained the situation. "Besides we can save money on the passage—by sharing one cabin."

Her suspicion was piqued. "But," she protested. "But—"

"Don't worry, l'il girl. Ya don't have ta fear me. Ah wouldn't touch a young 'un like ya. Ah don't aim to be put in the brig or face a firing squad. I know Mexican laws, ya hear? Besides it would be against my grain to molest a young 'un."

That afternoon, Madelaina Obregon and Peter Duprez

were married by a magistrate, in dismal, shabby surroundings, far from Madelaina's expectations. She told herself not to mind all this; that it was only an expedient to get to her country, that nothing mattered except returning to her father. So she closed her eyes and recited the vows as if by rote. Peter slipped a golden circlet around her third finger and hoped the magistrate hadn't noticed it was a golden earring.

Settled in the larger cabin which boasted twin beds and a small sitting room and bath, Madelaina relaxed and tried to devote herself to making their four weeks aboard ship as enjoyable as possible. None of the other passengers thought it strange when Mr. and Mrs. Peter Duprez remained in their cabin most of the trip—they were newlyweds. The captain had readily informed this message to the more inquisitive. At night after dinner in their cabin—when most of the other passengers had retired or remained in the lounge playing cards or socializing, Peter and Madelaina would walk along the promenade deck taking a vigorous walk, which usually wound down to a leisurely stroll after the first few minutes. Peter was insistent on the exercise to keep up bodily health. It was over the intimacy of dinner each night that they got to know more about each other.

* * *

In Lisbon Peter purchased an ample wardrobe for crossing the Atlantic, and she dressed exquisitely for him, knowing how it pleased him. The lights of appreciation in his eyes were telltale enough. She found herself doing more than she felt capable of doing for a stranger. Each day, she saw desire mount in him. He was superb at controlling his emotions and his desire, and he maintained a superb pose of aloofness and detachment. It was Madelaina who began to feel the pangs of desire shoot through her, something unfulfilled with Armando, which demanded attention. The low pains in her stomach left her nervous and high strung. Her body, awakened to pleasure, now craved it.

* * *

"I don't know what I'm trying to say. But it's terribly frustrating to be considered a child when you have the body and intelligence of a woman."

"So. Ya think yer a woman? Who put that into yer head—that there Armando fella?" he said with biting sarcasm. He drew her wrap up around her neck, closer to her face, tenderly. "It's getting cooler now, stay bundled up. I don want'cha ta be catching yer death before ah get ya to Mexico."

"Why do you keep speaking of him in such a bad way? Armando was my friend."

"Ah'll jus' betcha he was. Look, ya better get back to the cabin. If ya don't ah'm likely to start teachin' ya what life is really all about."

He was very close to her now. Her small flushed face tilted up to his. Dark fires burned brightly in her eyes and reached out into the depths of his heart, stirring him to high passion. He reached in toward her, held her face between his strong, scented hands that smelled of cologne and tobacco and kissed her lightly at first. Her response both startled him and delighted him. She kissed him back the way Armando taught her. "I want to know about life, Peter," she said quietly.

"Whooooa, little fox," he backed off. "Yer going a mite fast for this old cowhand. Ya hadn't oughta be doing me like that!" He whistled softly. "Let's walk for a spell." He swallowed hard at the increased sweep of passion surging through him. It happened so fast, Peter had no strength left to resist her. Besides the wench was asking for it like no one he'd ever met. It was a thoroughly new experience for him, to play the hunted rather than the hunter in the game of love.

* * *

For two weeks, he had examined the consequences and the implications of messin' around with the daughter of a respected Mexican General. One thing was certain, the kind of thoughts he labored under mightn't be considered best in the promotion of friendly relations between *gringos* and *latinos*. Ten minutes later, nestled in each others arms, Peter Duprez shouted aloud, "To hell with promoting relations between the *gringos* and *latinos*." He fairly startled Madelaina by such a declaration.

She lay naked, next to his warm, strong, clean body and inhaled the very presence of him in her arms. And Peter, inhaling her sweet, fragrant body odors and the scent of rose petals found his passion increasing.

For a time he just held her, doing nothing, just feeling her. He told her to do the same. After a few awkward moments, in which she had already begun to see the difference between Armando Cortez' bumbling sexual exertion in which she had felt nothing, she was confronted with so many new sensations, she didn't know which to record first.

"What shall I do? What do you want me to do, first?" she asked in innocence.

"Just lay there quiet like, little fox. Just feel me. Let your own feelings take hold, I swear mother nature will step in right after that ta tell ya what ta do."

He kissed her again. Madelaina let herself go. Here, was a master craftsman not a bumbling architect. In moments the warmth of his body fused into hers and she felt a rising excitement, a tingling sensation from head to toe. He lifted her raven tresses and fanned them out on the pillow and buried his face next to her neck. She could feel the warmth, the shivering sensation of his hot breath on her ears and neck. Her nipples stood out like flower petals unfolding in birth. Her skin tingled, the tiny hairs on her body stood on end.

His warm, passionate kisses began on her lips and traveled to the side of her face to her ears and throat. Shifting his position a bit lower than hers, he kissed her breasts, then began to nibble at them. How tender. How gentle he was, she thought. Yet he's setting me on fire, by all these light-fingered, light kisses and almost imperceptible movements. She wanted to speak, to tell him what she felt, but she felt certain he knew, so she concentrated on the feeling, which to her was the most exquisite, intoxicating sensation she'd ever experienced.

His expert hands, soft and sensuous moved slowly down her body caressing every curve, every soft graceful line, over her hips and down her thigh. With his mouth over her lips, now, he placed her hand over his manhood and felt her reaction. Her eyes fluttered open in amazement. He was built like some of the seed bulls on the *rancho*. Under her touch it seemed to expand and tremble with anticipation. She began to manipulate it in fast jerking movements as Armando had requested her to do. Instantly his hand clasped over hers and he slowed her down to a caressing touch. Slow, and sensuously up and down and around. "Easy, now, l'il fox, slow and gentle, that's it."

Madelaina had wanted this, never knowing she'd feel such exquisite delight. Peter placed his hand gently between her thighs stroking her lightly until he reached the velvety lips. She moved sensuously under his touch. So many new sensations crashed through her body and mind she was unable to distinguish them or feel them individually. She wanted all—at once. It was all too pleasurable—too scintillating.

If this was the coupling men and women did together, God! How beautiful.

Oh, she had so much to write Armando about. After all, he was only a boy. Peter Duprez was a man. *Madre de Dios!* What a man! She knew the difference between men, now. With a real man one doesn't think—one feels—feels—feels.

Peter swung her arms around his neck and whispered. "Cling to me, hold me tight, little one. Ya see jus' how ready ya are? The honey's jus' dripping from ya." He sighed heavily. "Ya can't know how much ah've been wantin' ya. From the moment ah first realized ya were a woman, like any red-blooded man, ah desired ya. When ah learned who ya were ah jus' pushed myself away from ya. Not cause ah didn't hanker after ya, ya sweet l'il thing."

"I'm glad for that, Peter," she whispered huskily.

"Ah don't want ya to be afraid, now. Yer almost like a l'il ole virgin, ya know. Ah'll not frighten ya. Ya hear?" He spoke softly to her, telling her sweet endearing things to make her feel she was his only concern in the world. She felt such a strong pull toward him. Their chemistry, working overtime and their bodies clung in such a magnetic pull it left them breathless, and quivering until both their bodies trembled with ecstasy.

"How much a fool you must have thought me," she said.

He cut her off sharply. "Shhh, sweet li'l thing. If yer mind's working like that ah haven't performed my artistry well enough. Just lay back and feel, let me communicate—let us both communicate what we feel."

Her hand slid down his back, feeling the strength of his muscles, the smoothness of his back, and its amazing warmth. Her hands moved around to his powerful chest and down his shoulders to the rippling biceps. She found her inexperienced hands gliding along with no forethought as to what they should be doing. And when he groaned excitedly with little small animal sounds as she touched certain sensitive areas, she found herself making mental notes of them, and would repeat the strokes. Again she got the desired response.

It was a powerful feeling knowing by her touch she could make a man respond to her, an exciting one, one which thrilled her and made her more receptive. She hadn't time to think. All she could do was feel.

"I've never felt so deliriously happy."

"On another night I shall lead ya further into the chambers of love, sweet little fox. But everything in moderation. First things first," he teased.

"You mean there's more than this?" she groaned. "I don't think I could take much more. I'm hurting right now," she whispered. "Inside my stomach are a thousand little humming-birds fluttering their wings, dying to escape."

Peter chuckled. "Ah know the feeling. It's like having yer guts bust wide open."

He slipped over her body, spreading her legs apart, and began to enter her, slowly, at first. She sighed with intense pleasure. He lifted her buttocks to meet him and began a series of slow, sensual thrusts. Madelaina felt a quiver shoot through her, tiny explosions burst inside her. Her eyes opened in frenzy. She looked up at him in the shaft of moonlight coming through the open porthole. His blue eyes were liquid fire, his body was like a lightning rod touching hers and making it do his bidding. Suddenly she exploded internally, time and again.

She must have had a half a dozen orgasms, something she hadn't experienced before and couldn't identify until later when Peter explained them to her. Only after she experienced these pleasures did Peter begin to make his thrusts deeper and even more sensual. Feeling him swollen inside her, she felt certain he had penetrated her up to her breasts. He leaned over her, began to kiss her breasts and suck them with long clinging kisses that drove her to the pinnacle of sensation, once more. Finally, she saw his eyes take on a half-crazed expression that seemed he was in agony. He uttered soft animal growls in his throat.

Certain neither he nor she could endure the agony any longer, it suddenly turned into ecstasy for them both. Peter spilled his juices into her and continued to experience such excitement, it took a while before either of them could move.

"Will ya ever forget this night? he said softly, nuzzling her neck.

"Never."

"Promise?"

"Will there be more nights like this before we get to Mexico?"

"Ya jus' try and stop me."

"Then, I'll never forget. Oh, *querido*—you know I won't."